CLASSIC
AUSTRALIAN

SHORT STORIES

Selected by
Walter Murdoch and
Henrietta Drake-Brockman

Melbourne

OXFORD UNIVERSITY PRESS

Oxford   Auckland   New York

OXFORD UNIVERSITY PRESS AUSTRALIA

Oxford New York
Athens Auckland Bangkok Bombay
Calcutta Cape Town Dar es Salaam Delhi
Florence Hong Kong Istanbul Karachi
Kuala Lumpur Madras Madrid Melbourne
Mexico City Nairobi Paris Port Moresby
Singapore Taipei Tokyo Toronto
and associated companies in
Berlin Ibadan

OXFORD is a trade mark of Oxford University Press

National Library of Australia
Cataloguing-in-publication data:

Australian short stories (1951).
Classic Australian short stories.

ISBN 0 19 550619 7.

1. Short stories, Australian – 19th century. 2. Short stories,
Australian – 20th century. I. Murdoch, Walter, 1874–1970.
II. Drake-Brockman, H. (Henrietta), 1901–68. III. Title.

A823.0108

Cover designed by Anitra Blackford
Cover photograph: 'Circular Quay West' by Harold Cazneaux
(National Library of Australia)
Printed by McPherson's Printing Group, Australia
Published by Oxford University Press
253 Normanby Road, South Melbourne, Australia

CONTENTS

CONTENTS

CONTENTS

CONTENTS

EDITORS' NOTE

THE stories here collected have been arranged in chronological order, with one or two exceptions deliberately made, where the subject appeared to demand a different placing. It seemed obvious, for instance, that 'Beereeun the Mirage Maker' should come first in the volume no matter what the birth date of Mrs. Langloh Parker, from whose admirable gleaning of Australian legends the story is selected.

Each story is a completed whole: none is an episode from a novel. References in the Table of Contents are to authors' own collections in which a story has appeared, or, if it has not yet appeared in any such collection, to the journal in which it was first published.

Our grateful acknowledgements are due to all the living authors for their permission to include their stories. Also to Mrs. William Hughston for her husband's work; to Mr. Eric Bedford, Mr. Samuel Furphy, and Mr. B. O'Reilly for the stories by their fathers; to her executors for the story by Mrs. Langloh Parker; to Messrs. Jonathan Cape and the author for 'The Grey Horse' from *Kiss on the Lips* by Katharine Susannah Prichard; to Messrs. Gerald Duckworth & Co. Ltd. for 'Scrammy 'And' by Barbara Baynton; and to Messrs. Reed and Harris for 'You Go, Florence Nightingale!' and 'The Man who Bowled Victor Trumper' from *The Courtship of Uncle Henry* by Dal Stivens, and 'Drift' from *Drift* by Peter Cowan.

Acknowledgements and thanks are also due to

The Bulletin (Sydney), 'The Lone Hand', *Steele Rudd's Magazine*, *The Adelphi* (London), *Southerly* (Sydney), *Meanjin Papers* (Melbourne), *The Argus* (Melbourne), *The Sydney Morning Herald*, *The Home* (Sydney), *The Sun* (Melbourne), *The Australian Journal* (Melbourne), *The Cosmopolitan* (U.S.A.), *Munsey's Magazine* (U.S.A.), *Chambers's Journal* (Edinburgh), *Good Housekeeping* (London), *The Sunday Times* (Sydney), *Australian New Writing*, *The A. I. F. News*, *Mademoiselle* (U.S.A.), *Art in Australia* (Sydney), *A. B. C. Weekly* (Sydney); in one or other of which periodicals one or more of the stories appeared.

We wish to thank Messrs. Angus & Robertson, Australasian Publishing Company, Dolphin Press, Dymock's Book Arcade, William Heinemann, Gerald Duckworth, and the N. S. W. Bookstall Co., for the use of copyright material.

For some omissions we are not responsible. One distinguished writer, in particular, would certainly have been represented had he himself been agreeable; and difficulties with the executors of two others seemed insurmountable.

Finally, we would express grateful appreciation to all those who have helped us to trace remote authors and books long out of print.

W. M.
H. D.-B.

PERTH, W.A.
1950

BEEREEUN THE MIRAGE MAKER

An aboriginal legend transcribed by
K. LANGLOH PARKER

BEEREEUN the lizard wanted to marry Bullai Bullai the green parrot sisters. But they did not want to marry him. They liked Weedah the mocking-bird better. Their mother said they must marry Beereeun, for she had pledged them to him at their births, and Beereeun was a great wirreenun and would harm them if they did not keep her pledge.

When Weedah came back from hunting they told him what their mother had said, how they had been pledged to Beereeun, who now claimed them.

'To-morrow,' said Weedah, 'old Beereeun goes to meet a tribe coming from the Springs country. While he is away we will go towards the Big River, and burn the track behind us. I will go out as if to hunt as usual in the morning. I will hide myself in the thick Gidya scrub. You two must follow later and meet me there. We will then cross the big plain where the grass is now thick and dry. Bring with you a firestick; we will throw it back into the plain, then no one can follow our tracks. On we will go to the Big River; there I have a friend who has a goombeelgah, or canoe, then shall we be safe from pursuit, for he will put us over the river. And we can travel on and on even to the country of the short-armed people if so we choose.'

The next morning ere Gougourgahgah had ceased his laughter, Weedah had started.

Some hours later, in the Gidya scrub, the Bullai Bullai sisters joined him.

Having crossed the big plain they threw back a fire-stick, where the grass was thick and dry. The fire sped quickly through it, crackling and throwing up tongues of flame.

Through another scrub went the three, then across another plain, through another scrub and on to a plain again.

The day was hot; Yhi the sun was high in the sky. They became thirsty, but saw no water, and had brought none in their haste.

'We want water,' the Bullai Bullai cried.

'Why did you not bring some?' said Weedah.

'We thought you had plenty, or would travel as the creeks run, or at least know of a goolahgool, or water-holding tree.'

'We shall soon reach water. Look even now ahead, there is water.'

The Bullai Bullai looked eagerly towards where he pointed, and there in truth, on the far side of the plain, they saw a sheet of water. They quickened their steps, but the further they went, the further off seemed the water, but on they went ever hoping to reach it. Across the plain they went, only to find on the other side of a belt of timber the water had gone.

The weary girls would have lain down, but Weedah said that they would surely reach water on the other side of the wood. Again they struggled on through the scrub to another plain.

'There it is !-I told you so ! There is the water.'

And looking ahead they again saw a sheet of water.

Again their hopes were raised, and though the sun beat fiercely, on they marched, only to be again disappointed.

'Let us go back,' they said. 'This is the country of evil spirits. We see water, and when we come where we have seen it there is but dry earth. Let us go back.'

'Back to Beereeun, who would kill you?'

'Better to die from the blow of a boondee in your own country than of thirst in a land of devils. We will go back.'

'Not so. Not with a boondee would he kill you, but with a gooweera, or poison-stick. Slow would be your deaths, and you would be always in pain until your shadow was wasted away. But why talk of returning? Did we not set fire to the big plain? Could you cross that? Waste not your breaths, but follow me. See, there again is water!'

But the Bullai Bullai had lost hope. No longer would they even look up, though time after time Weedah called out, 'Water ahead of us! Water ahead of us!' only to again, and again, disappoint them.

At last the Bullai Bullai became so angry with him that they seized him and beat him. But even as they beat him he cried all the time, 'Water is there! Water is there!' Then he implored them to let him go, and he would drag up the roots from some water-trees and drain the water from these for them.

'Yonder I see a coolabah; from its roots I can drain enough to quench your thirst. Or here beside us is a bingahwingul; full of water are its roots. Let me go; I will drain them for you.'

But the Bullai Bullai had no faith in his promises, and they but beat him the harder, until they were exhausted. When they ceased to beat him, and let him go, Weedah went on a little way, then lay down, feeling bruised all over, and thankful that the night had come and the fierce sun no longer scorched them.

One Bullai Bullai said to her sister: 'Could we not sing the song our Bargie used to sing, and make the rain fall?'

'Let us try if we can make a sound with our dry throats,' said the other.

'We will sing to our cousin Dooloomai the Thunder; he will hear us, and break a rain cloud for us.'

So they sat down, rocking their bodies to and fro, and, beating their knees, sang:

> 'Moogary, Moogary, May May,
> Eehu, Eehu, Doongairah.'

Over and over again they sang these words as they had heard their Bargie, or grandmother, do. Then for themselves they added:

> 'Eehu oonah wambaneah Dooloomai
> Bullul goonung inderh gingnee
> Eehu oonah wambaneah Dooloomai.'

Which meant:

> 'Give us rain, Thunder, our cousin,
> Thirsting for water are we,
> Give us rain, Thunder, our cousin.'

As long as their poor parched throats could make a sound they sang this. Then they lay down to die, weary and hopeless. One said faintly: 'The rain will be too late, but surely it is coming, for strong is the smell of the Gidya.'

'Strong indeed,' said the other.

Even this sure sign to their tribe that rain was near roused them not; it would come, they thought, too late for them. But even then away in the north a thundercloud was gathering. It rolled across the sky quickly, pealing out thunder calls as it came to tell of its coming. It stopped right over the plain in front of the Bullai Bullai. One more peal of thunder, which opened the cloud, then splashing down came the first big drops of rain. Slowly and few they came until just at the last, when a quick, heavy shower fell, emptying the thundercloud, and filling the gilguy holes on the plain.

The cool splashing of the rain on their hot, tired limbs gave new life to the Bullai Bullai and Weedah. They all ran to the gilguy holes. Stooping their heads, they drank and quenched their thirst.

'I told you the water was here,' said Weedah. 'You see I was right.'

'No water was here when you said so. If our cousin Dooloomai had not heard our song for his help we should have died, and you too.'

And they were angry. But Weedah dug them some roots, and when they ate they forgot their anger. When their meal was over they lay down to sleep.

The next morning on they went again. That day they again saw across the plains the same strange semblance of water which had lured them on before. They knew not what it could be, only they knew that it was not water.

Just at dusk they came to the Big River. There they saw Goolayyahlee the pelican, with his canoe. Weedah asked him to put them over on to the other side. He said he would do so one at a time, as the canoe was small. First he said he would take Weedah, that he might get ready a camp of the long grass in the bend of the river. He took Weedah over. Then back he came and, fastening his canoe, he went up to the Bullai Bullai, who were sitting beside the remains of his old fire.

'Now,' said Goolayyahlee, 'you two will go with me to my camp, which is down in that bend. Weedah cannot get over again. You shall live with me. I shall catch fish to feed you. I have some even now in my camp cooking. There, too, have I wirrees of honey, and durrie ready but for the baking. Weedah has nothing to give you but the grass nyunnoos he but now is making.'

'Take us to Weedah,' they said.

'Not so,' said Goolayyahlee, and he stepped forward as if to seize them.

The Bullai Bullai stooped, and filled their hands with the white ashes of the burnt-out fire, which they flung at him.

Handful after handful they threw at him until he stood before them white, all but his hands, which he spread out and shook, thus freeing them from the cloud of ashes enveloping him and obscuring his sight.

Having thus checked him, the Bullai Bullai ran to the bank of the river, meaning to get the canoe and cross over to Weedah.

But in the canoe, to their horror, was Beereeun— Beereeun, to escape whom they had sped across plain and through scrub!

Yet here he was, while between them and Weedah lay the wide river.

They had not known it, but Beereeun had been near them all the while. He it was who had made the mirage on each plain, thinking he would lure them on by this semblance of water until they perished of thirst. From that Dooloomai, their cousin, had saved them. But now the chance of Beereeun had come.

The Bullai Bullai looked across the wide river and saw the nyunnoos Weedah had made. They saw him running in and out of them as if he were playing a game, not thinking of them at all. Strange nyunnoos they were, too, having both ends open.

Seeing where they were looking, Beereeun said: 'Weedah is womba, deaf. I stole his doowee while he slept and put in its place a mad spirit. He knows naught of you now. He cares naught for you. It is so with those who look too long at the Eer-dheer, or mirage. He will trouble me no more, nor you. Why look at him?'

But the Bullai Bullai could not take their eyes from Weedah, so strangely he went on, unceasingly running in at one end of the grass nyunnoos, through it and out of the other.

'He is womba,' they said, but yet they could not understand it. They looked towards him and called to him, though he heeded them not.

'I will send him far from you,' said Beereeun, getting angry. He seized a spear, stood up in the canoe, and sent it swiftly through the air into Weedah, who gave a great cry, screamed 'Water is there! Water is there!' and fell back dead.

'Take us over! Take us over!' cried the Bullai Bullai. 'We must go to him, we might yet save him.'

'He is all right. He is in the sky. He is not there,' said Beereeun. 'If you want him you must follow him to the sky. Look, you can see him there now.' And he pointed to a star which the Bullai Bullai had never seen before.

'There he is, Womba.'

Across to the grass nyunnoos the Bullai Bullai looked, but no Weedah was there. Then they sat down and wailed a death song, for they knew well they should see Weedah no more. They plastered their heads with white ashes and water; they tied on their bodies green twigs; then, cutting themselves till the blood ran, they lit some smoke branches and smoked themselves, as widows.

Beereeun spoke to Goolayyahlee the pelican saying: 'There is no brother of the dead man to marry these women. In this country they have no relation. You

shall take one, and I the other. To-night when they
sleep we will each seize one.'

'That which you say shall be,' said Goolayyahlee
the pelican.

But the sisters heard what they said, though they
gave no sign and mourned the dead Weedah without
ceasing. And with their death song they mingled a cry
to all of their tribe who were dead to help them, and
save them from these men who would seize them
while they were still mourning, before they had
swallowed the smoke-water, or their tribe had heard
the voice of their dead. As the night wore on, the
wailing of the women ceased.

The men thought that they were at length asleep,
and crept up to their camp. But lo! it was empty!
Gone were the Bullai Bullai!

The men heaped fuel on their fire to light up the
darkness, but yet saw no sign of the Bullai Bullai.

They heard a sound, a sound of mocking laughter.
They looked round, but saw nothing.

Again they heard a sound of laughter. Whence came
it? Again it echoed through the air.

It was from the sky. They looked up. It was the new
star Womba, mocking them. Womba who once was
Weedah, who laughed aloud to see that the Bullai
Bullai had escaped their enemies, for even now they
were stealing along the sky towards him, which the
men on earth saw.

'We have lost them,' said Beereeun. 'I shall make
a roadway to the skies and follow them. Thence
shall I bring them back, or wreak my vengeance on
them.'

He went to the canoe where were his spears; having
grasped them, he took too the spears of Goolayyahlee,
which lay by the smouldering fire.

He chose a barbed one. With all his force he threw it up to the sky. The barb caught there, the spear hung down. Beereeun threw another, which caught on to the first, and yet another, and so on, each catching the one before it, until he could touch the lowest from the earth. This he clutched hold of, and climbed up, up, up, until he reached the sky. Then he started in pursuit of the Bullai Bullai, and he is still pursuing them.

Since then the tribe of Beereeun have always been able to swarm up sheer heights. Since then, too, his tribe, the little lizards of the plains, make, just like he did, the mirages to lure on thirsty travellers, only to send them mad before they die of thirst. Since then Goolayyahlee the pelican has been white, for ever did the ashes thrown by the Bullai Bullai cling to him, except where he had shaken them off from his hands, where are a few black feathers. The tribe of Bullai Bullai are coloured like the green of the leaves the sisters strung on themselves, in which to mourn Weedah, with here and there a dash of whitish yellow and red, caused by the ashes and the blood of their mourning. And Womba [1] the star, the mad star, still shines. And Weedah the mocking-bird still builds grass nyunnoos, open at both ends, in and out of which he runs, as if they were but his playground.

And the fire that Weedah and the Bullai Bullai made spread from one end of the country to the other, over ridges and across plains, burning the trees so that their trunks have been black ever since. Deenyi, the iron-barks, smouldered the longest of all, and their trunks were so seared that the seams are deeply marked in their thick black bark still, making them show out

[1] Canopus.

grimly distinct on the ridges, to remind the Daens of
Beereeun the mirage maker for ever.

GLOSSARY

wirreenun, *priest, doctor*.
Gougourgahgah, *kookaburra*.
boondee, *club*.
bingahwingul, *needle-bush*.

durrie, *bread made from grass seed*.
nyunnoos, *grass humpies*.
Daens, *black fellows*.

Untranslated song:

'Moogary, Moogary, May May,
Eehu, Eehu, Doongairah.'

'*Hailstones, Hailstones, Wind Wind,
Rain, Rain, Lightning.*'

THE JEWELLER'S SHOP
By Tom Collins (Joseph Furphy)

DURING the dreary winter of '70, Fred Schlapp and
Antoine Dubois had the one decent claim in the
vicinity of the Native Cat. And they deserved such
luck, if only for the spirit which had prompted each to
select a racial enemy as his working mate. For there
was a principle underlying their partnership. At a
time when Socialism presented itself to the average
mind as a crude and personal fad, rather than as an
evolutionary National policy, these men were Social-
ists; and, happy where no Rhenish trumpet sung, they
purposely made their fellowship an object-lesson to
the society of the Native Cat.

They lived in the hut nearest mine, and we were
intimate, though I was, in the most literal sense, an

Individualist. Abe Spoker—last of my three mates—
had cleared out, leaving me sole owner of the four
men's ground registered as No. 309. Not being able to
work a forty-foot shaft of my own, I just baled a bucket
of water every morning, by way of complying with the
labour conditions, and spent the rest of my time
partly in fossicking for half-tucker, and partly in
futile negotiations for a renewal of tick at the store. I
still believed in No. 309 as firmly as any Orangeman
believes in the Number of the Beast.

Returning to my hut one evening, I picked up one
of the Melbourne weeklies, which somebody had
dropped; and, reading as I went along, I found the
announcement of the Franco-German War. Thinking
that the news might have some interest for my
European friends, I looked into their hut as I passed,
and gave them half the paper. It might have been
fifteen or twenty minutes afterward—at all events, I
had just roused up the fire, and put my last three
spuds in the embers to roast—when I heard something like an altercation next door. I went outside,
and listened—

'*Sacré cochon de tête carrée! il y a longtemps que nous vous
avons donné une brûlée, cette fois-ci nous allons vous etouiller!*'

'Du bist ein meserabler Froschfresser, und ein
verdammter Constantinopolianer-schustergeselle! Das
nextema wen ir euth am Rhein shen, lasst dan werden
wir euth eure rote Hosen apziehen und den erseufen!'

Jupiter! had it come to this? Yes, and worse; for
there was a sound of trampling and scuffling, followed
by a clatter of tin table service on the floor, and more
confusion of tongues. I darted across, to act as referee,
but the door was fastened inside, and I could only
watch the misunderstanding through a crack in the
wall. The candle was out, but the bright firelight

showed my two friends dragging, pushing, swaying over the littered floor; not in body-holts, but each with his hands woven in the other's hair. No blows were struck; it was purely a question of the respective root-hold of Gallic and Teutonic thatch. Both varieties of roofing material gave way at the same time, and each combatant glanced round for a weapon. Antoine secured a long vinegar bottle, and Fred a short-handled frying-pan. At the next onslaught, the bottle smashed on the edge of the pan, and Antoine, now weaponless, made a tactical movement, head-foremost, through the calico window beside him.

But man is not constructed for sliding swiftly across narrow sills; and before Antoine's hands touched the ground outside, Fred pinned his feet against the wall inside, and fell furiously on his unprotected rear with the flat of the frying-pan—smote him hip and thigh, as the Scripture bluntly puts it.

I kicked at the door, demanding fair play, British or foreign, but Fred still spanked and spared not. At last I ran round to the window; but by this time Antoine had managed to kick loose and clear himself. Then he disappeared in the darkness, and I returned to my hut.

I had finished my three spuds, and was wondering where the next three would come from, when Antoine entered, and sat down by the fire, with danger in his eye. He sat there all night, declining to take the spare bunk, with one of my two blankets. The frying-pan had entered into his soul.

In the morning he went to the store, and presently brought back such a quantity of eatables as made me resolve to neither borrow nor lend. After breakfast, he accompanied me to Hungry Gully, where I had left my tub and tools. We worked and yarned together all day, and cleaned up at sundown for seven or eight grains of dull, water-worn gold.

After supper, leaving Antoine in my hut, I went across and had a long, friendly conversation with Fred. My friends' claim was about worked out, and I wanted them to join me in unearthing the half-ton of gold located just where the rainbow met the ground in No. 309. My proposal was that they should buy into the claim for a couple of notes each—and I wanted ten shillings of the money *down*.

Next day, Antoine and I shifted the fossicking plant, and tried the Mosquito, panning out a pinch of sharp, bright reef-gold—again about seven or eight grains. Antoine was disgusted; yet this was good compared with the average of the district—bar the solitary sluicing claim from which my two friends had taken sixty ounces in three months. Antoine forgot to give me our two days' gold, but that was neither here nor there; he had given me ten times its value in stores.

Fred, Antoine and I spent the evening together over a half-gallon of villainous ale from the shanty, and arranged to give No. 309 a fair trial in the morning, leaving the premium for after-consideration. The tiff between the two mates was smoothed over by this time. Blessed are the peacemakers.

After an easy forenoon's baling of the accumulated water, I lowered Fred and Antoine down the shaft, with some tools; then pegged the windlass—with the bucket just off the bottom—and followed by the rope. Fred was panning off a prospect in a pool of water up the north drive, while Antoine held the candle. I had barely time to see a fine show of gold in the dish, when Antoine caught sight of me over Fred's shoulder, and sharply ordered me to keep away. I returned up the rope, and waited.

Half an hour afterward, I pulled up the tools and the prospectors. On reaching the surface, Fred—who was the most deeply scientific man I ever knew—stepped aside to examine privately and minutely, by sunlight, the prospects which he had collected in a bit of paper. Whilst doing so, an involuntary exclamation broke from him, and he glanced furtively round; but I was occupied in detailing, and Antoine in hearing, how the claim had been wrecked through the pigheadedness of my former mates.

My friends kept together, and avoided me, for the rest of the day; but next morning, before daylight, Antoine came into my hut and woke me quietly—

'Ve vill vash damfine prospec' in you clem,' said he impressively. 'Olt Sauerkraut he vant grab de lot. Dat iss de Sherman for alvays time. Shoke me off; shoke me off. Ver vell. I haf vat you call "settle-me-up" vit him. You vill qvick, qvick, sell him you clem. Tventee note—no less—cash dan on de top of de nell. Tventee note, mind!' And Antoine slipped out as quietly as he had entered.

Early in the forenoon of the same day he packed his swag, bade good-bye to Fred and me, took the track toward Spring Creek; and the Native Cat knew him no more.

As Antoine disappeared across the hill, Fred, in casual conversation, depreciated No. 309 till my heart was in my boots. But he was a good sort. He would give me ten shillings to face the road with, and take the claim off my hands. Here was a change! However, remembering Antoine's counsel, I carelessly remarked that I should like to see some of the Gluepot fellows first. I could tell them something about the claim that would set them tumbling over each other in the race for shares. And I turned away toward the Gluepot.

Fred, starting afresh from that base, sprung to £2; then to £5; then, little by little, to £10; then, more slowly still, to an anguish-laden £20; and we closed the bargain. By his desire, we set off at once for the Mining Registrar's Office, which was on the Golconda, about a mile distant.

Now it happened that I had never been able to run a Miner's Right. The few pounds I embezzled on leaving home had been thrown away to the last penny in the greenhorn purchase of a fourth share in No. 309, from the original holder, who, according to custom, had merely handed me his paper, endorsed:

'To the mineing register Pleas transfer this Share too Thomas Collins and oblige yours truely

JOHN MILTOM'

But the transfer couldn't take place till I produced a Miner's Right; and you might as well have asked me to produce a patent of nobility. Of course, I held the other three shares on the same fragile tenure.

So, as we walked on together, I explained to Fred that he would have to advance me six shillings—the price of a Miner's Right—in order to bridge the gap between the original holders and himself. He readily consented; but shortly afterward found that he had forgotten his purse in the hurry. This meant postponement of the business till next day. Being, however, so far on the way, he thought he would go on to the Golconda, to see a man he knew. I therefore returned alone to the Native Cat.

I lay on my bunk for the rest of the afternoon; reflecting that the claim might be no good after all;

and investing my £20 in twenty different ways. In the evening, going out for firewood, I noticed four blue documents tacked on the uprights of the windlass. A closer inspection showed these to be formal applications by Frederick Schlapp, for the four men's ground registered as No. 309, and now abandoned by original holders. The claim was jumped.

Hungry as I was for satisfaction, I perceived that a subterranean policy would suit me best. I still held the ground by prior occupation, and until Fred's application was confirmed there was no law to prevent me putting improvements on the claim. I purposed beginning with the face of the south drive, where a leaking, dripping wall of five feet thick held back the mass of water which filled the old workings of the original Native Cat. These extended half a mile, shallowing up to the surface, and tapping no end of perennial springs.

To keep Fred out of the way, I interviewed him through a crack in his hut, to such effect that, for some weeks to come, he would certainly avoid all places favourable to ambuscade.

Powder, fuse, paper and pitch being inedible, I had the material for one good earthquaking cartridge. I lowered a gad-hammer, two drills and a tamping bar into the shaft; then followed down the rope, carrying my cartridge and candle. At the face of the south drive I threw off the corn-sack tunic with which poverty had made me acquainted, and got to work. Some time after midnight I set the fuse going, and lit out for the shaft, leaving my tunic and tools to puzzle antiquarians of future ages. Before I got half-way to the surface, the explosion came off, nearly smothering me with powder-smoke. But I heard the churning of the water as it came in with a forty-foot head, and returned to my hut filled with a great, silent peace. I am of Irish extraction.

The claim was granted to Fred. He hired a cheap man, and began baling.

Next day he rigged twenty-gallon hide buckets, and hired two more cheap men.

A few days later, he sacked his men, and hired a portable engine, with pumping plant.

After a week's continuous working, he sacked the engine, and, with incredible pertinacity, set to work taking levels for a tunnel. This would give him nearly two hundred yards of nasty slate to go through, but he tackled it single-handed; evidently determined to run the claim as a one-man enterprise. At last I began to pity his infatuation, and called round on him while he was putting in his second set.

'You're doing a foolish thing, Fred,' said I. 'I'm not interested in the claim now, and I know her for what she is; she's worse than a duffer; she's a stringer. She'd ruin Money Miller.'

'Der vogs mit der sour greps!' sneered Fred. 'Unt you schall der vater svamp mit—eh?'

'Yes; I put a bit of a shot in her before I left.'

'I veesh you will progue ¹ you neg mit. Bot der Gott schall pe ver goot. You pelong notteen mo you svag mit; unt minezelluf I pelong dot glaim mit der yeweller's yop.'

'Jeweller's shop!' I repeated, in dismay.

'Yoos so. Dot knog you—eh? I vill esplen: Vhen dwo rons golt come altogedder mit, unt after von py hezelluf, dhere schall pe der yeweller's yop,—eh?'

'Yes; that's the theory, Fred.'

'Teory pe plo!—I haf on Pallarat vorg.² Now you schall see,—mit hanse off, py yimgo!'

¹ broke.   ² work.

He produced a match-box, and from this, a prospect, enfolded in ply after ply of paper; then with a splinter of wood he separated the prospect into two fairly equal parts. One portion consisted of a few bits of dull, water-worn gold; the other of sharp, bright reef-gold; and there might have been a third of a dwt. in each lot.

'Dhere!' he continued, in ungenerous triumph. 'Minezelluf I schall dot brosbec' in der vorgins [1] vash yoos vhere I plattivell [2] blease, mit der nort' drife, unt mit der sout' drife. Dwo roms golt dhere—eh? Vot pig yackass dot Yermance vos! Youzelluf you schall dhree monse vorg mit dot yeweller's yop you nose onter, semple ass der A P C. Go vay unt posh you het in von pag!'

I could find no rejoinder. Like a ragged fossicker in a dream, I stood hazily contemplating the two samples—each so different from the smooth, scaly gold with which No. 309 had lured her former victims to ruin. But had I seen those two diverse prospects before—under other conditions, or in some former state of existence? Or was it merely a case of unconscious cerebration? Or was my brain softening under the cares of the world and the deceitfulness of riches?

'Minezelluf,' continued Fred, repacking his prospect, 'I schall pe mit von yare der yentlemans, mit der golt vatch unt der belldopper, unt you schall youzelluf mit plattivell zbite on der gom-tree hang. Soolim!'

---

[1] workings.   [2] bloody well.

Text corrected from Furphy's final typescript by R. G. Howarth, editor of his collected *Short Stories* (in preparation), University of Sydney. Explanatory notes added.

THE PARSON'S BLACKBOY
By Ernest Favenc

THE Rev. Joseph Simmondsen had been appointed
by his Bishop to a cure of souls in the Far North, in the
days when Queensland was an ungodly and unsancti-
fied place. Naturally, the Rev. J., who was young,
green, and zealous, saw a direct mission in front of him.
His predecessor had never gone twenty miles outside
the little seaport that formed the commercial outlet
of the district; but this did not suit Joseph's eager
temperament. Once he felt his footing and gained
a little experience, he determined on a lengthened tour
that should embrace the uttermost limits of his fold.

Now, although beset with the conceit and priggish-
ness inseparable from the early stages of parsonhood,
Simmondsen was not a bad fellow, and glimpses of his
manly nature would at times peep out in spite of himself. This, without his knowledge, ensured him a
decent welcome; and he got a good distance inland
under most favourable auspices, for, the weather being
fine, everybody was willing to lend him a horse or
drive him along to the next station upon his route. The
Rev. Joseph began to think that the roughness of the
back country had been much exaggerated.

In due course he arrived at a station which we will
call Upton Downs; beyond it there were only a few
newly-taken-up runs. On Upton Downs they were
busy mustering, and when the parson enquired about
his way for the next day the manager looked rather
puzzled. 'You see,' he said, 'we are rather short-
handed, and I can't spare a man to send with you; at
the same time the track from here to Gundewarra is

not very plain, and I am afraid you might not be able to follow it. However, I will see what I can do.'

Mr. Simmondsen was retiring to rest that night when a whispered conversation made itself audible in the next room. No words were distinguishable, but from the sounds of smothered laughter a good joke seemed to be in progress.

'I think I can manage for you,' said the manager at breakfast next morning. 'When you leave here you will go to Gundewarra, twenty-five miles. From there it is thirty-five miles to Bilton's Camp, and ten on to Blue Grass. From Blue Grass you can come straight back here across the bush, about forty miles. I will lend you a blackboy who knows the country well and will see you round safely.'

The young clergyman thanked his host, and, after breakfast, prepared to leave. The blackboy, a good-looking little fellow arrayed in clean moles and twill shirt, was in attendance with a led pack-horse, and the two departed.

For some miles the Reverend Joseph improved the occasion by a little pious talk to the boy, who spoke fairly good English, and showed a white set of teeth when he laughed, as he constantly did at everything the parson said. At midday they camped for an hour on the bank of a lagoon, in which Mr. Simmondsen had a refreshing swim. In the evening they arrived at their destination, and received the usual welcome.

'I see you adapt yourself to the customs of the country,' said his host at mealtime, and a slight titter went round the table. The Rev. Joseph joined in, taking it for granted that his somewhat unclerical garb was alluded to. In reply to enquiries he was informed that Bilton's Camp was a rough place, and Blue Grass even worse; and he was pleased to hear it, for until then his path had been too pleasant altogether; he hadn't had a chance to reprove anybody.

Bilton's Camp proved to be indeed a rough place. The men were civil, however, and as the parson had taken another exhilarating bath at the midday camp he appreciated the rude fare set before him; although here, as at the other place, there seemed to be a joke floating about that made everybody snigger.

The next day's journey, to Blue Grass, was but a short stage, and as the reverend gentleman had by this time become very friendly with Charley, the blackboy, the two rode along chatting pleasantly until they came somewhat unexpectedly on the new camp.

A very greasy cook and two or three gins in dilapidated shirts were the only people at home, and they stood open-eyed to greet the stranger.

Although Mr. Simmondsen had suited his attire to his surroundings, he still retained enough of the clerical garb to signify his profession. The cook, there-fore, at once took in the situation, and invited the parson under the tarpaulin which did temporary duty as a hut.

He informed his visitor, at whom he looked rather curiously, that 'everyone' was away, camped out, and that no one would return for a couple of days; that he was alone, excepting for two men who were at work in a yard a short distance off, and who would be in to dinner; in fact, they came up while he was speaking. Mr. Simmondsen took a great interest in this, the first real 'outside' camp he had seen; and as the two bush-men had gone down to the creek for a wash, and the cook was busy preparing a meal, he called Charley to ask him a few questions.

B

'What are these black women doing about the place, Charley?'

'O! all about missus belongah whitefellow,' was the astonishing reply.

It was some moments before Joseph could grasp the full sense of this communication; then he considered it his duty to read these sinners a severe lecture, and prepared one accordingly.

'Do you not understand,' he said, when the three men were together, 'the trespass you are committing against both social and Divine laws? If you do not respect one, perhaps you will the other.'

The cook stared at the bushmen in blank amazement, and the bushmen at the cook.

'I allude to these unfortunate and misled beings,' said the parson, waving his hand towards the half-clad gins.

A roar of laughter was the reply. 'Blest if that doesn't come well from *you*!' said the cook, when he could speak. The others chuckled in acquiescence.

'What do you mean?' said the indignant Joseph; 'I speak by right of my office.'

'Sit down and have some tucker,' said the cook; 'you're not a bad sort, I can see; but don't come the blooming innercent!'

The indignant pastor refused. He saw that his words were treated lightly, that no one would listen to him, and he left in high dudgeon. Charley had told him that there was a good lagoon about twelve miles on the road back to Upton Downs; he would go on there and camp—they had plenty of provisions on the pack-horse—and taking his bridle and calling the boy he went to catch his horse.

As he came back he overheard the fag-end of a remark the cook was making to the others. 'They came round the end of the scrub chatting as thick as thieves, and when I seed who it was—Lord! you could have wiped me out with one hand.'

This was worse than Greek to the Rev. Joseph. Greek he might have understood. In spite of a humble apology from the delinquent, he departed, and near sundown arrived at the lagoon Charley had spoken of. It was a lovely spot. One end was thick with broad-leaved water-lilies, but there was a clear patch at the other end promising the swim the good parson enjoyed so much.

When the tent was pitched he stood in Nature's garb about to enter the water, when Charley called to him. Pointing towards the lilies he told Mr. Simmondsen that he would get him some seed-pods which the blacks thought splendid eating. The clergyman had only got up to his waist when he heard a plunge behind him and saw Charley's dark form half splashing, half swimming towards the lilies. Presently his head emerged from a dive, and he beckoned towards the clergyman to come over and taste the aboriginal luxury. The Rev. Joseph paddled lazily over and investigated. The seed-pods proved of very pleasant flavour, and as the sun was nearly down, Mr. Simmondsen wended his way to the bank and emerged in the shallow water, with Charley a few paces behind him. For some reason he looked back. Shocking predicament! There was no shirking the fact; all the quiet laughter about 'the customs of the country', the unexplained allusions, the ribald manner of the cook, were intelligible in a flash. Charley was a woman!

The wicked manager of Upton Downs had started him on his travels with ('after the custom of the country') a black gin dressed in boy's clothes as a valet, and that gin had been recognized by everyone on the road. Mr. Simmondsen thought of the past and blushed. The night was spent in fervent prayer.

'My dear sir,' said Davis, the super. of Upton Downs, 'I did the best I could for you. Charlotte is as good as any blackboy, and knows all the country round here. Now, own up, didn't she look after you well?'

'You forget the scandal that may arise,' said the Rev. Joseph Simmondsen.

'Lord, man! who cares about what is done out here? Nobody will ever hear of it.'

Davis was wrong. Everybody did hear of it. The Rev. Simmondsen received indignant letters from his Bishop, his churchwardens, several missionary societies, and, last and worst, a letter of eternal farewell from the young lady to whom he was engaged to be married. Fortunately he inherited some money at the time, so he did the best thing possible—threw up the Church, went into squatting, and is now one of the most popular men in this district.

JOHN PRICE'S BAR OF STEEL
By Price Warung (William Astley)

THE sea-breeze fanned the symmetrical stems of the giant Araucaria transplanted by Colonel Foveaux to the front of a Government Cottage, and swept from its fronds a chord or two of the music which the undisturbed centuries had there garnered. The nearer face of Mount Pitt, alpine in its solitude, was dazzling in the pallor of a south sea moon; the blue of the

ocean lay intersected with broad, fan-like beams of
pearly radiance. It was such a night as poets dream
of and delight in, and, in other climes, as the nightingale sings to the listening rose; such a night as, in
this newest clime, John Price enjoyed to the utmost.

A born captain of men, and knowing the seamy side
of human nature, as (to the evil deities' sorrow) few
men who have visited these colonies have done, he
was so constituted as to intensely enjoy every form
of physical beauty. In the midst of any scenic splen-
dour, or in the presence of finely proportioned man,
convicted or not, as beautiful women, he would forget
even to fix his eyeglass; and the hard grey of his eyes
would lose that dreadful faculty of penetration in
which consisted the main source of his power over the
convict creature and the newer penal official. And
when John Price's face lost the use of the stony stare
of the crystal disc, and the metallic keenness of the
unveiled eye, then John Price was not himself.

There were frequent moments when he was not
himself. Take any of the sparse convict survivors of
the Old Regime, or any of the scarcely more numerous
representatives of the subordinate Penal Officialdom,
and they would deny this. They would assert that
John Price was never aught but himself—that is to
say, the sternest of disciplinarians, the most sceptical
of moralists, the most saturnine of humorists, and
the most exquisite of torturers. That drawing of him
is about as true in perspective as that other picture
limned by the partial hand of superior officers and of
personal friends, in which the figure of the commandant stands clothed with a majesty of character
little short, considering his temptations, of saintliness.
John Price was neither a saint, nor yet of that high
degree among demons which would entitle him to

a shout of 'Hail, brother!' from the sovereign and princes of the damned on his entrance into the nether world. He was, truly, a many-sided man, the majority of whose facets were, unfortunately for himself, shaped by the planing-steel of the System. The System put under its knife the material which, under other conditions, wielded as a sword against the nation's enemies, would have formed a general of inspired audacity, a leader of dauntless courage, and an administrator of unerring prescience. But—the Fates were just! If there was scarcely a convict whom the System and the Regime did not spoil more or less, neither did they spare the officials. And as John Price, from his varied service in three colonies, was the instrument of contamination to more destinies than was any other administrator, it was only to be expected that the loss he personally suffered should have exceeded that of all other servants of the System. The life which might have ended at the doors of Westminster Abbey was miserably let out by a felon's hand on Williamstown Pier. He whom the System created, died by the System. Which was justice according to the System.

On this night, when Despair, throned imperially in her realm of Norfolk Island, decked herself with the effulgence of Heaven in mockery of the twelve hundred kindred mortals who sweated terror-drops beneath their stamped blankets, or in the embrace of fetters which they nursed too deeply at night into the wounds it had punctured during the day; on this night John Price, Civil Commandant, passed, with a guest, from his dining-room to the veranda, and gazed on the glory.

He thrust the less known facets of his character into the view of his guest.

'A heavenly evening,' he said; 'I never saw a finer.'

'Nor I!' was the answer.

They exchanged no other word. Each steeped himself in the rapture of the moment, and forgot his companion. Price gazed in the direction of Phillip Island, his visitor to the zenith.

Then a child's voice broke the silence. A tiny, white-gowned figure glided out of the hall doorway, and called its father.

'Fa'ver! Where is you, fa'ver?'

'Here, sonnie. But, fie! Not in bed yet?'

The youngster trots on his naked feet half the length of the veranda, and, at his father's side, holds out his hands so that he might be lifted up.

'I t'udn't go to bed, fa'ver, not wi'out saying my new prayer.'

'A new prayer!'

A stern commandant stoops and gathers the little one within his arms. The guest thinks if he were the father he would have echoed the words ashamedly, for there is something discrepant between the position of an absolute ruler of twelve hundred slaves and the function of a father listening to the lisping of an infant's benison. Not so thinks John Price. With all his faults, he did not fear God, man, nor devil, and it is only the coward who insincerely gives heed to another's opinions. The whole world might have stood by, and John Price would have done just the same.

'Ees, a new prayer, fa'ver! Danny teached it me, an' I isn't to tell on'y you, fa'ver.'

'All right, little man, go on.'

The child slipped from the strong grasp, and knelt on the bare veranda boards.

'You believe in training up a child in the way he

should go, even if it isn't your way, eh, Price?' chuckled the guest.

The Civil Commandant, though Dr. Hampton was his official superior for the time being (inasmuch as that Lesser Providence to forty thousand souls, the Governor of Van Demonia, had entrusted to the ex-convict-ship-surgeon the potential duty of reporting on the 'moral state of Norfolk Island'), imperiously hushed him into silence.

'I believe in religion,' he said, 'for children and transports.'

And the doctor good-humouredly — for Price was a useful official—accepted the snub, with a rejoinder—

'Who, after all, are only children of a larger growth. They've to be fed, and put to bed, and whipped and locked up like children. But I'm interrupting—go on, my little boy!'

'I's not you's 'ittle boy—I's fa'ver's—isn't I, fa'ver?'

'Yes, yes! But say your prayers, sonnie! You'll get cold here. Hadn't you better say them to mamma or nurse, inside?'

'No, fa'ver, for Danny tol' me to say my new prayer to you wery ownself, fa'ver.'

'Well, well, go on!'

The child whispered the Lord's Prayer. His little head, curl-crowned, was reverently bent above his pressed palms.

After the one prayer, which has been the voice of all men in all ages of Christendom, he whispered his—

> 'Gentle Jesus, meek and mild,
>   Look 'pon 'ittle chil','

and thereafter, his piping struggling with drowsiness, his—

'God b'ess fa'ver, mu'ver, 'ittle sister, Sir John Fwan-in, where's he ever is, an' Lady Fwan-in, an' all —dear fr'ens . . . ' The curls, burdened by sleep, fell upon the loosened hands, and the childish accents dropped.

The father stooped to lift the boy, when Hampton, curious, said loudly:

'You haven't said your new prayer, my little man!'

The child, aroused, rubbed his knuckles into his eyes, and murmured a response.

'Oh, no—I's forgettin'. I'll say it now, fa'ver!'

He slipped again to the floor, and, putting himself once more into the posture of prayer, breathed, with a palpable reverence which made the words doubly terrible—

'God, p'ease damn John Price!'

It's a toss-up who developed a more refined capacity for cruelty—John Price or some of the transports whom John Price trained.

When Dr. Hampton was Governor of Western Australia he was accustomed to remark that never had he known or heard of John Price flinching, except on two occasions. The first was on a certain day in Tasmania, whose history we have yet to tell. The second was on this night.

The father shrank visibly as the child's voice breathed its innocent malediction. The pallor of his face was not that of the moonlight alone.

'Danny—taught—you—to say that?' he questioned the laddie.

But the child's head pressed against his knees in slumber. The father gathered the boy into his arms, and carried him into the house. As he placed the little fellow in his cot he paused, battled with himself for a moment as to whether he could touch those lips which had emitted so poignant a sting, and then, stooping, kissed the rich redness of their curves and dimples.

The child, semi-roused, stirred, and murmured caressingly, 'Fa-ver!'

'What are you going to do with the pris'ner who has put him up to saying that?' questioned Hampton, as the commandant came forth again to the veranda.

'Wait!'

'Why?'

'Because I can't punish the scoundrel now without confronting him with the child. Doing that would fix the—the—thing in the little cove's mind, and would help him to remember it. The words will slip away from his recollection if I do nothing to impress them upon him. Besides . . .'

'What?'

'To reveal to the pris'ner that he has——'

He paused again.

'Hurt you?' suggested Hampton, with that delicate malevolence, like a feline claw-scratch, which was one of his characteristics.

'If you like—sir!' Price was compelled to remind himself the doctor was not only his superior, but his guest. 'To let him know that he has hurt me—as you say—would be to incite every servant I have to play me the same trick. Don't you know, doctor, with all your experience of pris'ners, that the way to break 'em of a trick or practice not expressly prohibited by regulation is to say nothing about it? And that if you punish 'm for it, you'll give it an increased importance in their eyes?'

As an administrator in a large way, and truly merit-

ing Mr. Gladstone's encomium that 'he was
thoroughly qualified for the most responsible offices
in connexion with convict discipline', Hampton was
accustomed to consider himself John Price's superior,
but he deferred to the Civil Commandant in all
matters of precise knowledge. He said so now, and not
so much fearful that Price would be excited to an
unusual exercise of magnanimity, as curious as to the
way he should punish the convict who had invented
this newest devil's trick, asked the commandant, 'Was
he prepared to overlook the matter?'

'I said I would wait,' replied Price.

All things come to the man who waits.

Daniel Duncan, lifer, per *Westmoreland*, was one
of the four men allowed by Grace of the Authorities
to the commandant for domestic service. He had been
selected by the previous commandant, and Price had
retained him in the entourage of Government Cottage
till he had seen whether he could be replaced by a
more deserving man—that is to say, in the language of
the System, a man who was likely to be more useful
in the house.

Unfortunately for Danny, such a man was not long
in presenting himself to the commandant's august
notice. Somebody or other, who was so contemptible
a creature in the keen eyes of the Lords of Evil as
to be awarded by them a mere trifle of seven years'
confinement amid the beauties of the island, was
discovered to possess a pretty faculty for artistic
gardening. He had suggested one or two striking
means of improving the view from the cottage, and,
as the System was always anxious to improve upon
nature, he was to be granted a chance of gilding
refined gold, by being told off to reduce the tangled
exquisiteness of the pine-glades, and the honeyed

sweetness of the spice-land, to the order so beloved of penal officialdom.

Now, order is a very fine thing, and, as a vile body on which the Regime had performed countless experiments, with the object of instilling a sense of orderliness into his soul, Daniel Duncan should have been appreciative of Mr. Price's motive in superseding him by the other prisoner. But even so admirably devised a plan of morality, as was comprised in the Transportation System, could not eradicate from Duncan's nature that tendency towards selfishness which the less pious surroundings of his youth had encouraged. Instead of meeting Mr. Price half-way, so to speak, and welcoming his relegation to the gaol cell as an opportunity for enjoying that self-communion which is so essential to the culture of good character, he resented his removal. And, resenting it, had directed the innocence of the commandant's little child into the channel of cursing. Of course it was not prudent of Danny to act in this fashion, but wherever, since the epoch of Eden, did splenetic man act prudently?

He knew it was imprudent, and he knew, moreover, that it was damnable to teach child lips to syllable imprecations. And with all his knowledge, he risked the consequences of the imprudence for the sake of the damnableness. Which was a corollary of the System.

He knew it was the beginning of the consequences when, standing on the veranda steps, the morning after the night, the commandant said smilingly: 'Make the most of your last day, Duncan! You go into the gaol-gang to-morrow.'

The prisoner looked defiantly into the disc of unrimmed glass—and trembled as he saluted.

'Yes, sir!'

'And, Duncan——'

'Sir!'

'You are fond of children, Duncan?'

'Yes, sir.'

'Then, as you have, I believe, served the cottage pretty well, you shall have one indulgence, Duncan— the youngsters shall come over sometimes. But no more prayers, Duncan; no more prayers.'

Duncan, though the world was singing in its warm bath of sunlight, shivered again, and bowed his head over the mattock. He regretted his imprudence now.

Three days later the main guard—the gaol—turned out as Dr. Hampton and the commandant arrived to inspect.

'Muster!' ordered the Civil Commandant, speaking to Assistant-Superintendent Tuff.

The occupants of the gaol, saving those waiting trial, who were doubly ironed in the cells, were ranged in the corridor.

The authorities intended to 're-form the gangs' that day, and 'out' labour had ceased for the time being, a circumstance which was unpalatable to Tuff and disastrous to Danny Duncan. For the gaol-men were usually mustered by their gangs, and Tuff's special lot for muster could be comprehended by a glance, and he could rattle off the names from the muster-book as though he were reading them. Read them he could not, unless they were written in text-hand. With forty men, however, to call over, this mechanical process was impossible, and he could not read the names from the roll, because the entries were made in a running hand.

'Muster!' repeated the Civil Commandant.

Tuff, saluting, in deprecatory tones informed their Honours that 'the names wasn't large 'nuff for his weak eyes to see, yer Honours'.

'Weak eyes!' echoed the commandant. 'I didn't know you had weak eyes.'

'Yes, sir! But they're jest come on, sir! They'll be better shortly, sir!' And Tuff vowed to himself that he would give some of the hospital rations of rum and tobacco to some convict to coach him in reading 'small-hand'. 'Be better shortly, sir. An' shall one of the men read over, sir?'

The commandant took no notice of the question, but pursued his motive of inquiry.

'Just come on, has the weakness! Now, how weak are they? Look at Duncan there, Duncan 41—392. Duncan of the *Westmoreland*. Can you see that bar of steel—a dangerous weapon specially prohibited by regulation to be in the possession of pris'ners—which he has?'

Tuff looks stupidly at Duncan; Duncan regards himself as stupidly; there is a forward craning of necks down the line, as crows ranged on a rock might protrude their beaks to watch the turning of a living substance into carrion.

For a second there is nothing to be seen by any one; Duncan's hands are, as per regulation, clapped at his sides. Where, what, can be the bar of steel?

The Civil Commandant, John Price, steps forward, pauses an instant to adjust his eyeglass, and with his index-finger touches the fatal object.

'Present this pris'ner after muster for having in his possession a dangerous weapon, and report yourself to the doctor forthwith, Mr. Tuff, in order to have that weakness remedied. It's time something was done to correct your sight when you allow pris'ners—

and gaol-gangers above all others—to carry bars of steel on their persons. Give me the book!'

The muster began, proceeded, ended. And then Duncan, Daniel, No. 41—392, per *Westmoreland*, was presented at Court. Assistant-Superintendent Tuff presented, and Civil Commandant John Price, acting as magistrate, presided. And Dr. Hampton, as an interested spectator, was accommodated with a seat.

'Defence, pris'ner?' demanded the Court. 'What d'ye say?'

'Only that your boy brought it me. I was a-making him sails for his toy-boat when you transferred me, sir, and the little chap, when he see me yesterday, brought it me, sir, to finish 'em. From his mammy, he said, sir.'

'You admit another offence as well? Holding communication with free persons' children is illegal, and you know it. But we'll leave that to another day. No other defence?'

The prisoner held his breath. So did all the Court, save the commandant and Dr. Hampton. They breathed easily enough, you may depend. Only a Secretary of State could affect their respiration.

'Then fifty lashes—and the wet quarry for six months—and the article to be forfeited. May I ask your opinion, sir?'

'A very proper sentence in my judgement,' approved the inspecting officer. 'Very!'

And he gazed steadily into the eyeglass, and saw in the steely eyes an interpretation of the sentence which expressed his own mind. John Price had waited only three days.

Fame is a product of accident. So is infamy.

But it is questionable whether it was altogether by accident that Danny Duncan, per *Westmoreland*, became possessed of that common sewing-needle—size No. 2.

SCRAMMY 'AND

By BARBARA BAYNTON

ALONG the selvedge of the scrub-girt plain the old man looked long and earnestly. His eyes followed an indistinct track that had been cut by the cart, journeying at rare intervals to the distant township. At dawn some weeks back it had creaked across the plain, and, at a point where the scrub curved, the husband had stopped the horse while the woman parted the tilt and waved good-bye to the bent, irresponsive old man and his dog. It was her impending motherhood that made them seek the comparative civilization of the township, and the tenderness of her womanhood brought the old man closer to her as they drove away. Every week since that morning had been carefully notched by man and dog, and the last mark, cut three nights past, showed that time was up. Twice this evening he thought he saw the dust rise as he looked, but longer scrutiny showed only the misty evening light.

He turned to where a house stood out from a background of scrub. Beside the calf-pen near it, a cow gave answer and greeting to the penned calf. 'No use pennin' up ther calf,' he muttered, 'when they don't come. Won't do it ter-morrer night.' He watched anxiously along the scrub. 'Calf must 'ave got 'is 'ed through ther rails an' sucked 'er. No one else can't

'ave done it. Scrammy's gorn; 'twarn't Scrammy.'
But the gloom of fear settled on his wizened face as he
shuffled stiffly towards the sheep-yard.

His body jerked; there was a suggestion of the dog
in his movements; and in the dog, as he rounded up
the sheep, more than a suggestion of his master. He
querulously accused the dog of 'rushin' 'em, 'stead
er allowin' Billy (the leader) to lead 'em'.

When they were yarded he found fault with the
hurdles. 'Some 'un 'ad been meddlin' with 'em.' For
two pins he would 'smash 'em up with ther axe'.

The eyes of the sheep reflected the haze-opposed
glory of the setting sun. Loyally they stood till a grey
quilt swathed them. In their eyes glistened luminous
tears materialized from an atmosphere of sighs. The
wide plain gauzed into a sea on which the hut floated
lonely. Through its open door a fire gleamed like the
red, steaming mouth of an engine. Beyond the hut a
clump of myalls loomed spectral and wraith-like, and
round them a gang of crows cawed noisily, irreverent
of the great silence.

Inside the hut, the old man, still querulous, talked
to the listening dog. He uncovered a cabbage-tree
hat—his task of the past year—and laid upside down,
on the centre of the crown, a star-shaped button that
the woman had worked for him.

'It's orl wrong, see!' The dog said he did. '''Twon't
do!' he shouted with the emphasis of deafness. The
dog admitted that it would not. 'An' she done it like
thet, ter spile it on me 'er purpus. She done it outer
jealersy, 'cos I was makin' it for 'im. Could 'ave done
it better meself, though I'm no 'and at fancy stitchin'.
But she can't make a 'at like thet. No woman could.
They're no good.' The dog did not dispute this
condemnation.

'I tole 'er ter put a anker jes' there,' he continued. He pointed to the middle of the button which he still held upside down. 'Thet's no anker!' The dog subtly indicated that there was another side to the button. 'There ain't,' shouted the old man. 'What do you know about an anker; you never see a real one on a ship in yer life!' There was an inaudible disparaging reference to 'imperdent kerloneyals' which seemed to crush the dog. To mollify him the man got on his knees and, bending his neck, showed the dog a faded anchor on the top of the cabbage-tree hat on his head. A little resentment would have served the dog, but he was too eager for peace.

Noting this, the old man returned to the button for reminiscences. 'An' yet you thort at fust a thing like thet would do.' There was a sign of dissent from the dog. 'Yer know yer did—Sir. An' wot's more yer don't bark at 'er like yer used ter!'

The dog was uneasy, and intimated that he would prefer to have that past buried.

'None er thet now; yer know yer don't.' Bending the button he continued, 'They can't never do anythin' right, an' orlways, continerally they gets a man inter trouble.'

He had accidentally turned the button, he reversed it, looking swiftly at the dog. 'Carn't do nothin' with it. A thing like thet! Might as well fling it in the fire!' He put it carefully away.

'W'ere's 'e now?' he asked abruptly. The dog indicated the route taken by the cart.

'An' 'ow long as 'e bin away?' The dog looked at the tally-stick hanging on the wall. 'Yes, orl thet time! What does 'e care about me an' you, now 'e's got 'er! 'E was fust rate afore 'e got 'er. Wish I 'ad er gorn down thet time 'e took their sheep. I'd er seen no woman didn't grab 'im. They're stuck away down there an' us orl alone 'ere by ourselves with only ther sheep. Scrammy sez 'e wouldn't stay if 'e wus me. See's there any signs er 'em comin' back!'

While the dog was out he hastily tried to fix the button, but failed. 'On'y mist, no dust?' he asked, when his messenger returned. 'No fear,' he growled, "e won't come back no more; stay down there an' nuss ther babby. It'll be a gal too, sure to be! Women are orlways 'avin' gals. It'll be a gal sure enough.'

He looked sternly at the unagreeing dog. 'Yer don't think so! Course yer don't. You on 'er side? Yer are, Loo!'

The dog's name was 'Waderloo' (Waterloo) and had three abbreviations. 'Now then, War!' meant mutual understanding and perfect fellowship. 'What's thet, Warder?' meant serious business. But 'Loo' was ever sorrowfully reminiscent. And accordingly 'Loo' was now much affected and disconcerted by the steady accusing eyes of the old man.

'An' wot's more,' he continued, 'I believe ye'll fool roun', ye'll fool aroun' 'er wusser nor ever w'en she comes back with ther babby.' At this grave charge the dog, either from dignity or injury, was silent. His master, slowly and with some additions, repeated the prophecy, and again the dog gave him only silent attention.

"Ere she comes with ther babby,' he cried, flinging up his arms in clumsy feigned surprise. Loo was not deceived, and stood still.

'Oh, I'm a ole liar, am I? Yit's come ter thet, ez it? Well, better fer I ter be a liar 'n fer you ter lose yer manners—Sir.'

In vain Loo protested. His master turned round, and when poor Loo faced that way he drew his feet under him on the bunk, and faced the wall. When the distressed Loo, from outside the hut, caught his eye through the cracks, he closed his own, to stifle remorse at the eloquent dumb appeal.

Usually their little differences took some time to evaporate; the master sulked with his silent mate till some daring feat with snake or dingo on the dog's part mollified him. Loo, probably on the lookout for such foes, moved to the end of the hut nearest the sheep. Two hasty squints revealed his departure, but not his whereabouts, to the old man, who coughed and waited, but for once expected too much from poor Loo. His legs grew cramped, still he did not care to make the first move. It was a godsend when an undemonstrative ewe and demonstrative lamb came in.

Before that ewe he held the whole of her disgraceful past, and under the circumstances, "'er imperdence—'er blarsted imperdence!' in unceremoniously intruding on his privacy with her blanky blind udder, and more than blanky bastard, was something he could not and would not stand.

'None er yer sauce now!' He jumped down, and shook his fist at the unashamed, silent mother. 'Warder,' he shouted, 'Warder, put 'em out!'

Warder did so, and when he came back his master explained to him that the thing that 'continerally an' orlways' upset him was 'thet dam ole yeo'. It was the only sorrow he had or ever would have in life. 'She wusn't nat'ral, thet ole yeo.' There was something in the Bible, he told War, about 'yeos' with barren udders. 'An' 'twarn't as though she didn't know.' For that was her third lamb he had had to poddy. But not another bite would he give this one. He had made up his mind now, though it had been 'worritin'' him all day. 'Jes' look at me,' showing his lamb-bitten fingers. 'Wantin' ter get blood outer a stone!'

He shambled round, covered the cabbage-tree hat and the despised woman-worked button carefully; then his better nature prevailed. 'See 'ere!' and there was that in his voice that indicated a moral victory. He took off the cloth and placed the button right side up and in its proper place. 'Will thet do yer?' he asked.

After this surrender his excitement was so great that the dog shared it. He advised War to lie down 'an' 'ave a spell', and in strong agitation he went round the sheep-yard twice, each time stopping to hammer down the hurdles noisily, and calling to War not to 'worrit; they's orlright now, an' firm as a rock'.

Through these proceedings the ewe and lamb followed him, the lamb—lamb fashion—mixing itself with his legs. He had nothing further to say to the ewe, but from the expression of her eyes she still had an open mind towards him. Both went with him inside the hut. Were they intruders? the dog asked. He coughed and affected not to hear, went to the door, looked out and said the mist was gone, but the dog re-asked. 'I think, War, there's some er that orker'd little dam fool's grub lef',' he said, gently extricating the lamb from between his legs, 'an' it'll on'y spile. Jes' this once an' no more, min' yer, an' then you skiddy addy,' he said to the ewe. He carried the lamb outside, for he would not finger-suckle it that night before Waterloo.

From his bunk-head he took an axe, cut in two a myall log, and brought in half. He threw it on the fire for a back-log, first scraping the live coals and ashes to a heap for his damper.

He filled and trimmed his slush lamp, and from

a series of flat pockets hanging on the wall he took thread, needle, and beeswax. He hung a white cloth in a way that defined the eye of the needle which he held at long range; but vary as he would from long to longest the thread remained in one hand, the needle in the other. Needle, thread, light, everything was wrong, he told War. 'Es fer me, thenk a Lord I ken see an' year's well's ever I could. Ehm, War! See any change?' War said there had been no change observable to him. 'There ain't no change in you neither, War!' he said in gratitude to the grizzled old dog. But he felt that War had been disappointed at his failure, and he promised that he would rise betimes to-morrow and sew on the button by daylight.

'Never mind, War; like ter see 'em after supper?' Comradeship was never by speech better demonstrated.

From the middle beam the old man untied two bags. Boiled mutton was in one, and the heel of a damper in another.

'No blowey carn't get in there, eh?' The dog looked at the meat uncritically, but critically noted the resting-place of two disturbed 'bloweys'.

'No bones!' He had taken great care to omit them. 'Neow!' As ever, War took his word; he caught and swallowed instantly several pieces flung to him. At the finish his master's 'Eny?' referred to bones. War's grateful eyes twinkled, 'Not a one.' 'Never is neow!' had reference to a trouble War had had with one long ago.

It was now time for his own supper, but after a few attempts he shirked it. 'Blest if I evven fergot t' bile th' billy; funny ef me t' ferget!' He held his head for a moment, then filled the billy, and in a strange uncertainty went towards and from the fire with it, and in the end War thought there was no sense at all in putting it so far from the blaze when it had to boil.

'Tell yer wot, War, w'ile it biles us'll count 'em. Gimme appertite, ehm, War?'

War thought 'countin' 'em' was the tonic. Then together they closed the door, spread a kangaroo-skin on the floor, and put the slush lamp where the light fell on it. The man sat down, so did War, took off his belt, turned it carefully, tenderly, and opened his knife to cut the stitching. This was a tedious process, for it was wax thread, and had been crossed and recrossed. Then came the chink of the coins falling. The old man counted each as it rolled out, and the dog tallied with a paw.

'No more?' Certainly more, said War. A jerk, tenderly calculated, brought another among the seductive heap.

'All?' No—still the upraised paw. The old man chuckled.

'Ole 'en gets more b' scratchin'.' This was the dog's opinion, and a series of little undulations produced another, and after still further shaking, yet another.

War was asked with ridiculous insincerity, 'All?' and with ridiculous sincerity his solemn eyes and dropped paw said 'All.' Then there was the honest count straight through, next the side show with its pretence of 'disrememberin'', or doubts as to the number—doubts never laid except by a double count. In the first, so intent was the man, that he forgot his mate; though his relief in being good friends again had made him ignore his fear.

But the dog had heard an outside sound, and, moving to the door, waited for certainty. At this stage the man missed his mate's eyes.

He lay face downward, covering his treasure, when

he realized his friend was uneasy. And, as the dog kept watch, he thrust them back hurriedly, missing all the pleasure and excitement of a final recount.

With dumb show he asked several questions of his sentinel, and took his answers from his eyes. Then, when Warder, relieved, began to walk about, the old man with forced confidence chaffed him. He sought refuge from his own fears by trying to banish the dog's, and suggested dingoes at the sheep-yard, or a 'goanner' on the roof. 'Well, 'twas 'possum,' he said, making a pretence of even then hearing and distinguishing the sound.

But round his waist the belt did not go that night. Only its bulk in his life of solitariness could have conceived its hiding-place.

He bustled around as one having many tasks, but these he did aimlessly. With a pretence of unconcern he attempted to hum, but broke off frequently to listen. He was plainly afraid of the dog's keen ears missing something. But his mate's tense body proclaimed him on duty.

'I know who yer thort 'twas, Warder!' They were sitting side by side, yet he spoke very loudly. 'Scrammy 'And, Ehm?' He had guessed correctly.

'An' yer thort yer see 'im lars' night!' He was right again.

'An' yer thort 'twas 'im that 'ad bin ramsakin' the place yesterday, when we was shepherdin'. An' yer thort 't must 'ave bin 'im shook the tommy!' The dog's manner evinced that he had not altered this opinion. The old man's heart beat loudly.

'No fear, Warder! Scrammy's gone, gone 'long ways now, Warder!' But Warder's pricked ears doing double duty showed he was unconvinced. ''Sides, Scrammy wouldn't 'urt er merskeeter,' he continued.

'Poor ole Scrammy! 'Twarn't 'im shook the tommy, Warder!' The dog seemed to be waiting for the suggestion of another thief having unseen crept into their isolated lives, but his master had none to offer. Both were silent, then the man piled wood on the fire, remarking that he was going to sit up all night. He asked the dog to go with him to the table to feed and trim the slush lamp.

Those quavering shadows along the wall were caused by its sizzling flare flickering in the darkness, the dog explained. 'Thort it mighter bin ther blacks outside,' the man said. 'They ain't so fur away, I know! 'Twar them killed ther lamb down in ther creek.' He spoke unusually loudly. He hoped they wouldn't catch 'poor ole one-'anded Scrammy'. He said how sorry he was for 'poor ole Scrammy, 'cos Scrammy wouldn't 'urt no one. He on'y jes' came ter see us 'cos 'e was a ole friend. He was gone along ways ter look fur work, 'cos 'e was stony-broke after blueing 'is cheque at ther shanty sixty miles away'.

'I tole 'im,' he continued in an altered voice, 'thet I couldn't lend 'im eny 'cos I 'ad sent all my little bit er money (he whispered "money") to ther bank be ther boss. Didn' I?' Emphatically his mate intimated that this was the case. He held his head in his shaking hands, and complained to the dog of having 'come over dizzy'.

He was silent for a few moments, then, abruptly raising his voice, he remarked that their master was a better tracker than 'Saddle-strap Jimmy', or any of the blacks. He looked at the tally-stick, and suddenly announced that he knew for a certainty that the boss and his wife would return that night or early next morning, and that he must see about making them a damper. He got up and began laboriously to mix soda

and salt with the flour. He looked at the muddy-
coloured water in the bucket near the wall, and
altered his mind.

'I'll bile it first, War, same as 'er does, 'cos jus' neow
an' then t' day I comes over dizzy-like. See th' mist t's
even! Two more, then rain—rain, an' them two out
in it without no tilt on the cart.' He sat down for a
moment, even before he dusted his ungoverned floury
hands.

'Pint er tea, War, jes' t' warm ther worms an' lif'
me 'art, eh?'

Every movement of the dog was in accord with this
plan.

His master looked at the billy, and said ''twarn't
bilin'', and that a watched pot never boiled. He rested
a while silently with his floury hands covering his face.
He bent his mouth to the dog's ear and whispered.
Warder, before replying, pointed his ears and raised
his head. The old man's hand rested on the dog's
neck.

'Tell yer wot, War, w'ile it's bilin' I'll 'ave another
go at ther button, 'cos I want ter give 'im ther 'at as
soon as he comes. S'pose they'll orl come!' He had sat
down again, and seemed to whistle his words. 'Think
they'll orl come, Loo?'

Loo would not commit himself about 'orl', not
being quite sure of his master's mind.

The old man's mouth twitched, a violent effort
jerked him. 'Might be a boy arter orl; ain't cocky
sure!' His wagged irresponsibly, and his hat fell off
as he rolled into the bunk. He made no effort to
replace it, and, for once unheeded, the fire flickered
on his polished head. Never before had the dog seen
its baldness. The change from nightcap to hat had
always been effected out of his sight.

'War, ain't cocky sure it'll be a gal?'

The dog discreetly or modestly dropped his eyes, but his master had not done with concessions.

'Warder!' Warder looked at him. 'Tell yer wot, you can go every Sunday evenin' an' see if 'tis a boy!'

He turned over on his side, with his face to the wall. Into the gnarled uncontrolled hand swaying over the bunk the dog laid his paw.

When the old man got up he didn't put on his hat, nor even pick it up. Altogether there was an unusual-ness about him to-night that distressed his mate. He sat up after a few moments, and threw back his head, listening strainingly for outside sounds. The silence soothed him, and he lay down again. A faded look was in his eyes.

'Thort I 'eard bells—church bells,' he said to the dog looking up too, but at him. 'Couldn't 'ave. No church bells in the bush. Ain't 'eard 'em since I lef' th' ole country.' He turned his best ear to the fancied sound.

He raised himself from the bunk, and followed the dog's eyes to a little smoke-stained bottle on the shelf. 'No, no, War!' he said. 'Thet's for sickness; mus' be a lot worser'n wot I am!' Breathing noisily, he went through a list of diseases, among which were palsy, snake-bite, 'dropersy', and 'suddint death', before he would be justified in taking the last of his pain-killer.

His pipe was in his hidden belt, but he had another in one of those little pockets. He tried it, said ''twouldn't draw'r', and very slowly and clumsily stripped the edge of a cabbage-tree frond hanging from the rafter, and tried to push it through the stem, but could not find the opening. He explained to the intent dog that the hole was stopped up, but it didn't matter. He placed it under the bunk where he sat, because first he would ''ave a swig er tea'. His head kept wagging at the billy. No, until the billy boiled he was going to have a little snooze.

Involuntarily he murmured, looking at his mate, 'Funny w'ere ther tommy'awk's gone ter!' Then he missed the axe. 'My Gord, Warder!' he said, 'I lef' the axe outside; clean forgot it!' This discovery alarmed the dog, and he suggested they should bring it in.

'No, no!' he said, and his floury face grew ghastly.

He stood still—all his faculties seemed paralysed for a time—then fell stiffly on his bunk. Quite suddenly he staggered to his feet, rubbed his eyes, and between broken breaths he complained of the bad light, and that the mist had come again.

One thing the dog did when he saw his master's face even by that indifferent light, he barked low, and terribly human.

The old man motioned for silence. 'Ah!' His jaw fell but for a moment. Then a steely grimness took possession. He clung to the table and beckoned the dog with one crooked finger. 'Scrammy?' cunningly, cautiously, indicating outside, and as subtly the dog replied. Then he groped for his bunk, and lay with his eyes fixed on the billy, his mouth open.

He brought his palms together after a while. ''Cline our 'earts ter keep this lawr,' he whispered, and for a moment his eyes rested on the hiding-place, then turned to the dog.

And though soon after there was a sinister sound outside, which the watchful dog immediately challenged, the man on the bunk lay undisturbed.

Warder growling savagely went along the back wall of the hut, and despite the semi-darkness, his eyes, scintillating with menace through the cracks, drove from them a crouching figure who turned hastily to grip the axe near the myall logs. He stumbled over the lamb's feeding-pan lying in the hut's shadow. The moonlight glittering on the blade recalled the menace of the dog's eyes. The man grabbed the weapon swiftly, but even with it he felt the chances were unequal.

But he had planned to fix the dog. He would unpen the sheep, and the lurking dingoes, coming up from the creek to worry the lambs, would prove work for the dog. He crouched silently to again deceive this man and dog, and crept towards the sheep-yard. But the hurdles of the yard faced the hut, and the way those thousand eyes reflected the rising moon was disconcerting. The whole of the night seemed pregnant with eyes.

All the shadows were slanting the wrong way, and the moon was facing him, with its man calmly watching every movement. It would be dawn before it set. He backed from the yard to the myalls' scant screen. Even they had moulted with age. From under his coat the handle of the axe protruded. His mind worked his body. Hugging the axe, he crept towards some object, straightened himself to reach, then with the hook on his handless arm drew back an imaginary bolt, and stooping entered. With the axe in readiness he crept to the bunk. Twice he raised it and struck.

It was easy enough out there, yet even in imagination his skin was wet and his mouth was dry. Even if the man slept, there was the dog. He must risk letting out the sheep. He covered the blade of the axe and went in a circuit to the sheep, and got over the yard on the side opposite to the hut. They rushed from him and huddled together, leaving him, although stooping, exposed. He had calculated for this, but not for the effect upon himself. Could they in the hut see him, he would be no match for the dog even with the axe. Heedlessly, fear-driven, he rushed to where he could see the door, regardless of exposing himself. Nothing counted now, but that the dog or the old man should not steal upon him unawares.

The door was still closed. No call for 'Warder!' came from it, though he stood there a conspicuous object. While he watched he saw a ewe lamb make for the hut's shelter. He stooped, still watching, and listened, but could hear nothing. He crept forward and loosened the hurdles. Never were they noisier, he was sure. He knew that the sheep would not go through while he was there. He crept away, but although the leader noted the freed exit, he and those he led were creatures of habit. None were hungry, and they were unused to feeding at night, though in the morning came man and dog never so early they were waiting.

Round the yard and past the gateway he drove them again and again. He began to feel impotently frenzied in the fear that the extraordinary lightness meant that daylight must be near. Every moment he persuaded himself that he could see more plainly. He held out his one hand and was convinced.

He straightened himself, rushed among them, caught one, and ran it kicking through the opening. It came back the moment he freed it. However it served his purpose, for as he crouched there, baffled, he unexpectedly saw them file out. Then they rushed through in an impatient struggling crowd, each fearing to be last with this invader.

When he 'barrowed' out the first, he had kept his eyes on the hut, and had seen an old ewe and lamb run to it and bunt the closed door. But if there was any movement inside, the noise of the nearer sheep killed it.

They were all round the hut, for above it hung the moon, and they all made for the light. He crept after them, his ears straining for sound, but his head bobbing above them to watch the still closed door.

Inside, long since, the back-log had split with an explosion that scattered the coals near enough to cause the billy to boil, and the blaze showed the old man's eyes set on the billy. The dog looked into them, then laid his head between his paws and, still watching his master's face, beat the ground with his tail. He whined softly and went back to his post at the door, his eyes snapping flintily, his teeth bared. Along his back the hair rose like bristles. He sent an assurance of help to the importunate ewe and lamb. As the sheep neared the hut he ran to the bunk, raised his head to a level with his master's, and barked softly. He waited, and despite the eager light in his intelligent face his master and mate did not ask him any questions as to the cause of these calling sheep. Why did he not rise, and with him re-yard them, then gloatingly ask him where was the chinky crow by day, or sneaking dingo by night, that was any match for them, and then demand from his four-footed trusty mate the usual straightforward answer? Was there to be no discussion as to which heard the noise first, nor the final compromise of a dead-heat?

The silence puzzled the man outside sorely; he crouched, watching both door and shutter. The sheep were all round the hut. Man and dog inside must hear them. Why, when a dingo came that night he camped with them, they heard it before it could reach a lamb. If only he had known then what he knew now ! His hold on the axe tightened. No one had seen him come;

none should see him go! Why didn't that old fellow wake to-night?—for now, as he crept nearer the hut, he could hear the whining dog, and understood, he was appealing to his master.

He lay flat on the ground and tried to puzzle it out. The sheep had rushed back disorganized and were again near the hut and yard. Both inside must know. They were waiting for him. They were preparing for him, and that was why they were letting the dingoes play up with the sheep. That was the reason they did not openly show fight.

Still he would have sacrificed half of the coveted wealth to be absolutely certain of what their silence meant. It was surely almost daylight. He spread out the fingers of his one hand; he could see the colour of the blood in the veins. He must act quickly, or he would have to hide about for another day. And the absent man might return. To encourage himself, he tried to imagine the possession of that glittering heap that he had seen them counting on the mat. Yet he had grown cold and dejected, and felt for the first time the weight of the axe. It would be all right if the door would open, the old man come out and send the dog to round up the sheep. It was getting daylight, and soon shelter would be impossible.

He crept towards the hut, and this time he felt the edge of the axe. Right and left the sheep parted. There was nothing to be gained now in crawling, for the hostility of the dog told him that he could be seen. He stood, his body stiffened with determination.

Mechanically he went to the door; he knew the defensive resources of the hut. He had the axe, and the stolen tomahawk was stuck in the fork of those myalls. He had no need for both. The only weapon that the old fellow had was the useless butcher's knife.

His eyes protruded, and unconsciously he felt his stiffened beard.

He breathed without movement. There was no sound now from man or dog. In his mind he saw them waiting for him to attack the door; this he did not debate nor alter. He went to the shutter, ran the axe's edge along the hide hinges, pushed it in, then stepped back.

Immediately the dog's head appeared. He growled no protest, but the flinty fire from his eyes and the heat of his suppressed breath, hissing between his bared fangs, revealed to Scrammy that in this contest, despite the axe, his one hand was a serious handicap.

With the first blow his senses quickened. The slush lamp had gone out and there was no hint of daylight inside. This he noted between his blows at the dog, as he looked for his victim. It was strange the old fellow did not show fight! Where was he hiding? Was it possible that, scenting danger, he had slipped out? He recalled the dog's warning when his master was counting his hoard. The memory of that chinking belt-hidden pile dominated greedily. Had the old man escaped? He would search the hut; what were fifty dogs' teeth? In close quarters he would do for him with one blow.

He was breathing now in deep gasps. The keen edge of the axe severed the hide-hinged door. He rushed it; then stood back swinging the axe in readiness. It did not fall, for the bolt still held it. But this was only what a child would consider a barrier. One blow with the axe-head smashed the bolt. The door fell across the head of the bunk, the end partly blocking the entrance. He struck a side blow that sent it along the bunk.

The dog was dreadfully distressed. The bushman outside thought the cause the fallen door. Face to face

C

they met—determined battle in the dog's eyes met murder in the man's. He brandished an axe circuit, craned his neck, and by the dull light of the fire searched the hut. He saw no one but the dog. Unless his master was under the bunk, he had escaped. The whole plot broke on him quite suddenly! The cunning old miser, knowing his dog would show his flight by following, had locked him in, and he had wasted all this time barking up the wrong tree. He would have done the old man to death that minute with fifty brutal blows. He would kill him by day or night.

He ran round the brush sheep-yard, kicking and thrusting the axe through the thickest parts. He had not hidden there, nor among the myall clump where he had practised his bloody plot. The dog stood at the doorway of the hut. He saw this as he passed through the sheep on his way to search the creek. He was half-minded to try to invite the dog's confidence and co-operation by yarding them.

He looked at them, and the moonlight's undulating white scales across their shorn backs brought out the fresh tar brand 8, setting him thinking of the links of that convict-gang chain long ago. Lord, how light it must be for him to see that!

He held out his hand again. There was no perceptible change in the light. There were hours yet before daylight. He moulded his mind to that.

The creek split the plain, and along it here and there a few she-oak blots defined it. He traversed it with his eyes. There were no likely hiding-places among the trees, and it would be useless to search them. Suddenly it struck him that the old man might be creeping along with the sheep—they were so used to him. He ran and headed them, driving them swiftly back to the yard. Before they were in he knew he was wrong. Again he turned and scanned the creek, but felt no impulse to search it. It was half a mile from the hut. It was impossible that the old man could have got there, or that he could have reached the more distant house. Besides, why did the dog stay at the door unless on guard? He ran back to the hut.

The dog was still there, and in no way appeased by the yarding of the sheep. He swore at the threatening brute, and cast about for a gibber to throw, but stones were almost unknown there. A sapling would serve him! Seven or eight myall logs lay near for firewood, but all were too thick to be wielded. There was only the clump of myalls, and the few stunted she-oaks bordering the distant creek. To reach either would mean a dangerous delay. Oh, by God, he had it! These poles keeping down the bark roof. He ran to the back of the hut, cut a step in a slab and, putting his foot in it, hitched the axe on one of the desired poles and was up in a moment. He could hear the cabbage fronds hanging from the rafters shiver with the vibration, but there was no other protest from inside.

He shifted a sheet of rotten bark; part of it crumbled and fell inside on the prostrate door, sounding like the first earth on a coffin, in a way that the dog particularly resented. He knelt and carefully eyed the interior. The dog's glittering eyes met his. The door lay as it had fallen along the bunk. The fire was lightless, yet he could see more plainly, but the cause was not manifest, till from the myalls quite close the jackasses chorused. From his post the dog sent them a signal. Quite unaccountably the man's muscles relaxed. 'Oh, Christ!' he said, dropping the pole. He sprang up and faced the east, then turned to the traitorous faded moon. The daylight had come.

The sweat stung his quivering body. Slowly, he made an eye circuit round the plain; no human being was in sight. All he had to face was a parcel of noisy jackasses and a barking dog! He would soon silence the dog. He took the pole and made a jab at the whelping brute. One thing he noticed, that if he did get one home, it was only when he worked near the horizontal door. His quickened senses guessed at the reason. He could have shifted the door easily with his pole, yet feared, because, if the old man were under, he would expose himself to two active enemies. He must get to close quarters with the dog, and chop him in two, or brain him with the axe.

He ripped off another sheet of bark, and smashed away a batten that broke his swing. Encircling a rafter with his hooked arm, he lay flat, his feet pressing another just over the bunk, because only there would the dog hold his ground. One blow well directed got home. He planted his feet firmly, and made another with such tremendous force that his support snapped. He let go the axe and it fell on the door. He gripped with his hand the rafter nearest, but strain as he would he could not balance his body. He hung over the door, and the dog sprang at him and dragged him down. In bitten agony, he dropped on the door, that instantly up-ended.

It was daylight, and in that light the power of those open eyes set in that bald head, fixed on the billy beside the dead fireplace, was mightier than the dog. His unmaimed hand had the strength of both. He lifted the door and shielded himself with it as he backed out.

But that was not all the dog wanted. At the doorway he waited to see that the fleeing man had no further designs on the sheep.

It was time they were feeding. Though the hurdles were down, even from the doorway, the dog was their master. He waited for commands from his, and barked them back till noon.

Several times that day the ewe and lamb came in, looked without speculation at the figure on the bunk, then moved to the dead fireplace. But though the water in the billy was cold, the dog would not allow either to touch it. That was for tea when his master woke.

There was another circumstance. Those blowflies were welcome to the uncovered mutton. Throughout that day he gave them undisputed right, but they had to be content with it.

Next day the ewe and lamb came again. The lamb bunted several irresponsive objects—never its dam's udder—baaing listlessly. Though the first day the ewe had looked at the bunk, and baaed, she was wiser now, though sheep are slow to learn. Around that dried dish outside the lamb sniffed, baaing faintly. Adroitly the ewe led the way to the creek, and the lamb followed. From the bank the lamb looked at her, then faced round to the hut and, baaing disconsolately, trotted a few paces back. From the water's edge the mother ewe called. The lamb looked at her vacantly, and without interest descended. The ewe bent and drank sparingly, meaningly. The lamb sniffed the water and, unsatisfied, complained. The hut was hidden, but it turned that way. Again the ewe leisurely drank. This time the lamb's lips touched the water, but did not drink. Into its mouth raised to bleat a few drops fell. Hastily the mother's head went to the water. She did not drink, but the lamb did. Higher up, where the creek was dry, they crossed to tender grass in the billabong, then joined the flock for the first time.

Through the thicker mist that afternoon a white-tilted cart sailed joltingly, taking its bearings from the various landmarks rather than from the undefined track. It rounded the scrub, and the woman, with her baby, kept watch for the first glimpse of her home beyond the creek. She told her husband that there was no smoke from the nearer shepherd's hut, but, despite his uneasiness, he tried to persuade her that the mist absorbed it.

It was past sundown, yet the straggling unguarded sheep were running in mobs to and from the creek. Both saw the broken roof of the hut, and the man, stopping the horse some distance away, gave the woman the reins and bade her wait. He entered the hut through the broken doorway, but immediately came out to assure himself that his wife had not moved.

The sight inside, of that broken-ribbed dog's fight with those buzzing horrors, and the reproach in his wild eyes, was a memory that the man was not willing she should share.

THE FUNERALS OF
MALACHI MOONEY
By EDWARD DYSON

A NUMBER of Bungaree farmers, called from the fields, stood bareheaded about the sick-bed in attitudes of grievous constraint. Mrs. Mooney, seated on a low stool, wept sluice-heads, with wailing and querulous protestations. She had been replenishing the fountain of tears with whisky, and now cherished a great grievance against Malachi for dying, and the time chosen, and the manner thereof.

'There's hwhisky by the jar, min,' said the dying man in a thin wheeze. 'Be dhrinkin'.'

Hogan gravely assumed authority over the jar, and filled up for the company with judicial impartiality.

'Good luck to ye, Mullocky!' said Hogan, raising his cup.

Malachi waved his thin hand in expostulation. He was beyond all chances of fortune in this world, and knew it. Hogan temporized.

'Good luck to ye, Mullocky, fwhere ye're goin'.'

'How dar' ye doi, Mooney—how dar' ye do id?' wailed Mrs. Mooney, throwing her apron over her head, and rocking her body to and fro.

The company drank with one action, quite military in its precision, and then looked towards Malachi Mooney for further orders, and Malachi lay peacefully, happily dead with a smile on his lips, and the half-drained mug in his wasted fingers.

'Oh, ye divil! T' be dyin' on me like dthis,' moaned Mrs. Mooney under her apron. 'I'm disaved in yeh, Mooney!—disaved!—disaved! Whurra whroo!'

Presently, perceiving that Malachi was beyond argument, she lifted up her voice and filled the house with dolorous cries, and wailed dutifully and monotonously far into the night, when the chant was taken up by eerie, wrinkled old crones, smoke-dried grandmothers, lent for the occasion by sympathetic families from the four quarters of the wilderness.

What a wake that was! It lasted all night, and right up to the time fixed for the funeral. There was no end to the willing drinkers, and no limit to the whisky. Indeed, the miraculous manner in which tiny kegs, loaded to the bung, rolled from under the bed on demand, confirmed the local opinion that 'Mullocky' Mooney had more than a finger in the snug still, the smoke from which curled so artfully up from a charred trunk on Peter's Hill, and was thoughtfully given a supernatural origin by the neighbourly people of the district.

The funeral was advertised to move from the home of deceased at ten a.m. sharp. It was a long march to the´Ballarat old cemetery, and an early start was deemed necessary in consideration of the fact that Hooley's funeral, which happened a month earlier, had been fined for furious driving, by reason of the anxiety of the mourners to reach the graveyard before closing time.

The vehicles began to arrive at seven in the morning, the farmers and settlers driving, and their wives and 'childer' loaded in behind. A funeral was a 'trate' that didn't happen every day, and it would have been considered a sin to deprive the 'byes' and 'gurrls' of a bit of 'enjymint' that cost nothing. But many of the mourners had been at Mooney's all night, 'kapin' the carpse company', and daybreak disclosed a baker's dozen scattered about the farm, sleeping where they fell. One hung over the dog-leg fence 'forninst' the house, like an old shirt, with down-swinging arms. Canty, recumbent against the butt-end of a gum, rigid as a stump, slept so profoundly that the old guttural Brahmapootra had perched on his bald and awful head, and was defying creation with senseless repetitions of a cracked clarion. Others reposed curled against the house, and several dotted the paddock like quaint hieroglyphics, objects of wonderment and noisy speculation to the familiar pigs.

Michael Morrissey was the first to drive up. Michael was to occupy an honourable and responsible position at the head of the procession. He had generously offered the use of his trap as a hearse, and it was appropriately draped for that solemn office. This vehicle was an American wagon, and it had been roofed over about two feet from the floor, and was ordinarily used for the conveyance of meat; Michael being a butcher. There was a door at the back, and just room within for Mooney's coffin. Quinn's trotter, The Imp, was in the shafts. The Imp had been borrowed for the occasion because he was the only black horse in the district; but although his complexion was satisfactory his disposition quite unsuited him for so grave a duty. He was old and had a semi-bald tail; but there was a peculiar and aggressive jauntiness about the beast altogether out of harmony with his years and the situation in which he found himself. He held his head high, and pricked his ears, and his tail had a perky elevation that exhibited the bald butt to the worst advantage, and excited popular derision wherever he went.

When the friends of the late Malachi Mooney arrived, they walked reverently into the room where Malachi lay still on the bed amidst his monumental candles, and gazed on him for a moment with pensive sadness, as in duty bound.

'Pore mahn, he have the peaceful shmile on him!'
'He have, he have!'

After repeating the sentiment several times, with nodding heads and much wise clicking of tongues, thus having paid their respects to the dead, they withdrew to the kitchen, and devoted themselves to the whisky.

The coffin had been delivered, and stood on two bush stools in the kitchen, decently covered with a black shawl. Mrs. Mooney sat at the foot, adjacent to a pannikin, and continued to upbraid Mooney for his inconsiderate conduct in dying, and 'lavin' a lone lorn widdy'.

The funeral moved at eleven, when it was quite certain that only one baby keg remained. This keg Morrissey took with him on the improvised hearse, as a wise provision for the first half of the journey, which lay through a barren land.

Many of the mourners had to be helped into their vehicles, and after the start many remained in only by a miracle. Morrissey led the way, The Imp stepping along with a frivolous kind of a four-footed jig that robbed the *cortège* at the outset of any pretence to dignity. O'Connor's old wagonette followed, O'Connor driving carefully strapped down; and Mrs. O'Connor and the 'widdy' occupying the back seat. Then came Clark in his spring-cart driving The Imp's rival, Colleen. After him two or three miscellaneous vehicles, and then a long string of wood drays, each in charge of an unnaturally rigid and solemn Irishman perched on a candle-box, and each containing one or two women and three or four children, the former squatting composedly on the bottom of the dray with their substantial feet swinging out behind. A dozen sleepy, unshaven, unshorn agriculturists brought up the rear, riding two abreast on large, morbid horses that shuffled moodily through the dust with drooped heads and sagging under-lips.

The women in the drays maintained a shrill conversation along the line, but for the most part the men observed an owl-like decorum until the Travellers' Rest was reached—that is, if the puffing of abbreviated black clays be not considered derogatory from true reverence. Meanwhile, the day being hot and the way dusty, a couple of short halts had served to drain the keg on the hearse. It was a gritty, drought-stricken funeral that descended upon the Travellers' Rest, and when it moved again it left the wayside inn as dry as a powder-mill, having drunk up everything in the bar, and demolished the water-butt.

And now a great spirit of unrest took possession of many of the mourners, and there was much whooping and many manifestations of a wild and unholy desire to convert the procession into something like a steeple-chase. The Imp was stepping out gaily with his deceitful double-shuffle, game as a pebble, despite his age and infirmities, but it was Clark with Colleen who led the breakaway.

Springing up with a whoop and whooroo, Clark whipped his mare alongside the hearse.

'Morrissey,' he cried, 'I can bate that bumble-footed ould crock to the Pint beyant fer tin bob!'

'Ye can't!' roared Morrissey, all the sportsman stirring within him.

'Ye loi!' Clark fairly shrieked, laying the whip on.

Michael lashed The Imp, and the veteran, scenting a contest, snorted defiance, and hit out with all four afflicted legs at once. Then, bounding over ruts, jumping the boulders, rocking and rearing, the two vehicles went thundering through the dust, Colleen leading and The Imp following, flinging wide his legs with the action of a startled tarantula as he rushed down the hill, his body working with the antic spasms of two pigs in a bag.

The other drivers flogged their stolid horses into unwonted activity, and in this way the mad funeral, strung out a mile long, tore through one affrighted township, scattering sows and sucklings, goats, dogs, poultry, and shrieking children, raising a dust that blotted out half the landscape, and filling men and women with a wonderment that lasted many days. Half a mile beyond, The Imp, with a triumphant tail and starting eyeballs, flung past Colleen with a rush and a roar, neatly carrying away Clark's near wheel, which went humming ahead down the well-worn track.

Morrissey obtained control over his blood horse and succeeded in pulling up about a mile further on, and there he waited for the rest of the funeral in a humble and contrite frame of mind. The procession arrived in sections, the heavy horses spent and reeking, and the mourners coated thickly with powdered clay that caked rapidly in the sun on their perspiring faces. The women, particularly the stout ones, tumbled and bumped out of all knowledge and restraint, were loud and fierce in their complainings; and the men agreed that it was 'ondacent' and 'agin religion' to conduct a funeral at a hard gallop. So Michael led away again, holding his trotter hard, and proceeded as reverently and demurely as possible with such a horse and so much whisky.

Matty Clark was reported unharmed, and busy fixing a skid in place of the lost wheel. It was expected that he would turn back, and be no more a disturbing element in his neighbour's funeral.

The procession travelled into the outskirts of Ballarat without any further misadventure. In fact, most of the drivers and several of the ladies were asleep, and the weary plough-horses drowsed along at their own gait. The Imp, in spite of the apparent sprightliness of his action, was a very slow walker, for the reason that he generally dropped his hoofs in almost the spots from which he had just lifted them, and sometimes behind.

But at this point, cries of warning and of wonderment and disgust ran along the line, and looking back, Morrissey beheld Matty Clark in the distance, erect in his cart, gesticulating like a maniac, and rapidly overhauling the funeral. Matthew had fixed a sapling under his trap for a skid, and on this and one wheel he presently rattled up alongside the hearse again, oblivious to the threats and expostulations of the mourners.

'Mike Morrissey, ye divil ye!' yelled Mat, red, panting, and furious, 'to the cemmethry fer a quid!'

'Niver a won av me,' replied Morrissey, hanging on to The Imp.

'Yis, be the powers!' roared Clark, shooting ahead, and slashing viciously at the hearse-horse as he passed.

Michael clung to the reins, and hauled with all his might, but The Imp was not to be denied. Squealing shrilly in reply to the challenge, he broke into his old, ungainly, link-motion combination of canter, amble, and trot, and spread himself all over the road in pursuit of Colleen.

A couple of horsemen put their nags to a gallop to head-off Matty Clark, and in this way the funeral broke in upon Ballarat, careering down Humphrey Street, and stirring the city to its depths.

Fortunately Colleen was headed just before reaching the main thoroughfare, and Daly and O'Mara seized upon Matty, who was a small, bristly Hibernian, and fought like a peccary. They got him down and tied him up. Then, after throwing their turbulent captive into the cart, O'Hara sat on his chest and led the horses, and Daly, driving Colleen, now blown and humbled, took up a subordinate position at the tail of the procession; while the funeral, which had paused to collect itself once more, moved on, followed by a delighted crowd of children and many envious adults.

Many astonishing funerals had come up out of

Bungaree into Ballarat East, but Malachi Mooney's funeral was the most weird and wonderful that ever invaded any town on the Australian continent, and news of it seemed to have electric passage through the place. The improvised hearse with the well-intentioned effort to rig a pair of plumes of cocks' feathers upon it, the strange, jocund horse that hauled it, and the great, red, clayed-up, hairy, wild-eyed Galway man driving were alone sufficient to have brought the whole population into Bridge Street; but with the added attractions—the awful procession of drays, their dusty kiln-dried occupants, and the last vehicle riding jauntily on its skid—the funeral simply stopped business, took possession of the town, and drew the people after it in crowds.

Morrissey had the reins wound about his wrists, and with his heels dug in, his eyes protruding, and all his faculties intensely concentrated, hung to The Imp. The matrons still swung their stout feet, and here and there a worn-out mourner slept in his dray—Heffernan and Moore with their heads suspended over the tail and their mouths open. The police followed too, and eyed the procession dubiously, half inclined to arrest the whole funeral; but by exercising the severest self-restraint and the greatest caution the mourners contrived to pull through, and arrived at the cemetery at half-past four, with the coffin in good order and condition.

After the usual preliminaries the coffin was carried to the graveside by four of the late Mooney's most intimate friends, and, considering all things, their progress down the path was not as devious as might have been expected, but they landed the pine casket with a dump that produced the greatest sensation of the day. The coffin-lid had not been screwed down.

and it slipped to one side, making a revelation. There were many cries and much commotion when it was seen that the coffin contained packages of sugar and tea and miscellaneous groceries, and nothing more. Malachi Mooney was not there! Consternation sat whitely on every face, and the women crossed themselves vigorously.

'He's bin shpirited away!' wailed the 'widdy'.

'Did annywon see us dthrop him?' asked the dazed Morrissey in a small, awed voice.

Flynn now remembered that he had packed the groceries in the coffin the day before. He it was who carted the casket out from Ballarat; and having goods to carry at the same time he packed them into the 'piner' for 'convanience', and by reason of the thirst that came upon him, and possessed him for two days, 'disremimbered ivirything aftherwards'.

In truth the late Malachi Mooney still lay undisturbed upon the bed in his humble home in Bungaree, and the last of the yard-long candles guttered in the brass-sockets at his head. *The corpse had been forgotten!* And this is how Malachi Mooney came to have two funerals.

SEND ROUND THE HAT
By HENRY LAWSON

Now this is the creed from the Book of the Bush—
Should be simple and plain to a dunce:
'If a man's in a hole you must pass round the hat—
Were he jail-bird or gentleman once.'

'Is it any harm to wake yer?'

It was about nine o'clock in the morning, and,

though it was Sunday morning, it was no harm to wake me; but the shearer had mistaken me for a deaf jackeroo, who was staying at the shanty and was something like me, and had good-naturedly shouted almost at the top of his voice, and he woke the whole shanty. Anyway he woke three or four others who were sleeping on beds and stretchers, and one on a shakedown on the floor, in the same room. It had been a wet night, and the shanty was full of shearers from Big Billabong Shed which had cut-out the day before. My room-mates had been drinking and gambling overnight, and they swore luridly at the intruder for disturbing them.

He was six-foot-three or thereabout. He was loosely built, bony, sandy-complexioned and grey-eyed. He wore a good-humoured grin at most times, as I noticed later on; he was of a type of bushman that I always liked—the sort that seem to get more good-natured the longer they grow, yet are hard-knuckled and would accommodate a man who wanted to fight, or thrash a bully in a good-natured way. The sort that like to carry somebody's baby round, and cut wood, carry water and do little things for overworked married bushwomen. He wore a saddle-tweed sac suit two sizes too small for him, and his face, neck, great hands and bony wrists were covered with sun-blotches and freckles.

'I hope I ain't disturbin' yer,' he shouted, as he bent over my bunk, 'but there's a cove——'

'You needn't shout!' I interrupted, 'I'm not deaf.'

'Oh—I beg your pardon!' he shouted. 'I didn't know I was yellin'. I thought you was the deaf feller.'

'Oh, that's all right,' I said. 'What's the trouble?'

'Wait till them other chaps is done swearin' and I'll tell yer,' he said. He spoke with a quiet, good-natured drawl, with something of the nasal twang, but tone and drawl distinctly Australian—altogether apart from that of the Americans.

'Oh, spit it out for Christ's sake, Long-un!' yelled One-eyed Bogan, who had been the worst swearer in a rough shed, and he fell back on his bunk as if his previous remarks had exhausted him.

'It's that there sick jackeroo that was pickin'-up at Big Billabong,' said the Giraffe. 'He had to knock off the first week, an' he's been here ever since. They're sendin' him away to the hospital in Sydney by the speeshall train. They're just goin' to take him up in the wagonette to the railway station, an' I thought I might as well go round with the hat an' get him a few bob. He's got a missus and kids in Sydney.'

'Yer always goin' round with yer gory hat!' growled Bogan. 'Yer'd blanky well take it round in hell!'

'That's what he's doing, Bogan,' muttered Gentleman Once, on the shakedown, with his face to the wall.

The hat was a genuine 'cabbage tree', one of the sort that 'last a lifetime'. It was well coloured, almost black in fact with weather and age, and it had a new strap round the base of the crown. I looked into it and saw a dirty pound note and some silver. I dropped in half a crown, which was more than I could spare, for I had only been a green hand at Big Billabong.

'Thank yer!' he said. 'Now then, you fellers!'

'I wish you'd keep your hat on your head, and your money in your pockets and your sympathy somewhere else,' growled Jack Moonlight as he raised himself painfully on his elbow and felt under his pillow for two half-crowns. 'Here,' he said, 'here's two half-casers. Chuck 'em in and let me sleep for God's sake!'

Gentleman Once, the gambler, rolled round on his shakedown, bringing his good-looking, dissipated face from the wall. He had turned in in his clothes and, with considerable exertion, he shoved his hand down into the pocket of his trousers, which were a tight fit. He brought up a roll of pound notes and could find no silver.

'Here,' he said to the Giraffe, 'I might as well lay a quid. I'll chance it anyhow. Chuck it in.'

'You've got rats this mornin', Gentleman Once,' growled the Bogan. 'It ain't a blanky horse race.'

'P'r'aps I have,' said Gentleman Once, and he turned to the wall again with his head on his arm.

'Now, Bogan, yer might as well chuck in somethin',' said the Giraffe.

'What's the matter with the —— jackeroo?' asked the Bogan, tugging his trousers from under the mattress.

Moonlight said something in a low tone.

'The —— he has!' said Bogan. 'Well, I pity the —— ! Here, I'll chuck in half a —— quid!' and he dropped half a sovereign into the hat.

The fourth man, who was known to his face as 'Barcoo-Rot', and behind his back as 'The Mean Man', had been drinking all night, and not even Bogan's stump-splitting adjectives could rouse him. So Bogan got out of bed, and calling on us (as blanky female cattle) to witness what he was about to do, he rolled the drunkard over, prospected his pockets till he made up five shillings (or a 'caser' in bush language), and 'chucked' them into the hat.

And Barcoo-Rot is probably unconscious to this day that he was ever connected with an act of charity.

The Giraffe struck the deaf jackeroo in the next room. I heard the chaps cursing 'Long-'un' for waking them, and 'Deaf-'un' for being, as they thought at first, the indirect cause of the disturbance. I heard the Giraffe and his hat being condemned in other rooms and cursed along the veranda where more shearers were sleeping; and after a while I turned out.

The Giraffe was carefully fixing a mattress and pillows on the floor of a wagonette, and presently a man, who looked like a corpse, was carried out and lifted into the trap.

As the wagonette started, the shanty keeper—a fat, soulless-looking man—put his hand in his pocket and dropped a quid into the hat which was still going round, in the hands of the Giraffe's mate, little Teddy Thompson, who was as far below medium height as the Giraffe was above it.

The Giraffe took the horse's head and led him along on the most level parts of the road towards the railway station, and two or three chaps went along to help get the sick man into the train.

The shearing season was over in that district, but I got a job of house painting, which was my trade, at the Great Western Hotel (a two-storey brick place), and I stayed in Bourke for a couple of months.

The Giraffe was a Victorian native from Bendigo. He was well known in Bourke and to many shearers who came through the great dry scrubs from hundreds of miles round. He was stakeholder, drunkard's banker, peacemaker where possible, referee or second to oblige the chaps when a fight was on, big brother or uncle to most of the children in town, final court of appeal when the youngsters had a dispute over a foot-race at the school picnic, referee at their fights, and he was the stranger's friend.

'The feller as knows can battle around for himself,' he'd say. 'But I always like to do what I can for a hard-up stranger cove. I was a green-hand jackeroo once meself, and I know what it is.'

'You're always bothering about other people, Giraffe,' said Tom Hall, the Shearers' Union Secretary, who was only a couple of inches shorter than the Giraffe. 'There's nothing in it, you can take it from me—I ought to know.'

'Well, what's a feller to do?' said the Giraffe. 'I'm only hangin' round here till shearin' starts agen, an' a cove might as well be doin' something. Besides, it ain't as if I was like a cove that had old people or a wife an' kids to look after. I ain't got no responsibilities. A feller can't be doin' nothin'. Besides, I like to lend a helpin' hand when I can.'

'Well, all I've got to say,' said Tom, most of whose screw went in borrowed quids, etc.—'all I've got to say is that you'll get no thanks, and you might blanky well starve in the end.'

'There ain't no fear of me starvin' so long as I've got me hands about me; an' I ain't a cove as wants thanks,' said the Giraffe.

He was always helping someone or something. Now it was a bit of a 'darnce' that he was gettin' up for the girls; again it was Mrs. Smith, the woman whose husban' was drowned in the flood in the Bogan River lars' Crismas, or that there poor woman down by the Billabong—her husban' cleared out and left her with a lot o' kids. Or Bill Something, the bullocky, who was run over by his own wagon, while he was drunk, and got his leg broke.

Toward the end of his spree One-eyed Bogan broke

loose and smashed nearly all the windows of the
Carriers' Arms, and next morning he was fined
heavily at the police court. About dinner-time I
encountered the Giraffe and his hat, with two
half-crowns in it for a start.

'I'm sorry to trouble yer,' he said, 'but One-eyed
Bogan carn't pay his fine, an' I thought we might fix
it up for him. He ain't half a bad sort of feller when he
ain't drinkin'. It's only when he gets too much booze
in him.'

After shearing, the hat usually started round with
the Giraffe's own dirty crumpled pound note in the
bottom of it as a send-off, later on it was half a
sovereign, and so on down to half a crown and a
shilling, as he got short of stuff; till in the end he would
borrow a 'few bob'—which he always repaid after
next shearing—'just to start the thing goin''.

There were several yarns about him and his hat.
'Twas said that the hat had belonged to his father,
whom he resembled in every respect, and it had been
going round for so many years that the crown was
worn as thin as paper by the quids, half-quids, casers,
half-casers, bobs and tanners or sprats—to say nothing
of the scrums—that had been chucked into it in its
time and shaken up.

They say that when a new governor visited Bourke
the Giraffe happened to be standing on the platform
close to the exit, grinning good-humouredly, and the
local toady nudged him urgently and said in an awful
whisper, 'Take off your hat! Why don't you take off
your hat?'

'Why?' drawled the Giraffe; 'he ain't hard up, is
he?'

And they fondly cherish an anecdote to the effect
that, when the One-Man-One-Vote Bill was passed

(or Payment of Members, or when the first Labour Party went in—I forget on which occasion they said it was), the Giraffe was carried away by the general enthusiasm, got a few beers in him, 'chucked' a quid into his hat, and sent it round. The boys contributed by force of habit, and contributed largely, because of the victory and the beer. And when the hat came back to the Giraffe he stood holding it in front of him with both hands and stared blankly into it for a while. Then it dawned on him.

'Blowed if I haven't bin an' gone an' took up a bloomin' collection for meself!' he said.

He was almost a teetotaller, but he stood his shout in reason. He mostly drank ginger-beer.

'I ain't a feller that boozes, but I ain't got nothin' agen chaps enjoyin' themselves, so long as they don't go too far.'

It was common for a man on the spree to say to him:

'Here! here's five quid. Look after it for me, Giraffe, will yer, till I git off the booze.'

His real name was Bob Brothers, and his bush names, 'Long-'un', 'The Giraffe', 'Send-round-the-hat', 'Chuck-in-a-bob', and 'Ginger-ale'.

Some years before, camels and Afghan drivers had been imported to the Bourke district; the camels did very well in the dry country, they went right across country and carried everything from sardines to flooring boards. And the teamsters loved the Afghans nearly as much as Sydney furniture makers love the cheap Chinese in the same line. They loved 'em even as union shearers on strike love blacklegs brought up-country to take their places.

Now the Giraffe was a good, straight unionist, but in cases of sickness or trouble he was as apt to forget his unionism, as all bushmen are, at all times (and for all time), to forget their creed. So, one evening, the Giraffe blundered into the Carriers' Arms—of all places in the world—when it was full of teamsters; he had his hat in his hand and some small silver and coppers in it.

'I say, you fellers, there's a poor, sick Afghan in the camp down there along the——'

A big, brawny bullock driver took him firmly by the shoulders, or rather by the elbows, and ran him out before any damage was done. The Giraffe took it as he took most things, good-humouredly; but, about dusk, he was seen slipping down towards the Afghan camp with a billy of soup.

'I believe,' remarked Tom Hall, 'that when the Giraffe goes to heaven—and he's the only one of us, as far as I can see, that has a ghost of a show—I believe that when he goes to heaven, the first thing he'll do will be to take his infernal hat round amongst the angels—getting up a collection for this damned world that he left behind.'

'Well, I don't think there's so much to his credit, after all,' said Jack Mitchell, shearer. 'You see, the Giraffe is ambitious; he likes public life, and that accounts for him shoving himself forward with his collections. As for bothering about people in trouble, that's only common curiosity; he's one of those chaps that are always shoving their noses into other people's troubles. And as for looking after sick men—why! there's nothing the Giraffe likes better than pottering round a sick man, and watching him and studying him. He's awfully interested in sick men, and they're pretty scarce out here. I tell you there's nothing he likes better—except, maybe, it's pottering round a corpse. I believe he'd ride forty miles to help and sympathize and potter round a funeral. The fact of the matter is that the Giraffe is only enjoying himself with other people's troubles—that's all it is. It's only vulgar curiosity and selfishness. I set it down to his ignorance; the way he was brought up.'

A few days after the Afghan incident the Giraffe and his hat had a run of luck. A German, one of a party who were building a new wooden bridge over the Big Billabong, was helping unload some girders from a truck at the railway station, when a big log slipped on the skids and his leg was smashed badly. They carried him to the Carriers' Arms, which was the nearest hotel, and into a bedroom behind the bar, and sent for the doctor. The Giraffe was in evidence as usual.

'It vas not dat at all,' said German Charlie, when they asked him if he was in much pain. 'It vas not dat at all. I don't cares a damn for der bain; but dis is der tird year — und I vas going home dis year — after der gontract — und der contract yoost commence!'

That was the burden of his song all through, between his groans.

There were a good few chaps sitting quietly about the bar and veranda when the doctor arrived. The Giraffe was sitting at the end of the counter, on which he had laid his hat while he wiped his face, neck and forehead with a big speckled 'sweat-rag'. It was a very hot day.

The doctor, a good-hearted young Australian, was heard saying something. Then German Charlie, in a voice that rung with pain:

'Make dat leg right, doctor—quick! Dis is der tird pluddy year—und I must go home!'

The doctor asked him if he was in great pain.

'Neffer mind der pluddy bain, doctor! Neffer mind der pluddy bain! Dot vas nossing. Make dat leg well quick, doctor. Dis vas der last gontract, and I vas going home dis year.' Then the words jerked out of him by physical agony: 'Der girl vas vaiting dree year, und—by Got! I must go home.'

The publican—Watty Braithwaite, known as 'Watty Broadweight' or, more familiarly, 'Watty Bothways' —turned over the Giraffe's hat in a tired, bored sort of way, dropped a quid into it, and nodded resignedly at the Giraffe.

The Giraffe caught up the hint and the hat with alacrity. The hat went all round town, so to speak; and, as soon as his leg was firm enough not to come loose on the road, German Charlie went home.

It was well known that I contributed to the *Sydney Bulletin* and several other papers. The Giraffe's bump of reverence was very large, and swelled especially for sick men and poets. He treated me with much more respect than is due from a bushman to a man, and with an odd sort of extra gentleness, I sometimes fancied. But one day he rather surprised me.

'I'm sorry to trouble yer,' he said in a shamefaced way. 'I don't know as you go in for sportin', but One-eyed Bogan an' Barcoo-Rot is goin' to have a bit of a scrap down the Billybong this evenin', an'——'

'A bit of a what?' I asked.

'A bit of fight to a finish,' he said apologetically. 'An' the chaps is tryin' to fix up a fiver to put some life into the thing. There's bad blood between One-eyed Bogan and Barcoo-Rot, an' it won't do them any harm to have it out.'

It was a great fight, I remember. There must have been a couple of score blood-soaked handkerchiefs (or 'sweat-rags') buried in a hole on the field of battle, and the Giraffe was busy the rest of the evening helping to patch up the principals. Later on he took up a small collection for the loser, who happened to be Barcoo-Rot in spite of the advantage of an eye.

The Salvation Army lassie, who went round with the *War Cry*, nearly always sold the Giraffe three copies.

A new-chum parson, who wanted a subscription to build or enlarge a chapel, or something, sought the assistance of the Giraffe's influence with his mates.

'Well,' said the Giraffe, 'I ain't a churchgoer meself. I ain't what you might call a religious cove, but I'll be glad to do what I can to help yer. I don't suppose I can do much. I ain't been to church since I was a kiddy.'

The parson was shocked, but later on he learned to appreciate the Giraffe and his mates, and to love Australia for the bushman's sake, and it was he who told me the above anecdote.

The Giraffe helped fix some stalls for a Catholic church bazaar, and some of the chaps chaffed him about it in the union office.

'You'll be taking up a collection for a Joss-House down in the Chinamen's camp next,' said Tom Hall in conclusion.

'Well, I ain't got nothin' agen the Roming Carflics,' said the Giraffe. 'An' Father O'Donovan's a very decent sort of cove. He stuck up for the unions all right in the strike anyway.' ('He wouldn't be Irish if he wasn't,' someone commented.) 'I carried swags once for six months with a feller that was a Carflick, an' he was a very straight feller. And a girl I knowed turned Carflick to marry a chap that had got her into trouble, an' she was always jes' the same to me after as she was before. Besides, I like to help everything that's goin' on.'

Tom Hall and one or two others went out hurriedly to have a drink. But we all loved the Giraffe.

He was very innocent and very humorous, especially when he meant to be most serious and philosophical.

'Some of them bush girls is regular tomboys,' he said to me solemnly one day. 'Some of them is too cheeky altogether. I remember once I was stoppin' at a place—they was sort of relations o' mine—an' they put me to sleep in a room off the verander, where there was a glass door an' no blinds. An' the first mornin' the girls—they was sort o' cousins o' mine— they come gigglin' and foolin' round outside the door on the verander, an' kep' me in bed till nearly ten o'clock. I had to put me trowsis on under the bed-clothes in the end. But I got back on 'em the next night,' he reflected.

'How did you do that, Bob?' I asked.

'Why, I went to bed in me trowsis!'

One day I was on a plank, painting the ceiling of the bar of the Great Western Hotel. I was anxious to get the job finished. The work had been kept back most of the day by chaps handing up long beers to me, and drawing my attention to the alleged fact that I was putting on the paint wrong side out. I was slapping it on over the last few boards when—

'I'm very sorry to trouble yer; I always seem to be troublin' yer; but there's that there woman and them girls——'

I looked down—about the first time I had looked down on him—and there was the Giraffe, with his hat-brim up on the plank and two half-crowns in it.

'Oh, that's all right, Bob,' I said, and I dropped in half a crown.

There were shearers in the bar, and presently there was some barracking. It appeared that that there woman and them girls were strange women, in the local as well as the Biblical sense of the word, who had come from Sydney at the end of the shearing season, and had taken a cottage on the edge of the scrub on the outskirts of the town. There had been trouble this week in connexion with a row at their establishment, and they had been fined, warned off by the police, and turned out by their landlord.

'This is a bit too red-hot, Giraffe,' said one of the shearers. 'Them ——s has made enough out of us coves. They've got plenty of stuff, don't you fret. Let 'em go to ——! I'm blanked if I give a sprat.'

'They ain't got their fares to Sydney,' said the Giraffe. 'An', what's more, the little 'un is sick, an' two of them has kids in Sydney.'

'How the —— do you know?'

'Why, one of 'em come to me an' told me all about it.'

There was an involuntary guffaw.

'Look here, Bob,' said Billy Woods, the Rouse-about's Secretary, kindly. 'Don't you make a fool of yourself. You'll have all the chaps laughing at you. Those girls are only working you for all you're worth. I suppose one of 'em came crying and whining to you. Don't you bother about them. *You* don't know them; they can pump water at a moment's notice. You haven't had any experience with women yet, Bob.'

'She didn't come whinin' and cryin' to me,' said the Giraffe, dropping his twanging drawl a little. 'She looked me straight in the face an' told me all about it.'

'I say, Giraffe,' said Box-o'-Tricks, 'what have you been doin'? You've bin down there on the nod. I'm surprised at yer, Giraffe.'

'An' he pretends to be so gory soft an' innocent too,' growled the Bogan. 'We know all about you, Giraffe.'

'Look here, Giraffe,' said Mitchell the shearer. 'I'd never have thought it of you. We all thought you were the only virgin youth west the river; I always thought you were a moral young man. You mustn't think that because your conscience is pricking you everyone else's is.'

'I ain't had anythin' to do with them,' said the Giraffe, drawling again. 'I ain't a cove that goes in for that sort of thing. But other chaps has, and I think they might as well help 'em out of their fix.'

'They're a rotten crowd,' said Billy Woods. 'You don't know them, Bob. Don't bother about them— they're not worth it. Put your money in your pocket. You'll find a better use for it before next shearing.'

'Better shout, Giraffe,' said Box-o'-Tricks.

Now in spite of the Giraffe's softness he was the hardest man in Bourke to move when he'd decided on what he thought was 'the fair thing to do'. Another peculiarity of his was that on occasion, such for instance as 'sayin' a few words' at a strike meeting, he would straighten himself, drop the twang, and rope in his drawl, so to speak.

'Well, look here, you chaps,' he said now. 'I don't know anything about them women. I s'pose they're bad, but I don't suppose they're worse than men has made them. All I know is that there's four women turned out, without any stuff, and every woman in Bourke, an' the police, an' the law agen 'em. An' the fact that they is women is agenst 'em most of all. You don't expect 'em to hump their swags to Sydney! Why, only I ain't got the stuff I wouldn't trouble yer. I'd pay their fares meself. Look,' he said, lowering his voice, 'there they are now, an' one of the girls is cryin'. Don't let 'em see yer lookin'.'

I dropped softly from the plank and peeped out with the rest.

They stood by the fence on the opposite side of the street, a bit up towards the railway station, with their portmanteaux and bundles at their feet. One girl leant with her arms on the fence rail and her face buried in them, another was trying to comfort her. The third girl and the woman stood facing our way. The woman was good-looking; she had a hard face, but it might have been made hard. The third girl seemed half defiant, half inclined to cry. Presently she went to the other side of the girl who was crying on the fence and put her arm round her shoulder. The woman suddenly turned her back on us and stood looking away over the paddocks.

The hat went round. Billy Woods was first, then Box-o'-Tricks, and then Mitchell.

Billy contributed with eloquent silence. 'I was only jokin', Giraffe,' said Box-o'-Tricks, dredging his pockets for a couple of shillings. It was some time after the shearing, and most of the chaps were hard up.

'Ah, well,' sighed Mitchell. 'There's no help for it. If the Giraffe would take up a collection to import some decent girls to this God-forgotten hole there might be some sense in it. . . . It's bad enough for the Giraffe to undermine our religious prejudices, and tempt us to take a morbid interest in sick chows and Afghans, and blacklegs and widows; but when he starts mixing us up with strange women it's time to buck.' And he prospected his pockets and contributed two shillings, some odd pennies, and a pinch of tobacco dust.

'I don't mind helping the girls, but I'm damned if

I'll give a penny to help the old ——,' said Tom Hall.

'Well, she was a girl once herself,' drawled the Giraffe.

The Giraffe went round to the other pubs and to the union offices, and when he returned he seemed satisfied with the plate, but troubled about something else.

'I don't know what to do for them for to-night,' he said. 'None of the pubs or boardin'-houses will hear of them, an' there ain't no empty houses, an' the women is all agen 'em.'

'Not all,' said Alice, the big, handsome barmaid from Sydney. 'Come here, Bob.' She gave the Giraffe half a sovereign and a look for which some of us would have paid him ten pounds—had we had the money, and had the look been transferable.

'Wait a minute, Bob,' she said, and she went in to speak to the landlord.

'There's an empty bedroom at the end of the store in the yard,' she said when she came back. 'They can camp there for to-night if they behave themselves. You'd better tell 'em, Bob.'

'Thank yer, Alice,' said the Giraffe.

Next day, after work, the Giraffe and I drifted together and down by the river in the cool of the evening, and sat on the edge of the steep, drought-parched bank.

'I heard you saw your lady-friends off this morning, Bob,' I said, and was sorry I said it, even before he answered.

'Oh, they ain't no friends of mine,' he said. 'Only four poor devils of women. I thought they mightn't like to stand waitin' with the crowd on the platform, so I jest offered to get their tickets an' told 'em to wait round at the back of the station till the bell rung. . . . An' what do yer think they did, Harry?' he went on, with an exasperatingly unintelligent grin. 'Why, they wanted to kiss me.'

'Did they?'

'Yes. An' they would have done it, too, if I hadn't been so long. . . . Why, I'm blessed if they didn't kiss me hands.'

'You don't say so.'

'God's truth. Somehow I didn't like to go on the platform with them after that; besides they was cryin', and I can't stand women cryin'. But some of the chaps put them into an empty carriage.' He thought a moment. Then:

'There's some terrible good-hearted fellers in the world,' he reflected.

I thought so too.

'Bob,' I said, 'you're a single man. Why don't you get married and settle down?'

'Well,' he said, 'I ain't got no wife an' kids, that's a fact. But it ain't my fault.'

He may have been right about the wife. But I thought of the look that Alice had given him, and——

'Girls seem to like me right enough,' he said, 'but it don't go no further than that. The trouble is that I'm so long, and I always seem to get shook after little girls. At least there was one little girl in Bendigo that I was properly gone on.'

'And wouldn't she have you?'

'Well, it seems not.'

'Did you ask her?'

'Oh, yes, I asked her right enough.'

'Well, and what did she say?'

'She said it would be redicilus for her to be seen trottin' alongside of a chimbley like me.'

'Perhaps she didn't mean that. There are any amount of little women who like tall men.'

'I thought of that too—afterwards. P'r'aps she didn't mean it that way. I s'pose the fact of the matter was that she didn't cotton on to me, and wanted to let me down easy. She didn't want to hurt me feelin's, if yer understand—she was a very good-hearted little girl. There's some terrible tall fellers where I come from, and I know two as married little girls.'

He seemed a hopeless case.

'Sometimes,' he said, 'sometimes I wish that I wasn't so blessed long.'

'There's that there deaf jackeroo,' he reflected presently. 'He's something in the same fix about girls as I am. He's too deaf and I'm too long.'

'How do you make that out?' I asked. 'He's got three girls, to my knowledge, and as for being deaf, why, he gasses more than any man in the town, and knows more of what's going on than old Mother Brindle the washerwoman.'

'Well, look at that now!' said the Giraffe slowly. 'Who'd have thought it? He never told me he had three girls, an' as for hearin' news, I always tell him anything that's goin' on that I think he doesn't catch. He told me his trouble was that whenever he went out with a girl people could hear what they was sayin'— at least they could hear what she was sayin' to him, an' draw their own conclusions, he said. He said he went out one night with a girl, and some of the chaps foxed 'em an' heard her sayin' "don't" to him, an' put it all round town.'

'What did she say "don't" for?' I asked.

'He didn't tell me that, but I s'pose he was kissin' her or huggin' her or something.'

'Bob,' I said presently, 'didn't you try the little girl in Bendigo a second time?'

'No,' he said. 'What was the use? She was a good

D

little girl, and I wasn't goin' to go botherin' her. I ain't the sort of cove that goes hangin' round where he isn't wanted. But somehow I couldn't stay about Bendigo after she gave me the hint, so I thought I'd come over an' have a knock round on this side for a year or two.'

'And you never wrote to her?'

'No. What was the use of goin' pesterin' her with letters? I know what trouble letters give me when I have to answer one. She'd have only had to tell me the straight truth in a letter an' it wouldn't have done me any good. But I've pretty well got over it by this time.'

A few days later I went to Sydney. The Giraffe was the last I shook hands with from the carriage window, and he slipped something in a piece of newspaper into my hand.

'I hope yer won't be offended,' he drawled, 'but some of the chaps thought you mightn't be too flush of stuff—you've been shoutin' a good deal; so they put a quid or two together. They thought it might help yer to have a bit of a fly round in Sydney.'

I was back in Bourke before next shearing. On the evening of my arrival I ran against the Giraffe; he seemed strangely shaken over something, but he kept his hat on his head.

'Would yer mind takin' a stroll as fur as the Biller-bong?' he said. 'I got something I'd like to tell yer.'

His big, brown, sunburnt hands trembled and shook as he took a letter from his pocket and opened it.

'I've just got a letter,' he said. 'A letter from that little girl at Bendigo. It seems it was all a mistake. I'd like you to read it. Somehow I feel as if I want to talk to a feller, and I'd rather talk to you than any of them other chaps.'

It was a good letter, from a big-hearted little girl. She had been breaking her heart for the great ass all these months. It seemed that he had left Bendigo without saying good-bye to her. 'Somehow I couldn't bring meself to it,' he said, when I taxed him with it. She had never been able to get his address until last week; then she got it from a Bourke man who had gone South. She called him 'an' awful long fool', which he was, without the slightest doubt, and she implored him to write, and come back to her.

'And will you go back, Bob?' I asked.

'My oath! I'd take the train to-morrer only I ain't got the stuff. But I've got a stand in Big Billerbong shed an' I'll soon knock a few quid together. I'll go back as soon as ever shearin's over. I'm goin' to write away to her to-night.'

The Giraffe was the 'ringer' of Big Billabong shed that season. His tallies averaged 120 a day. He only sent his hat round once during shearing, and it was noticed that he hesitated at first and only contributed half a crown. But then it was a case of a man being taken from the shed by the police for wife desertion.

'It's always that way,' commented Mitchell. 'Those soft, good-hearted fellows always end by getting hard and selfish. The world makes 'em so. It's the thought of the soft fools they've been that finds out sooner or later and makes 'em repent. Like as not the Giraffe will be the meanest man out-back before he's done.'

When Big Billabong cut out, and we got back to Bourke with our dusty swags and dirty cheques, I spoke to Tom Hall.

'Look here, Tom,' I said. 'That long fool, the Giraffe, has been breaking his heart for a little girl in Bendigo ever since he's been out-back, and she's been breaking her heart for him, and the ass didn't know it till he got a letter from her just before Big Billabong started. He's going to-morrow morning.'

That evening Tom stole the Giraffe's hat. 'I s'pose it'll turn up in the mornin',' said the Giraffe. 'I don't mind a lark,' he added, 'but it does seem a bit red-hot for the chaps to collar a cove's hat and a feller goin' away for good, p'r'aps, in the mornin'.'

Mitchell started the thing going with a quid.

'It's worth it,' he said, 'to get rid of him. We'll have some peace now. There won't be so many accidents or women in trouble when the Giraffe and his blessed hat are gone. Anyway, he's an eyesore in the town, and he's getting on my nerves for one. . . . Come on, you sinners! Chuck 'em in; we're only taking quids and half-quids.'

About daylight next morning Tom Hall slipped into the Giraffe's room at the Carriers' Arms. The Giraffe was sleeping peacefully. Tom put the hat on a chair by his side. The collection had been a record one, and, besides the packet of money in the crown of the hat, there was a silver-mounted pipe with case—the best that could be bought in Bourke, a gold brooch, and several trifles—besides an ugly valentine of a long man in his shirt walking the room with a twin on each arm.

Tom was about to shake the Giraffe by the shoulder, when he noticed a great foot, with about half a yard of big-boned ankle and shank, sticking out at the bottom of the bed. The temptation was too great. Tom took up the hair-brush, and, with the back of it, he gave a smart rap on the point of an ingrowing toe-nail, and slithered.

We heard the Giraffe swearing good-naturedly for a while, and then there was a pregnant silence. He was staring at the hat, we supposed.

We were all up at the station to see him off. It was rather a long wait. The Giraffe edged me up to the other end of the platform. He seemed overcome.

'There's—there's some terrible good-hearted fellers in this world,' he said. 'You mustn't forgit 'em, Harry, when you make a big name writin'. I'm—well, I'm blessed if I don't feel as if I was jist goin' to blubber!'

I was glad he didn't. The Giraffe blubberin' would have been a spectacle. I steered him back to his friends.

'Ain't you going to kiss me, Bob?' said the Great Western's big, handsome barmaid, as the bell rang.

'Well, I don't mind kissin' you, Alice,' he said, wiping his mouth. 'But I'm goin' to be married, yer know.' And he kissed her fair on the mouth.

'There's nothin' like gettin' into practice,' he said, grinning round.

We thought he was improving wonderfully; but at the last moment something troubled him.

'Look here, you chaps,' he said hesitatingly, with his hand in his pocket, 'I don't know what I'm going to do with all this stuff. There's that there poor washerwoman that scalded her legs liftin' the boiler of clothes off the fire——'

We shoved him into the carriage. He hung—about half of him—out the window, wildly waving his hat, till the train disappeared in the scrub.

And, as I sit here writing by lamplight at midday, in the midst of a great city of shallow social sham, of hopeless, squalid poverty, of ignorant selfishness, cultured or brutish, and of noble and heroic endeavour frowned down or callously neglected, I am almost aware of a burst of sunshine in the room, and a long form leaning over my chair, and—

'Excuse me for troublin' yer; I'm always troublin'
yer; but there's that there poor woman . . .'

And I wish I could immortalize him!

FOURTEEN FATHOMS BY QUETTA ROCK

By Randolph Bedford

The palm-fronds threshed softly. Nigh to midnight
the land breeze became too strong for anything but
the frangipani scent; the palm-fronds threshed
through the air saturated with moonlight; the red
lamp on the jetty showed as a purple stain.

The last of the pilots of Torres Straits went to bed;
the Grand Hotel of Thursday Island closed its bar;
but the two barefoot men on the veranda talked on
the topic that had lasted since dusk—the wreck of
the *Pandora*—and one man, Pipon, tried to soothe the
other, Moresby, who talked without ceasing of the
wreck and twenty thousand pounds' worth of pearls.

'Can we get a launch, Jim?' he asked.

'I told you no,' replied Pipon. 'Bear up, old man;
y' can have a lugger.'

'A lugger and a dead calm? It would be worse than
waiting here.'

'Well, quiet a bit!'

'Quiet! How can I be—when I am in a fever to be
there?'

He looked south as if trying to make out the coast of
Australia, now the ghost of a shadow in the moon haze
and sea blur.

'What could you do if you were, Martin?'

'I could stand by the wreck; I could——'

'You couldn't do any good. It's lucky Phil Regard is coming to-morrow. He's the British India diver. He'll do all there is to be done.'

'My pearls, Tom! The big one and nine ounces of little ones. Oyley was bringing them up. What depths did the *Pandora* sink in?'

'Nobody knows, old man, or how she went. The skipper was a good man—exempt, too. Knew every key and every inch of reef—and there's millions of 'em.'

'It was my rotten luck, Tom, to miss the *Pandora* by five minutes and then pick up the *Maranea* to catch her here, and find when I did get here that she'd sunk fifty or a hundred miles south. And there's my pearls —Oyley was taking charge of them—and then I missed the ship. Oh, gimme a raft and I'll start!'

'Not you! Come on, take a fool's advice and sleep. You'll leave it all to Phil Regard.'

The grass trees rustled softly to the poinciana as the men went to bed; the breeze strengthened to a wind and replaced perfume with a taste of salt; from the veranda above a man began to whimper—a man that had seen death and terror and was now dreaming it all over again and shrieking out the story in his recurrent nightmare—the one survivor of the *Pandora*, who had been picked up by a pearling lugger.

'She's going! Two minutes—you can't get the boats out of the chocks. Why didn't they have boat practice? You can't! You can't! Don't scream, women—dear women, don't scream—it's better to drown than—— Ah, my God, the sharks! the sharks!'

Druce, the pilot of Torres Straits, boarded that slow, comfortable, old-time high-pooped steamer of the tea-clipper type, the *Airlie*, at Goode Island, and brought her up in the early dawn to the wharf at Thursday. A big, brown-eyed man was the first to land; he was a man in a hurry—in a hurry for news, at least. He waited for neither bath nor breakfast, but aroused an irritated postmaster and begged so for telegrams that the postmaster gave him his mail long before the beginning of office hours. There were many newspapers, and he did not look at them; a dozen letters, all man-directed and official, and he put them in his pocket. A bitter disappointment settled on his face— the letter from the beloved was not there. He found new hope in the telegrams. Alas! They were as the letters; and his heart was heavy then. This diver, who knew no fear that he could not fight down, fought against his disappointment and could not conquer it.

'I telegraphed her from Darwin, and she hasn't wired a reply. She's thoughtless, not cruel, not cruel— my girl.'

He took from his pocket-book a photograph; looked at it and put it back again.

'God bless her! I'll telegraph again, and in seven days we'll be together—for a month, anyhow. But— she might have made sure of not missing the post; a letter would make me a king to-day.'

He returned to duty by taking a telegram from his pockets, and a fierce resentment held him for a moment as he read it:

'*Pandora* sunk; locate wreck; if not impossible, recover gold, ship's papers. B.P. provide tug and tender; made splendid terms.'

So he would not see her in a week—happiness was to be postponed again. He thought of the long two months of salvage diving in the Flores Sea. Three months since he had seen her, and now there was to be another fortnight of hunger for her!

But hope came to his comfort. 'Another year and I'll have made enough to retire on, with this new chance. Then no separation!'

So he went to Burns Philp and arranged for the departure of the little steamer, hired diving tenders and had his diving gear brought from the *Airlie*'s hold. It was then that Moresby found him—Moresby of the drowned pearls; and the commission made Phil Regard almost gay.

'Oyley had 'em,' said Moresby. 'I gave them to him to mind because I was going on a spree in Brisbane.'

'Was he straight, d'ye think?'

'I think so. He put 'em in a little steel box in his trunk—he had his own pearls in the box—and his wife had the key on a chain round her neck.'

'What was the number of his cabin, and what was he like?'

'A dark, red-moustached chap—cabin number 41–43 B, port side, near the music room.'

'You know the ship?'

'I tell you I sailed on her from Sydney to Brisbane and lost my passage at Brisbane through going to the races. I gave the pearls to Oyley when I was going ashore. But you will get 'em again, mate?'

'I don't know. Nobody knows where she foundered. But if I do?'

'Five hundred pounds.'

With the lack of ceremony characteristic of the latitude, every man in the bar joined in the conversation.

'Five hundred pounds!' said Druce, the pilot. 'Five hundred pounds for dredgin' fifteen or twenty thousand pounds out o' the Pacific Ocean! It's worth that to find the old hulk that hit the rock somewhere, and did me out o' pilot fees.'

'I thought it wouldn't be hard to find the wreck,' said Moresby. 'If——'

'Oh,' replied Druce, 'if your aunt had whiskers she'd be your uncle. Why, I know ten wrecks about here that no man knows the name of—ships that were never missed. You know, too, don't you, Dan'l?'

An old man, bent and wizened, replied quaveringly, 'I've seen below me—when I've been down—old Spanish ships an' old Dutch ships an' old Portugees down below; me in twenty fathoms water an' them deep below, me man——'

'Twenty fathoms—too much,' said the big diver. 'I've got a girl at home and she wants me. Fifteen fathoms is all I care to go.'

'Aa—ah!' said the old diver, nipping with his strong and crooked fingers the arm and leg muscles of Phil Regard, 'I was as strong and straight as ye; but deep divin' an' showin' off above the other min, an' takin' no notice o' the shootin' pains in me legs— callin' it rheumatics, an' all the time 'tis the paralyser warnin' ye. An' then twenty-three fathom I went, an' hauled up—I was a cripple.'

He laughed as he spoke, but there was in his eye a tear of sorrow for his own dead strength; and, to cover his self-pity, he said, with a feeble attempt at gaiety:

'But 'tis only here I am a cripple! Put me down in fifteen or twenty fathom and give me the pressure on me skin again an' a four-knot tide, an' I'll fly along the floorin' of the sea like a sunbird.'

'And you're offering five hundred pounds for the chance of that?' said Druce to Moresby. 'Open your heart, Moresby.'

'A thousand, then,' said Moresby. 'I want to be fair, and it's all to nothing.'

'It isn't,' said Phil Regard. 'I've got to go below on

another contract, and you think I've only got to open a cabin door and take a key from some poor dead woman and open a box. But that means two extra corners to go round, and the more corners the more chances of fouling. It's your pearls to my life. I want a certainty.'

'Here y' are, then,' said Moresby. 'A hundred pounds for opening the cabin door and I'll take your word for it, and a thousand if you bring back the pearls.'

'It's a deal,' agreed Phil Regard.

The warning bell of the *Airlie* clanged, and Druce departed to his pilotage. Phil Regard, as yet only half resigned, saw the steamer that should have borne him south disappear down the channel, rounding the Residency, and so away to open sea, then he resolutely put regrets behind him and went to his tug and tender to prepare for his attempt to find a few thousand tons of foundered metal in an immensity of blue.

The survivor of the *Pandora* had become quiet enough to talk of the wreck.

'I was steerage steward,' he said. 'Mister, I can't think! Stay by me, mister—don't leave me alone.'

'Hold on to my coat, if you like. I'll stand by.'

'We never had a boat practice—rottin' in the chocks, the boats were. It was about eleven at night —moonlight, quiet; y' could hear the scrapin' of shovels in the stoke-hole on the flat sheets, and the noise came up the ventilators. An' not a ripple. An' there I'm smoking by the rail, waitin' till I can sneak out on the boat deck to sleep—the glory hole being so hot. An' then it comes. It seemed to get her amidships —that was because she was drawing a lot more water aft. Only one man came out of the engine-room. The quiet people in the cabins had the best death. Sharks got all the deck lot. She ran a minute or two an' I saw the water risin' closer up—an' loosed a raft and went over. It was like hell, mister, the howls. Her decks blew up amidships. . . . An' then on the raft I see white fire cutting the water all over, criss-crossin' it. It was sharks. An' then a yell, an' more criss-crossin' of fire, an' another yell.'

'I know! I know!' said Phil Regard, soothingly. 'Don't think of it! Help me. Tell me where you think she went down.'

'I can't help thinkin' of it. Oh—oh!'

'Steady! Steady! Take a pull at yourself. Where did she go down?'

'A girl of twenty or so—I heard her singing in the saloon the night before—a song about 'Mine, for ever Mine', an' her husband lookin' at her as if he was dyin' for her while she was singin'. He was swimmin' with her when the sharks took him; an' I beat the sea with me 'ands an' brought the raft close, an' I was bringin' her up to the raft—swish! comes the shark fire, an' she went, too.'

The diver's eyes grew moist at that; he thought of his beloved safe at home, and the tragedy touched him nearly. But he said again:

'Where's the *Pandora*?'

'I drifted to an island, an' then I went mad, an' the lugger found me.'

'To-day is Wednesday. When did the *Pandora* sink? Now, think—listen! We may pick up somebody yet. Tell me.'

'She sank on Monday night.'

'Where?'

'We made twelve knots to Cape Grenville; then we slowed to ten.'

'What time at Cape Grenville?'

The survivor of the *Pandora* wrinkled his brows as if thought were a physical pain, and replied: 'Twelve o'clock in the mornin'. Y' can't find her—she'd got no masts, on'y hydraulic winchpoles.'

Phil Regard, with the dividers in his hand, said inquiringly:

'And she struck at eleven in the night?'

'It might have been later.'

'We'll go on that. Where were you picked up?'

'The lugger came from Bushby Island.'

Regard pricked off one hundred and ten miles on the chart. 'Somewhere east of Newcastle Bay,' he said.

Before noon he had left Thursday Island, taking the direct track with his light-draught tugboat east between Tuesday and Horn Islands; and then, after easting Mount Adolphus Island and thridding the reefs to the south of it, steering south through the turquoise of shallow water and into the sapphire of deep sea, he ran south to Bushby Island and then east over reefs and then north again, and then west, and then zigzag. And the next day he drove slowly over a blackness in the coral bed; a monstrous black thing surrounded by lazy sharks; the *Pandora*—almost on an even keel and sunk in fourteen fathoms.

With a little reluctance, Regard made the preparations necessary for such as dive in dress and helmet, and shaved the moustache that had grown since he had dived in Flores Seas. The growing of the moustache had been an innocent vanity for the pleasure of his wife, who objected to his professionally beardless face, just as the new suit was for her benefit and not to be worn until the day of happy meeting, that he might shine all freshly in her eyes. Then, in the warm shadow of the white awning he stripped and donned the many woollen undergarments and the canvas dress, with its watertight red-rubber bands at wrists and ankles.

The tender put on his feet the great brass-toed boots of twenty-eight pounds weight; and when he had climbed to the ladder and placed his feet upon the rungs, they screwed his twenty-eight-pound copper helmet on the collar-ring and hung thirty-eight pounds of lead upon his breast and thirty-eight pounds of lead at his back. Lifeline, piping, corselet, helmet, brass boots and leaden weight complete, the men at the pump began to turn; the tender screwed the face-glass into the helmet and tapped upon it as a signal; the pumps lifted the pressure of the weights from the diver's chest. The air thudded irritatingly into the copper prison that was the helmet; the sense of confinement and the close smell of the natural breathing element of man unnaturally compressed, returned to Phil Regard. He thought of the wife in Sydney—the last thought of the divinity before bracing himself to work that had the chance of death in it always, though use had brought danger into contempt; then he opened the valve and dropped easily and gently into the caresses of the water.

The black corpse of the *Pandora* seemed to rise to him. He closed the valve and sank as through a cataract of feathers. Avoiding the deck, he dropped to the bottom for a survey of the hull. Moving lightly as a featherweight, Regard studied the situation.

All about him stretched tangles of seaweed and coral with white walks between the spongy copses and the brakes. A yellow water-snake followed his every movement with curious imitation, and white fish circled around his helmet so that a green hand must have become dizzy. From a rift in the rock wavered the tentacles of a devil-fish, feeling its way to crime with every cup and sucker. . . .

The weight of ocean pressed the diver softly in his armour of the air; his body felt as if stroked by the silky hands of the caressing sea. And then from the great tunnel in the hull of the *Pandora* came floating the horrors of the deep.

Used as he was to these cruel cowards, in the light of the story of the bride who had died in the wreck, they held for him a new horror, and for a moment he was afraid. Their gorged habit, their slow, plethoric movements, their dull eyes, forgetting for a moment to be greedy, told the tale. Regard felt almost physically sick. All those eyes looked at him threateningly, contemptuously; the little fish that swam up to his face-glass and gazed at him did not seem to be frightened as quickly as usual by the movement of his hands.

The sharks came nearer, and Regard, lifting the rubber wristband, shot air at them in a succession of silver bullets, and the cowards became energetic and fled. A carpet-bag shark, the incarnation of filthy malevolence, hovered above him until Regard turned the escape-valve on his helmet and shot a madness of fear into the horrible thing.

He finished his survey of the hull with difficulty. For an hour Regard rested and fed; then he went to the ladder, and was loaded and imprisoned again, and sank to the deck of the *Pandora*.

His retinue of enemies left him at the entrance to the saloon; but the small fish, their brilliance seeming to light the half-gloom, swam into the depths and in and out at the portholes—'like schoolboys playing a game', thought Phil Regard. Even there some little things had begun already to benefit by the fall of greatness; little pearl shells as big as a thumb-nail had here spun their byssus to tie them to the saloon stairs, hiding their weakness in this unexpected asylum.

'All this death to make a safe hiding-place for a shell', thought Regard bitterly, as he walked on tiptoe through this silent world where all values of vision were distorted.

He talked to himself, and the words reverberated to him from the helmet: 'I'll bring dynamite and a wire down and blow the specie-room open, rig a winch, and haul out the gold-boxes. That'll be to-morrow. And while I'm here I'll do the horrible job—Moresby's pearls.'

He went back to the saloon stairs. Above it a great grey shape hung watchfully, patiently, as if it had all eternity to wait in. Regard, with never a quickening of the pulse, fired the silver bullets from his wristband, and the grey shape backed and fled. Regard laughed and went on to find Moresby's pearls.

He opened a cabin door; two fish fled through the porthole and the body of a woman came at him in the swirl of the water. The dead face struck his helmet. Regard cried out in horror, and backed away. But in a moment he caught his courage and closed the porthole; then he shut the cabin door again and went to the next. He could not distinguish the letter denoting the corridor, nor the number either.

He opened an inner cabin and a drowned man came out and struck him. He opened another, and there were in it a dead man and a dead woman trying with her floating skirts to hide a little child from the sea. Horror gripped the diver as with fingers of cold steel.

Yet his duty was to be done, and he did it. He found B corridor, and the first cabin had in it a dead girl with her hands clasped as if she still prayed. He closed the cabin reverently and came to another, in which an old man and an old woman had died in their bed-places; and then to an outer cabin opposite the one he had first entered. The light was better there; he saw that this was B 41 at last.

The lock of B 41 did not yield to the lifting of the handle, so Regard inserted the point of his small axe between the door and the beading and levered it open. Two bodies, those of a man and a woman—the man's as if he had died standing, the woman's in the lower berth floating up against the wires of the upper berth—moved queerly in the disturbed liquid, as if they were alive.

'Porthole closed,' muttered Regard to himself, try-ing not to look at the dead for a moment. 'He had the fan going—the lever's on the top speed.'

He looked at the body of the man, and turned him around in the water.

'That'll be the man Moresby gave the pearls to. Oyley was the name, and he looks it. There's the trunk under the berth. And this poor soul has the key round her neck. I can't do it. But I promised. I'll do it to-morrow. No; better now—get it done with. For-give—whoever you are, forgive me. Young, too, and pretty.' With a shaking hand, and covering his face, he touched the woman's neck, and there he felt the necklet and the key.

'It's horrible. I'll have to use both hands for the fastening.'

As if he were physically afraid of it, he looked back at the sinister dead man floating near the porthole; then, swiftly and without looking, he unfastened the necklet and held it up—a necklet and a key. The movement floated the body from its position against the springs of the upper berth; it turned upright, floating by his head—through the little circle of the face-glass its dead eyes looked sorrowfully into his own.

And then—madness! Unbelief! Doubt! Unbelief again! And again madness, clamoured through his brain. The air seemed to be withdrawn; the helmet became a mountain of copper; the weights upon his back and breast were each a ton of lead. He looked at the necklet—yes, it was so! He had given it. He released it, and it sank to the ooze upon the sodden carpet. He looked at the bracelet of opal before the mirror, and recognised it too; and then at the dead woman gazing at him mournfully with eyes that seemed to plead: 'Forgive; I have been punished and repented so; forgive.'

Still unbelieving, but stunned, he pushed the dead man through the door. Then he turned back and re-entered the cabin. There could be no doubt—no doubt!

He left her there and fastened the cabin door behind him. And then his heart broke.

He could not live! With his last conscious instinct he hacked with uncertain hand at the airpipe and missed it; then the weight of all the ocean settled on his heart and he wavered to the floor.

He had a conscientious tender. At that sudden jag upon the lifeline the tender hauled carefully, and by that luck which shames the best judgement, drew Philip Regard safely through the alleyway to the deck of the *Pandora*, and up to sunlight.

But they might as well have left him there, for the strong man who had dived never returned to the surface.

'Beats me!' said Druce, looking pityingly at the withered wreck that sat every day through all the daylight hours of every day, upon the veranda of Thursday Island Hospital. 'Can't understand it. A fine, big, strong world-beater of a man paralysed in fourteen fathoms. It beats me!'

THE NIGHT WE WATCHED
FOR WALLABIES
By 'Steele Rudd' (Arthur H. Davis)

It had been a bleak July day, and as night came on a bitter westerly howled through the trees. Cold! Wasn't it cold! The pigs in the sty, hungry and half-fed (we wanted for ourselves the few pumpkins that had survived the drought), fought savagely with each other for shelter, and squealed all the time like—well, like pigs. The cows and calves left the place to seek shelter away in the mountains; while the draught horses, their hair standing up like barbed wire, leaned sadly over the fence and gazed at the green lucerne. Joe went about shivering in an old coat of Dad's with only one sleeve to it—a calf had fancied the other one day that Dad hung it on a post as a mark to go by while ploughing.

'My! it'll be a stinger to-night,' Dad remarked to Mrs. Brown—who sat, cold-looking, on the sofa—as he staggered inside with an immense log for the fire. A log! Nearer a whole tree! But wood was nothing in Dad's eyes.

Mrs. Brown had been at our place five or six days. Old Brown called occasionally to see her, so we knew they couldn't have quarrelled. Sometimes she did a little housework, but more often she didn't. We talked it over together, but couldn't make it out. Joe asked Mother, but she had no idea—so she said. We were full up, as Dave put it, of Mrs. Brown, and wished her out of the place. She had taken to ordering us about, as though she had something to do with us.

After supper we sat round the fire—as near to it as we could without burning ourselves—Mrs. Brown and all, and listened to the wind whistling outside. Ah, it was pleasant beside the fire listening to the wind! When Dad had warmed himself back and front he turned to us and said:

'Now, boys, we must go directly and light some fires and keep those wallabies back.'

That was a shock to us, and we looked at him to see if he were really in earnest. He was, and as serious as a judge.

'*To-night!*' Dave answered, surprisedly; 'why to-night any more than last night or the night before? Thought you had decided to let them rip?'

'Yes, but we might as well keep them off a bit longer.'

'But there's no wheat there for them to get now. So what's the good of watching them? There's no sense in *that*.'

Dad was immovable.

'Anyway,' whined Joe, '*I'm* not going—not a night like this—not when I ain't got boots.'

That vexed Dad. 'Hold your tongue, sir!' he said; 'you'll do as you're told.'

But Dave hadn't finished. 'I've been following that harrow since sunrise this morning,' he said, 'and now you want me to go chasing wallabies about in the dark, a night like this, and for nothing else but to keep them from eating the ground. It's always the way here, the more one does the more he's wanted to do,' and he commenced to cry. Mrs. Brown had something to say. *She* agreed with Dad and thought we ought to go, as the wheat might spring up again.

'Pshah!' Dave blurted out between his sobs, while we thought of telling her to shut her mouth.

Slowly and reluctantly we left that roaring fireside to accompany Dad that bitter night. It *was* a night!— dark as pitch, silent, forlorn and forbidding, and colder than the busiest morgue. And just to keep wallabies from eating nothing! They *had* eaten all the wheat—every blade of it—and the grass as well. What they would start on next—ourselves or the cart-harness —wasn't quite clear.

We stumbled along in the dark one behind the other, with our hands stuffed into our trousers. Dad was in the lead, and poor Joe, bare-shinned and bootless, in the rear. Now and again he tramped on a Bathurst-burr, and, in sitting down to extract the prickle, would receive a cluster of them elsewhere. When he escaped the burr it was only to knock his shin against a log or leave a toe-nail or two clinging to a stone. Joe howled, but the wind howled louder, and blew and blew.

Dave, in pausing to wait on Joe, would mutter:

'To *hell* with everything! Whatever he wants bringing us out a night like this, I'm *damned* if *I* know!'

Dad couldn't see very well in the dark, and on this night couldn't see at all, so he walked up against one of the old draught horses that had fallen asleep gazing at the lucerne. And what a fright they both got! The old horse took it worse than Dad—who only tumbled down—for he plunged as though the Devil had grabbed him, and fell over the fence, twisting every leg he had in the wires. How the brute struggled! We stood and listened to him. After kicking panels of the fence down, and smashing every wire in it, he got loose and made off, taking most of it with him.

'That's one wallaby on the wheat, anyway,' Dave muttered, and we giggled. *We* understood Dave; but Dad didn't open his mouth.

We lost no time lighting the fires. Then we walked through the 'wheat' and wallabies! May Satan reprove me if I exaggerate their number by one solitary pair of ears—from the row and scatter they made there was a *million*.

Dad told Joe, at last, he could go to sleep if he liked, at the fire. Joe went to sleep—*how*, I don't know. Then Dad sat beside him, and for long intervals would stare silently into the darkness. Sometimes a string of vermin would hop past close to the fire, and another time a curlew would come near and screech its ghostly wail, but he never noticed them. Yet he seemed to be listening.

We mooched around from fire to fire, hour after hour, and when we wearied of heaving fire-sticks at the enemy we sat on our heels and cursed the wind, and the winter, and the night-birds alternately. It was a lonely, wretched occupation.

Now and again Dad would leave his fire to ask us if we could hear a noise. We couldn't, except that of wallabies and mopokes. Then he would go back and listen again. He was restless, and, somehow, his heart wasn't in the wallabies at all. Dave couldn't make him out.

The night wore on. By and by there was a sharp rattle of wires, then a rustling noise, and Sal appeared in the glare of the fire. '*Dad!*' she said. That was all. Without a word, Dad bounced up and went back to the house along with her.

'Something's up!' Dave said, and, half-anxious,

half-afraid, we gazed into the fire and thought and thought. Then we stared, nervously, into the night, and listened for Dad's return, but heard only the wind and the mopoke.

At dawn he appeared again, with a broad smile on his face, and told us that Mother had got another baby —a fine little chap. *Then* we knew why Mrs. Brown had been staying at our place.

KATE'S WEDDING
By 'Steele Rudd' (Arthur H. Davis)

Our selection was a great place for dancing. We could all dance—from Dad down—and there wasn't a figure or a movement we didn't know. We learned young. Mother was a firm believer in early tuition. She used to say it was nice for young people to know how to dance, and be able to take their part when they went out anywhere, and not be awkward and stupid-looking when they went into society. It was awful, she thought, to see young fellows and big lumps of girls like the Bradys stalk into a ballroom and sit the whole night long in a corner, without attempting to get up. She didn't know how mothers *could* bring children up so ignorantly, and didn't wonder at some of them not being able to find husbands for their daughters.

But *we* had a lot to feel thankful for. Besides a sympathetic mother, every other facility was afforded us to become accomplished. Abundance of freedom; enthusiastic sisters; and no matter how things were going—whether corn wouldn't come up, or the wheat had failed, or the pumpkins had given out, or the water-hole run dry—we always had a concertina in the house. It never failed to attract company. Paddy Maloney and the well-sinkers, after belting and blasting all day long, used to drop in at night, and throw the table outside and take the girls up, and prance about the floor with them till all hours.

Nearly every week Mother gave a ball. It might have been every night only for Dad. He said the jumping about destroyed the ground-floor—wore it away and made the room like a well. And whenever it rained hard and the water rushed in *he* had to bail it out. Dad always looked on the dark side of things. He had no ear for music either. His want of appreciation of melody often made the home miserable when it might have been the merriest on earth. Sometimes it happened that he had to throw down the plough-reins for half an hour or so to run round the wheat paddock after a horse or an old cow; then if he found Dave or Sal, or any of us, sitting inside playing the concertina when he came to get a drink, he would nearly go mad.

'Can't y' find anything better t' do than ever-lastingly playing at that damn thing?' he would shout. And if we didn't put the instrument down immediately he would tear it from our hands and pitch it outside. If we *did* lay it down quietly he would snatch it up and heave it out just as hard. The next evening he would devote all his time to patching the fragments together with sealing-wax.

Still, despite Dad's antagonism, we all turned out good players. It cost us nothing either. We learnt from each other. Kate was the first that learnt. *She* taught Sal. Sal taught Dave, and so on. Sandy Taylor was Kate's tutor. He passed our place every evening going to his selection, where he used to sleep at night (fulfilling conditions), and always stopped at the fence to yarn with Kate about dancing. Sandy was a fine dancer himself, very light on his feet and easy to waltz with—so the girls made out. When the dancing subject was exhausted Sandy would drag some hair out of the horse's mane, and say, 'How's the concertina?' 'It's in there,' Kate would answer. Then turning round she would call out, 'J—*oe*, bring the concer'.'

In an instant Joe would strut along with it. And Sandy, for the fiftieth time, would examine it and laugh at the kangaroo-skin straps that Dave had tacked to it, and the scraps of brown paper that were plastered over the ribs of it to keep the wind in; and, cocking his left leg over the pommel of his saddle, would sound a full blast on it as a preliminary. Then he would strike up 'The Rocky Road to Dublin' or 'The Wind Among the Barley', or some other beautiful air, and grind away untiringly until it got dark—until mother came and asked him if he wouldn't come in and have supper. Of course, he always would. After supper he would play some more. Then there would be a dance.

A ball was to be held at Anderson's one Friday night, and only Kate and Dave were asked from our place. Dave was very pleased to be invited; it was the first time he had been asked anywhere, and he began to practise vigorously. The evening before the ball Dad sent him to put the draught horses in the top paddock. He went off merrily with them. The sun was just going down when he let them go, and save the noise of the birds settling to rest the paddock was quiet. Dave was filled with emotion and enthusiastic thoughts about the ball. He threw the winkers down and looked around. For a moment or two he stood erect, then he bowed gracefully to the saplings on his right, then to the stumps and trees on his left and, humming a tune, ambled across a small patch of ground that was bare and black, and pranced back again. He opened his arms and, clasping some beautiful imaginary form in them, swung round and round like a windmill. Then he paused for breath, embraced his partner again, and 'galloped' up and down. And young Johnson, who had been watching him in wonder from behind a fence, bolted for our place.

'Mrs. Rudd! Mrs. Rudd!' he shouted from the veranda. Mother went out.

'Wot's—wot's up with Dave?'

Mother turned pale.

'There's *something* . . . !'

'My God!' Mother exclaimed. '*Whatever* has happened?'

Young Johnson hesitated. He was in doubt.

'Oh! what *is* it?' Mother moaned.

'Well' (he drew close to her), 'he's—he's *mad*!'

'*Oh-h!*'

'He *is*. I seen 'im just now up in your paddick, an' he's clean off he's pannikin.'

Just then Dave came down the track, whistling. Young Johnson saw him and fled.

For some time Mother regarded Dave with grave suspicion, then she questioned him closely.

'Yairs,' he said, grinning hard, 'I was goin' through th' *fust set*.'

It was when Kate was married to Sandy Taylor that we realized what a blessing it is to be able to dance. How we looked forward to that wedding! We were always talking about it, and were very pleased it would be held in our own house, because all of us could go then. None of us could work for thinking of it —even Dad seemed to forget his troubles about the corn and Mick Brennan's threat to summon him for half the fence. Mother said we would want plenty of water for the people to drink, so Sandy yoked his horse to the slide, and he, Dad, and Joe started for the springs.

The slide was the fork of a tree, alias a wheel-less water-trolly. The horse was hitched to the butt end, and a batten nailed across the prongs kept the cask from slipping off going uphill. Sandy led the way and carried the bucket; Dad went ahead to clear the track of stones; and Joe straddled the cask to keep her steady.

It always took three to work the slide.

The water they brought was a little thick—Old Anderson had been down and stirred it up pulling a bullock out; but Dad put plenty ashes in the cask to clear it.

Each of us had his own work to do. Sandy knocked the partition down and decorated the place with boughs; Mother and the girls cooked and covered the walls with newspapers, and Dad gathered cow-dung and did the floor.

Two days before the wedding. All of us were still working hard. Dad was up to his armpits in a bucket of mixture, with a stack of cow-dung on one side, and a heap of sand and the shovel on the other. Dave and Joe were burning a cow that had died just in front of the house, and Sandy had gone to town for his tweed trousers.

A man in a long, black coat, white collar, and new leggings rode up, spoke to Dad, and got off. Dad straightened up and looked awkward, with his arms hanging wide and the mixture dripping from them. Mother came out. The cove shook hands with her, but he didn't with Dad. They went inside—not Dad, who washed himself first.

Dave sent Joe to ask Dad who the cove was. Dad spoke in a whisper and said he was Mr. Macpherson, the clergyman who was to marry Kate and Sandy. Dave whistled and piled more wood on the dead cow. Mother came out and called Dave and Joe. Dave wouldn't go, but sent Joe.

Dave threw another log on the cow, then thought he would see what was going on inside.

He stood at the window and looked in. He couldn't believe his eyes at first, and put his head right in. There were Dad, Joe, and the lot of them down on their marrow-bones saying something after the parson. Dave was glad that he didn't go in.

How the parson prayed! Just when he said 'Lead us not into temptation' the big kangaroo-dog slipped in and grabbed all the fresh meat on the table; but Dave managed to kick him in the ribs at the door. Dad groaned and seemed very restless. When the parson had gone Dad said that what he had read about 'reaping the same as you sow' was all rot, and spoke about the time when we sowed two bushels of barley in the lower paddock and got a big stack of rye from it.

The wedding was on a Wednesday, and at three o'clock in the afternoon. Most of the people came before dinner; the Hamiltons arrived just after breakfast. Talk of drays!—the little paddock couldn't hold them.

Jim Mullins was the only one who came in to dinner; the others mostly sat on their heels in a row and waited in the shade of the wire fence. The parson was the last to come, and as he passed in he knocked his head against the kangaroo-leg hanging under the veranda. Dad saw it swinging, and said angrily to Joe: 'Didn't I tell you to take that down this morning?'

Joe unhooked it and said: 'But if I hang it anywhere else the dog'll get it.'

Dad tried to laugh at Joe, and said loudly: 'And what else is it for?' Then he bustled Joe off before he could answer him again.

Joe didn't understand.

Then Dad said (putting the leg in a bag): 'Do you want every one to know we eat it, —— you?'

Joe understood.

The ceremony commenced. Those who could squeeze inside did so—the others looked in at the window and through the cracks in the chimney.

Mrs. M'Doolan led Kate out of the back room; then Sandy rose from the fireplace and stood beside her. Everyone thought Kate looked very nice—and orange blossoms! You'd think she was an orange-tree with a new bed-curtain thrown over it. Sandy looked well, too, in his snake-belt and new tweeds; but he seemed uncomfortable when the pin that Dave put in the back of his collar came out.

The parson didn't take long; and how they scrambled and tumbled over each other at the finish! Charley Mace said that he got the first kiss; Big George said *he* did; and Mrs. M'Doolan was certain she would have got it only for the baby.

Fun! there *was* fun! The room was cleared and they promenaded for a dance—Sandy and Kate in the lead. They continued promenading until one of the well-sinkers called for the concertina—ours had been repaired till you could only get three notes out of it; but Jim Burke jumped on his horse and went home for his accordion.

Dance! They did dance!—until sunrise. But unless
you were dancing you couldn't stay inside, because
the floor broke up, and talk about dust!—before
morning the room was like a drafting-yard.

It was a great wedding; and, though years have
since passed, all the neighbours say still it was the best
they were ever at.

THE WIDOW DARE
By H. Stone (William Hughston)

MR. TREGEAR and his daughters were just come in
for breakfast, after milking in the cold starlight dawn
of an autumn morning.

'But, gurls,' the old man was saying, as he held his
hand to the fire, 'I can't never feel for to do it, like.'

'Feel to do it! And is she to stick on there for ever,
not payin' a farthin' of rent, because you don't feel to
do it? My word! Some folks' feelin's make rare pets
for 'em.'

The new day was penetrating the dusky kitchen,
and as Sarah Ann spoke she turned and blew out the
tallow-dip, which gave out its pungent smoke.

'But, Sareh, couldn't some of 'ee women-folk go?
Seem to me more fitty than for old widow-man like I
be. Thyself or Adelaide or Janey.'

'Oh, yes! Of course! I was expectin' that. "Couldn't
some of us women-folk go!" Same old story. My! it's
easy bein' good and pop'lar if the women-folk'll do
all the nasty work for you. Just like the other day,
when that Joe had to be cleared out. Couldn't say a

rough word to him for the world, could you? The women-folk might do it, though, if they liked, and so they did. Come to breakfast.'

'Now, now, Sareh,' replied Mr. Tregear, sitting down, but not beginning to eat. 'Haven't I often 'splained to 'ee about this blessed old coffee palace of ourn, and why do you be harpin' 'pon it still? Can't 'ee see since railway comed along up here the port have all goned to pot? There don't belong to be no coffee palace down there, where nobody do come. I tell 'ee nuther Mrs. Dare nor nobody else you do think to put in will ever make it pay—not even thee thyselves; I defy 'ee to do it.'

'Make it pay!' retorted Sarah Ann, with a sort of exultation of her meagre visage. 'Didn't us girls make it pay for two years? And saved money out of it, too. But it wasn't by settin' down and lookin' tired and interestin', like that Mrs. Dare. We slaved and con-trived, and got our due and paid our due. And look here, Father,' she added emphatically, 'we wouldn't be afraid to do the same to-morrow.'

''Es, 'es,' answered the old man conciliatingly. 'No doubt, Sareh, thee and thy sisters did nobly by that coffee palace, and made it pay, too, p'r'aps. Wonder-ful buskers you were to think and plan, and wonderful workish in the 'ouse; but 'ee see there be some as 'an't got your gifts. And then times be different.'

'Well, then, Father, will you go or not?'

'But them scrub-cutters,' answered the old man, hard bested. 'They do need constant watchin'.'

'Scrub-cutters!' replied Sarah Ann derisively. 'Why, you only keep them back with your talk, Father.'

'But that milk to the factory, Sareh. Ben't fitty for 'ee——'

'Milk to the factory! Well! I guess it won't sour if Janey takes it for once, will it? Or is your drivin' anythin' partic'ler for milk? Or p'r'aps it's the gossip round the tip you'll be missin'.'

'But, Sareh! Can't 'ee spare a thought to the poor wida 'ooman 'erself? I, as knowed her 'way back along, and your mother did, too. Fancy, to go for to turn 'er out of 'ouse and 'ome. Sim terrible mean.'

'It's a terrible sight meaner, I call it,' said Sarah Ann, thoroughly exasperated, 'to turn and twist and excuse yourself all round to put a thing on your daughters as you ain't willin' to do yourself. Course, some of us 'll haft to go. A fifteen-mile ride's nothin' to us through the bush, as long as we can think how nice it is for your feelin's. 'Tisn't nothin' to count. None of us won't be able to get a new bonnet nor nothin' for Mr. Peters's annerversary.'

'Bonnet for annerversary!' repeated Mr. Tregear, looking pained and puzzled. 'Didn't know it were that a-makin' 'ee so set on to it, Sareh. Shoarly we can manage new bonnets for th' annerversary 'ithout turnin' Mrs. Dare into street.'

'Well! it wasn't that altogether,' replied Sarah Ann, nodding her head sidewise. 'But how are we to get bonnets or anything else if every bit of business about the place is managed like this? I'm sure we'd been a long way better off if we'd stayed at the coffee palace, 'stead of comin' up here to slave for nothin'.'

'Now! Now! Hush! Sareh, my dear,' replied the old man anxiously. 'Don't 'ee be pullin' things up by roots that a-way, nor say such words to thy old da. 'Twere good of 'ee to come, when I were lonely after thy poor mother . . . Howsomdever,' he added, 'if 'ee be so bent, I'll go for 'ee. P'r'aps it be my place! —p'r'aps it be. I'll go. There! See else.'

At this a general movement of satisfaction seemed to pass round the table.

'Very well, then, Father,' said Sarah Ann briskly. 'Go on with your breakfast. You know what's to be done. Just give her notice in the usual way. One week's enough. You can say Mrs. Webster is going in by then. She hasn't spoken definitely yet, but I know it's all right.'

'But, Sareh, do you think he'd better say anything about Mrs. Webster?' asked the cautious Adelaide.

'Oh, yes,' replied Sarah decisively. 'Let him tell her that, and if there's any hitch—which I know there won't be—perhaps we may think of takin' it ourselves.'

Sarah Ann at this glanced meaningly at her father, who, however, did not observe the innuendo.

'And if she shows any of her tantrums,' said Janey, 'just tell her, Father, that under your daughters' management the place paid handsomely.'

'Yes!' said Sarah Ann. 'Come, now, Father, you must get yourself ready and be off at once, and you can be back before night. And mind, you ain't to go the Polglazes' comin' back. You promise? Put on your Sunday best. Where are your boots? I'll make Dick polish 'em to see 'is face in 'em.'

The little mountain farm—carved out of the heart of the forest—with its steep grassy slopes steaming grey in the early sun, and its scrubby paddocks dark and dewy under the shadow of the range, seemed to be awakening to a Sabbath freshness as Mr. Tregear rode away that luminous autumn morning.

A lyre-bird from the depths of some gully was sending out its strong, ringing whistle, but the old man, adorned in his smooth broadcloth, shiny boots, and high hat, heard it not. His pleasant face was screwed up into an expression of puzzlement and concern, and

E

as he rode down his hand sought his chin irresolutely. At the slip-rails, feeling sorely the need of some ally, he paused and felt anxiously about for his pipe, but those stiff virgin pockets knew naught of pipes, and his efforts only brought to light a new pocket-handkerchief.

He turned and looked hesitatingly back to the house, but at the door he could see Sarah Ann's rigid figure still looking after him, and he hastily resumed his journey.

'Derned if this ben't an errand,' he said to himself. 'How ever did I get 'pon it? Don't see how I be a-goin' to scrooge through, 'tall, 'tall.'

His way took him into the heart of the forest, along a slippery, slushy corduroy track, undried for months under the crowding trees.

With a loose rein he mounted the hills and plunged down into the dank aromatic air of the gullies, sometimes emerging into a rough clearing, and again entering the forest; and the sun was already well past its noon when he came out upon the coast, and saw way below him, between the long slope of forest and the sea, the scattered roofs of the little town of Port Karimba.

As he went down the old man's mind became more and more rebellious to the duties of the task he had undertaken. 'I be come to give 'ee waernin', Mrs. Dare,' he rehearsed reflectively to himself. 'How do that sound for down souse? Seem terrible suddent and queer. Won't do; won't do.'

He dismounted in the street before the coffee palace, a shabby blistered building displaying an enormous sign, and knocked. His profound hopes that the Widow Dare might not be 'to hum' were disappointed by the sound of a step within and the opening of the door.

A tall, youngish woman stood there, with kindly eyes and a mouth a little pinched, as by a struggle beyond her strength.

'Mr. Tregear, I do declare,' she said, but with a touch of anxiety in her smile.

A wrinkle was on the old man's brow, and he nodded awkwardly, and hesitated a moment with his hand.

Mrs. Dare noticed his uneasiness. 'Won't you come in, Mr. Tregear?' she said, holding out her hand frankly.

It was grasped with the warmest friendliness. 'Ben't it glorus weather, ma'am?' said Mr. Tregear.

As he stepped inside he noticed that things did not seem to wear the old harsh cleanliness of Sarah Ann's rule. The sitting-room, which had always been associated in his mind with repression—abstinence from smoking, stiff-backed chairs, antimacassars (not to be moved), anxiety about the state of his boots, etcetera—now struck him as a snug and pleasant spot. He sat down on the big sofa, which seemed a respectable relic of better days, with an unlooked-for sense of comfort after the strain of his long ride.

'And you've been riding since early morning, Mr. Tregear? You must be real tired, and in need of some dinner.'

'No, no,' protested Mr. Tregear. 'Dinner ben't thing I be partial to 'tall, 'tall, Mrs. Dare. I assure 'ee 'tis so; just cup tea all I do need, if 'ee be so kind.'

The hot strong tea and sweet scones were very comforting to the old man, but they somehow made the object of his visit much less manageable. They produced on his mind the dangerous illusion of a 'company-call, friendly-like'.

'Well, now,' he said, as he finished, 'that be prime

tea, and they scones remind me of old Cornish saffern cake, if I d' live.'

Mrs. Dare smiled, but her smile was without brightness. Her needle flew faster.

Mr. Tregear looked out of the window. 'And what be the luck of the sea 'ith the fishers?' said he genially. 'Seed old Nickey Muffat fixin' his preens in th' lobstar-pots as comed down. Wonderful old fisher Nickey be, ben't 'ee, ma'am? A real tremenyeous old man.'

'Yes, he's a very nice old man. He sometimes brings me up a fish.'

'Do he now? That's the sort he be, and talk. 'Tis a hollerday to 'ear en. And old Benny Trembath,' continued the old man, fearing a pause, 'an' so he be gone. 'Twere like a knife to me to 'ear it. Won't see him down 'pon quay no moor—spurticles 'pon his nose.'

'No, poor old man.'

'And how be Mrs. Trewells a-fadgin' now? A fine and thumpin' dame she were in her time, full o' jokes and condudles.'

On went Mr. Tregear from one thing to another with much liveliness. Mrs. Dare listened and nodded, but did not help him much in the conversation. Under her attention of manner the old man soon perceived an anxious preoccupation, which, as he talked on, he became more and more determined to remove.

'What do'st think of that last preacher, Mrs. Dare?' he asked. 'That Peters; he do drive along forthy, don't he? Sarah Ann be greatly taken up 'ith en. A real power, she do call en. He do remind me of our young rooster when th' oats be hoved down. He be a-callin' all the world to come and feast.'

After a while, lack of matter brought a pause to

Mr. Tregear's flow, and Mrs. Dare said in a strained voice:

'Mr. Tregear—about my rent. I am sure you and Miss Tregear must be annoyed about it.'

The old man felt himself unexpectedly reminded of his duty, and a feeling of great respect came over him for conscientiousness like this.

'Rent, ma'am!' he said. 'Rent! Well, now you speak of it, there were some little tok about rent, I do believe.' He scratched his head as if to remember. 'But homsomdever, ma'am,' he went on, 'don't 'ee——'

Mrs. Dare, seeing his drift, and unwilling to take advantage of it, interposed, 'Well, Mr. Tregear, I wanted to say to you that if only you will have patience I hope to be able to do something later. I know how unsatisfactory it is for you, but then you see the place has gone down so.'

''Es, 'es, to be sure, ma'am. That's what I do say to my gurls. 'Tain't reasonable to expect no rent; I do know how you be fixed here. No traffic like 'twas in old days 'ith the boat. No summer visitors like there be to Highville. No nothin'. 'Tis enough, Mrs. Dare, if you do make a livin' out of et 'ithout rent, and I hope you do. That's what I try to explain to my gurls. But dern et—— Homsomdever,' he added, checking himself, 'mine be grand gurls, grand buskers. I belong to uphauld en for that. But I can see, ma'am, how this yer coffee palace be a-makin' of 'ee thin and pale. And us do wish, ma'am,' he hurried on to say, 'Sarah and the gurls and all us do wish that 'ee take no more trouble 'bout rent. That's like much as anything else what I comed for to-day, ma'am.'

Mr. Tregear had gone far indeed on the downward path thus boldly to couple Sarah Ann's and the girls' names with his crimes. Mrs. Dare, however, was not deceived, but she felt keenly the old man's kindly feeling, and spoke to him freely as an old friend of her worries and anxieties. Mr. Tregear became so sympathetic that he formed in his mind a grand scheme for sending down a cart-load of farm stuff next day. As this project came to him he began feeling about his smooth person with the heels of his hands for his pipe—that first confident of his cogitations.

'You have forgotten your pipe, Mr. Tregear,' said Mrs. Dare, smiling. 'I'll call Tommy, and he'll run down to the store and get you a new one, and some tobacco if you'll tell him what sort.'

'Well, now,' he said, with slow smiling emphasis; 'that be like 'ee, I do declare, Mrs. Dare. That pure roagish face and all.'

The little thoughtful touch of the widow's had quite won the old man's heart; as he wrung her hand he conjured her again to keep up heart and think no more about rent; he hinted mysteriously 'that somethin' ed be sure-like to turn up'.

Mr. Tregear was surprised as he looked round after mounting to see how late it was. Grey evening was already over the sea, and the mountains stretched out above him in gloomy sable masses. Time had indeed passed quickly, in chat with Mrs. Dare, but his warmth of heart grew a little chill as he addressed himself to the track, and the pipe he had been puffing with excited vigour went out in the mental pause in which his thoughts flew homewards. 'Goodness me!' he said to himself in a sort of whisper. 'They'll be that mad; they'll be fair mazed 'ith anger.'

Midway up the black hillside he paused to think, and looked back, as if the sight gave him pain, over the waters of the bay, dyed to their depths with the red and sullen reflection of the afterglow.

Slowly he turned and resumed his journey, with his eyes on the ground. 'They'll never let it stand, I do fear. No! 'Twill be put down to her as old man's tok and fullishness. Not to be considered on, snuffed out like—a—thing. Sareh 'erself 'ill be comin' to settle all up sharp and quick, and 'noy her 'ith her plain tok— my heart——'

Soon he was travelling in the narrow forest aisle already growing black as night under the masses of foliage. Dimly the boles of the trees stood in the wooded depths. All was hushed and silent, save for the small occasional clitter-clitter of a dead leaf falling. The horse pushed on with forward-flinging nose, eager to be home; Mr. Tregear, sunk in his reflections, heeded nothing. 'If could only think o' somethin' 'for leavin' en knaw,' he ruminated. 'And then give en out down souse. But one and all again me, could I haul me awn? Could I haul me awn? 'Twould be just rousin' of en again 'er more bitter.

'My life,' he added after a long mental chase after different expedients. 'I would like for to see Cousin Polglaze 'pon it. He would knaw a plan. He would fotch a compass about en.'

By this time Mr. Tregear was about half-way on his journey, and was crossing a creek under a high black ridge, on which the moonlight was faintly rising. It was just here that the Polglazes' track turned off. The old man pulled up slowly, half stopping and half going on, and thinking of his promise of the morning.

'Perhaps there'll be time fur both,' he said to himself hastily, as he turned into an unseen but familiar track going off along the creek side. After a mile or so he caught sight of a lighted window through the timber, and was saluted by the baying of dogs. He made his way to the door and knocked, while the dogs, after preliminary sniffs, began leaping and bounding about him, and yawning with satisfaction.

After the old man's departure that morning things were pushed on with even more than their usual briskness, for Sarah Ann was anxious to be done early in order to go and transact a very important little bit of business with Mrs. Webster, the prospective tenant.

So in the afternoon, the buggy having been got out by Dick, and the old mare harnessed up, Sarah was driven off, attired for the occasion, and promising the girls, with a touch of dignity, to be back by milking-time. Dignity was with Sarah Ann inseparable from the sensation of best clothes.

She came back, however, somewhat before her time, and with a very disturbed countenance. Mrs. Webster, it seemed, had for some reason or other changed her mind, and would have nothing to do with the coffee palace. Moreover, she had declared that if Mrs. Dare were turned out the Tregear girls would be the talk of the district for meanness and hard-heartedness. There was in that a menace which touched them to the quick. Mrs. Webster was a noted talker, and a leading light at chapel.

'Of course I declared to her,' said Sarah Ann excitedly, 'that Mrs. Dare was not going to be turned out. That we'd no intention of doing so. That it was only in case she left of herself like. My word! I didn't leave her much to say about it, I can tell you.'

'But, Sarah, what's changed her? Why don't she want it herself no longer?'

'Oh, I don't know. She's been stayin' at Port Karimba, and they've been holdin' a revival down there. That's it. I think she reckons on going to heaven at our expense.'

'But, Sarah, how could you make it out like that to her when Father's gone to——'

'Well, what else could I do? Somethin' 'ill have to be done to stop it. Can't any of you suggest anythin' 'stead of starin' there like scrub heifers?'

'If Father only were back. Perhaps he's not turned her out after all.'

'Oh, trust him for that now that we don't want it. But it isn't that so much. It's it getting all over the place. That's it,' said Sarah. 'Go now, girls,' she added testily. 'The cows must be milked whatever happens. We'll think of somethin' milkin'.'

But it was a silent milking-shed that evening. Dick had been sent off to help the scrub-cutters, lest any deliberations should arise, but nothing was forthcoming.

Adelaide at last broke out from her cow: 'I don't know what Father was in such a hurry for, goin' off like that. I never saw him so easy persuaded before. He just seemed bent to be off, didn't he?'

'Yes, and anyway 'mongst all his 'scuses did anyone ever hear him say anything about folks talking about it, or anything like that? 'Twas just his own feelin's he was always on.'

Every now and then Sarah would go to the end of the shed and look out down the track, only to come back shaking her head to the girls' anxious eyes.

But the afternoon wore away and brought no Father.

'It's shameful, girls,' cried Sarah Ann almost tear-fully as they were washing the buckets in the twilight. 'He's gone off to them Polglazes again, and leavin' us here like this. It'll be all over the place before we hardly know it ourselves, and all the church folk'll have it, and Mr. Peters.'

Vexation prevented Sarah from saying more. She turned away and they went on with their work in silence.

'Sarah,' cried Adelaide, at last pausing with a sudden inspiration. 'Why wait for Father to come home? He'll be all hours to-morrow. Why not write to Mrs. Dare, sayin' it's all a mistake; that Father acted like without warrant—isn't that it?—in turnin' her out, and that there's no occasion for her to go. And we'd feel obliged if she'd kindly stay on, knowin' she ain't got another place to go to. That it was only an old man's business way like, and didn't need to be taken notice of.'

Adelaide's face beamed with her own cleverness, and Sarah Ann saw at once that this was the thing.

So, without delay, by the lamp, in the little parlour, as was fitting, the letter was taken in hand, and with much discussion and care of wording—for the impression it was to convey was a delicate one—it was written, recopied on pink notepaper, and sealed in an envelope adorned with a flower.

Next morning early it was sent off by the hand of Dick, who had instructions to return without delay with Mrs. Dare's answer.

The girls breathed easier as he rode off. It was calculated that, by hard riding, he could be back by three in the afternoon. Till then impatience must be dulled by hard work.

But the morning had scarcely worn past and the twelve-o'clock dinner on the fire when Dick came riding into the yard with the announcement that he had overtaken Mr. Tregear on the road to the port, who had sent him back, promising to deliver the letter himself. Further, he was to say that Mr. Tregear would be home by nightfall.

The girls looked at each other. What portent was this? What was he up to? Why was he going back to the port, anyway? Did he say it was on account of the letter he was going? Did he ask anything about what was in the letter? Dick could explain nothing.

The sun was flooding the farm with his low level beams, and after milking the cows were peacefully straying out in the rich light, when Mr. Tregear was descried coming up the hill homewards.

'Girls! Girls! Here he's comin'.'

As he came nearer it was difficult to read his face in the bright haze, but he took no notice of the dogs, which went wagging and barking down to meet him.

'Now, girls, we'll wait till he comes right in, and not make any great thing of it at first. Just go on settin' tea natural like.'

Dick took the horse, and Mr. Tregear entered the kitchen, noisy with the rattle of delf and wavering in the red light of the fire.

'Well, Father, you're back. How is Mrs. Dare?'

All stood still.

'Well, gurls, she be simmingly bearin' up reasonable well.'

'And it's all right about——'

'Oh, 'es, gurls. 'Tis all right. Just as you do wish. I may say,' he added, with a peculiar complacency, 'she dedn't go for to make no serus objection.'

'You mean she's willin' to stay on, then?'

'Stayin',' repeated the old man. 'I thoft goin' were the word, gurls.'

'Then you've turned her out?' they cried shrilly, closing in around him as he stood with his back to the fire.

He looked from one to the other with an extraordinary quaint geniality.

'Why, gurls, what a takin' you be in! Nothin' I d' do don't seem to please 'ee. What be the meanin' of et?'

'Do you mean to tell us straight that you've arranged to turn Mrs. Dare into the street?'

'Well,' said Mr. Tregear, 'she have arranged to leave thickey coffee palace o' thine, Sareh. First time, gurls,' he hurried on to say, 'I did rather mess things up, but second time I did make all shoar and certain.'

'And that's the meanin' of your second visit,' said Sarah Ann, tall and withering. 'You went to them Polglazes, and they advised you to go back and turn her out.'

'Well, 'es, in a manner of speakin',' assented Mr. Tregear, turning to look after his hand, as he held it to the fire. 'Leastways, Benjamin did give his censure for delay, and so, thinkin' to please all, I gone and done it, and now this!'

'And did it never strike you,' cried Sarah Ann, with eyes of steel, 'that it 'ed be all over the district; that everybody would have hold of it, and Mr. Peters and all?'

'Have 'old o' what?' said Mr. Tregear, flushing a little.

'That we'd turned Mrs. Dare into the street, of course! What else?'

'Oh! that,' replied he, apparently much relieved.

'But, Father!' interrupted Adelaide, coming nearer and pressing a bundle of plates to her breast. 'What about our letter to Mrs. Dare? Didn't that make all right? Had she nothin' to say to that?'

'Oh, 'es, that letter,' replied the old man, coming out of his peculiar mood. 'What were in that letter,

any'ow, gurls? Mrs. Dare made sort o' great mystery
to me 'bout en. Simmed disposed to laff greatly over
'en to 'erself.'

'Laff! Did she?' cried Sarah Ann, lifting her chin
with resentment and surprise. 'What could the woman
find to laff at in that letter? Seems to me a queer thing
for a person what's bein' turned out of house and
home to be so ready for laffin'! That letter,' she added,
looking hard at the old man, 'was simply tellin' her
she needn't take no notice of this turnin' of her out,
that you say you've been so quick and clever with.'

'Oh!' cried Mr. Tregear, with a long drawl of
enlightenment. 'Oh! Oh! I do see why Mrs. Dare be
humoursome.'

And he, too, went off into a loud laugh.

The girls gazed at him helplessly, in a sort of trance
of apprehension and shame. What had they done?
What had they done? Hot blushes spread all over
their faces. The disgrace of having openly turned Mrs.
Dare into the street seemed nothing to this.

Sarah Ann, however, found refuge in wrath. 'Stop
this fool's laffin',' she cried. 'Stop it! Stop it! It's all
put on, both yours and that Dare woman's. Seems to
me,' she added witheringly, 'two such great laffers
ought to make a match of it.'

Mr. Tregear sobered instantly. He laid his hand
upon his chin, and said, 'Well, gurls, that's just et.'

'The Misses Tregear beg to announce that they
have resumed the management of the Coffee Palace,
Port Karimba. Special arrangements have been made
for the reception of summer visitors, who will have
all the advantages of a seaside residence, together
with the comforts of a private home. Refurnished
throughout. Bath, piano. Terms strictly moderate.'

THE CHAMPION BULLOCK-DRIVER

By Lance Skuthorpe

We were sitting outside old Tallwood cattle-station, in our white moleskin trousers, elastic-side boots, and cabbage-tree hats, watching two stockmen shoe a very wild brumby mare. We were all slaves to the saddle and bridle, and there was nothing too heavy or hard. The boss squatted on a new four-rail fence. There were twenty panels of this fence, strong ironbark post-and-rails. The first rails were mortised into a big ironbark tree, and there were four No. 8 wires twisted around the butt, passed through the posts and strained very tightly to the big strainer at the other end.

As though he had dropped out of the sky there appeared on the scene a very smart-looking man carrying a red-blanket swag, a water-bag, tucker-bag, and billycan. He put them down and said, 'Is the boss about?'

We all pointed to the man on the fence. The new chap took his pipe out of his mouth and walked up, a bit shy-like, and said:

'Is there any chance of a job, boss?'

'What can you do?' asked the boss.

'Well, anything amongst stock. You can't put me wrong.'

'Can you ride a buckjumper?'

'Pretty good,' said the young man.

'Can you scrub-dash—I mean, can you catch cattle in timber on a good horse before they're knocked up?'

'Hold my own,' said the young man.

'Have you got a good flow of language?'

The young man hesitated awhile before answering this question. So the boss said:

'I mean, can you drive a rowdy team of bullocks?'

'Just into my hand,' said the young man.

The boss jumped down off the fence.

'Look here,' he said. 'It's no good you telling me you can drive a team of bullocks if you can't.' And pointing to a little graveyard he added, 'Do you see that little cemetery over there?'

The young man pulled his hat down over his eye, looked across, and said, 'Yes.'

'Well,' continued the boss, 'there are sixteen bullock-drivers lying there. They came here to drive this team of mine.'

I watched the young man's face when the boss said that to see if he would flinch; but a little smile broke away from the corner of his mouth, curled around his cheek and disappeared in his earhole, and as the effect died away he said, 'They won't put me there.'

'I don't know so much about that,' said the boss.

'I'll give you a trial,' the young man suggested.

'It would take too long to muster the bullocks,' said the boss. 'But take that bullock-whip there'— it was standing near the big ironbark—'and say, for instance, eight panels of that fence are sixteen bullocks, show me how you would start the team.'

'Right,' said the young man.

Walking over he picked up the big bullock-whip and very carefully examined it to see how it was fastened to the handle. Then he ran his hand down along the whip, examining it as though he were searching for a broken link in a chain. Then he looked closely to see how the fall was fastened to the whip. After that he stood back and swung it around and gave a cheer.

First he threw the whip up to the leaders, and then threw it back to the polers. He stepped in as though to dig the near-side pin-bullock under the arm with the handle of the whip, then stepped back and swung the big whip around. He kept on talking, and the whip kept on cracking, until a little flame ran right along the top of the fence. And he kept on talking and the whip kept on cracking until the phantom forms of sixteen bullocks appeared along the fence—blues, blacks and brindles. And he kept on talking and the whip kept on cracking till the phantom forms of sixteen bullock-drivers appeared on the scene. And they kept on talking and their whips kept on cracking till the fence started to walk on, and pulled the big ironbark tree down.

'That will do,' said the boss.

'Not a bit of it,' said the young man, 'where's your wood-heap?'

We all pointed to the wood-heap near the old bark kitchen.

And they kept on talking and their whips kept on cracking till they made the fence pull the tree right up to the wood-heap.

We were all sitting round on the limbs of the tree, and the young man was talking to the boss, and we felt sure he would get the job, when the boss called out, 'Get the fencing-gear, lads, and put that fence up again.'

'Excuse me for interrupting, boss,' said the young man, 'but would you like to see how I back a team of bullocks?'

'Yes, I would,' said the boss.

So the young man walked over and picked up the big bullock-whip again. He swung it around and called out:

'Now then, boys, all together!'

And the phantom forms of the sixteen bullock-drivers appeared on the scene again; and they kept on talking and their whips kept on cracking, till every post and rail burst out into flame, and when the flame cleared away each post and rail backed into its place, and the phantom forms of the sixteen bullock-drivers took off their cabbage-tree hats to the young man, and they backed and they bowed, and they bowed and they backed right into their graves, recognizing him as the champion bullock-driver.

'AND WOMEN MUST WEEP'

By Henry Handel Richardson (Ethel H. Lindesay Richardson)

1870–1946

'For men must work'

SHE was ready at last, the last bow tied, the last strengthening pin in place, and they said to her—Auntie Cha and Miss Biddons—to sit down and rest while Auntie Cha 'climbed into her own togs': 'Or you'll be tired before the evening begins.' But she could not bring herself to sit, for fear of crushing her dress—it was so light, so airy. How glad she felt now that she had chosen muslin, and not silk as Auntie Cha had tried to persuade her. The gossamer-like stuff seemed to float around her as she moved, and the cut of the dress made her look so tall and so different from everyday that she hardly recognized herself in the glass; the girl reflected there—in palest blue, with a wreath of cornflowers in her hair—might have been a stranger. Never had she thought she was so pretty

. . . nor had Auntie and Miss Biddons either; though all they said was: 'Well, Dolly, you'll *do*,' and 'Yes, I think she will be a credit to you.' Something hot and stinging came up her throat at this: a kind of gratitude for her pinky-white skin, her big blue eyes and fair curly hair, and pity for those girls who hadn't got them. Or an Auntie Cha either, to dress them and see that everything was 'just so'.

Instead of sitting, she stood very stiff and straight at the window, pretending to watch for the cab, her long white gloves hanging loose over one arm so as not to soil them. But her heart was beating pit-a-pat. For this was her first real grown-up ball. It was to be held in a public hall, and Auntie Cha, where she was staying, had bought tickets and was taking her.

True, Miss Biddons rather spoilt things at the end by saying: 'Now mind you don't forget your steps in the waltz. One, two, together; four, five, six.' And in the wagonette, with her dress filling one seat, Auntie Cha's the other, Auntie said: 'Now, Dolly, remember not to look too *serious*. Or you'll frighten the gentlemen off.'

But she was only doing it now because of her dress; cabs were so cramped, the seats so narrow.

Alas! in getting out a little accident happened. She caught the bottom of one of her flounces—the skirt was made of nothing else—on the iron step, and ripped off the selvedge. Auntie Cha said: 'My *dear*, how clumsy!' She could have cried with vexation.

The woman who took their cloaks hunted everywhere, but could only find black cotton; so the torn selvedge—there was nearly half a yard of it—had just to be cut off. This left a raw edge, and when they went into the hall and walked across the enormous floor, with people sitting all around, staring, it seemed to Dolly as if every one had their eyes fixed on it. Auntie Cha sat down in the front row of chairs beside a lady-friend; but she slid into a chair behind.

The first dance was already over, and they were hardly seated before partners began to be taken for the second. Shyly she mustered the assembly. In the cloakroom, she had expected the woman to exclaim: 'What a sweet pretty frock!' when she handled it. (When all she did say was: 'This sort of stuff's bound to fray.') And now Dolly saw that the hall was full of *lovely* dresses, some much, much prettier than hers, which suddenly began to seem rather too plain, even a little dowdy; perhaps after all it would have been better to choose silk.

She wondered if Auntie Cha thought so, too. For Auntie suddenly turned and looked at her, quite hard, and then said snappily: 'Come, come, child, you mustn't tuck yourself away like that, or the gentlemen will think you don't want to dance.' So she had to come out and sit in the front; and show that she had a programme, by holding it open on her lap.

When other ladies were being requested for the third time, and still nobody had asked to be introduced, Auntie began making signs and beckoning with her head to the Master of Ceremonies—a funny little fat man with a bright red beard. He waddled across the floor, and Auntie whispered to him . . . behind her fan. (But she heard. And heard him answer: 'Wants a partner? Why, certainly.') And then he went away and they could see him offering her to several gentlemen. Some pointed to the ladies they were sitting with or standing in front of; some showed their programmes that these were full. One or two turned their heads and looked at her. But it was no good. So he came back and said: 'Will the little lady

do *me* the favour?' and she had to look glad and say:
'With pleasure', and get up and dance with him.
Perhaps she was a little slow about it . . . at any rate
Auntie Cha made great round eyes at her. But she felt
sure every one would know why he was asking her. It
was the lancers, too, and he swung her off her feet at
the corners, and was comic when he set to partners—
putting one hand on his hip and the other over his
head, as if he were dancing the hornpipe—and the
rest of the set laughed. She was glad when it was over
and she could go back to her place.

Auntie Cha's lady-friend had a son, and he was
beckoned to next and there was more whispering. But
he was engaged to be married, and of course preferred
to dance with his fiancée. When he came and bowed—
to oblige his mother—he looked quite grumpy, and
didn't trouble to say all of 'May I have the pleasure?'
but just 'The pleasure?' While she had to say 'Certainly', and pretend to be very pleased, though she
didn't feel it, and really didn't want much to dance
with him, knowing he didn't, and that it was only out
of charity. Besides, all the time they went round he
was explaining things to the other girl with his eyes
. . . making faces over her head. She saw him,
quite plainly.

After he had brought her back—and Auntie had
talked to him again—he went to a gentleman who
hadn't danced at all yet, but just stood looking on. And
this one needed a lot of persuasion. He was ugly, and
lanky, and as soon as they stood up said quite rudely:
'I'm no earthly good at this kind of thing, you know.'
And he wasn't. He trod on her foot and put her out of
step, and they got into the most dreadful muddle,
right out in the middle of the floor. It was a waltz and,
remembering what Miss Biddons had said, she got

more and more nervous, and then went wrong herself, and had to say : 'I beg your pardon', to which he said : 'Granted.' She saw them in a mirror as they passed, and her face was red as red.

It didn't get cool again either, for she had to go on sitting out, and she felt sure he was spreading it that *she* couldn't dance. She didn't know whether Auntie Cha had seen her mistakes, but now Auntie sort of went for her. 'It's no use, Dolly, if you don't do *your* share. For goodness' sake, try and look more agreeable !'

So after this, in the intervals between the dances, she sat with a stiff little smile gummed to her lips. And, did any likely-looking partner approach the corner where they were, this widened till she felt what it was really saying was : 'Here I am ! Oh, *please*, take *me* !'

She had several false hopes. Men, looking so splendid in their white shirt fronts, would walk across the floor and *seem* to be coming . . . and then it was always not her. Their eyes wouldn't stay on her. There she sat, with her false little smile, and *her* eyes fixed on them; but theirs always got away . . . flitted past . . . moved on. Once she felt quite sure. Ever such a handsome young man looked as if he were making straight for her. She stretched her lips, showing all her teeth (they were very good), and for an instant his eyes seemed to linger . . . really to take her in, in her pretty blue dress and the cornflowers. And then at the last minute they ran away—and it wasn't her at all, but a girl sitting three seats farther on; one who wasn't even pretty, or her dress either. But her own dress was beginning to get quite trashy, from the way she squeezed her hot hands down in her lap.

Quite the worst part of all was having to go on sitting in the front row, pretending you were enjoying

yourself. It was so hard to know what to do with your
eyes. There was nothing but the floor for them to look
at—if you watched the other couples dancing they
would think you were envying them. At first she made
a show of studying her programme; but you couldn't
go on staring at a programme for ever; and presently
her shame at its emptiness grew till she could bear it
no longer, and, seizing a moment when people were
dancing, she slipped it down the front of her dress.
Now she could say she'd lost it, if anyone asked to see
it. But they didn't; they went on dancing with other
girls. Oh, these men, who walked around and chose
just who they fancied and left who they didn't . . .
how she hated them! It wasn't fair . . . it wasn't fair.
And when there was a 'leap-year' dance where the
ladies invited the gentlemen, and Auntie Cha tried to
push her up and make her go and said 'Now then,
Dolly, here's your chance!' she shook her head hard and
dug herself deeper into her seat. She wasn't going to ask
them when they never asked her. So she said her head
ached and she'd rather not. And to this she clung,
sitting the while wishing with her whole heart that her
dress was black and her hair grey, like Auntie Cha's.
Nobody expected Auntie to dance, or thought it
shameful if she didn't: she could do and be just as she
liked. Yes, to-night she wished she was old . . . an
old, old woman. Or that she was safe at home in bed
. . . this dreadful evening, to which she had once
counted the days, behind her. Even, as the night wore
on, that she was dead.

At supper she sat with Auntie and the other lady,
and the son and the girl came, too. There were lovely
cakes and things, but she could not eat them. Her
throat was so dry that a sandwich stuck in it and nearly
choked her. Perhaps the son felt a little sorry for her

(or else his mother had whispered again), for after-wards he said something to the girl, and then asked *her* to dance. They stood up together; but it wasn't a success. Her legs seemed to have forgotten how to jump, heavy as lead they were . . . as heavy as she felt inside . . . and she couldn't think of a thing to say. So now he would put her down as stupid, as well.

Her only other partner was a boy younger than she was—almost a schoolboy—who she heard them say was 'making a nuisance of himself'. This was to a *very* pretty girl called the 'belle of the ball'. And he didn't seem to mind how badly he danced (with her), for he couldn't take his eyes off this other girl; but went on staring at her all the time, and very fiercely, because she was talking and laughing with somebody else. Besides, he hopped like a grasshopper, and didn't wear gloves, and his hands were hot and sticky. She hadn't come there to dance with little boys.

They left before anybody else; there was nothing to stay for. And the drive home in the wagonette, which had to be fetched, they were so early, was dreadful: Auntie Cha just sat and pressed her lips and didn't say a word. She herself kept her face turned the other way, because her mouth was jumping in and out as if it might have to cry.

At the sound of wheels Miss Biddons came running to the front door with questions and exclamations, dreadfully curious to know why they were back so soon. Dolly fled to her own little room and turned the key in the lock. She wanted only to be alone, quite alone, where nobody could see her . . . where nobody would ever see her again. But the walls were thin, and as she tore off the wreath and ripped open her dress, now crushed to nothing from so much sitting, and threw them from her anywhere, anyhow, she could hear the two voices going on, Auntie Cha's telling and telling, and winding up at last, quite out loud, with: 'Well, I don't know what it was, but the plain truth is, she didn't *take*!'

Oh, the shame of it! . . . the sting and the shame. Her first ball, and not to have 'taken', to have failed to 'attract the gentlemen'—this was a slur that would rest on her all her life. And yet . . . and yet . . . in spite of everything, a small voice that wouldn't be silenced kept on saying: 'It wasn't my fault . . . it wasn't my *fault*!' (Or at least not except for the one silly mistake in the steps of the waltz.) She had tried her hardest, done everything she was told to: had dressed up to please and look pretty, sat in the front row offering her programme, smiled when she didn't feel a bit like smiling . . . and almost more than anything she thought she hated the memory of that smile (it was like trying to make people buy something they didn't think worthwhile). For really, truly, right deep down in her, she hadn't wanted 'the gentlemen' any more than they'd wanted her: she had only had to pretend to. And they showed only too plainly they didn't, by choosing other girls, who were not even pretty, and dancing with them, and laughing and talking and enjoying them. And now, the many slights and humiliations of the evening crowding upon her, the long-repressed tears broke through; and with the blanket pulled up over her head, her face driven deep into the pillow, she cried till she could cry no more.

ADVENTURE
A Fantasy of the Ranges
By Hugh McCrae

I REMEMBER my grand-uncle—an octogenarian—
sad automaton of what he used to be, stooping under
eucalyptus-trees with a gun in his hand. The neighbours' houses, abutting on our yard, left him little
room; yet he imagined limitless space in some barren
part of Australia, and the companionship of a dog,
visible only to himself. Each night, the old man left
out a plate of bones for 'Shag'; and, regularly, one of
us emptied the dish, then put it back again.

In 1840, this ancient (before he became an ancient),
staggering across stringybark ranges, had all but died
of starvation. Nothing to eat. Nothing to drink. Without powder, his 'Joe Manton' wasn't any use to him;
so he knocked out the flints, and, dropping them into
his mouth to moisten it, went in search of a waterhole.

By the light of the moon his dog killed a snake; and,
after the man had cooked it, they ate it between them.
Two days subsequently they were still sucking at the
spiny vertebrae: the dog with his thick tail wound up
over his back, happy enough; and my grand-uncle,
meditative, feeling hungry again. He recollected the
dingo—how that beast, when no other food is obtain-
able, devours his own anatomy. Experimentally,
G.-U. searched his body, but, because there was no
fat, gave up that idea. Even his arm, separated, hadn't
meat enough to make foundation broth for *soupe aux
choux*. Besides, there were no *choux*!

So his thoughts returned to civilization, via cutlets
in curl-papers, and jelly pudding with cream. Claret,

too . . . deliciously cool. Repeating Dr. Maginn's advice: 'A glass of brandy after every four glasses of claret corrects the frigidity', my grand-uncle took the gun-flints out of his mouth and continued in a dream.

Shag lay before him, inelegantly spread, showing legs, shoulders, neck, and saddle; all the best cuts there were. The temptation became too great for G.-U., who dragged a tomahawk from his belt. (He could do it in one stroke, or a couple at the most!)

With the axe up-ended in the air, Shag leaned sideways, his tail draping itself over a log. Such a beautiful tail! Such a fat one!

My grand-uncle made a lightning change in the direction of the blade. The axe fell, and Shag disappeared into the jungle, leaving his appendage behind. The latter, scraped, then broiled on red-hot gum branches, proved to be rank eating, yet it stayed the stomach for a day at least.

After my grand-uncle had satisfied his hunger he whistled for Shag to return to him; but the dog was afraid. Nevertheless, his master, who did not like to be alone, kept on whistling. While he did so he grew aware of a curious motion about his interior—a motion which coincided with the notes of his call. From the first 'phew-phew!' to the last, this mysterious something vacillated inside him. When he stopped—it stopped. When he began again—it began also.

Then, it dawned upon him that this must be Shag's tail, signalling affectionate answers. Because the result was uncomfortable he never whistled any more; or if, by accident, he did, a gruff 'Lie down, sir!' brought him effectual peace.

THE GOOD GRANDMOTHER
By Hugh McCrae

WHEN I was seven I visited my grandmother for the last time. She sat in a room upstairs with her face towards the sunset; and, to reach her, I had to pass a bed made mysterious by curtains and increasing darkness.

My grandmother put her arms about me, and kissed me.

I felt uncomfortable in the embrace; but it was Death's strength that held me; her mouth, pressed against my own, took my breath away, and I wanted to be elsewhere . . . imagining myself a tiger up our sycamore.

After she had let me go I could still feel the kiss; as if it had been nailed into me.

And, I remember, there were roses on the window-sill; not enough of them to hide the smell of iodoform —although I was too young to understand the signals of mortality.

The old lady pressed into my hand something hard, wrapped in tissue paper. 'Get a book,' she said, 'to remember me by.'

That night she died; and, on the next day, with the guinea she had given me, I bought a child's tricycle.

A week later this plaything was broken under a carrier's cart; but I returned home unperturbed, emotionless; until pride setting in I said to myself: 'Within a little while I have lost a tricycle . . . and a grandmother. . . . How important I am!'

Then I realized I had bought the tricycle to remember my grandmother by; and wondered whether, in the absence of this memorial, she would become forgotten.

At once my grandmother kissed me again.

That unsquanderable kiss . . . Richer than the guinea. I began to study her portrait in our drawing-room; I read her diaries, and looked at her water-colour sketches . . . learned to love them . . . to adore her.

Soon she gave me my first book.

I mean I saved up five shillings, and bought a copy of *Paul and Virginia*.

After I had made sure of this possession I wrote across the flyleaf: 'For dear little Noel, from his affectionate Grandmama, 4th October, 1887.'

Since that time the old lady has methodically filled my shelves; and, at odd intervals, she still subscribes herself in a handwriting singularly like my own.

CROWS
By Dowell O'Reilly

THE 'Pommy' parson made good, as a good man always will, and when the long drought closed down on the ten thousand square miles of sheep-run that he called his 'parish' the sufferings of man and beast overwhelmed him. His grief at his parishioners' profanity and irreligion soon passed in pity for their losses and admiration of their courage. They seldom spoke, and then only about stock—feed—water. They toiled incessantly. The railway sidings were congested with trucks laden with fodder purchased at famine prices from the coastal farmers. This feed, with vast quantities of greenstuff lopped from the river-belts, was carted miles to the dying flocks.

The new chum saw with horror the famished brutes licking the very dust—as he thought; in reality, nosing for the seeds and dead stalks of vanished herbage. He rode a bicycle, and his flying black coat-tails were soon familiar in the district. A feverish pity and a longing to help drove his wheel far out on the plains. The hateful crows flapped heavily and cawed curses as he spurted past dead sheep, and pedalled slowly through thousands that could not die. The wicked blue mirage came and went about him; silent little waves of impalpable dust leapt from under his tyres; rhymes from the *Ancient Mariner* rang in his ears —he, too, was adrift in a silent sea of phantoms, and death, and corruption.

One day he came upon a stockman stooping over a young ewe, still alive, but lying helpless. Her exposed eye was picked out, and her lamb lay near, dead— both eyes gone, the kidneys ripped out. The man lifted her on her legs, but she was too weak to stand.

'Kargh—kargh—kar-r-gh.'

'Look,' said the stockman.

The parson glanced up.

'No—here!' The man pointed at the ground. The ewe lay in a dusty circle of innumerable hoof-prints. He shook his fist fiercely in the clergyman's face.

'She faced them bloody crows for two days—round and round—her little 'un beside her all the while suckin' her strength—but they got it at last!'

Swete rode on, sick at heart.

'Hey, parson——'

He glanced back over his shoulder. The man was holding up the dead lamb by the tail.

'Feed my lambs!'

As his head again bowed forward the little carcass thudded almost under his wheel and rolled over and over in the dust. He spurted in horror—the insult was not meant for him.

At some of the larger tanks pumping engines had been rigged to lift what water remained into radiating troughs, but at the smaller hole he now approached there was other work forward.

The thirst-maddened sheep had staggered by scores into the quagmire and, too weak to return, had remained bogged; some still living, others trampled underfoot. Three men worked in the stinking slime, dragging out the living sheep, and building a protecting wall round the bog with the swollen carcasses; from these the wool would easily be plucked by hand —later. He dismounted on the blistered brink and looked down.

There was something eerie, inhuman, abominable, in the scene—the yellow pit quivering in white light —the mud-plastered men so active among the shapeless, silent, grey things. It was like a glimpse through a microscope at a drop of putrid water, swarming with elementary life.

'Storm comin',' said one of the men, looking up, and trying to wipe his forehead on his shoulder. A cylindrical dust-cloud was rolling from the west. He had spoken cheerfully; dust was preferable to stench and flies. The others scrambled to the brink to look.

'I've brought the Sydney papers.' The parson threw a roll on the ground. They nodded thanks, and returned to their work; he remounted and followed his shadow homeward.

The white sunlight suddenly fled before him. He looked back and saw that all the west was blotted out by a billow of red dust; it seemed as though the plains themselves were upheaving in a tidal wave.

He loved Nature; despite Oxford, and gold crosses, and ascetic illuminations, they twain were still one flesh, and her rising passion thrilled him. He dismounted and leaned on his wheel, waiting. The lamb, the tainted slough, were forgotten in the thought that whenever Creation thus appealed to him he heard the voice of the Creator.

Scattered puffs of dust trailed towards him as catspaws fleck an oily sea—then the storm burst. He turned his back to the wind that licked the baked soil bare as concrete. The heavier particles, driving along the ground, tinkled against the steel spokes, and piled to windward of the tyres. He moved his foot, and already its outline was ridged in dust. He looked at it curiously, remembering the strange heaps of red earth against the western side of every post. He pictured the fate of a sick or drunken man lying there, the earth-tide rising against him—rippling over—

'Kargh-kargh-kar-r-gh!'

He could not see the black wings driving and wheeling in the blinding dust, nor the wicked eyes that had found them, but the lightning thought of a dead lamb with bloody eye-sockets seared his soul— he became conscious of an obscene power of which the evil birds were a manifestation—a power malefic, wide-winged, triumphant, with cruel beak, and tearing talons—

'Kar-r-gh!'

He stared up into the murk—dull red, like dry blood—and shook his fist at the accursed cry. An imprecation tore his soul and distorted his face—

'God . . .' He stopped.

The Great Name rang through his horror in a

voice that was not his own—he flung down his machine and fell on his knees, his hands clasped, sobs shaking him—

'Then the Lord answered Job out of the whirlwind.'

THE HAND
By M. L. Skinner

IT was winter, and bitter cold when the sun was hidden. There was little doing in the mining-town hospital back there in the west. The evenings were long, the light from the old kerosene-lamp dim to read by, and the Matron was good at telling a story.

She had been through the war, but it was not of her war-time experiences we persuaded her to talk, rather of her days in peace. We would draw our slippery leather chairs to the fire, and ask her how she had come to be a matron so young, and how she had got herself appointed to those posts way back in the interior, where she had managed so well.

'I was trained young,' she told us modestly. 'And then my father was a doctor; he suggested my taking a course in dispensing. That was how I dropped into these positions. You see, there are no chemists out back there, and if there is a doctor, he has no time for dispensing. So I could do it.'

'It was an awfully lonely life for a young nurse.'

'I loved it.'

'But weren't you ever frightened?'

'Of what?'

'Well—the loneliness. And bad white men, and bad

blacks. Of patients in delirium. Or some awful maternity case you couldn't handle!'

'I didn't think about it. I did what I could. I *was* frightened once, though: and that, really, by a nurse screaming. A nurse shouldn't scream.'

We agreed in silence.

'It was in that outpost hospital between Ashthorp and Boolong, out there on the far edge of the goldfields, twenty miles from Ashthorp and thirty from Boolong—a rough half-way. We served the mining camps as well as the settlers. It's a great sheep country, and the station people used to call in and give us Coo-ee! when they were going down to the coast.

'It wasn't so lonely. There were two nurses and a cook on the staff, as well as myself. Then the big well, with the water-supply for everybody, and the half-way house, and a blacksmith's, and the public-house, all lay in a jumble between the railway and the road. The publican had a wife and a boy, and the blacksmith's wife had three little girls. The trail came through, from up-country, and every buggy or wagon stopped at the blacksmith's, or at the public-house, or at the hospital. We weren't so lonely, at all.

'They were fine people, the people from the sheep stations. As a rule they brought us eggs, poultry, or mutton, kangaroo and wild turkeys, going down; and coming back from the coast the newspapers, and books, and chocolates.

'Nurse Hammer—you remember her, don't you?— she was a regular town girl, very attractive, but unstable, untried. Nurse Smith was a staunch little thing. They were both in the men's ward this particular evening, playing cards. The hospital was a wooden, ramshackle, **L**-shaped bungalow, without fence or anything, lying open to the bush on one side,

F

the road on the other side, the railways going beyond
the road, and somebody's boundary fence beyond the
railways. The men's ward was at the bend of the **L**,
and our bedrooms opened out on to the veranda on
one wing, the kitchen and stores at the other end.

'This night I'm telling you about, I was sitting
doing accounts in my room, and my mind kept
wandering—I am like that, very practical, really, and
then liable to feel things in the air, things that other
people don't seem aware of. My father called it
"unwarranted inference"; and told me to taboo it.
But it gets hold of me sometimes: and this evening I
was uneasy, aware of "something". I could not get
on with my work. There seemed to be a sound. . . .

'It was hot; all the doors were open on to the
veranda. The moon was up, a brilliant white night,
white and black, and still. From where I sat I could
see the bush, mysterious under the bright moon,
drawing itself into itself, as if the blazing hot sun all
day long had been enough, without now the moon. It
fascinated me, yet I could understand why the blacks
were so terrified after sundown. It was frightening.

'I wanted to get on with my work and ignore the
night, but I kept stopping and staring outside, just
gazing. I could hear the nurses laughing and chatting
with the patients, and an old mopoke booing—a most
reassuring sound. And I knew that cook was not far
off, out on the wood-heap, perhaps, with her young
man, a respectable sandalwood-getter who was "in"
from his camp with a load of trucking. The sound I
imagined could not come from them, because if there
was any sound at all it was a breath-held, creeping
sound, a stifled sound. I heard nothing, really, yet I
made myself get up and look along the veranda, and
round the clearing. Shadowy emptiness was all there

was, except that I saw the mopoke that had been sitting on the stump fly away. So I went back to the table and tried to add up those figures. My little clock chimed ten. I heard Nurse Hammer coming to bed. There came the scrape of her match striking, and suddenly, a blood-curdling scream.

'I jumped from my chair and ran out on to the veranda. I couldn't run along the shadowy veranda itself, after that terrible scream, yet my instant thought was to reach the patients. One had just recovered from an attack of D.T.s and I had him immediately in mind. So I had to jump further, to the ground, and run beside the dark veranda until I came into the lamplight that flooded out from the ward.

'It wasn't Sam Jones who had screamed. He met me with a sheepish grin—nervous but quiet. The other men were all right, rousing up from their pillows with inquiring glances. Sam had slipped into his dungarees, and both he and Nurse Smith looked at me with relief, as if my presence in the doorway would solve the mystery.

'Relief vanished in the moment, for the scream was repeated. We stood paralysed, until Nurse Smith gasped: "Hammer!" Then we all ran along the veranda together to her room.

'There was no light coming from her open door, though I had distinctly heard her strike a match: but terror seemed to sweep out like a blast of cold wind.

'"Hammer!" cried Nurse Smith; and then in the gloaming we could see the figure of the girl standing motionless by the bed. "Wait a minute," said Nurse Smith, and she ran back to get a hurricane lantern.

'I went in and put my arms round Nurse Hammer.

She began to sob: "*I can't move! I can't move! Something has got me by the foot.*"

'I felt the terror emanating from her, and I went cold. "Hurry up with the lantern!" I called. "There might be a snake in the room."

'"Is it a snake?" panted Hammer. "It feels like something else."

'"Hurry up with the lantern!" I cried again.

'"It clutched me," whispered Nurse Hammer. "I dropped the candle."

'She did not move. She stood inside the ring of my arm, utterly rigid. I felt as if some dreadful thing would rise in the dark and envelop us both.

'Then a curious thing happened to me. I became conscious, not only of Hammer's terrible fear, but of a deeper source, dark and secret, within herself. I remembered how lovely she was. How men in the wards watched with furtive eyes as she walked past. I remembered the way she walked—and how she avoided those eyes. I knew then that the girl had herself been tempted, that she was powerless, now, in this darkness, because in her own life she was passing through crisis.

'I found I was praying, under my breath, that whatever we found in this room would not be evil. It seemed to me hours that I prayed.

'In the doorway Sam remained transfixed, a dim shadow. We heard Nurse Smith's quick footsteps. She ran in, trembling, with a lantern. She swung it round. Light revealed the solid chest of drawers under the window, the bed unruffled, the wardrobe mirror reflecting weirdly our motionless figures. Then, as Smith dipped the lantern to the floor, it went out, as hurricane lanterns do, when suddenly dipped.

'We were again in horrifying darkness and silence. Tension mounted, became almost unbearable, for

Hammer's fear was immense. It charged the air. And there *was* something else.

'With fumbling fingers Nurse Smith relit the lantern. I saw, by the flicker of flame from match and wick, that Hammer's blue eyes were staring and blank. Afraid she would scream again and add hysteria to the listening patients in the ward, or set Sam into renewed delirium, I took the lantern and, still holding Hammer, lowered the light myself.

'A human hand clasped the girl's ankle.

'Still no less fearful of Hammer's reactions, I was amazed, as I touched the hand, to find it icy cold. And I thought: if some man has been trapped here he may act viciously trying to get away. . . .

'Grimly I pushed back the bed. We saw first an arm, then a torso, then a head. The face was gentle in spite of a bluey-brown growth of beard. It was marked by exhaustion, sun-bitten, the eyes closed, the lips drawn back over white clenched teeth. A lost man who looked dead; he was naked, unconscious, helpless, his feet had bled.

'I glanced at Hammer. The Nightingale light was flooding her face. I dropped my arm from round her. She took a cup of water from the table by the bed and, kneeling quickly and easily, moistened the parched lips without a word. She was very pale, her own lips bloodless, but her beauty was melting, tender. As she bowed over that tortured naked form, strange words rose in my mind: *Here, then, were the women to attend him.* . . .

'Abruptly, I sent Nurse Smith off to prepare a bed, and sent Sam with her. When I looked back at Hammer, the man had released his clutch and taken hold of her fingers. How can I describe that hand-clasp? His hand lay in hers confidingly, like a child's hand. As he slowly opened tormented eyes, Hammer put the hand gently down. She lifted his head and pressed the cup again to his lips.

'When the water was finished he became crazed for more. Demented, he seized the girl and began to wrestle. I felt again afraid for her. But Hammer did not flinch; quickly, resolutely, she struggled, forgetful of self. Suddenly he fell back, limp, with closed eyes.

'"He's dying!" exclaimed Sam in an awestruck voice, as he returned with Nurse Smith, their terror and dismay gone.

'All Hammer ever said to me later was, "Sorry I screamed, Matron. A nurse shouldn't scream."'

Matron stopped, as if she had finished her story.

'Did he?' we asked, at last.
'What?'
'Die?'
'Of course not.'
'So you heard all about him?'
'Yes—and no romance. A station hand from Toobooroo. Lost his horse, wandered in the scrub, lost himself, couldn't find water, threw away his clothes, then by good chance stumbled on the settlement and crawled into shelter. That's all. Nothing, really. Unless . . . I often wonder,' she added strangely, '*why?* Why should chance let *Hammer* be the one to find him, to save him, in such need?'

Again we waited. But Matron did not say another word; she stared at the fire.

THE LOBSTER AND
THE LIONESS
By 'Kodak' (Ernest O'Ferrall)

AT eleven o'clock Thomson, who had broken his glasses during a last whirling argument *re* the chances of the Liberal candidate, was pushed gently out the side door and told to go home. Instead of taking the barman's advice, he sat on the horse-trough, and held an indignation meeting with himself until Sergeant Jones happened along.

'Good night, Mr. Thomson,' said the sergeant kindly.

Thomson pushed his boxer hat to the back of his head. 'Good evenin',' he returned sulkily.

'Are ye comin' down the street?' ventured the sergeant.

'Cert'nly not!' said Thomson. 'I've lost me glasses, an' me eyesight's 'stremely bad. I can't see what I'm doin'!'

'Well, come along and walk with me. I'll see ye as far as the gate.'

Thomson rose unsteadily. 'I tol' you before I've broken me glasses. Do you mean to 'sinuate I'm *drunk*?'

'I do not!' said the sergeant. 'I never saw a soberer man in my life! But come along now, an' I'll tell ye somethin' I heerd to-day about Prince Foote f'r th' Cup. I'm goin' your way!'

On those honourable terms, Thomson condescended to take up his lobster, and allow Jones to pilot him gently toward his lodgings.

According to Thomson's reckoning, they had

trudged through 283 deserted streets, and turned 1834 strange and unexpected corners, when he found they were both standing still on a vacant piece of land, in front of an enormous board with 'For Sale' on it.

'Whasser matter?'

'I heerd a strange sound,' answered the sergeant. 'Be quiet a minit! Maybe we'll hear it agin!'

They waited breathlessly. . . .

A deep, muffled grunt arose close by.

'That's it!' said the sergeant excitedly.

'Somebody's drunk,' sighed Thomson wearily. 'Sailor prob'ly.'

The sergeant snorted. 'No sailor ever made a sound like that! Look, it's gettin' up! Is it a dog? . . . *Run, man! run for your life!*' he yelled, and ran heavily up a dark lane.

Thomson, swaying on his feet, patted his leg and called encouragingly to the approaching thing, 'Goo' dog!'

Two yellow eyes glowed in the darkness.

'Goo' dog!' cooed Thomson encouragingly, and patted his leg again.

A deep, hungry growl.

'Come on, ole feller. I won't hurt yer!'

The thing with the smouldering yellow eyes came a step nearer, and Thomson cried out in delight, 'By George! that's finest mastiff I've ever seen! I'll get him to foller me back to boarding-house!' He staggered off sideways, murmuring endearments, and stopping every few yards to flick his fingers or pat his leg. And the escaped circus lioness followed him as if he had been another Daniel.

They went slowly up the long, flat street that stretched away to a plain of burnished silver—the sea. The moon had slipped from her cloud dressing-room, and was hurrying down the sky like a woman going in search of a policeman.

Thomson staggered on, hugging his lobster, till he reached a lamp-post. Then he sat down, and calling affectionately to the lioness, started to eat. 'Here ye are, ol' boy,' he cooed. A claw hit the lioness on the nose and dropped to the pavement. The beast growled at the indignity, but ate the fragment, and licked her chops with evident pleasure.

Thomson methodically dissected the food with his hands and chewed stolidly, occasionally throwing a bit over his shoulder with a mumbled word of encouragement. The lioness sat on her haunches and growled between courses, but accepted the scraps with a sort of eager humility. This went on till the lobster was no more. Thomson then wiped his mouth with the back of his hand, leant against the lamp-post, and closed his eyes. In a minute he was asleep. In another thirty seconds, he gave a long, whistling snore like the wail of a distant siren.

The wild beast, sitting erect like a thing of stone, growled nervously.

Thomson snored again.

The lioness growled angrily.

Thomson awoke with a start. 'Who said that?' he demanded. 'Who denies that Wade's done more f'r th' d——d country than th' blanky Labour party—*eh*?' He turned slightly and beheld the enormous beast. 'Goo' dog!' he cooed. 'Goo' dog!'

Faintly, from the distant sea of city lights, came the clear chimes of a clock, followed by twelve deep, solemn notes. Brother timepieces to right and left answered it like watchful guardians of the hours.

Thomson rose slowly with a look of determination and flicked his fingers. 'Come on, ol' boy! Mus' be

gettin' home!' He staggered along for about twenty
yards, and the lioness, her head down and her tail
straight out, tracked him step by step. Then he paused.
The beast stopped dead, with her glowing, yellow eyes
fixed on his face. Thomson didn't notice her; his mind
was grappling with some tremendous problem.
'Where did I leave it?' he moaned at last. 'I'll go back
an' look!' With tremendous care, he steered a wavering course back to the lamp-post, moored himself to it,
and peered all round the circle of light. The thing he
sought was nowhere to be seen. 'Dammit! I wonder
where I lef' that lobster? . . . I'm certain I had it—an'
I can *smell* it now! . . . Somebody's done me for it!'

Far up the street, approaching boot-heels made a
clear, crisp clatter in the still night. 'I'll ask this chap
if he's seen it!' murmured Thomson, and took a
firmer grip of the post.

The lonely pedestrian came up rapidly, and proved
to be a slight young man in evening dress.

Thomson raised his hat. ''Scuse me, did you notice
a 'stremely large lobster as you came 'long?'

The stranger stopped dead, stared past Thomson
into the gloom beyond, and, with a muffled cry of
horror, turned in his tracks. He ran with amazing
swiftness into the night.

'Hol' on!' yelled Thomson after him, but there was
no answer—merely the sound of a man running.

The lobster-loser turned disconsolately and found
the lioness looking intently in the direction the stranger
had taken. 'Served him right if I sooled th' dog on
him!' he reflected bitterly. Then, with an air of
resignation, 'Come on, Carlo, ol' boy; if coffee-stall's
open, I'll get a pie.' Once more he set sail, and
the immense beast of prey followed stealthily in his
footsteps at a distance of three paces.

Down the road they went, round two corners and across an unoccupied grassy lot, then along a dark, shop-lined street. At the far end, near the kerb, gleamed the headlights of a coffee-stall. As Thomson drew near, the proprietor was seen leaning on the counter absorbed in reading, by the light of his big lanterns, the account of the previous night's fight.

Out of the darkness a command came to him : 'Hey! give's a pie an' 'nother f'r th' dog!'

The proprietor looked up cheerily. 'Right-oh!' He put down his paper and turned to fill the order. As he opened his oven door a delicious whiff of hot meat perfumed the frosty air. The lioness in the shadow growled loudly.

''Oo did *that*?' asked the hot-pie man suspiciously.

'Sorright,' Thomson assured him; 'th' dog won't hurt yer.'

'Wot sorter dorg *is* it?' persisted the pieman, vainly endeavouring to see what species of animal was beyond the light.

'Mastiff,' explained the amateur lion-tamer wearily. 'Prize mastiff—mos' 'fectionate beast. Gimme two pies!'

The pie artist extracted two of his finest works from the oven, and placed them on the counter just as the lioness growled hungrily again.

'Better give us another pie f'r th' dog,' said Thomson, putting a shilling down on the counter, and taking up one of the bandboxes of nourishment.

The coffee-stall man ignored the order, and, leaning far over the counter, looked into the shadow. His eyes bulged with apprehension. '*That* ain't no mastiff,' he breathed at last. 'It looks more like a—GORSTRUTH!' With one mad bound he was over the counter and away. Thomson howled after him indignantly, and waited for five minutes to see if he would come back. He didn't. At last, Thomson climbed carefully over the counter, threw two sizzling pies to the lioness, and recommenced on his own. Fortunately the lioness's share fell into the gutter, and was thereby cooled, otherwise tragedy would probably have happened then and there.

After the light refreshments had been consumed, Thomson climbed down and invited Carlo to follow him again. Some blind instinct guiding his feet, he at last came by devious ways to the terrace house where he wasn't a star boarder.

Hanging on to the frost-cold railings in the moonlight, he communed with himself thus : 'If I take th' dog roun' back, I'll wake up all th' dogs in th' place and fall over dust-box. Let's see! . . . Yes, I better take ole Carlo in fron' door and go through house. That's it! That's what'll do. Come on, ol' chap!'

With extreme care and patience he at last found the keyhole, and flung wide the door. Then he lit a match and cooed encouragingly, but in vain, until the flame burnt his fingers. '*I'll* get him in!' he muttered, and, stumbling through to the kitchen, he found a large piece of raw steak. After opening the back door, he returned to the front and waved it at the lioness. 'Come on, Carlo!' he commanded. The beast, growling slightly, started to follow him. He backed into the hall, intending to lure his prey right through; but she was too quick for him. At the foot of the stairs she darted forward, and snatched the steak from his outstretched hand.

'Give it here, d——n yer!' he hissed, and made a wild grab at the goods.

The brute snarled horribly, and thumped the floor

angrily with her heavy tail. Thomson staggered back and his match went out.

A door on the first landing opened explosively, the wavering light of a candle illumined the upper part of the staircase, and a quavering soprano voice cried, 'Is anyone there?'

'Sorright. It's only me!' replied Thomson irritably. 'I've gotter dog!'

The candle, a wrapped-up head, and a long thin arm appeared over the banisters. 'Do you mean to say you are bringing a dog through the *house*, Mr. Thomson?'

'It won't hurt th' d——n house!' retorted the bringer-home-of-lions, staring upward defiantly.

'Mr. Thomson,' chattered the partially hidden land-lady, 'you are not in a fit state to argue. I will speak to you in the morning!' The hand that held the candle shook with rage, and, as a natural consequence, the light wavered considerably.

'I *am* fit t' argue, and I *will* argue 'slong as I please! An', what's more, I'll do what I d——n well please in th' rotten house, and bring as many dogs as I want inter it! Why, yer know yerself it's only *fit* f'r dogs! Come on, Carlo, ol' chap!'

He made a grab at the lioness's head, but missed. The brute snarled again, louder than the largest-sized dog.

'If you have any respect for yourself,' wailed the landlady, 'I say if you have any *respect* for yourself, you will take that bloodthirsty brute out of the house!'

'Gorrer bed!' shouted Thomson. 'Gorrer bed, an' mind yer own bizness, you—you *ole meddler*!'

'How *dare* you!' shrieked the landlady, and fled horror-stricken to her room.

Then, alone and unseen in the hall, Thomson

performed a really fine taming feat. Lighting his
second last match to see what he was doing, he walked
behind the lioness and gave her a hearty kick.
'*Gerrout!*' he yelled, and the lioness, with an ugly
shriek, ran lightly down the hall, and out into the
yard. Thomson then shut both doors, back and front,
and stumbled heavily upstairs to his room, where,
without troubling to undress, he climbed solemnly
into bed.

On the stroke of three he awoke and muttered,
'Warrer! I wonder if warrer-bottle's been filled.' He
struggled sadly out of bed, and blinked at the wash-
stand, dimly visible by the light of the waning moon.
He could not make out a water-bottle, but something
white and round like a china bowl gleamed invitingly
by the wash-basin. 'I dunno what's in it, but I'll
drink it, whatever it is!' he sighed, and made dry-
mouthed for the waiting refreshment. He seized the
bowl, and conveyed it half-way to his lips, then dashed
it to the floor. It bounced lightly under the bed.
'*Blast th' collar!*' he shouted, and started to fumble for
matches. He persevered nobly until the water-jug
meanly bumped against his elbow and smashed with
a terrific sound on the floor.

'That settles it!' he said, and plumped down on the
bed. 'I'm not goin' t' degrade meself by gettin' drink
for meself in soap-dish!' For five wrathful minutes he
sat and savagely wondered how best to revenge himself. Finally he opened his room door and bawled:
'Where's my shavin' water?'

The house remained submerged in sleep.

'Where's my *shavin' water*?' he howled again.

The dumb walls flung the echoes back at him; and
outside in the yard the iron dust-box rolled to and fro

in agony. Something hungry was ransacking it for nourishment.

'D'ye think I'm goin' t' wait all day f'r my *shavin' water*?' roared the mastiff-finder for the third time.

The landlady's door flung open, and she appeared on the threshold, done up like a sort of original mixture of Lady Macbeth and the Worst Woman in Sydney after a gas explosion. 'How *dare* you?' she cried tragically. 'How *dare* you make such a noise at this hour? What do you *mean* by asking for shaving water at this hour?'

Thomson, not at all abashed, lurched to the lobby railings, and leant over like a candidate addressing an election crowd from the balcony of an hotel. 'What do I want *warrer* for? *I'll* tell yer why! I *want t' drink it!!* I've decided t' reform and join th' No-Licence crowd. I'm goin' t' be a Wowser! That rotten ole paper y' gave me last week with picture of two horses at a trough sayin' "We only drink warrer" has made me better man! I'm goin' t' vote No-Licence! I think pubs are curse to *ev'ry* man! If there were no pubs, you'd have t' keep beer in th' house, and we wouldn't have t' go *out* f'r it. D'ye understan' that, missus? D'yer see?'

'You forget yourself, sir!' trumpeted the landlady.

'Forget *who*?'

'I say you *forget* yourself!'

'Oh no, I don't! But I wish *you* wouldn't forget t' put warrer in my room! Look here, it's all d——n fine t' gas 'bout 'totalism, but why don' you s'ply some warrer? Has warrer gone up?'

'This is too much!' wailed the wretched landlady. She turned and tapped sharply with her bony knuckles on the door of the next room, and a sleepy male voice said: 'All right! Be there directly.'

Thomson leaned far over the railings and sniffed suspiciously. His nose wrinkled in disgust, and he said something in an undertone about the place smelling like the Zoo.

'Who's keepin' bears?' he demanded excitedly at last. 'I'm not goin' t' stay in place if you're goin' t' take in bears!'

'You are drunk!' chattered the landlady furiously. 'How *dare* you say there are animals in the house?'

Thomson sniffed again. 'Why, th' house stinks like a circus! It's bears, or tigers, or somethin'!'

The landlady raised a shaking hand, and pointed an accusing finger at him. 'If there is anything in the house you brought it in yourself!' she intoned.

A sudden gust of rage shook Thomson to the foundations of his being. 'Same ole gag!' he roared. 'That's exactly what y' said when I found th' what-d'ye-call-it! "Muster brought it in yourself!" I tell yer I didn't bring *anything* in! There's bears in th' house, an' I'll leave it t'morrer! D'ye think I'm going t' live in a m'agerie? S'pose you'll tell me nex' I don't know what a bear *smells* like!'

The door of the other room opened, and a tall, thin, spectacled man, in a purple dressing-gown, stepped out. 'What is all the noise about?' he inquired bitterly, holding his candle on high like the Torch of Liberty.

'I say that there's *bears* in th' house!' repeated Thomson.

The tall man inhaled deeply. 'There certainly *is* a strong odour of animals,' he remarked acidly.

'What did I tell yer?' cried Thomson triumphantly. His voice rang through the house, and two more doors were heard to open slightly.

The tall, embittered man turned to the landlady. 'I suppose, Mrs. Tribbens, Mr. Thomson has brought home a monkey or something of the kind. He seems to be able to do just as he pleases in this house. I dare say we shall become used to the smell in time; but I really must object to being called up in the middle of the night to talk about the matter. Surely it would have done in the morning!'

'You don't understand, Mr. Pyppe,' retorted the landlady with fearful hauteur.

'No, I'm afraid I don't,' said Pyppe irritably. 'The whole thing seems ridiculous to me. Why on earth I should be called out of bed at this hour of the night to talk about an unpleasant smell with a man who is obviously——'

Crash! The tinkle of glass falling on stone told the landlady that the kitchen window had succumbed.

'*What's that?*' she gasped. Down the pitch-dark hall they heard sounds which suggested a burglar in stockinged feet dragging the body of a murdered boarder over the linoleum.

'I will see what it is!' Pyppe announced in a loud voice, and went cautiously downstairs, a step at a time.

Thomson and the landlady stared after him.

'*Who is there?*' cried the brave investigator, holding his candle far out over the railings.

There was no answer.

'*Who is there?*' he snapped. His candle tilted, and a drop of hot wax detached itself, and fell into the well of gloom. A grating, bestial roar of rage rang through the place, and a lithe, yellow animal sprang into the lighted radius, and stood lashing its tail.

'*My God, it's a lioness!*' shrieked Pyppe, really shaken for the first time in his life. His candle clattered

from his hand, and he rushed upstairs into his room
and slammed and bolted the door. . . .

'I *tol*' yer so!' shouted Thomson exultantly outside the landlady's door, from behind which came
hysterical sobs and the shrieking of castors. 'I *tol*' yer
there was bears in th' house!'

'The police!' wailed the distracted woman. 'The
telephone! Ring for the police!'

'I give you notice now,' continued Thomson, above
the sounds of hurried barricading. 'I think it's dis-
gustin'! *Why, your d——d lion might have eaten my dog!*
I'm going t' leave t'morrer, d'ye *hear*? I'm not goin' t'
live with lions! I'm *sick* of yer stinkin' house!'

A deep, menacing growl floated up the staircase.

Thomson sprawled over the rails. '*Shurrup!*' he
commanded, and the lioness, absurdly enough, was
still. 'Stinkin' brute!' he muttered, without the
slightest sign of fear, and made for the telephone on
the landing.

In a minute or so he had the police station, and was
speaking: 'That th' p'leece station? Yesh. Well, this is
Thomson speakin' here. Eh? Yesh, Thomson, of
Gladstone Manshuns (*I don't think!*). Can you hear?
. . . I say, there's a lion in th' hall here waitin' t' be
fed. . . . Eh? . . . Yes, a *lion*! . . . No, I'm wrong,
ol' chap—it's th' lion's wife. Are you there? . . . Well,
it's waitin' t' be fed. I dunno who it b'longs to, but I'm
goin' t' leave in mornin'. It's stinkin' th' place out.
Eh? . . . *What's* that? . . . Yesh, Gladstone Manshuns—you know th' place near th' Town Hall! Eh?
. . . No, nobody's killed; there's nothin' here t' eat
but boarders—never is! Are you comin' along? . . .
Right-oh!' The bell tinkled hurriedly in the darkness.
Thomson fumbled his way into his room and shut the
door.

It was a lovely, peaceful morning. There wasn't a sound until two policemen and a little man, in the ring-costume of a tamer, trotted round the corner.

Thomson waved frantically to them from his window. 'Go roun' side an' get in th' scullery window!' he howled. 'Look out f'r my dog in th' back yard—he's big mastiff, but he won't hurt yer. If he growls give him a bit o' lobster—he loves lobster!'

HOODOO JO
By Bernard Cronin

JO ASGARD was a small man and very active. Like most of the Swedes in the timber camps he kept his head shaved, and his scalp was red and rough from the sun and wind. He had big sandy eyebrows and a sandy tuft under each ear. His eyes were blue, and his cheek-bones were high and shining. He was a silent man. He was turned thirty, and was married to the eldest daughter in a Danish family that had come to settle in Trowutta, share dairy-farming.

Until there came a series of fatalities which eventually branded Jo as a pariah, he was the smartest cant-dog man in the Tasmanian north-west big timber. The duty of a cant-dog man is to orient the logs in their original chaotic setting of tangled scrub, and then make fast the cable for a sharp haul into the clear. Jo knew to a hairbreadth the exact centre of gravity where the point of the big steel hook should be tapped to a turning grip with the back of his axe, before the strain was taken up by the cable. Bullock chains or a wire rope winding on the drum of a steam winch were all one to him.

It looked easy, but it wasn't. The cant-dog man lives in the shadow of danger. A snapped link, made brittle with frost, or a loosened dog point could mean a broken limb—or a broken back. Jo knew when to jump . . . and when to stay. It was intuition, rather than judgement. Either you had it, or you hadn't. Jo handled the chains, or it might be the wire cable, as though he had been born to it.

When the first of the fatalities occurred Jo had actually no share in it. A strand of the wire cable broke and ran up, as the drum wound, and then the whole rope parted. There was a feller named Peter Moss, who was heading past for the camp to get a new axe-handle, and the wire cable whipped back on the recoil and cut him literally in half. Jo happened to be standing close to Moss, but just outside the line.

That was nothing, of course. But when Jack Emery, the foreman's mate, was killed by a flying maul-head a month later, and Jo was alongside him, men remembered the first time and began to look at him a little askance. And then it happened again. The billyboy, who had been down to the creek for water for the eleven-o'clock scran, stumbled and fell in the line of a big red myrtle. His right leg was broken in two places. It was Jo Asgard who picked him up.

That night the foreman gave Jo his time. He didn't say why, and Jo didn't ask him. There was no need. Both men were embarrassed. They shook hands, and Jo got his few things together and went off down the track to look for a new camp. He went off shaking his head, as though he didn't understand what was happening. The winchman, who was Irish, said maybe Jo had trod on the little people when they were at play. The little people were very vindictive, he said, and never let up once they got to dislike you.

Jo got a job with the Grahams, who were cutting out a stand of celery-top. The first day Bill Graham himself lost two fingers by mistiming the give of a saw-cut in standing timber. By the time a wedge was driven in to take the lift, Graham's fingers were a pulp.

Jo's record had come down the line, and Graham wouldn't listen to reason. He sacked Jo with a week's wages, and told him the sooner he got going the better he'd be pleased. It was a case of giving a dog a bad name.

So Jo went on the hunt again. His shoulders began to get a droop, and his blue eyes seemed somehow to become faded. He went home to Trowutta and talked it over with his wife. She was a sensible sort of girl and she explained how ridiculous the whole thing was, blaming Jo like that. She didn't know anything about bush superstitions. She had very little English, and Jo had very little of Swedish, and no Danish at all. He was born in Sweden, but came to Tasmania when he was only just able to walk. All the language Jo and Hedda had between them was the common language of affection. But what is ample for love-making is no good at all for abstract argument. So Jo gave over and talked instead of the baby that was coming. That was something both of them could understand.

Old Saul Ribash, who had the contract for putting down corduroy over Archer's swamp, heard Jo was out of work, and sent for him. Ribash wanted a cant-dog man who didn't get drunk every second night or so, and call him for nothing and for a so-and-so son of a Jew. Ribash didn't believe in good luck or bad luck. Things just came along, and they were one way or another way, but never all the same way. Ribash had

heard of the hoodoo on Jo Asgard, just as every man
on the timber line had heard of it, but he only
laughed. Ribash was a big man and his laugh was a
big laugh. It began deep down in his stomach and
came roaring out of his wide-open mouth.

All that had been wrong with Jo, Ribash said, was
coincidence. Ribash was very fond of ascribing everything to coincidence. It was his favourite word. He
was great on working out percentages, and things like
that; and he proved to everybody that the chance of
an accident happening when Jo was around now was
about one in 10,000,000. He took a timber chalk and
set the figures down on a bit of planking for everybody
to see.

The men didn't say much because they were afraid
of what Ribash might do to them. He was as strong as
any three of them. Besides, he was the boss. But Jo
brightened up quite a lot. He thought probably
Ribash was right; all his bad luck was only coincidence. But he was extra careful, just the same. He
kept away from the other men as well as he could, and
showed no interest in any part of the work but his own.

As the days went by he began to regain his old
confidence. He had his dog fast on the timber almost
as soon as the chains came down to him, and the logs
went out in a steady stream. At the end of a fortnight
Ribash sought Jo out and shook his hand.

'There—you see,' he said, 'what did I tell you? A
coincidence is a coincidence. It's a matter of mathe-
matics. Things happen and then they don't happen.'

He grinned at Jo, and Jo grinned back. He was
feeling happy for the first time in months. It was a
Saturday afternoon and the camp was almost
deserted. Some of the men were resting in their bunks,
but most of them had gone down the line to the sly

grog shanty. Ribash's young wife had driven out in the jinker to fetch her husband home for the week-end. The Ribashes lived just out of Green Point, about ten miles south over the button-grass plains.

Mrs. Ribash brought her little girl with her. While Ribash was tidying up, the child wandered over to where Jo was sitting mending his leggings with kangaroo sinews. Jo was fond of kids. He had a way with them. He told her stories out of Hans Andersen until Mrs. Ribash came looking for her. Ribash came out of his tent, all spruced up, and shiny with soap and water, and began to walk over to where the horse and jinker were waiting. The little girl ran to meet her mother.

Dry timber will always give warning, however slight, but a tree-limb waterlogged over successive winters knows no such compassion. High overhead the arm of a stringy-bark parted from its fork and overweighed to the earth. Ribash saw it coming and staggered back, his hands lifting to cover his eyes. Jo Asgard stood paralysed. The mass of timber by a miracle fell clear of both mother and child, but the taint of death was in the air.

Mrs. Ribash's scream had brought the men from their bunks into the open. Ribash, seeing his wife and child unharmed, knew the inevitable reaction. Anger kicked out of him like a bolting horse, and he came for Jo Asgard, roaring.

Jo ran. Ribash was crazy, real dirty crazy. Jo ran with the wind in his ears and blood beating at the back of his eyes. His face looked broken. His breath came in sucks and bursts. He ran until he dropped exhausted. The wave of fear rolled over him and vanished. A blankness came. He put his head on his arm and began to cry.

That finished Jo Asgard on the timber line. He became a pariah. The odd part of it was that people liked him. Everybody liked him. But they feared him, too. And fear is stronger than liking. Only Hedda stuck to him. Jo had a little money saved, so they weren't likely to starve for a time, anyhow.

For the first few weeks Jo sat at home, with his head in his hands. One moment he felt sick and dejected; the next, anger spurted up inside him. He wanted to go out and get drunk and curse and break things, but he would think of Hedda and the baby that was coming, and that quietened him. After a time he felt his sickness leaving him. He became restless. He was an active man and he couldn't bear to be idle for long. So now on Monday mornings he got Hedda to put up a pack of food, and he would go camping along the timber line, hunting for new timber stands whose locations he might sell to the millers, perhaps, and doing a little prospecting along the creeks and gutters. Men would pass the time of day with him, but that was all. They were too scared of him to invite him to a drink of tea. The timber line had put a tail on Jo, and it had a fork at the end of it.

So matters stood at the end of the following summer. A new government road was being cleared through the back country and the contract had been let in two sections. Ribash had up to the five-miles peg on the start in from the plain, and the Graham brothers were covering the section on to the made road at Red Flag. By agreement the contractors began operations each at his own end, so that they would eventually meet at the five-miles. There was method in this, for the contracts specified a fine of £50 a day for each day over the allotted time for completion, less the usual three days of grace.

It was Ribash's idea for the gangs to work toward each other, so that if either of them fell short the two gangs could pool on the last lap. It proved a wise provision, for the winter had been one of the worst on record. With a month to go the racing gangs were still half a mile apart. They had applied for an extension, but had been turned down.

At the start of the final week both gangs mixed in. To save time, the Grahams piled the roughage into one huge kiln on their end of the five-miles peg. It looked what it was—an insecure mountain of straight and twisted logs, held together more by good luck than good management.

Rufe Spinks had the subcontract for the drays and scoops. He was cranky and mean. He didn't drive himself, but spent most of his time keeping a red, suspicious eye on his men, in case they tried to steal the holes out of his harness straps. Rufe was cat-napping in the shade of the big kiln one afternoon when some of the top logs shook loose. One of them rolled flat over Rufe and pinned him to the ground. He wasn't crushed or anything, but just solidly wedged. Only his head and shoulders could be seen; his red, surprised face lay on its back in the caked mud, eyes staring, and his head tilting up like a grey sponge.

The gangs, summoned by the winchman's whistling, could only stand in helpless inaction. Half-way up the kiln a key-log had swung loose. It hung by a hair, ready to bring down a landslide of jagged timber. A mistouch would have done it. Not one of the cant-dog men there dared attempt to straighten the loose log because of the risk to Rufe.

Word spread that Jo Asgard was camped down by the creek and a dozen men ran to get him. Jo came.

He was bewildered and angrily protesting. Wasn't it enough that all men shunned him like a yaller dog, through no fault of his own, but now they must make him take the blame for killing Rufe Spinks. He wouldn't have anything to do with it. It wasn't fair. . . . He shook himself free of their persuading hands and walked to the end of the kiln and looked down at Rufe. The old man was groaning with terror. His eyes seemed to implore Jo.

Jo made a little pathetic gesture of resignation. It wasn't fair; but he couldn't see any decent way out of it. Someone had to bust that key-log back into holding place, or Rufe's life wouldn't be worth the price of his dirty, mean, snooping old carcass. He turned to the watching men and began to snap orders, with all his old-time eager authority.

'Gimme the chains. Ben . . . back a yoke your side. Baldy and Speck . . . they're the steadiest.'

The bullocky knew his cattle. They stepped like cats under the scorch of his rumbling blasphemies. A dozen poles meantime ferried the chains over the kiln to Jo, who stood balanced half-way up the timber. An inch to the right, or an inch to the left; the death potential lay in a hairbreadth. Jo's practised eye felt itself along the bole of the quivering log until halted by his unerring intuition. He held the heavy cant-dog in place with his two hands, sighed deeply, and gave the signal. The bullocky spat. He laid the long handle of his whip lightly on the necks of the two old leaders. The chain came taut as smoothly as though it were a rope of oil. For an instant the log hung; then the hook bit. And then suddenly the miracle was won. The huge haunch of timber swung over and fell into place; the whole kiln shuddered, and there came the rasp of resting wood. . . .

Saul Ribash, laughing his big laugh, pushed through the shouting crowd to where Jo sat weakly on the ground. He roared: 'What did I always tell you? It's this way or that way, but it's never all the one way. Haven't I told you you can't get away with the law of averages? Look here . . . I can prove it in black and white.'

Men were slapping Jo on the back, but Ribash cursed them away. He grabbed a plank-end and pulled out his timber chalk. He said: 'See here, Jo. . . .'

Jo grinned. He looked around the circle of friendly faces and his heart swelled. His luck had clicked into place with the key-log. Everything was going to be fine from now on . . . fine.

'You know,' Ribash complained, busy with his sums, 'I never stood for that rot about you, Jo. . . .

A BED OF RUBIES
By H. E. RIEMANN

'ROT!' snorted Publican Lanfred, throwing down the month-old newspaper, and turning to the open door. 'Precious stones indeed—sheep is the wealth of this country!'

Outside, the sinking sun, its torrid power waning, cast a brilliant red radiance on the heated wooden structures that housed the inhabitants of Peepingee. The township contained little to examine. The official portion was represented by the snug post office, the aristocratic, high-verandaed hospital and, lastly, the lock-up. This was a roofless, stone-walled edifice, which stood up uncompromisingly, even above the hospital, its top bristling with fragments of broken bottles. Under a normal nor'-western sun, a single day's incarceration in it would have been sufficient to mend the ways of a bigamist.

Besides the ten dwelling-places, there was a store, a smoke-begrimed blacksmith's premises, and an embarrassed-looking church. The most important building—Lanfred's Evening Star Hotel—was the shrine to which all Peepingee turned its eyes.

The publican's eye wandered listlessly down the main 'street', which tapered off into the 280-mile River Mail-track, and vanished in the distant haze of heat and smoke. There were dry throats on the sun-baked stations inland, he knew—throats that got no nearer to Perth than Peepingee, and fondly referred to that township as the 'Port', although four miles of blistering landscape lay between it and the actual sea-line. Dry throats, too, were down at the cobra[1]-eaten jetty; and every moment the ancient, obsolete, seldom-greased horse-truck, rails for which manoeuvred through the sandhills, was expected to burst into view.

Suddenly the languidness left Lanfred; his head jerked a foot higher, and his eyes narrowed with intense interest. In the blurred distance a cloud of dust arose. Up sprang the publican; out through the doorway he rushed, and seizing a shovel handle commenced to bang an empty, bullet-riddled tank.

The uproar created great activity. Lanfred's wife looked out of a window and inquired who was coming; the Chinaman cook ordered Jim, the blackboy, to climb the wood-heap and count how many; Curtis and his two men deserted the goods-shed platform; burly Brannon, the blacksmith, flung down hot iron;

[1] toredo worm.

Gammy-leg Springer came limping from his tent, and the horse-truck, emerging from the sandhills, became light by reason of its riders jumping off like rats from a sinking ship. All hurried towards the hotel, shading their eyes in a vain endeavour to conquer the dazzling glare of the sun.

Down at the post office Postmaster Powell sat in his receiving-room, transmitting a telegraphic message. He cursed and ground his teeth as he snatched glances at the hotel, where, it seemed, all the world—his little world—had congregated. From his position he made out the object of interest to be a camel, coming in at a swinging gallop.

As the new-comer neared the hotel, McBride, the Pinyinnie teamster, identified the animal by its lopped ear as the property of his boss.

Onward came the camel, a galloping grotesque object, laden with square boxes, strapped on each side like balconies, and crowned with a white man. Suddenly, at a tug from the single rein, it slowed to a steadier pace, and stalked down the 'street' with ponderous majesty.

The watchers then saw a travel-stained, florid-faced, golden-bearded man, comfortably seated, who looked steadfastly ahead, and passed the motley assemblage without as much as a glance.

They were flabbergasted. That a white man coming down from the reaches of the river should shun the 'Port' hotel filled their minds with gloomy apprehension. Silently, they watched the camel come to a standstill by the slender, white-painted post office flagstaff that pencilled the sky.

Scarcely waiting for his steed to kneel, the new-comer sprang lightly to the soft sand, and dived, unceremoniously, into Powell's receiving-room.

'My name's Rice—John Rice,' he jerked out. 'Is there a telegram here for me?'

'John Rice.' The name flashed across Powell's memory. 'Are you—' suddenly he remembered, and adroitly substituted, 'expecting a wire?'

'Cable,' corrected the other, impatiently, 'via Broome.'

The postmaster glanced at the 'R' pigeon-hole. 'No,' he said, 'there is nothing, Mr. Rice.'

The golden-bearded jaw fell, and there was a tone of keen disappointment in the visitor's voice. 'I suppose,' he said, 'it'll come later. Can you direct me to the policeman of this place?'

'Faulity? Yes, over at the hotel. Wait a second and I'll——'

'And a teamster named—er—McBride?'

'Pinyinnie man—over at the hotel, too—I'm coming now.'

'You might pick them up and bring them into the bar,' suggested Rice, as he and the postmaster, with the camel following, walked across.

A roguish smile lit up Powell's features as he passed through Peepingee's puzzled ranks, and spoke low to McBride and Faulity.

A hum of disapproval arose among the others.

'It's as much our bar as theirs,' exclaimed Brannon. 'Come on in.'

They filed in after McBride and Faulity.

'You're McBride, eh?' Rice was saying. 'Well, I'm just down from Pinyinnie, with a camel belonging to Mr. Campbell. He asked me to turn it over to you, to bring back on your return.'

'Awfully kind—of him,' drawled the teamster. 'P'raps he'd like me to take a mob of sheep with the teams, too?'

'I know it's awkward, and I'm willing to pay——'
Rice paused, and produced a leather pouch from his
pocket. 'Here, take this.' Into McBride's open hand
he put a dull-gleaming, waterworn pebble, about the
size of a pea, which the teamster promptly let fall.
Rice stooped quickly and recovered it.

'What the devil is it?' asked McBride, bewildered.

'What . . . is it?' repeated the man with the
golden beard. He rolled it on the tip of his tongue. 'A
gem!' he cried, holding the pebble up to the lamp
the publican had just lit. 'A ruby! An Oriental ruby!
Matchless as the orb of day at dawn! See here is car-
mine and cochineal fire, more brilliant than the aurora-
red ruby of the Kyat Pyen mines of Mandalay——'

A howl of derisive laughter checked his enthusiasm.

'Why,' exclaimed Brannon, failing to catch the
postmaster's warning gesture, 'you must be Ruby-man
Rice?'

The other looked him up and down.

'The bloke what sent samples of rubies to Streeter
in London?' pursued the blacksmith, breaking off
into a boisterous laugh.

'My name happens to be Rice,' said the golden-
bearded man, staring hard. 'How comes it you know
so much of my private affairs?'

Instantly, Powell pushed his way in between
Brannon and Rice. He didn't want it reported that
Peepingee possessed a post official cursed with
unscrupulous inquisitiveness. Powell had opened the
parcels as they passed through his hands, as the whole
township knew. He had extracted a couple of stones
and sent them to Perth, and these were worthless.

'It happened this way, Mr. Rice,' he lied. 'That old
Squarehead coach-driver had a smash-up in front of
the hotel here, and one of your parcels burst the

wrappings. The note inside gave us your name. But anyhow, it don't matter, they're worthless.'

'How do you know?'

Powell coughed uneasily; and the publican came to his rescue. 'Experience,' he said. 'Years ago, when we had only a few tents here, a blackboy came along with a handful of those same stones. We thought we'd struck it rich, but we found out from the jewellers in Perth they were only garnets or spinels. Not fit to load a gun with.'

'Matter of opinion,' said Rice briefly, and turned to the policeman. 'Mr. Faulity, I want you to take charge of my rubies. There's two hundredweight on the camel outside. The equivalent in gold is colossal! Will you take delivery now?'

When Faulity recovered his breath, he stared fixedly at Rice. 'Peepingee has no thieves, and no locks either, except the lock-up; but there's a mad hatter in there. Your safest plan would be to bury your rubies in one of the sandhills behind the pub—and sleep on 'em! I'll guarantee you immunity from theft.'

A hush fell upon the company at the policeman's solemn suggestion. The joke was not to be spoilt by even a smile!

Faulity's plan was accepted. As the twilight fell, McBride, Gammy-leg Springer, and Faulity helped Rice unload the camel. During the process, a big box fell on Springer's foot—with profane results.

Peepingee had seen many jokes, but none so good as the sight of an able-bodied, sober-minded, florid-faced, golden-bearded man sitting on a sandhill, guarding two hundredweight of worthless pebbles.

The night heard many tank-beats, and saw

stealthy figures creeping among the sandhills. But as they drew near, Rice growled like a big dog in his kennel with a bone, and when he growled the figures fled, choking back derisive laughter.

Postmaster Powell's eyebrows uplifted, as he stared at the words he had just deciphered from the telegraph tape.

'Gee!' he whistled, and drew a roll of bunting from a locker. There were other rolls inside. The flag idea was his own invention—a method for saving time and trouble. He had persuaded each permanent inhabitant of the township to provide a differently designed flag, and when in receipt of a telegraphic message he flew the one belonging to the addressee.

Powell leaned out of his window, attached the bunting to the flagstaff halliards, and hoisted it up. Within ten minutes, Publican Lanfred appeared at the door.

Powell's eyes turned to the telegraphic form again. 'Lanfred,' he said slowly, 'that Perth jeweller who said those stones were no good is a fool! Look here! This is Streeter's reply to Rice.'

The publican examined the slip of paper. 'Great Scott!' he ejaculated, and looked up. Their eyes met. 'We all know where they are kept,' Lanfred continued. 'He's not over-careful and the sun drives——'

'No robbing,' hastily interposed the postmaster. 'Faulity said we weren't thieves; and we're not. Rice calls here less frequently now, Lanfred. If I held this message three days, do you think you could extract . . . rubies—legitimately?'

'Easy,' grinned the other. 'He's half-decided they are valueless already.'

'Well, I'll alter the date on this to the eighteenth.

G

One condition, Lanfred—a half-share, with a half-cost of the liquor consumed, will be necessary for me. You understand?'

Lanfred understood perfectly. He strolled back to the hotel, accosted Rice, and came straight to the point.

'My word, it's hot!' he exclaimed. 'Come and have a drink. Oh, about those stones, Rice—garnets—rubies—call 'em what you will. My little niece in Perth is always bothering me to send her something pretty from the Nor'-West. Now, you'll never get rid of your stones. I'll sell you liquor at a ruby per drink, and make up a parcel for the kiddie.'

Rice looked curiously at the publican. The dull expression of his eye brightened to a quaint gleam of devilry. A half-hundredweight would make Peepingee blue-blind drunk for a year, he reflected. Well, why shouldn't he? It was only a flea-bite of his wealth! 'Beat the tank, Mr. Lanfred!' he cried.

Before twenty-four hours had elapsed, the astounding news that Peepingee had embarked on a mad, mad spree was heard a hundred miles away. All along the river, men shelved their jobs, and saddled station horses. Moullip Station emptied out all hands to participate in the overflow; Mittayong lost four shearers and the cook; Youlang was left with only the manager and a string of lazy blackboys; Wig Hill became the sole charge of a buck-toothed Mongolian. The mail-coach arrived at 'Port' a day before scheduled time, heavy with human freight.

With wonder-dazed eyes the new arrivals saw the drinks put up; saw the dull-red pebbles trundled across the counter, and gasped.

Such a furious, elephantine drunk Peepingee had never known. It was a ruby-red drunk. It eclipsed for

ever the far-famed Cleopatra's banquet, and her
great pearl drink with Antony.

They drank! The flow of liquor ebbed not, though
lower sank the source—until suddenly, unexpectedly,
there came a cessation. Peepingee staggered—an
enormous gap where its heart had always been. The
Evening Star Hotel had run dry!

John Rice sat on the veranda step, dejectedly
supporting his bursting head with two flabby hands.
Gammy-leg Springer lay prone on the bare boards,
groaning laboriously. Presently he spoke.

'Rice,' he said, 'this thing's settling in me bones—
I mean where your infernal box hit me foot. You
oughter recognize your responsibility—er—compensation an' all that. I'd accept a thousand rubies
willin'——'

'Man, you don't know what you ask!'

'Stuff!' Springer snapped. 'A thousand drinks isn't
much to soothe an injury that'll carry me to me grave.'

Rice pondered. 'I'll give you one hundred,' he
compromised.

Springer's violent expostulation brought the
publican to the door, and Powell, too, appeared
unexpectedly.

'Here you are, Mr. Rice,' said the postmaster
breezily, 'your cable's come.'

Rice's hands came quickly from his head; he
snatched the missive; his trembling fingers tore it open,
and he read. His eyes bulged; his breath came short,
and an involuntary exclamation escaped his lips. The
pain was gone from his head.

'By God!' he cried, deliriously, lifting his arm like
a warrior who has won a fight, 'I was right!'

The paper fell fluttering to the floor. He staggered
to the wall. 'Gammy,' he said, 'I'll bring the number

down to fifty—and that's fifty fortunes rolled in one.'
Then he stepped from the veranda, and walked away
in the dusk. To the eyes of Lanfred and Powell,
his passage to the sandhills bore an uncommon
resemblance to a triumphant cakewalk.

Lanfred tugged the postmaster's sleeve. 'I've saved
a bottle of Scotch,' he whispered. 'Come and
celebrate.'

Rice awoke with a start, dispelling the luxuries his
dreams had pictured. Slowly his mind came back to
immediate surroundings. As he raised himself on his
elbow, he caught an indistinct glimpse of a prowling
figure, that hurried away with a curious hopping run.

'Gammy-leg, by God,' he muttered, recalling the
cable he had dropped. So, he thought, Peepingee was
not the honest town Faulity had imagined. Anyone
could have stolen his gems—if they had thought it
worth their while. Now, the substance of his cable
had leaked out. The rubies?—were they safe beneath
him? Could he trust them with the policeman? Men
in higher positions than Faulity had fallen! And himself? Was he safe? Gammy-leg could come along any
night—could knock him on the head! Springer, with
the bulging neck, the low, bristling brow, the drooping
lips! Springer was capable of murdering him!

Rice sat up. Over at Gammy-leg's tent a light
flared up and went out again, as if a pipe had been
lit. Gammy-leg was awake all right—probably
planning. An idea occurred to Rice. He smiled and
stood up. Good!—the south wind would obliterate
his tracks in the sand.

He would set Peepingee at its own throat with
suspicion. In the turmoil, he hoped to hold his rubies
safe until the steamer called.

While half Peepingee yet slumbered in the early light of morn, a thunderous onslaught on Constable Faulity's door brought him tumbling out of bed. In a moment his blinking eyes took in Rice, frenzied and almost incoherent of speech.

'My rubies! My rubies!' Rice cried wildly. 'I've been robbed! My rubies are gone!'

'Nonsense,' laughed Faulity. 'Some joke!'

'Joke!' echoed Rice. 'Call it a joke! Cable came last evening—specimens ninety carat—fortune in each! I lost the message—woke up in the hollow instead of on the hill—rubies gone!'

At once the case assumed a serious aspect, and Faulity frowned, although he still considered it a possible joke. 'You sit quiet, Mr. Rice,' he said, 'and I'll soon produce your rubies.'

But from each blear-eyed, whisky-sodden person he visited, only head-shakes and protests of innocence were extorted.

When Powell heard of the robbery he glared at the publican and said something under his breath. To which Lanfred retorted with a veiled accusation, causing the postmaster to stumble angrily to his office.

Faulity buzzed about like a disturbed hornet. 'Leave it to me,' he reassured Rice. 'I'll give' em one more chance,' and he proceeded to the hotel. Presently the tank resounded with blows.

When Peepingee had assembled in full force, Faulity marched them to the sandhill that had been burglarized.

'I've called the roll,' said the policeman, 'to give you a final chance to save Australia ringing with the news of the greatest gem robbery on earth. It's no laughing matter! You know how Rice came amongst us, and how I guaranteed him immunity from theft.

That immunity has been disgracefully broken. In short, some cow has nicked the rubies! It's a good joke, I'll admit; but the seriousness of the sequel will allow it to go no further. Mr. Rice has received intelligence, confirming his opinion of the value of the stones. Now—ten minutes for the joker to own up and save a scandal!'

Murmurs of astonishment were superseded by cries of indignation. Peepingee was no thief! The publican's name was shouted out; but Rice spoke up and proclaimed Lanfred's dealings honourable.

'Now, be swift,' went on Faulity sharply. 'Make no mistake, I'll mark the man! I haven't lived among you for six years without knowing——' He stopped abruptly, and his eyebrows lifted.

The crowd, following the look, saw Postmaster Powell striding towards them. His very gait seemed portentous. Without a word, he handed an official-red envelope to Rice, who immediately broke the seal.

Rice's face broadened, and he gave vent to a short, metallic laugh as he read. He turned and, swiftly, his eyes searched the crowd until they alighted on Gammy-leg Springer, who stood sullenly in the background. Rice strode up to him.

Excitement ran high. The air became electric.

'Gammy,' said Rice, 'yesterday, you demanded a thousand rubies compensation for your damaged foot. I offered a hundred. While you argued Streeter's cable came. In my excitement I let fall the message and walked away. Is that correct?'

'Ye—es, b—but——'

'You wanted compensation,' interrupted Rice. 'You weren't satisfied with a big helping of an enormous fortune—you wanted all! Gammy, will that sore foot allow you to walk a quarter of a mile across these sandhills?'

'Yes—b—but I didn't steal——'

Threatening faces had ringed around the unfortunate Springer, indignant voices clamoured. Cries of 'Don't give him a chance!' 'Don't give him a start!' were deafening. His townsmen, it seemed, were ready to lynch him the moment an accusation was launched.

Rice held up his hand for silence. 'Go,' he said, when order was restored. 'Make a bee-line for that bush yonder'—he pointed—'count, twelve sandhills, and in the next hollow—dig! That which you so much desired awaits you!' And with another hard, mirthless laugh Rice dramatically thrust the second cable he had received into Springer's hand.

Completely mystified, the men, who a moment before would have driven the suspected man from the township, now peered over his shoulder to fathom the meaning of Rice's words. They read: 'Rice, Peepingee, via Broome—Previous cable referred African diamonds yours to read—garnets worthless—Streeter, London.'

THE GREY HORSE
By KATHARINE SUSANNAH PRICHARD

HE was young, a draught stallion, grey, and Old Gourlay worked him on the roads.

Old Gourlay kept the road in order on the back of Black Swan and lived with his housekeeper in a bare-faced, wooden box of a house beside the road, where it loped over the mountain to Perth, by way of the river and half a dozen townships scattered across the plains. Gourlay was a dry stick of a man, and deaf; but Grey Ganger—the beauty of him took the breath like a blast of cold wind. There was nothing more beautiful in the ranges, not the wild flowers, yellow and blue, on the ledges of the road, nor the tall white gums gleaming through the dark of the bush from among thronging rough-barked red gums and jarrah.

A superb creature, broad and short of back, deep-barrelled, with mighty quarters, the grey stallion carried Old Gourlay, on the floor of the tip-dray, uphill in the morning, curveting with kittenish grace, as though the tip-dray were a chariot; prancing and tossing his head so that silver threads glinted in the spume of his mane. He brought loads of gravel down-hill, gaily, prancing still, with an air of curbing his pace to humour the queer, fussy insect of an old man who clung to the rope reins stretched out beside and behind him.

Wood-carters who worked on the Black Swan road envied the old man his horse. They wanted to buy him; but Gourlay would not sell the Ganger. Their great, rough-haired horses laboured along the bush tracks and came slowly down the steep winding road, sitting back in the breeching, the roughly split jarrah for firewood stacked on the carts jabbing their haunches.

O'Reilly had offered good money, cash down, for Grey Ganger; he had told Gourlay to name his own figure. But Old Gourlay shook his head. Nothing but cussedness, it was, O'Reilly declared. Gourlay had not enough work for the Ganger: a less powerful horse would suit him better, cost less, and be easier to manage. O'Reilly would have liked to mate the Ganger with his Lizzie when he found he could not buy the horse. Lizzie was a staunch enough working mare, shaggy and evil-smelling, with a roach back, and splay feet, but she had been 'a good 'un in her day', he said.

Gourlay would have none of that either.

'Aw—aw,' he stuttered; 'she's rough stuff. He's only a baby. There'd be no holding him if ——'

Old Gourlay had pride in his horse, enjoyed crying his measurements, the size of his collar. The Ganger was always in good condition, close-knit and hard, his hide smooth and sheeny as the silk of a woman's dress. Not that Gourlay seemed to have any affection for him: rather was there hostility, a vague resentment in his bearing. He nagged at Grey Ganger as though he feared and had some secret grudge against him.

But no one envied Old Gourlay his horse more than Bill Moriarty, who, against the advice of every fruit-grower in the district, had taken up the block of land adjoining Gourlay's, and had planted vines and fruit-trees to make an orchard there, a few years before Gourlay, Mrs. Drouett and the grey stallion had come to live on the Black Swan road. As he cleared and grubbed, burnt off, and cultivated his land, Young Moriarty had watched Gourlay and Grey Ganger.

On the wildest, wettest nights he had seen the flickering, loose golden star of Gourlay's lantern as he went to feed the Ganger and shut him into his stable for the night. He had been up when the old man pulled the board from across the stable door in the morning, and the Ganger, released, dashed round the small, muddy square of the yard, flinging up his heels, snorting and gambolling joyously, with such a clumsy, kittenish grace that Moriarty himself would laugh, and sing out to old Gourlay: 'He's in great heart, this morning, all right.'

Gourlay would mutter resentfully, and swear at the Ganger, clacking the gate of the stable-yard to, as he went up to breakfast. Nothing annoyed him more than to see Grey Ganger disporting himself.

When first he and his housekeeper had come to live at Black Swan, Old Gourlay had made those trips to feed and shut the Ganger in his stable for the night with zest, swinging his lantern religiously and whistling. And he had gone afterwards into the shed beside the stable, where a bed was made up, put the light out there and slammed the door. But Young Moriarty had seen him stumble uphill in the starlight, or when he thought all Black Swan was sleeping, open the back door quietly, and go into his house.

Black Swan people did not appear to mind where Old Gourlay slept, really. They were too busy in their orchards or clearing and cultivating land for vines to bother much about what their neighbours were doing. Besides, Gourlay's and Mrs. Drouett's story had gone before them. Nobody expected Old Gourlay to sleep in the shed beside the stable. Even the children going along the road to school, as they passed Gourlay's, said mysteriously to each other: 'He's got one mother up-country . . . and living here with another.'

The neighbours were kind and friendly enough when they met either Gourlay or Mrs. Drouett. Their story had created a slightly romantic sympathy. It was said Old Gourlay had been a well-to-do farmer with a wife and family when Laura Drouett had come his way. He sold his farm and left his family to go away with her. They had wandered about for years and grown old together.

Mrs. Drouett had been a comely woman and still kept her figure tight at the waist. Her hips were thrust out from it, plump and heavy; she had a bosom and a fringe of brown curly hair, which she wore above the withered apple of her face when she was dressed for the afternoon, or going driving with Mr. Gourlay. She was older than he, perhaps, but better preserved; deaf also, and nervy, under the strain of living with Mr. Gourlay, 'seeing how I am placed', as she explained to Young Moriarty when he hopped over the fence to talk to her, and cheer her up, sometimes.

Old Gourlay did not like Bill Moriarty hopping over the fence to talk to Mrs. Drouett.

'He's as mad as a wet hen if he finds me having a yarn with the old girl,' Bill explained to O'Reilly. 'She's a decent sort . . . a bit lonely . . . and I've been trying to get round her to make the old man lend me his horse, now and then.'

O'Reilly laughed. He thought he guessed what was at the back of Old Gourlay's mind. Bill was a good-looker, thick-set and swarthy, with crisp dark hair and blue eyes set in whites as hard as china, and so short-lashed that they stared at you unshaded from the bronze of his face. Though he was still more or less coltish, Young Moriarty, O'Reilly knew, was working too hard, and too much in love with a girl who lived down on the flats, to be bold with any woman or give Tom Gourlay cause for doubting the fidelity of his Laura. But O'Reilly could not resist rubbing it in when, a few days later, the old man stopped him on the road, not far from where Bill was pruning his vines.

'Good cut of a fellow, that,' he shouted, waving an arm towards Moriarty. 'Isn't a better made man in the ranges. Ever seen him stripped? By God, he's got good limbs on him.'

In the evening, mean-spirited and vindictive, Gourlay gave Mrs. Drouett the benefit of that praise of Bill and the gall he had stewed in all day. The old woman cried; but she was coy and self-conscious with Young Moriarty next time she saw him. She put on her brown hair in the morning and pulled the strings of her corsets tighter. Old Gourlay guessed what he had done, and was madder than a wet hen, though Bill, for all Laura's youthful figure and hair, saw only her poor grandmother's face. He was soaked with the sight and shape of Rose Sharwood, her warm bloom; thirsty with desire for the sound and the smell of her. He was all a madness for Rose. So when he could not get a horse to do his spring ploughing, he went again to Old Gourlay. He had asked before for the loan of his horse, and the old man had refused him, churlishly enough, but with excuses. And Bill had not pressed him. But this was different. It meant a great deal to him, getting that ploughing done.

Black cockatoos had whirled about the clearing, shedding their wild cries high in the air that morning. A long spell of dry weather was breaking and Bill Moriarty needed a horse to cultivate between his vines after the rain.

'How's it for a loan of the Ganger to plough my orchard?' he asked Old Gourlay, leaning over the weatherworn saplings of the stallion's yard.

'Nothing doing,' Old Gourlay growled.

Moriarty explained the difficulty he was in. He was hard up. He could not buy a horse: he could pay for the hire of one by the day. But every man in the district with working horses was waiting for the rain and required his horses to plough, and make the most of the ground while it was soft. Young Moriarty could not get the promise of a horse from anyone. And it

meant everything to him, to have the earth turned
and sweetened about his vines, this year; all the
difference between a good, or a poor, yield of grapes.
Bill let Old Gourlay know, with all the sentiment he
could muster, that he was praying for a good harvest
because he wanted to get married. He soft-pedalled
about Rose, and the skinflint of an aunt who
threatened to take her away to the Eastern States at
the end of the autumn if Bill had not built a house and
married the girl before then.

Old Gourlay pretended not to hear half of what he
was saying.

'T-too busy to do any ploughing,' he said. 'Rain'll
w-wash away half the road up by The Beak. . . .
Couldn' spare the Ganger . . . plenty of work for him
to do on the road. . . . Too much for one man and
one horse.'

He stuttered away from the subject, irritably.
Moriarty let him go, watching the stallion as he
frisked and plunged about the yard where the grey
sapling posts and rails, silvered by the early light,
shook as he bumped against them.

'Ever mate him, Mr. Gourlay?' Young Moriarty
yelled.

'No!' The old man's eyes leapt, sharp and startled
in the weathered fallow of his face. 'There'd be no
holding him if ever I did.'

So that was it, Bill thought. He and the Ganger
were in the same boat. Old Gourlay would thwart
them both if he could; defeat their instincts. Vaguely
Bill understood that what Gourlay resented in the
Ganger, and in himself, was their youth and virility,
when the sap had dried in his old man's bones.

It was beginning to rain as Bill went back to his work.

'Mean old blighter,' he muttered. 'Had two women

himself, and won't give a handsome animal like
that his dues. Him breaking his neck . . . and me
too.'

Young Moriarty went out to the road to meet
O'Reilly as the wood-carts came downhill that
evening, looking top-heavy, the wood piled high on
them red and umber with rain, the shaggy, brown-
furred horses stepping warily for fear they might
come down on the slippery road beside which the
feather-white torrents of rain-wash were flying.

Moriarty asked the wood-carter for the loan of his
mare, Lizzie, some Sunday soon, when he was not
using her. He told O'Reilly how Old Gourlay had
refused to let him have the Ganger although the
stallion spent most of his time on Sundays galloping
up and down and cavorting about his yard beside the
stable; and how he had explained to Gourlay what
it meant to him to get his ploughing and harrowing
done just then.

O'Reilly knew about Rose Sharwood and that Bill
wanted to marry her.

The rain beat around them as they talked, Bill hatless, hugging himself in the coat of his working clothes
buttoned up to the throat; O'Reilly, his tarred
overalls shining, his ruddy, unshaven face with
dropped lip and lit eyes laughing from under his
sodden hat. The raindrops quivering on its brim ran
and fell as he laughed, getting the gist of Young
Moriarty's grievance, and the way he proposed to pay
for the hire of old Lizzie.

Squalls swept up over the purple and green of the
plains all the week, flung themselves against the
ranges, scattering hailstones, and passed on inland.
A film of fine, chill rain veiled the timbered hills
about Black Swan for days. Then the sunshine of late

spring leapt, shimmering on the water lying down on the flats, and drying the land in the hills quickly.

O'Reilly did not appear with Lizzie that Sunday. Moriarty was desperate. Rains had lashed the blossom from the almond-trees along the boundary of his fences. The tooth of green was everywhere; the flame of young leaves. Down near Grey Ganger's stable and yard, where Moriarty had put a row of nectarines below the vines, pink flowers were spraying widespread, varnished branches. It would soon be too late to conserve moisture for the vines. And the thought that Rose would go away with her aunt if he did not do well out of his grapes that year, overhung Young Moriarty like a doom.

But the next Sunday morning, while the Ganger was galloping about his yard, just from his stable, as fresh and beside himself as Bill had ever seen him, O'Reilly brought old Lizzie to cultivate the orchard.

O'Reilly and Bill stood watching the Ganger's gambollings for a moment, laughing and exclaiming their admiration. Then they got to work. O'Reilly drove the mare as they ploughed, across the crest of the hillside, while Bill, stooping along before Lizzie, cleared stones and pruned branches out of the way. O'Reilly ploughed well down the slope before he swung Lizzie from an upper to a lower furrow, uphill and along, downhill and along.

The Ganger came to the end of his yard as he sighted them. He watched Lizzie curiously, snorted as she passed, and galloped up and down, throwing himself about to attract her attention. When they had finished ploughing that side of the hill, Moriarty and O'Reilly spelled Lizzie while they went up to the lean-to Bill lived in, for a meal.

They left her down near the fence where the young

nectarines were in blossom. The grey stallion was trembling against his yard as they did so; taut, the breath blowing in gusty blasts from his nostrils. Lizzie swung her bland, white-splashed face towards him and blinked at him from behind her wide black winkers. Her tail moved gently. A hot, herby aroma reached the men. Young Moriarty went to lead her away, as if to avoid trouble and propitiate Old Gourlay. But it was too late. Grey Ganger rushed and broke his fences. He whirled round Lizzie, charging Moriarty. Bill got away from his plunging fury and flung heels. He picked up the dead branch of a fruit-tree as though to defend himself, or beat off the Ganger. O'Reilly ran away over the broken earth of the hillside.

The noise of the breaking fence and the stallion's whinnied blast brought Old Gourlay running from the house. Mrs. Drouett jiggled marionette-wise on the back veranda for a moment; then when she saw what was happening at the bottom of the paddock, near Young Moriarty's flowering fruit-trees, she put her hands over her face and scuttered into the house again.

Old Gourlay writhed beside the fence, brandishing his whip and shrieking in a frenzy of rage. Moriarty tried to explain, but Gourlay would have no explanations. He was deaf to what Moriarty was saying, though he heard O'Reilly laughing up under the almond-trees. He knew well enough there was only one explanation, Old Gourlay, and Moriarty was not likely to give that.

'It's a put-up job,' he spluttered; 'a buddy put-up job. I'll have the law of ye for it. Taking the bread out of a man's mouth. There'll be no holding him now.'

And there was not. Gourlay was right about that.

At the sidings there was no keeping the Ganger from passing mares; and he was as flighty as a brumby, on the roads. He dragged Gourlay, powerless at the end of his reins, behind the tip-dray as they came down-hill, the old man looking more than ever like some dry, twiggy insect as he jogged there, shrilling fiercely. He was at his wits' end, and went in danger of his life, trying to manage the stallion. He could talk of nothing but the life the horse was leading him; and worry about each new incident in his career, as if an only son had kicked over the traces and was disgracing him in the district.

Mrs. Drouett got nerves with it all. She went about with her head in a shawl and said she was ill. She and Old Gourlay quarrelled incessantly. Their voices could be heard cracking and rattling at each other in the evening. Nothing seemed left of their old passion except its animosities. But when Mrs. Drouett took to her bed, Old Gourlay became alarmed. He thought she might die, and he threw up his contract for mending the road to stay at home and nurse her.

Without telling anyone in Black Swan what he was going to do, or where the horse was going, he sold Grey Ganger then. O'Reilly called him by every name he could think of. But Gourlay would not have forgone his vengeance for a fiver. As it was, he had taken less for the horse than O'Reilly, and many another man round Black Swan, would have given. He sold his house and land too; and he and Mrs. Drouett went to live nearer town, where, if people were not as kind and friendly, at least they were less free with their neighbours' property.

Moriarty married Rose Sharwood soon after old Lizzie had foaled in O'Reilly's paddock beyond The

Beak. At the end of the winter it was. His vines did
well in that fifth year: he had expected so much from
them. He dried currants, raisins, sultanas, and sold
them at top prices on the London market. Even Rose's
aunt was satisfied with the cheque he showed her from
his agents.

It was not until the following season that 'the
bottom fell out of the market for dried fruit', as
fruit-growers about Black Swan said. And about the
same time Rose gave birth to a son.

Bill was not sorry when the baby died, a few months
afterwards during the summer. He believed it was
better for a weakly child, as for a sick chicken or calf,
to die. But the birth, brief screaming existence and
death of the small puckered red creature were a shock
to him. He had not reckoned on a child from him
being a weakling; and Death, like a hand out of the
dark, had gripped, shaken, and squeezed life out of the
youngster. There was something brutal and unfair
about the whole business. If the thing was to die, why
had it ever been born? Young Moriarty was dazed,
numb and angry under the shock.

As he worked out of doors, milked the cows he had
bought to make up for the falling price of dried fruit,
fed pigs and fowls, ploughed and harrowed the
orchard, or cleared land for fodder crops, he still
glanced often down to the Ganger's yard. Through his
numbness and anger about the child, the cleaning of
sties and cowyards, breaking of earth, slopping of
milk into pig-troughs, thoughts of the stallion were
fugitive.

Life with Rose was not what he imagined it would
be. It was mostly a fitting-in of domestic jobs, talking
about the cost of things, eating frugally, and sleeping
without touching her. He had taken her as he wished,

sometimes; and now she pushed him away, saying he was 'low . . . a lustful brute'.

Moriarty was depressed about it. He had not expected Rose to be like that; his joy in her to fade so soon. As he toiled, ploughing, harrowing and pruning, he was conscious of belonging to the fecund earth and life, and yet of being apart from them.

Rose did not want any more children; she dreaded having another baby. It seemed simple and natural enough for a man and woman to have children. But not for Rose, or for him. . . . He snipped the shoots from a budding fruit-tree. . . . Perhaps they were burnt cats who feared the fire, he and Rose.

He noticed that grass had grown in the Ganger's yard and under his stable door.

Rose herself had no strong feelings, he was sure, except for the things that did not matter : dust in out-of-the-way corners, pennies spent unnecessarily. But she was keen on the scent of any hankering Bill might have for another woman, and so shrewish about it that for the sake of peace, at least, he had come to heel. He no longer sought other women.

But Lord, what was there to live for? His days tasted all the same to him, from dawn till dark, flat and dull. He worked hard but without the old zest. Couch had made its appearance in his orchard, his tilth was not what it had been. He invariably struck a bad day if he had cows to sell; and he missed the best price for eggs.

He was a fool, Moriarty told himself, as Rose had often said. He had been wrong about Rose; he had made a mistake about the orchard. There was no money in fruit, fresh or dried. He worked as hard as any of O'Reilly's draught horses for food and a roof over his head : and that was all there was to it. He was sick to death of pottering about pigsties, cowyards, fowl-houses, fruit-trees; and he supposed he would go on pottering among them, and being sick to death of them. It was the rut of life he had made and must stay in.

As he sprawled before the fire that evening, morose and weary, this was swarming over him, the thoughts crawling in and out of his brain and breeding, as did fruit-fly on rotting nectarines in his orchard.

O'Reilly swung into the kitchen.

'That draught stallion of Old Gourlay's,' he said, 'he's been bought by Purdies. Standing the season at The Beak farm and will travel the district. Be up at my place this day next week. . . . Thought you'd like to know.'

Moriarty went to see the horse when he was at O'Reilly's stables. As the groom led him out, the stallion came, arching his neck and tossing his head.

Grey Ganger was more beautiful than he had ever been; no longer skittish, but imperious, his quarters moulded to perfection, the grey satin of his skin sheening under its dapples as he moved. Bill walked across and stood beside him, rubbing a hand over his shoulders, the anguish of his dissatisfaction with life breaking.

'I wish it was me, old man,' he groaned. 'I wish it was me. It's all I'm fit for really.'

THE STUMP
By Vance Palmer

'See that stump!' Old Svenson used to say to any stranger he could get hold of. 'Somet'ing like a stump, ain't it? It belong to the biggest tallow-wood you ever set eyes on, an' I lopped it off when I first come here. T'irty feet from the ground.'

And little Oscar, hanging on to his grandfather's hand, would repeat with the same perky tilt of the chin:

'T'irty feet from the gwound.'

He didn't know what the height meant, but he was sure it reflected some vague glory on them both. Besides, he had become so used to echoing his grandfather that he did it when he was half-asleep or thinking about something else.

It was, indeed, a mammoth stump. It caught the eye of everyone who came up the steep slope to the cleared tableland, for it was about the only relic of the tall timber left. There were orange-trees, of course, arranged as neatly in their ordered rows as soldiers on a parade-ground, with the earth showing red and bare between. They provided a miracle of blossom that made the very bees drunk in the early months of the year, but usually their atmosphere was merely that of a tame prosperity. Small orchards abutting on one another, white-painted fences, growers who might be retired land-agents, flitting from the store to the post office in their saucy cars. And a few imported shrubs along the front, protected by palings from the night-wandering cow. The forest and the scrub had gone, picked over first by the timber-getters for pine and cedar, and then hacked down wholesale by settlers hungry to make use of every inch of the rich, volcanic soil, so that now there was no evidence of the great giants that had once grown there.

Except Svenson's stump! It stood on a grassy space between the church and the school, and could be seen from the flat country below, raising itself up like some white pillar of stone.

'T'irty feet from the ground,' old Svenson said,

as though he had taken the measurements to an inch.

There had been no point in cutting it off so high up. None at all, for the stump was nearly as thick at the top as at the butt. In those days, though, old Svenson had taken a pride in going one better than the next man. He had been a sailor and was not so expert as some of them with the axe, so he evened matters up by putting his footboards in higher than the most fool-hardy would have dared to venture. There was a triumph in stepping from his precarious perch on to the bare stump as the great tree heeled over and crashed, risking annihilation if it caught in another tree or kicked. It gave a fillip of excitement and adventure to the day's work.

Besides, it provided something to boast about, and that had always been a necessity to the little man. For forty years he had been boasting of one quality or possession after another, and his flickering eyes that peered out from behind their glasses still had a challenge in them. Didn't his smallholding of ten acres produce better oranges than any on the range? Hadn't his white Leghorns a record for laying? Wasn't his wife, when she was alive, known all over the district for her cooking? His trim, upright figure, with its stiff back and pointed, grey moustaches, was in itself an aggressive note of interrogation as he moved about the front by the store, holding little Oscar by the hand.

'Old Svenson—he'd shrivel up and die if he couldn't find something to skite about,' people said.

But he had been forced to give up one source of pride after another, conducting a strategic retreat down the years. His firstborn, Emil, who had promised to be such a brilliant youngster, had contracted a

disease of the hip that had cut short his schooling and
had left him lame and a little heavy-witted. He earned
his living as yardman and billiard-marker in an hotel
down the line, and would lick the boots of anyone who
would buy him a drink. The old man had long ceased
to boast about Emil.

Then his wife, that marvel among housekeepers,
had died in hospital after a lingering illness. Hardly a
memory was left of the days when she whisked one
triumph after another from the oven. The second boy,
Chris, was working in the canefields and never came
south; and as for Anna—well, no one quite knew what
had happened to Anna. After creating some scandal
by the way she carried on at dances with the young
fellows who came up for the fruit-picking, she had
gone to town as a waitress, and old Svenson was
evasive when inquiries were made about her. At one
time he implied that she had married an officer on an
overseas liner, and at another that she was playing in
the orchestra of a big cinema. But people ceased asking
about her when the old man went surreptitiously
to town one week-end and brought back Oscar, a
little, puny fellow of eighteen months, who looked as
if he had been reared at a baby-farm on separated
milk. That satisfied them finally about Anna.

Yet in spite of these subtle and treacherous blows of
Fate, Svenson still kept his aggressive old head up in
public. There remained the stump, durable and
securely-rooted, a testimony to all sorts of things—his
daring, his skill, the fact that he had been one of the
pioneers.

'Forty year ago', he would say, thrusting out his
chin, 'there was not'ing in the way of risks I wouldn't
take them days.'

He despised the men who had bought their orchards

for cash and knew nothing of the long struggle with the timber. They were hardly more than immigrants, in spite of the way they took the lead in everything, running the Progress Association and electing themselves to the local council. While the stump remained, he would be able to look over the heads of people like these.

And, in addition to the stump, there was little Oscar. He fussed over the boy like an old hen over a single chicken and hardly ever let him out of his sight. Something inexplicable had happened to his own children, but he was going to make sure nothing of the sort happened to little Oscar.

'Hey, Oscar, come away from that grass,' his voice echoed out as he chipped among his orange-trees. 'Do you want for to get bitten by a snake?'

Or, when he was sitting on the veranda reading his newspaper:

'Now then, Oscar, don't climb any more on that fence. How many times do I tell you not to play the monkey like that!'

Oscar was a mild, flaxen-haired youngster, a little cowed by his early life in an institution, and didn't rebel against this martinet discipline. He even seemed to thrive and grow robust under it. His admiration for his grandfather took the form of aping him even in the smallest things, and when he was swaggering in front of the butcher-boy, telling him how many eggs he had collected, or what a big water-melon was growing at the bottom of the garden, he might have been the old man himself. The same perky walk, the same tilt of the chin, the same inflexions of the voice. Svenson never had the slightest difficulty in shaping him in his own image.

But it was not so easy to guard the stump. As the

township in front developed, and became known as a
holiday resort, there were attacks on the stump from
all sides. First it was the proprietress of the new
boarding-house, a prim, suburban lady with a fringe
and eyeglasses, who argued that it was an eyesore and
blocked the view from her veranda.

'Such a beautiful view it would be, too, if that
thing wasn't planked down in the middle distance.
Catching the eye and holding it like some ghastly
tombstone. My guests all complain that it's a blot on
the landscape.'

The schoolmaster was with her, not merely on
aesthetic grounds, but because the youngsters had a
habit of trying to climb it at playtime and there was
always a danger of accidents. Other people wanted
the relic removed for various reasons. It seemed to
have the stigma of an earlier life about it, a crude,
hand-to-mouth life, like the first attempts at building
homes that most of them had turned into kitchens or
outhouses covered with greenery.

The most formidable enemy of the stump, though,
was the local councillor, for he had power and
authority, and he wanted the obstacle cleared away
for the deviation of a new road. A progressive type of
man who had come late on the scene and bought his
property instead of pioneering it, Rainey had no
sympathy with sentimental ideas or associations.

'Old Svenson's been skiting about that stump for
Lord knows how long,' he said. 'He's just about got
his money's worth out of it by now. Anyhow he has no
property rights over it, and it's a public nuisance.'

And the reply of the storekeeper, the land-agent, and
his other henchmen on the council, was always:

'That's so, Mr. Rainey: you're right there.'

But Svenson was militant in defending the stump's

right to remain, and he had his supporters. They were mainly drawn from the original settlers, and they didn't talk much, but their tenacity could be relied on:

'Why can't Rainey let it alone?' one of them growled. 'The place wouldn't be the same if that old stump went down. It's a landmark.'

And the others, with an obscure sense of loyalty to the past, repeated:

'That's right. It's a landmark.'

The subject was always being raised when Svenson came out to the front for his mail, or sat in the store waiting for Oscar to be let out of school. Even his friends had a good-humoured way of barracking him about it, and their jokes never failed to make the old man bristle aggressively. A ruffled fighting-cock, he looked, with his white moustaches waxed at the points and his pale eyes glinting behind their glasses. Since the rheumatics had come on him he was less inclined to boast about his orange-trees, which were running to wood, or his fowls, now being killed off because of the price of corn, but any attack on the stump always roused his fighting blood. They would see whether Rainey was game to remove it! If he tried, he would raise a storm that would sweep him out of his place on the shire council. Yes, there were enough of the old hands left to counter such an attack; they could make their minds easy about that.

And so the stump remained. Even Rainey didn't seem anxious to take the first step towards removing it, in spite of his talk. He knew there was a considerable amount of feeling liable to be aroused if he acted —more than if he did nothing. Having political ambitions, he was aware of the risks of offending even the least of his future constituents, for it was easier to

make enemies than gain supporters. As well let
sleeping dogs lie—for a while, anyway. Svenson was
growing old. You could see it in his figure, no matter
how he tried to keep his head up and his spine straight
when people were looking at him. There would come
a day . . .

It did come, sooner even than Rainey expected. Old
Svenson was chipping among his orange-trees one
afternoon when the schoolmaster and the boy from
the store edged down the track, bearing little Oscar
on an improvised stretcher. They laid their burden
down by the gate, hesitating. They seemed to be
waiting for the two women who were following
behind.

It was some time before the old man could take in
what had happened. Oscar had been climbing the
stump in the lunch-hour, it appeared, and had slipped
at the top niche, 't'irty feet from the ground', as his
grandfather had so often said. The schoolmaster
didn't attempt to drive home the moral, but he had
foreseen some such accident if the stump remained,
and his long, solemn face said plainly enough:

'There, what did I tell you? Your own grandson.
You see how chickens come home to roost.'

While the others were present the old man made
light of the accident. Things like this were always
happening. How many bad tumbles hadn't he had
himself when he was a youngster! Tumbles from trees,
from cliffs, and, later on, from the spars of sailing-ships
rolling in gales round the Horn! Oscar would be back
at school in a day or two, he affirmed, and the boy
repeated in a dim voice that he would be back at
school in a day or two. Not even a bone broken, the
old man said, and the echo repeated that there wasn't
even a bone broken. But when, next morning, he

complained of his back, his grandfather rang up the ambulance and had him taken down to the railway, making up his mind in the train that he would consult the best specialist. Oh yes, the very best! Money—that was of no account. Emil hadn't seen a doctor soon enough; that was the trouble with him; but there were going to be no risks with little Oscar.

It was nearly a month before he returned, and during that time a few more wrinkles had accumulated on his forehead and his moustaches had lost their spiky aggressiveness. Little Oscar had injured his spine, the specialist had told him, and would have to lie on his back for at least a year; indeed, it was doubtful whether he would ever walk again. Old Svenson had become hard of mental hearing, and it took some time for the news to sink into him. When it did, he decided to sell his orchard, then come back to town so that he would be near the boy. No use trying to let the place! He wouldn't be likely to find a man who would look after it with the same care as he had. And what pleasure would it be to come back in a year's time and find the trees a mass of wood, with weeds round them three feet high?

There was no car to meet the train, and as he walked up the five miles of steep road in the moonlight he had time to ponder on all that had happened since he first made the ascent. The people he had loved and taken a pride in—his wife, the two boys, Anna, and now little Oscar. Not much left to boast of now! . . . But he didn't want to think or look back; it gave him a pain in the head and made the climb more slippery. With all their talk of progress they hadn't improved the grades much since he first struggled up with a sailor's kit on his back behind Doherty's bullock-team.

As he rested after the last abrupt rise, he was faced by the stump, looking white in the moonlight and durable as stone. For a long while he stood peering at it with his short-sighted eyes, his chin thrust out aggressively as of old, and his body rigid as hardwood. Then a little vein seemed to burst in his head, and he stumped off to where Rainey lived among his orange-trees in the big white house overlooking the lower slopes.

'You can root out that stump,' he said, when Rainey appeared at the door.

The local councillor was in his pyjamas and already half-asleep. He looked at Svenson, whose eyes seemed pale and blind in the glare of light from the hall.

'Eh?' he said thickly.

'That stump,' repeated the old man. 'You can root it out now. I give you leaf. Yes, I myself give you leaf. You can burn it or root it out. It's stood too dam' long already.'

It was his final surrender to life.

'Too dam' long already,' he could hear Oscar echo faintly as he drifted off through the orange-trees.

CHOICE
By Henry G. Lamond

With the first keen touch of winter which came on the endless wind from the south-east, the wild dogs began to seek new habits. The packs split as the bitches roved singly. They sought places which provided good hunting near at hand, which were handy to secluded gorges in which burrows could be dug, places in which a litter of pups could be reared in reasonable safety.

The moon hung half-high, the stars twinkled like chips of illuminated ice, the winds poured in a constant stream, shivering the grey gidyas and shaking the coolabahs on the creeks. A dingo bitch sat on her haunches, merging with her surroundings, as she told her longing in a mournful howl. She pointed her nose to the skies, bellied her cheeks, drew her flanks and poured forth her long-drawn wail of desire. Softly, plaintively, rising and falling, it floated on the air. Mellow, yet crisp, it spread even as ripples widen on water, and almost by its intensity the bitch poured her soul into that call.

The reply came from a thick patch of gidyas at the base of a distant hill. The bitch replied, her call seductively plaintive, alluring, soft yet penetrating. The reply was dominant, bell-like in its clarity, impatient, masterly. The bitch listened, sitting motionless, showing as nothing more solid than a deeper shadow in the shades. The call sounded again. This time it was nearer. She replied softly, rose from her haunches and nervously turned and trotted towards where the call came.

They met. She was timid, sensing her surroundings, trusting to her nose and other finer senses rather than to her eyes, darting from shadow to shadow, hiding behind tree-trunks and rocks ere she showed herself. He was eager, daring yet fearful, and, though he cringed like a snake in open spaces, he stood up boldly and showed himself in the shadows.

He was a red dog with a slash of white over one shoulder—the scar of an old-time wound—massive without being heavy; muscular without being cumbersome. She also was red, with a white tuft on her tail, lithe where he showed strength, quick on her feet, alert to every sound and smell. She hesitated as she went to meet him.

The dog advanced with eager strides, his neck arched, his eyes shining, whimpering softly, his tail held jauntily while his flanks were drawn. She pretended to cringe in terror from him. She offered her nostrils to his; she cowered, almost seeming to shrink in on herself, as the dog towered above her. She submitted him to nose her affectionately, and then, jumping away, she fled, bending her backbone with an exaggerated elastic action as she raced. But she galloped in a circle. No matter by how much she outdistanced her pursuer, she never got any farther away from him.

The dog tired of that game. He dropped to his belly, his forepaws crossed in front of him, laid his jowls on the ground and was motionless. She understood: she, too, dropped to the ground and gazed at him. When the dog rose and came to her she trembled in pretended fear of him; wriggled her four legs helplessly in the air as she rolled; twisted suddenly and bounded to her feet. She picked up an old bone lying on the ground. She clawed at it as she galloped in a circle, tossing it in the air and pouncing on it again as it fell to the ground.

He was expected to play. He did. But he short-cut her on one circle, took her on the ribs with his shoulders, sent her spinning to the ground. The game was over. She picked herself up, looked back at him over her shoulder as she trotted away in the direction of the hills. He had courted her; he had been accepted. He turned and ran by her side.

The pair stopped suddenly as the heavily sweet scent of sheep came to them. They ran up that track in the wind, slipping from place to place almost, it would seem, merely by the power to wish themselves there— no sound was made, no action noticeable, and the dingoes were only discernible when they stood at one vantage-point to pick out the next place at which they would halt.

When they came to the mob the dog swung in with fine abandon. He took one sheep by the throat, left it gasping on the ground. To show his prowess, and to satisfy his killing instinct, he raced up the wing of the stringing sheep and laid body after body in a twitching heap on the grass. When he was satisfied he returned to the bitch. She was starting to tear chunks of flesh from the first sheep he had slain. White Stripe had other notions.

Though he took only a flashing grip in passing, the rich blood which spurted from one particular sheep had tickled his palate. He led the bitch to it, shouldered her from other bodies on which she would feast, ripped the skin from the shoulder of his selected meal, stood back and obviously invited her to eat. She tore slivers of quivering flesh from the warm corpse, gulped them hideously, gorged to swelling obesity. When she had finished, the dog had his turn. He ate till he was bloated, till he gasped as he breathed, till his swollen belly was an ill-balanced thing supported on four legs.

They waddled as they ran together towards the gorge. And they had no more than left the body of the sheep a hundred yards behind them when another dingo showed in front of them.

White Stripe never hesitated. He knew he had to fight for his mate. He launched himself with the suddenness of an arrow released. The dogs reared as they came together, with white fangs clicking as they met, with hot breaths mingling, with hate in their reddened eyes and murder in their hearts. They wrestled for a few seconds as each tested the other's strength; then they dropped to the ground with rumbling growls deep down in each throat. The hair along each back was raised in a bristling hedge; both walked proppily on tiptoes; they were alert; lips drawn back, muscles tensed and taut, they circled each other to seek an opening.

The bitch was interested; more, she was entertained. This was a worth-while spectacle. She sat at the base of a tree, licked her chops, composed herself and prepared to watch her champions fight for her favours.

The dogs sprang simultaneously. There were a pair of blurred red lines drawn in the moonlight, the thud of bodies meeting, the clash of fangs striking. They whirled in an eddy of sprayed dust, a maelstrom of tossed leaves and spurned grass. They slashed and tore, striking with the pecking motions of a snake stabbing. An aura of sprayed blood showered above them; deep breaths came from them; hair and flesh were torn in streaking ribbons.

Then they stood back by mutual agreement. They were panting, dishevelled, with flanks pumping great gallons of fresh air to burning lungs through parched throats. They reeled as they stood; but their eyes were as red as before, their wills as determined.

White Stripe was in a deplorable state. Owing to his recent full feed his breath came in strangling sobs; his glazed eyes rolled; his legs shivered as he shook to the gasp of his pantings. But he was the first to commence the fight again.

He lunged at the other's throat, lunged and ripped, all in one action; then, as the other quivered, he stood with a spray of blood spouting from inside his front

H

leg, with a strip of skin hanging from his shoulder, with the exposed nerves in a raw wound quivering as the air bit them and played on them. He was spent, braced on four widespread legs, exhausted to the point of finality.

Without hesitation the bitch went to the victor. She licked him tenderly, whimpered softly as she told her sympathy, played about him. She lay beside him when he rested; sprang to defend him when any strange movement or sound disturbed her.

As the sky in the east was reddening slightly she coaxed the dog to his feet to follow her. She led the way slowly, picking her way carefully. White Stripe followed. He was sore, stiff, weak from loss of blood, exhausted by his efforts. But he was the victor. He followed his mate as she led him to her home.

As they ran up a broken gully a strange dog stepped out from behind a boulder. He advanced to meet the pair. He was a big fellow, a blue with brindle markings. He approached the bitch, his eyes shining, with a low whimper of desire sounding deep down in his throat. He had but advanced his nostrils to hers and sniffed but once when White Stripe sprang at him— sprang with the same zeal as before, but with a little less of the dash and ginger with which he had commenced his previous fight.

Bluey reared as the other lurched through the air. He caught the red dingo in his arms, wrestled with him while striking his balance. Then he threw the red dog from him and let him roll over and over on the ground while he turned his attention to the bitch.

White Stripe came again to the attack. By all the laws of his caste he had earned his mate—slain for her, fought for her, won her on his merits. And as he charged his sore leg stumbled as he tripped on a pebble. He fell to his chest, skated along the ground. His mate which he had won fawned upon the blue dog which had usurped his place. White Stripe blundered between the two dogs, separating them. He turned to the bitch as he slipped from beneath the charge of Bluey—his eyes had picked up a break in the gully through which they could both dodge, evade the blue fellow and get away.

White Stripe looked back over his shoulder as he slid through the gap in the gully. He half-turned, expecting to find his mate beside him. Then he limped dejectedly from the place, of no further interest to the two dogs on the creek-bed below him. The bitch was fawning upon the new dog, playing before him, inducing him to chase her as she ran from him.

MEMOIRS OF A PROFESSIONAL ESCAPER

By Les Robinson

WE had so often got the sack, either separately or both together, that we were inured to a life of leisure and led it at all times and as often as possible. We had answered innumerable advertisements in the Slaves Wanted column of the newspaper and had been ignored. Pretending to be energetic fatigued us.

We were both of us what, in the back country, are called 'warbs', meaning confirmed and irredeemable loafers. We were experts at dodging responsibility of all possible kinds. We knew all the shortest cuts to all the nearest river-banks; all the best rocks to fish off; all the ways of existing without work, whilst being paid slightly now and then; all the culverts that were within easy walking distance and rainproof. We knew how to 'detain' and cook a fowl that had strayed from someone's backyard, by baking it in wrappings of wet newspaper, under the heaped-up ashes of our camp-fire. We had narrowly escaped prosecution for habitual vagrancy so often that we no longer took to our heels whenever we saw a policeman. Business men disliked us. Men of standing in the community, with some of whom we had gone to school, passed us with the glassy stare that denotes entire lack of recognition plus disapproval.

Metaphorically speaking, we had often asked for bread and been handed stones.

We were the absolute limit in languidity and most dreadful bone-weariness. It was so long since either of us had done what the most languorous would consider a day's work that the memory of it had ceased to be painful. The sight of a horse pulling a heavy load caused us to shudder. If anybody had shouted 'Work!' anywhere near us, in a loud voice, we'd probably have dropped dead. It would have been such a shock to our twin systems.

Lying on our beds of grass, gum leaves, ferns, news-papers, or sand, we dreamt of sofas, sedan-chairs, palanquins, cushioned divans, and sultanesque surroundings.

Town began to bore us. We were sick to death of leaning against veranda posts waiting for something to turn up, and of lying in the parks or, on unfriendly days, of sheltering from the ill-humour of the elements in the reading-room of the Public Library.

Our tattered and torn old clothes had been patched so often that very little of the original material used in their construction remained. A hole in the brim of my companion's weather-stained felt hat attracted the sunbeams. Shining through it on to his hard and scarred visage, they lent this playground of humorous and, at times, cynical smiles a most peculiar and bizarre appearance.

On wet days he covered the hole with a large green Moreton Bay fig-leaf, which he pinned to the felt.

Well, we found one day that we had enough money to take us into the country. Where we got it from I forget. Joe's uncle, the bookmaker, may have sent it to him for a birthday present. Perhaps we would get work out back. Joe said that he had read in the papers that the farmers were becoming impoverished because they couldn't get anybody to do their work for them. For the first time for months we talked about work. We wished to delude ourselves, and, if possible, to imbue each other with the belief that we were earnestly about to seek for it at last. In this we were partially successful, and became most exhilarated at the thought of a change of scene. Joe, in a moment of purposefulness, said he would borrow a sketch-book from a certain friend of his, in case of accidents. I asked him what he meant by accidents. He said, if the landscape proved irresistible from an artistic stand-point, that would be one. He then apologized for having forgotten for the moment that we were about to look for work.

We wandered up into the park to talk matters over. A more perfect day it would be difficult to imagine. The sun smiled tranquilly and there was just that tinge of spring in the air that induces romantic thoughts.

We never seemed to be able to do anything or to go anywhere without considerable argument. Frequently, or nearly always, we disagreed with each other's theories and contentions so persistently that the argument, on the instalment principle, lasted for months.

On this occasion, birds were responsible for an unusually prompt decision.

Joe had been gazing aimlessly round him as usual, and for some few moments had been staring intently at the sky.

'Watch where they go,' he said suddenly.

'Where what go?' I queried.

'Those birds,' he replied.

'What birds?' I said.

'See that cloud up there, the one that looks like a mountain of petrified cigarette smoke?'

'Yes.'

'Well, just above it. There! Now watch where I'm pointing.'

'Over there?' I hazarded.

'No, bonehead, no! Up there! Up! Up! Up! Higher still!'

Then I saw them, mere specks in immensity.

'Well?' I said.

'Ducks,' said Joe.

'Can't hear them quacking,' I replied.

'They're luckier than me,' growled Joe. 'They can't hear you.'

'Which way are they going?'

'South-west,' said Joe.

'Let us follow them,' I said. 'I'm extremely fond of duck.'

So we followed them. All the way up in the train Joe talked. He laughed derisively at the idea that a man was master of his fate and captain of his soul— his own soul. He became extremely wordy concerning the influence of environment on character, which the individual struggled against, but vainly. Any remarks I made merely added fuel to the fire. 'Striving uselessly for the unattainable,' he said, 'unless under exceptionally favourable circumstances, merely wore a man out just as he had arrived at an age when he should be more fully appreciative of life's pleasures than at any other period of his existence. How did I think the world would end?'

I did not know, and, shortly after saying so, fell asleep. When I woke again, about an hour later, Joe was still talking.

'It is a singular thing,' he said, apropos, evidently, of a chapter on natural history, 'that the favourite fluid beverage of seagulls, which are supposedly intelligent, should be salt water.'

'What does that prove?' I asked.

'It proves,' said Joe, 'that the sagacity of the seagull has been greatly overrated.'

Looking out of the window, there was nothing to be seen but gum-trees. If there had been anything else to see, you wouldn't have been able to see it. Gum-trees would have prevented you. There were millions of them, stretching for hundreds, if not thousands, of miles. Then the train ran past some partially cleared land, with here and there, at more and more infrequent intervals, a lonely-looking shanty, the kind of a shanty in which loose boards, loose screws, and loose nails would be prevalent, and loose sheets of iron that would rattle in windy weather. There would be cracks stuffed with ancient yellowed newspapers, leaks under which treacle tins and kerosene-tin buckets would have to be stood when it rained. Some, if not all, of the windows would be the non-opening kind; and there would be wasps' nests in their sashes and in the keyhole of the door; white ants' nests in the floor and walls; swallows' nests under the veranda and wherever else the roof projected; spiders' nests in the upper top ceiling corners; more spiders' nests; fowls' nests; rats' nests, lizards' nests and beetles' nests underneath the creaking floor.

Coloured Christmas supplements from weekly papers, depicting the delights of a rural existence, would be pasted on the walls. There would be a large sheet of looking-glass, in a frame made of corks or of corn-cobs, glued three deep all round it, and nailed to the wall above the fireplace in the living-room. There would be a noisy man who shuffled his feet when up and about, and snored frightfully all the rest of the time, and a hard-featured, garrulous, and heavy-footed woman; a galah parrot; an anaemic-looking, asthmatic, and watery-eyed cat; wailing infants, probably, and a dog that howled at night.

Gaunt and stark, round all such shanties, stood tall, dead, and spectral trees, inhabited by grey-plumaged, silent birds that resembled animate pieces of bark.

The occupants of the shanties were nowhere to be seen. Tired, doubtless, by working incessantly, they were, we concluded, lying down asleep on their packing-case beds and sofas.

I began to feel depressed, I did not know why, and to wish that we were back in our cave in the scrub by the sea.

Joe began a dissertation on the many and varied uses of the gum-tree and the curative virtues of eucalyptus. This deepened my depression.

Just as I was dozing off again, we reached our destination. I felt no desire to get out of the train. Neither did Joe. We got out, nevertheless, and looked around us helplessly. We had half a mind to wait on the platform for a train back, but reminded each other that we were about to look for work. There would be no train for Sydney, the porter informed me, until next day. This strengthened us in the determination to proceed with our quest.

They told us at the hotel that there was a dairy-farmer at Kidgewidgee Creek, about six miles from the railway station, and that he wanted several hands. We decided to walk out and see him.

'It's no good hurrying,' said Joe.

'Of course not,' I replied.

When we had walked about a mile and a half, we saw such an excellent place—or we thought we did—to camp for the night, that we decided not to go any further.

'We'll see him first thing in the morning,' said Joe.

'Not too early,' I suggested. 'It would be better to wait until he has milked all the cows, delivered the milk to the butter factory, and fed his pigs, fowls and foals. We'll catch him just when he is going back to bed for the rest of the day.'

Joe, for once, raised no objection. His suggestion that we should see the man first thing in the morning was only half-hearted. It lacked sincerity.

We camped for the night in what looked like a battlefield where two armies of trees had been fighting, leaving the dead and the wounded to lie where they fell. Huge logs, stumps, shattered branches, and fragments of bark littered the ground in all directions, and in the dim light of evening took on a fantastic appearance, seeming almost to glower at us menacingly. To prove its resentment at our intrusion, a branch I tripped over barked my shin, and a root waited for Joe, giving no indication of its presence until it hurt his toe when he blundered on to it. Joe's language was awful to listen to.

After our evening meal, which consisted of tinned herrings in tomato sauce, some bread and cheese we'd brought with us, and a billy of tea, Joe accused me of being a futile fellow who led others into undergoing unnecessary fatigue. My address in reply, followed by Joe's endeavours to prove that my views on things in general were nearly all wrong-headed, whereas his own were 'those held by intellectual people whose attainments are such as to command the respect of the serious-minded and the studious', together with several of those long-winded, personal reminiscences of his, which are so unlimited numerically and so varied in character as to seem like the experiences and recollections of half a dozen different kinds of men, made us both feel sleepy.

We were awakened during the night by scuffling bandicoots and by some nocturnal bird with a long-drawn-out, mournful cry; or was it the voice of the locality wailing for forgiveness?

At daylight we were again aroused, not by one bird, but by hundreds, shrieking, laughing, chattering, twittering, squawking, singing, screaming, cawing, squabbling, chasing one another; flying on to and off the trees round about us, hovering and swooping, darting hither and thither in the fallen timber; hurtling this way, then, at top speed, back again; as volatile as dreams and fancies; quickly speeding, whole flocks of them, full of excitement, full of intensity, feverishly flittering, exultant, inconsequent, ecstatic.

'Birds,' said Joe, poking his head out from under his coat, which he had used as a blanket, 'have been unduly praised by poets and romanticists. While useful to man, perhaps, in some ways, they are nothing but a source of annoyance to him in others. The inventor of the aphorism "A bird in the hand is worth two in the bush" was either an unparalleled self-deceptionist, meant wilfully to be misleading, or had been grossly deceived by incompetent observers. A bird in the hand can be controlled, but a bird allowed to wander at will in the bush wastes much of its time in senseless ejaculation, and in flying haphazardly from one tree to another. Notable for uselessly tiring themselves in this way, and for incessantly rearing families, with a view to filling the universe with birds, as though birds were not already far too plentiful, who could possibly regard these feathered creatures otherwise than with a scornful kind of pity?'

'It would be hard to say,' I said.

'Do you know,' said Joe, frowning, 'that you are the most abjectly ignorant man I've ever met in the whole course of my life?'

Ants, flies, and spiders trooped towards where we lay. They thought we'd been presented to them by the Almighty and they came to measure us and to arrange for our removal. They were jubilant, and concluding, no doubt, that we were about to be sold at auction among them, were keen to sample different parts of us before bidding.

We had to get up at last.

Joe was most irritable. He said that I was a dilettante as well as a futilitarian; that all such persons were nothing more than warts on the good nature of society; that I seemed to pride myself on being consistent when consistency was nothing so much as a virtue of fools, that, unless one wished to do without everything perpetually that most people enjoyed having, it was necessary to emulate certain kinds of fish and reptiles that were able to change colour as expediency, or their immediate environment, demanded.

Only, instead of changing colour, one should change one's views. To remain inflexible of purpose, when flexibility of it meant comfort and the elimination of fatigue, was to be considered, and most justly so, deficient in sagacity. Life, he reminded me, is not a supremely delightful hall of glamorous illusions, as I, at all times, with irritating erroneousness, seemed to imagine, through which one strolls aimlessly, with the pleased and fatuous smile that denotes inability to think and to differentiate between the actual and the non-existent or wholly imaginary.

'What is it then?' I asked.

'It is a gigantic shop-window,' said Joe, 'stuffed with everything we want but can't have, because our pockets are empty.'

'Why are our pockets empty?'

'They're empty,' said Joe, 'because we're both of us especially gifted for some occupation not yet invented.'

'Such as trapping silver-fish in a sack factory,' I suggested.

'More arduous, perhaps, than you imagine. In which case we'd be almost sure to get the sack.'

'If the nights were at all cold,' I said, 'we could be relied upon to get several.'

'As far as jobs go,' said Joe, 'there is only one that would be likely to suit me.'

'Guessing is a bore,' I said. 'What is the ideal job?'

'Breaking in sofas for the worn-out backs of the wealthy,' Joe replied.

'It's time we saw the dairy-farmer,' I said, 'and, in

exchange for a small trifle weekly, offered him our services.'

'Don't you think it would be better to wait until this evening? He'd have finished work for the day then,' said Joe, 'and would be more inclined to talk to us.'

'No,' I said. 'If we start now, we'll just catch him as he's getting out of bed to have his lunch. Refreshed by several hours' repose, he'd be likely to have forgotten his annoyance, for the time being, with an occupation that necessitates rising at dawn, and would therefore be almost good-humoured enough to treat us with civility.'

So we started and, without once lying down to rest, walked, with pretended tirelessness, along a dray-made track, in the blisterous heat. We were pursued by countless carnivorous flies, and annoyed by the incessant repetition of the same incoherent phrase by hundreds of leather-lunged birds.

Topping a rise, we came in sight, at last, of Kidgewidgee Creek and the farm sloping down to it.

There wasn't a cow to be seen.

'Wonder where they are?' said Joe.

'Up in the ranges at the back, most likely,' I said.

'We'll go down, anyway,' said Joe listlessly.

The place seemed deserted. No smoke ascended from the chimney. No dog barked. All was as silent and motionless as the reflections of the she-oaks in the creek.

Scribbled in chalk, on the back door of the ramshackle domicile, was the following :—

THIS FARM FOR SALE. SEE THE MISSUS AT TOM'S PLACE, OR ME WHEN I COME OUT OF THE HORSPITTAL.

BILL BUTLER.

I expected to be sworn at; to be told that men like

I

me were a nuisance to everybody—particularly to their friends—and, by reason of their accursed ineptitude, a menace to households and communities, that to follow such men, to listen to their advice, or to allow oneself to be influenced by them in the slightest degree, was simply to court discomfort and disaster. But, much to my surprise, Joe seemed not displeased. In fact, his spirits were unmistakably rising. He appeared to shed the depression occasioned by fear that he might have to work, a fear that had darkened his thoughts all the tramp through the morning.

'We'd have been roused out of bed before daylight, wet or fine, to milk all the cows,' he observed. 'And we'd have had to find them first, in about two thousand five hundred acres of mountain-side, and that would have tired us exceedingly.'

OUR NEW PROPERTIES
By James Hackston

A FEW hundred acres! We'd have sheep and a wind-mill—especially a windmill; it stamps a place. Father got a sheet of drawing-paper and measured off our acres with a footrule, then with strokes of the pen fenced it. Next he inspected the paper for a spot to build on. Choosing a site on which to build a house requires much foresight. 'Must have the right out-look.' When we'd strolled over the paper and finally chosen the exact location, he got a set-square, pencil and rule and erected the house. It had a wide veranda round three sides of it like a squatter's, so that he could sit and watch his burgeoning property;

sheep turning out wool and mutton, the grass putting on condition, and the sun or the rain hard at it, according to which shift they were on.

Afterwards I got the pen and, with a family of fat, prosperous-looking dots, stocked the place with sheep. It was a great feeling to jump suddenly from our very small roadside cottage to a squatter-like home with acres. I was proud of the new home with the long row of big pine-trees that my father had planted with a row of crosses. People would say, 'See those big pines; that's where they live.' He next made a road from the front fence to the house, and then with a few deft strokes of the pen put up a most impressive front gate so that people could say, 'Go in by the big front gate, and drive on until you come to the homestead.'

My father addressed most of his remarks concerning our new place to me and not to my mother. We would sit of a night going into details, my mother saying nothing, while she patched the children's clothes, or fought valiantly with a darning-needle to conquer the holes in Father's worn-out socks. From sixteen to hundreds of acres was a big rise in life, and we soon forgot our old home. I could almost hear the windmill clanking.

Now that Father was a station-owner, he, of course, looked down on gold-mining. He'd be a miner no more, he said; he'd finance the venture some other way. With this backsliding on his old self the two big red books on metallurgy (six instalments behind) that had dominated our mantelpiece were evacuated to a little shelf in a corner. In their place was a new volume on sheep-raising; the book, standing up, title showing, proclaiming to the world that Father was a sheep man.

Then one night Father shoved the lambing season

on and our flock increased. The fat, round dots on the paper lambed in the comfort of our room, without loss. No crows perched on the rafters overhead; there were no prowling foxes under the table, or wild dogs skulking behind the sofa. Next night we sheared, too, without having the expense of feeding our champion shearers like fighting cocks.

We were getting on well when Father came across an article in a paper in which it said that sheep up north were dying for want of feed, and that squatters were facing ruin. 'Most discouraging,' he said. 'A most depressing article.' Then he leaned back and looked into space. 'You know, this sheep business has its drawbacks; it's not all beer and skittles. In fact, I think it might be a good idea if I went in for something not quite so risky.'

That was the end of the station. I rolled it up and shoved it away on the back shelf—deserted. Mother said it was too bad Father having to walk off the property like that; and just when we were all getting settled, too. But he took no notice. He'd go in for something smaller; an orchard—just enough land to keep us comfortably, without ostentation. This time we'd have cows, poultry and pigs as well, and, as if to buck us up after our recent loss, he promised us poultry on the table, tons of fresh eggs, and cream and gallons of milk for the children. 'Just think how they'll thrive! And we'll have a regular income—the orchard itself will see to that.' When my mother asked him how he was going to find such a haven of milk and honey he said (making a note of bees, too, and their output) that there were lots of small properties, places with a good house, orchard planted, land fenced and cleared—no untamed selection in fiercely timbered bush—waiting to be worked scientifically. And it would be easier to finance the smaller concern. The loss of the big pines was a blow to me, but Father's picture of an orchard exploding with blossom and then fruit softened the loss.

As an orchardist he was an even greater success than he had been as a sheep man, for that same night— when he gave up the station—he pruned, sprayed, admired the blossom and picked the fruit. You could almost eat the luscious fruit off our table and see the rosy glow of health coming to our cheeks. And, with Father's promised glut of good things for the table, the children must have been putting on weight in anticipation. Before going to bed that night he had disposed of his crop and got his cheque, and all without one ha'p'orth of worry.

Then one day, having to go into the town about a small, welcome job (putting up some shelves for a shopkeeper), Father said as we drew flush with a land-agent's office, 'Shakespeare's right. There is a tide in the affairs of men which, taken at the flood, leads on to fortune.' And letting himself go with his tide he flowed in the agent's door, saying as he went, 'No harm in making a few inquiries, is there—even if we haven't the money yet—so long as I don't sign anything?'

I hung round the entrance door listening, and when I heard him tell them that he was looking for a property to buy, and—out to make a good impression, as usual—that it was to be a 'cash transaction', I thought he was certainly taking things at the flood. I saw him instantly swirled away from the counter like a twig in a swollen stream and carried ruthlessly on and into the inner sanctum, where the door slammed behind him.

After I'd waited a long time outside he ebbed out

looking swamped, with a big man pumping him up and down in a parting, very friendly handshake.

'Forceful fellow,' he said, joining me. 'A gentleman, though; and he treated me as one, too. Wanted me to inspect a place to-day, but I told him I had some important business to do at the bank.'

'Bank!' I said.

'Yes,' he said, seeing my look. 'Might as well put a bold front on it—you never know what might turn up.' Then he looked helplessly at me. 'He made me promise to call back and see him on Monday though, at twelve sharp, to—er—view a place. But I can't very well go as far as that, can I? Unless . . .' and he looked up longingly at the heavens. Nearing home he said, 'I had to give him my address, of course, and when I—er—don't turn up on Monday and he writes to me give me the letter on the quiet; I don't want Mother to know—not yet.'

He got the letter—something unforeseen must have cropped up to prevent his keeping the appointment and would he kindly make another appointment to view the property? 'Perhaps I should have waited a while before making inquiries—not been so hasty.' He burnt the letter. A few days later another one came. 'Oh,' he said as he read it, 'what a pity. He says here that this place is just the kind of property I'm looking for, but'—he sighed—'what's the use of my looking at it when I haven't a feather to fly with—not for the moment, anyway.' He paused. 'But, all the same, I would like to see it; you know it would give me some idea on which to base my future plans. But there you are, for the moment it's not opportune, is it? No use getting too entangled with things until I feel my feet on firmer ground—still, it's most tempting.' This letter found the fire, too, unanswered.

My mother now came back to the business of the shopkeeper's shelves and asked Father when he was going to clinch the job, so we tidied ourselves and set off for town again, Father saying he'd better give the agent's place a wide berth—for the time being; must not view any property yet, not in any circumstances— might become involved in some way. But the fates would have it otherwise; we ran into the agent driving along the road. 'Quick, duck!' Father hissed. But in the same breath he countermanded the order. 'No, he's seen us.' He then strode forward openly and gallantly to meet the agent as he bore down on us.

The agent didn't look put out as I thought he would, but on the contrary was all smiles, and again took Father's hand and nearly shook his teeth out.

'Been called away on business?' he asked pleasantly.

'Er—yes,' said my father; 'and just got back to-day.' Then, as an excuse for not keeping the appointment, 'I was—er—on my way in now to see you.'

Father was evidently not the only man in the district who gathered strength from Mr. Shakespeare. The agent must have also believed that there is a tide in the affairs of men which should be taken at the flood, for before you could say Jack Robinson he had whisked us up into his turnout and was bowling us along the road at such a breakneck speed that Father could not have escaped had he wished to.

'Lucky we met, wasn't it?' said the agent, as the trees and fences danced past us in a dizzy row. 'Instead of you wasting all this time getting to my office, here you are on your way to view the property.'

'Yes,' said my father lamely, looking down on the road and to the sides of it as if at any moment he might make a sudden, desperate dash for freedom.

Things had now suddenly changed to reality. First Father viewed the orchard, passing along the lines of trees like a general taking the salute, stopping and staring at odd ones. Had you seen him you'd have almost expected him to salute. Next the rest of the place stood to attention, Father picking up clods of earth and inspecting them as he went along, as he used to pick up bits of quartz and spit on them and look for signs of gold. I was hoping he wouldn't forget himself and spit on the clods of earth by mistake. The house was then put through its paces, and as we stalked it I saw their kids peeping wonder-eyed from one of the windows—they'd been shut up in a rear room while the man with the money looked at their home.

We had not long been inspecting the place before Father had completely forgotten that he hadn't a feather to fly with, and was imagining himself as its new owner. He beamed on everything, talked and showed such interest and evident satisfaction that I saw the agent looking at the owner and the owner looking at the agent. Then the man went away and brought his wife out. I reckoned he'd rushed in to her and said 'I think it's sold!' the way she came and smiled on Father.

Then Father, finding himself in their front room, with the wife looking hopefully into his face, the man fiddling with his fingers as if handling the money my father hadn't got, and the agent with one eye cocked at the ceiling counting up how much of it would be his commission—well, Father looked at this moment as if he'd have liked the floor to give way or an earthquake destroy everything. He could not say now that the place was not what he wanted, so what could he do but say that he would have to think it over. Pressed, he wanted a fortnight to decide. I thought of the poor owner and his poor wife spending that fortnight—waiting. I hoped they wouldn't get into debt in advance.

When we got home Father told Mother that he expected to hear from the shopkeeper (whom he had not seen) in about a week's time.

When I asked him later what he was going to do when the fortnight was up, he again looked longingly at the heavens and told me never to cross my bridges until I came to them; that one never knew what might happen in the meantime; a man could be poor to-day and well off tomorrow. He ended up with his comforting 'While there's life there's hope.'

Next day, by way of giving hope a hand (not having found the 'other way' of financing it), he again went up to One Stump Hill with the sole and steadfast objective of getting out of that gaunt, bitter, selfish hill the tempting orchard property.

The agent, a tide-and-flood man, too, did not let the long fortnight crawl by. One afternoon when Father had come home tired and dusty, and had taken his boots off and gone into the bedroom to have a rest, the agent called. As it turned out, Mother thought he was the shopkeeper come to see Father about the shelves job, and wishing to be nice to him asked him in, and then called out to Father.

Father, suddenly awakened, flustered and not knowing that there was anybody in the front room, did not put his boots on again, and stepping through the cane curtains came face to face with the agent. He looked flabbergasted; then, suddenly becoming conscious of the fact that he was in his socks, he reddened up with anger and mortification. I reckoned that he saw at that moment, in his mind's eye (he didn't dare look at them), his white toes poking out brazenly and shamelessly from—as it would happen that day—his most destitute-looking pair of socks.

The agent also looked a bit bewildered. Watching him, I saw him try not to see Father's socks, looking away quickly as if he did not wish to have his faith and confidence shattered. His eyes sought something more heartening and he looked hurriedly to the left.

Unfortunately, they came right into line with the old couch where the spring poked through. Refusing to see the couch he turned his eyes to the end of the room, where was our old moth-eaten armchair. Hurriedly he stampeded his eyes away from this fresh evidence of our poverty, and escaped to the floor, where the bare boards with the small square of worn lino hit him in the eye. But he wasn't yet beaten, and his escaping eyes turned to the ceiling, where there'd be nothing else to shake his sorely tried confidence. But there was no ceiling; only rafters, cobwebs, and a tarantula stalking flies. He pulled some papers out of his pocket and kept looking at them to keep his morale up, as if not daring to let his eyes escape again. Staring at the papers, he told Father that he had felt (you'll notice the 'had') that, as Father had been so satisfied with the place, he had probably made up his mind by this time to buy it.

Then he looked gingerly up from the papers, keeping his eyes in check, and forced a smile, as if having just made up his mind that people who look hard up are not always so.

Father was still standing in the same spot during these few seconds, as if not daring to move; held spellbound by his feet. All hope, tide taken at the flood and you never know what might turn up were now gone, and he looked now as if he hadn't a feather to fly with. The holes in his socks had submerged him. I knew what was in his mind. He had been found out —disgraced. What was the use of his pretending? He knew that. It would be just as well for him to finish the matter and get it over. 'Oh, about the property,' he said. 'Well, I'm sorry to have given you so much trouble, but—er—well, the deal's off.'

The agent never said a word.

'Anyway, for the time being,' Father went on. 'Yes; for the moment it's definitely off.'

The agent's eyes found my father's.

Father stumbled on, 'However, when the time is ripe I shall——' But he didn't get any further, for suddenly, maliciously and cruelly the agent looked deliberately and despicably at Father's seven naked toes. Then he looked nastily at the sofa, snobbishly at the armchair, disdainfully at the floor and unbelievably at the rafters, cobwebs and the tarantula, and at last, focusing his hard eyes on those seven toes, he put his papers back in his pocket and left.

There was no parting friendly handshake this time. When the agent got outside he turned and looked our little weather-beaten kipsie over, as if to prove to himself that his first impression had been right and that he had been a mug. And just before he got up into his turnout he stopped and gave the place a long, contemptuous stare.

'Well,' said my mother, 'how did all this come about?'

'Oh, quite simply,' said Father. 'I was passing his place and saw no harm in making a simple inquiry. You know, there is a tide in the affairs of——'

'I know,' said Mother, 'which, taken at the flood,

and so on. Well, all I can say is that it was a great pity the author didn't put a PS. to it and say something about drowning as well. It would save some people a lot of trouble and waste of time.'

Father said that perhaps, after all, it would be better for him to keep on as he was going. When all was said and done there'd be more money in his inventions. For instance, there was his deep-sea diving-dress. No diver at present could go down more than a certain depth, whereas his diving-dress would enable a diver to go down to the very depths of the ocean deep. Mother was looking hard at him. 'And as you know, Mother, there's billions of pounds of bullion and valuables lying in old wrecks at the bottom of the sea. Why, there's a veritable fortune waiting for the man who——'

'What about the shelves job, Walter?' she said.

I think Father must have seen some look in Mother's eye, for he said suddenly, 'Oh, yes, I must see to that job at once. The diving-dress invention can—er—wait for the moment.' That same afternoon he toddled off to town to see about the shelves job.

After he had gone, I was out in the backyard, and while I was gawking about there Mother came out and began to look about the place. It was looking pretty untidy now. I used to rake up all the rubbish and keep the yard and surroundings nice and tidy, but of late I'd neglected it all, and it was beginning to look as if nobody lived in it. Then I reckoned I saw the look in Mother's eyes that Father must have seen, so I toddled off, too, and got the rake and began to spruce up the old home again.

THE DINKUM AUSTRALIAN
By Harley Matthews

For Private Frederick Pearson there was only one
country in the world—Australia. The most favoured
locality in all that glorious land was Sandy Creek.
'But you should see the grass at Sandy Creek—the
gums,' he would say. The goannas there were almost
like the crocodiles of the Northern Territory. Sandy
Creek rabbit-skins brought the highest prices of all.
So the tent, and afterwards the battalion, called him
Sandy.

As their stay in Egypt lengthened, his outlook
widened. No longer did Sandy delight merely to
compare one locality against another. Now it was
Australia against the rest of the world—Egypt
generally, as that was the land responsible for their
hardships and, as it appeared to most Australians then,
their unrenown.

'Should White Australia defend Black Egypt?'
demanded Sandy one evening. They were sitting in
the tent, on their equipments, just back from a long
desert march.

The others said nothing. They had uttered the same
disgust many times before—particularly this day
while returning to camp through the sandstorm.

Scotty came into the tent, cool, fresh, and clean. He
had only joined the battalion about a week now—one
of the reinforcements—but he had proved to be the
oldest soldier of the lot. Let Scotty hear there was to be
a big day and he would 'go sick' to get a job with the
armourer sergeant cleaning rifles.

'And have ye had a nice quiet day?' Scotty asked

the dusty, perspiring, listless faces. He was grinning derisively, but Sandy wanted an answer to that question of his, and Scotty, the unwearied, was the only one likely to give it.

'Should White Australia defend Black Egypt?' he demanded again.

'If those in the high command expect it of you it's your duty to defend fellow-subjects,' Scotty answered weightily. 'But, anyway, the Australians will never make soldiers. They're not disciplined.'

'No; and they don't go sick or fall out the first mile,' said Bill Adams.

'But, Bill, we would if we were disciplined—like Scotty,' Diablo said.

'Look here!' said Sandy, lifting his head up and sighting Scotty along his thin nose. He was proud of that nose—not for its beauty, but all the family at Sandy Creek had it. 'We came away to fight, not to——'

'No, you did not,' Scotty interrupted. 'You came to do your duty by the Motherland and for the great Empire and to uphold the honour of the glorious old flag.'

'Rot!' cried Sandy. 'We came for a fight, and for Australia.'

Scotty's fat face flared up. 'The man who says he didn't come to do his duty by his king and country and the glorious old flag is no man at all,' he howled. 'He's a traitor.'

'Well, I came to fight,' said Sandy fiercely. 'What did you come for?'

'To do my duty like a loyal soldier. And to put some good British stamina and discipline into the Australian Army. That's why Captain Mac put me in this tent. He knew what you were badly in need of.'

That got them all talking—wearied out as they were. There were shouts of: 'Australia for us!' and a voice crying: 'Bonny Scotland and the Highlanders!' and further shouts of: 'Wait until the Australians get into action.' Above it all boomed Sandy's demand: 'What's Scotland to do with us? This is the Australian Army.'

Scotty pointed a scornful finger at him. 'And ye're glad to be known by a Scottish name,' he said— 'Sandy.'

'Scottish!' yelled Sandy. 'That's Australian if anything is. There are hundreds of Sandy Creeks at home.'

'And they're all called after one great Scotsman. It shows how the stamina of the race triumphs wherever it goes.'

So fierce and bitter did the dispute become that Scotty was not in the party that afterwards moved off to the canteen. All through the song and merriment of that evening there was much doubting and wondering in the mind of Sandy—was that right about his name?

He spoke at last. 'Anyway, you're not going to call me Sandy any more,' he said.

But somehow the name stuck.

At last it appeared that White Australia was going to be allowed to fight. On the ships in harbour and on the green slopes of Lemnos Island it was waiting and preparing for the day.

'It can't be long, now,' Diablo would say. 'Did you see the revolver that long Lanky Mac was wearing when we were ashore? It's got a barrel as long as his arm.'

'Must be the one he had when he was fighting in

Mexico,' said Sandy. 'He's fought in every war there's been.'

'That's a Scotsman for you,' said Scotty.

'He's an Australian,' Sandy asserted.

'A Scot!'

'An Australian, I tell you.' And that was as close to an agreement as ever they got.

'Ah!' the Old Man would say as they sat on a hill during a spell in their practice manœuvres. 'Where would you see a sky like that? Look at the green of that grass. And those dear little youngsters playing about. Look at those sheep on the hill over there. It's the most beautiful place I've ever seen.'

'I've seen better,' Sandy began. 'You ought to see the gums around Sandy Creek—and the paddocks there after the rain. And the sheep there—why there are thousands and thousands of them.'

'All the same, look at that big, long, lanky Mac looking at those sheep over there,' Bill Adams directed. 'He's wondering what they'd be like to shear. I knew I'd seen him in a shed outback once. That's why when he joined up his toes were sticking out of his boots. If ever I strike him in the same shed again I'll see that he gets all the old wrinkly rams to shear, the ——.' Bill never forgot when Lanky Mac had once, as O.C., fined him three days' pay.

Three days later. 'Wooish—crash!' warned the shrapnel on the crest continually as they struggled up the first hill off the beach. Lanky Mac was leading them, a pack on his back like the rest, that long revolver in his hand. Half-way up, he looked back. His men were some feet beneath him, struggling and pulling themselves up as best they could. Big as he was, he was already feeling the weight of that useless pack, and he did not, like the men, have to carry 300 rounds of ball amunition.

'Boys,' he called, 'off with these things.' He undid the straps and let his pack fall to the ground. The men did the same—gladly.

'Who'll volunteer to stay behind—to collect and guard them?'

'I will, sir.' That was Scotty. And Scotty it was who stayed behind. No one else had spoken.

'That's good old British stamina for you,' Sandy muttered to the boy Diablo as they lay under the ridge.

'Open the breeches for your rifles to cool,' Lanky Mac shouted.

'And how about the Australians' discipline now?' said Diablo as he looked at the intent faces on either side of him.

A week later Sandy, Bill Adams, and Diablo were walking back along the beach, their water-bottles swung around them. Bill carried an empty pack in his hand.

'Scotty might have done his duty for his king and country,' Bill said. 'But he forgot all about his mates.'

'Not an overcoat or a fag left,' Sandy growled.

They had been fighting ever since the day of the landing. This was the first time they could get away to recover their packs. They had found Scotty sitting in a hole dug in the hillside. They dragged him out to ask what had become of their property, but all they could get from him was: 'Terrible. Oh, it's terrible.' Their packs had been opened, everything they had wanted was gone—taken by the men who had landed afterwards. The rest was scattered about and trampled into the earth.

'They've been bombarding me night and day. Oh, it's terrible,' Scotty had moaned.

'Anyway,' said Diablo, as they walked along the beach now, 'we've had a good drink of water and our bottles are full.'

After that Sandy blamed the British nation and its army for all the failures. 'If there had been Australians at Cape Helles instead of Tommies, we'd have been in Constantinople now.' He said that and other hard things so often that when they heard that Scotty had gone to hospital with rheumatism he could say nothing. But it convinced him; so that when he was wounded he repeated his convictions on the hospital ship. He told them what he thought in the hospital in London—told the visitors even. To his disgust they were rather amused at him for it. 'We have heard about you Australians. How fond you are of pretending,' they said. 'All the time you know our men are splendid.'

What could a man say to that? And he had to admit that some of the Jocks and Tommies from France were fine fellows. They would do anything for him as he lay with his leg in splints, helpless. One night a Jock, back from a tea-party, brought him in a nip of Scotch. Still, when it came to fighting there was only one soldier in the world—the Australian. Next to him came—no, not the Jock or Tommy, nor the French poilu, but Jacko Turk. Because he had made a stand against the Australians at times.

Some evenings fellow-Australians would come round his bed. No one knew him there, and he let the name of Sandy remain unknown. 'Cobber,' they would say, 'the girls here are all right. You ought to see the crowds of them down the street. They stand out there looking up at the windows, and we throw notes with our names and ward numbers to them. Then next day they come in and ask the sister if they can take us out to tea. It'll do me—this country for the duration. Pity you can't get up yet. Couldn't we give some of them your name and they could come in and see you? They'd bring you in fags—anything you want. Then you can take your pick out of twenty or so, and you're fixed for a girl on your furlough. They stick like wattle-gum—the girls here.'

'The Australian girls will do me every time,' said Private Pearson. 'Australia for the Australians and Australian girls for the Australian soldiers. That's what I say.'

'That's all right,' they would tell him. 'But you might as well have a good time while you can.'

'I'll have it in Australia,' he replied.

At last he was hobbling about on a stick. Then he was out on furlough. London and its storied corners and its historic piles—'*poof!*' The Houses of Parliament were not bad—they might look well if they were at the new Federal capital in Australia.

Then, a few months afterwards, to France. There nothing suited except the fighting. The cobbled roads were only made to give blisters to Australian soldiers. Always it was either snowing or raining; why, as a country, Egypt even was better.

But in France he had to admit that the Jocks and Tommies could fight at times. They didn't have the dash of the Australians in the hop-over, and when it came to holding out to the last, he knew whom he'd sooner be with.

'There,' he said one day, as he worked his Lewis gun, 'Tommies wouldn't have it in them to wait till the Fritzes got close and shoot 'em down like this.'

'Rat-tat-tat-tat,' replied his mate's gun alongside.

Then—Sandy can only surmise what had happened

—he found himself floating in the air. He felt as big as a sausage balloon. Everything below seemed pygmy-size. The smoke from the ground rushed up at him and bore him higher. Another shell exploded below him noiselessly. He seemed to be floating about for a long time. Then he grew rigid and fell.

When he woke three days later he could just see with one eye. The rest of him was bandages. A sister was busy at a table at the foot of his bed. An English sister, he noticed. Then he remembered floating about in the air, that time. The sister looked up. 'You must keep very quiet,' she said softly.

A couple of days afterwards he was well enough to learn that he was in an English hospital—in the provinces this time. He was the only Australian there, the sister told him—the only one that had ever been in that town. People, absurdly interested, came to see him. He didn't mind that. It gave him a chance to tell them about Australia—what a wonderful place it was. Why, where he came from, Sandy Creek . . .

He certainly interested them. Even the nurses were always talking to him about Australia—especially the first one he had seen.

'She be a pretty one—the ward sister,' a Tommy patient said to him one evening.

'Oh, not bad. But you ought to see the girls in Australia.'

'There'll have to be a bit of skin-grafting done here,' the doctor said one morning, as the pretty sister lifted the bandages from his face. 'Here, and right along here.'

Next day she brought some new instruments to the table at his bedside. The doctor clapped something to his nostrils and he remembered no more. When he awoke his face was feeling stiff in patches—particularly along his nose. 'Taken beautifully—every graft,' the doctor said a few days later. 'A week or so and you can leave the bandages off, Sister.'

More and more visitors flocked in to see him. What with being the only Australian soldier the town had had in their hospital, and the wonderful surgery that had been performed on his face, he was the wonder of the country. He was sick of answering questions—even about Australia.

At last the sister let him look in a glass. There was a big patch of colour on one cheek, and his nose was red —a merry, shining red. It made him grin to see it— until he thought, 'They'll never believe in Australia that I didn't have a good time in England with a nose like that! Looks as if I'd been on a spree without stopping ever since I left school.'

People—girls, women, and old men—crowded in to see him. The locker by his bed was crammed with gifts—cigarettes, sweets, and books. Though he divided the spoils royally amongst them, some of the Tommy patients grew jealous of all this attention.

'Anyhow, what's Australia?' one of them said one night, as they sat by the ward stove.

'I'm Australian and proud of it,' Sandy replied.

'But it's all British blood in you,' two or three told him.

'I was born in Australia, and so were my two grandfathers. I'm Australian—every bit of me.'

A Tommy laughed. 'All except your nose,' he said. 'That's English, anyway.'

He thought this rather brutal. 'It might be a bit red,' he defended, 'but——'

'Yah. Most of it belongs to the pretty sister,' the Tommy kept on.

'*What?*'

'Well, it's her skin they've grafted on to your nose, isn't it?'

He had never thought of it that way—he had only worried about the colour. Still it must be true, what the Tommy said, he thought. She did have a very fresh complexion. Not all Australian! What had he to be proud of now?

'You! Australian?' the Tommies jeered at him, sitting silent.

He could say nothing. What he did do was to marry the pretty sister four months later. He doesn't have so much to say about Australia now.

THE PISÉ HOUSE
By BRIAN JAMES

A LONG time ago, Peter Browne built a house. Great fellow was Peter, a good deal different from the rest of us, and something of a poet. Some of the young fellows said Peter was a bit queer—a wide term to account for any degree of difference. Perhaps Peter *was* queer.

On Sundays and holidays Peter would take his Winchester ·32 and stride off for the hills, and as like as not would spend the time on some high point gazing down on the wide valley, shaped like a saucer, with the blue and purple range on the far side of it. That valley was always filled with mystery, though Peter knew every foot of it. Then Peter would try to set down the thoughts and feelings that craved utterance—and often missed finding it. Still, Peter did write a lot of verse, and filled some large exercise-books with his poems on the valley, the purple ranges, the quiet creek with its giant oak-trees, and of other things, too. He made a special trip to Sydney one time to see about having some published. Nothing much seemed to come of it.

Peter was very impulsive. At twenty-four he made the discovery that he wasn't married, and also that he had never been in love. He decided to do both forthwith. So he oiled the Winchester, fitted a cork in its muzzle, strapped it on the wall of his bedroom, and then laid vigorous siege to the heart of Mary Ann across the creek. The siege lasted less than a month, and seems to have been lifted by Mary Ann's father and Peter's mother. Both these were people of remarkably strong character, entirely devoid of poetry.

Peter's heart wasn't broken, as he thought it was at first. A sight of Polly a few weeks later told him that. The wooing was even more vigorous and might easily have ended well, if Polly's mother and two clergymen hadn't seen fit to intervene.

Three other campaigns followed in quick succession, but each was a complete failure.

Then Peter took down the Winchester ·32, pulled the cork out of the muzzle, ran a rag through the barrel, and went out slaughtering wallabies and hares. Also, he looked out a suitable site for a small log-cabin where a recluse might drag out his few sad remaining years. The rock formation of the hills didn't favour caves, so he had to forgo that luxury. All the while he turned over in his mind a fit poetic work to go with the log-cabin.

Then he saw Rose, and all other visions vanished at the sight of her, and along with them the log-cabin. He knew Rose was made to be adored, and that Mary Ann, Polly and the rest were but the appointed steps leading to the shrine. The course did run smooth at last; no mothers and fathers to interfere, no clergymen to intervene. Peter loved and was loved. Happiness in the clouds!

But Peter's mother was always practical; she ignored the white clouds floating above.

'You and Rose can have the two end rooms', she said, 'and eat with us.' Then she added, 'Of course, Rose will remember it is *my* house.'

There was a legal fiction that the house belonged to Peter's father, but Peter's father had long since ceased to worry about such minor points of existence.

Peter thought the arrangement was quite all right: he and Rose could be happy anywhere. He knew that. But Rose didn't think so. In secret she thanked God fervently that Peter wasn't like his mother. Then she told Peter he must build a home for her, which brought Peter against the stark question of ways and means. He had little money, and his hope of living was on the farm. Unless, of course, he could sell some of his poetry. The local newspaper printed some of it in its columns on a strictly honour and glory basis—and made it clear that you don't get much more for poetry anywhere. Sometimes not even that.

So Peter held counsel with his mother and father. His mother presided. Peter, she said, could have the top end of the farm and erect such a dwelling there as his humble means would allow. She also mentioned that she had once lived in a tent herself, and when she started married life it was in a small slab and bark hut. And look at her now! Peter was too depressed to look.

He told Rose, and she said, 'Borrow the money.' Peter asked where from. 'From the old folk, you goose!' said Rose. 'They have plenty.'

But Peter's mother now remembered that the tent had been a draughty one, and that the slab hut used to leak. Further, there had been no one to lend her money—even if she had been poor-spirited enough to try to borrow it. So that was that.

Then came a great idea to Peter.

At one end of the long paddock was a large section of whitish soil, sprinkled throughout with small round pebbles. A barren, hungry piece of soil it was, sodden and spewy in winter, and hard as iron in summer. It was never worth the ploughing for all the return it gave. No good for crops, someone said, but it would 'grow cherries like one thing'. Perhaps so, but wouldn't it also make great walls if you rammed it hard? Of course it would!

Peter rushed the horses out of the plough, and bare-backed one of them over to Rose's place. Rose said 'Um!' Though certainly it seemed better than slab and bark—and just as cheap, if not cheaper.

Peter made an experimental block by ramming the stuff, mixed with water, into a butter-box. It made a fine, firm block.

And so the house was commenced. It was a big house, since the walls would cost nothing, as it were. There were six rooms of generous proportions. Peter's mother came along to see the foundations marked out on the ground. She found it difficult to speak with restraint—not that she often tried to speak with restraint. But she made inquiry as to the cost of roofing and flooring. Peter said that would be all right, and tried to look wise. But his mother had no great faith in his wisdom, and went off grumbling loudly to herself—and *at* Peter.

Peter had no conception—at first—of the labour involved in the building of those walls. But he soon came to realize it. The pisé earth had to be dug, wheeled in a barrow to the house site, mixed and kneaded with water, shovelled into the frames, rammed thoroughly and then left to set. Then the frames had to be removed and raised another foot, and the whole slow process gone over again. And again, and again, with the labour increasing with every lift, and complicated by doors and windows and chimneys. The walls had to be very thick, and that meant more pisé to be mixed, and lifted and rammed. Hundreds and hundreds of tons of it—and one man to do it all! In the period of this building activity, Peter had to do his usual jobs on the farm; so, much of the raising of those walls was done at night—moonlight nights especially, when he often worked till all hours.

The earth was dug some fair distance from the house, and Peter shaped a dam, or tank, rather, of the excavation. He said you couldn't make that too close to the house, for the children might easily get drowned in it. It made a good sound waterhole eventually, but rather shallow, for the pisé earth was only a few feet thick, and the clay beneath was no good for the walls.

Peter was proud of those walls that rose so slowly, grey-white in the sun and misty-white under the moon. Rose was proud of them, too, and of Peter with his strong arms and stout heart. There was something chivalric about the building of that house—a knightly deed as brave in its way as the slaying of a dragon

On Sundays, Peter would drive Rose over to see the walls, and sometimes on a moonlight night she would drive over herself, and give cheery support, and boil a billy of tea, and spread out scones and sandwiches, or perhaps roast some potatoes in the ashes. Then she

would try to help with the endless pisé, and fail in all
departments of it, most of all in lifting the heavy
bucket up to the frames. She would say 'Ooh!' and
'How do you?' And Peter would be prouder than
ever.

Great nights, these, and, if they but knew it, the
happiest they could ever know. But Poetry suffered in
output—it just went into the walls along with the
sweat and brawn.

At long, long last, the walls were completed and
given a rough coat of plaster for protection against the
rain. Then for the roof and floor. Peter cut timber on
the hills, and snigged it down with the plough horses.
Cypress pines by the hundreds, in various sizes, for all
the plates, joists, rafters and battens. Long, straight
poles they were, and they took many an hour with
adze and saw to fit them for their places. That left to
buy only the roof iron, floorboards and doors and
windows. Even at that, the cost was as much as Peter
could stand. But he managed somehow. The enclosing
veranda he couldn't floor on account of expense, but
he and Rose decided that an earth floor for the
verandas, if raised a little, looked quite distinctive.
The chimneys had cost a bit, too, even if the bricks
were cheaply got second-hand, for he had to pay a
man to build them.

Finished at last—and a triumph. The finest house
for miles around, though a little raw-looking in its
newness. The iron roof didn't quite harmonize with
the pisé walls, and looked like a rakish hat on a
reverend head. Peter's mother came and had a look at
the house, and sniffed loudly and meaningly. Peter's
father was pleased, however, and he didn't sniff.

Peter and Rose were married before the plaster was
properly dry in three of the rooms. This arrangement

was a variant of the time-payment system, and no
doubt had much to commend it.

Peter was gaunt and thin from the building of the
house, but he was full of wiry, restless energy, and had
a hundred schemes that individually were much easier
of accomplishment than those walls. He planted
cherries—hundreds of them—in the end of the long
paddock; he put in a vineyard; he raised vegetables
that made Hop Sing from the river flat say 'welly,
welly ni!' when he saw them. He grew crops of wheat
and corn that filled his mother with nettled concern—
'never did anything like it when he was at home!'
But his poetic output again suffered, and now went
into cabbages, beans, wheat and twins. The twins
arrived with the first wheat harvest.

Then Peter's mother mentioned the matter of rent,
which she said she had overlooked earlier, but thought
it high time to bring up. Peter had never thought of
rent at all, and went into secret conference with his
father about it—behind the haystack. Peter's father
listened sadly, and said he'd speak 'to your mother'
about it. No doubt that was his intention, but it is not
too certain that he ever found courage to do it. Then
Peter told Rose about it, and she told her father, who
was reputed a wise man. Also he was a bush lawyer.
Rose's father came along to see Peter, and primed him
with plans. The first of these was counter-attack. 'See
the old woman', said Rose's father, 'and threaten her
with suit-at-law for wages unpaid.'

Peter didn't quite see, and Rose's father was more
explicit. 'You worked for her for years and years,
didn't you? And what did you get for it? See?'

Then Rose's father worked it out on paper—so
many years at so much a week. The amount was
staggering.

'Of course it *is* a lot, my boy, but you earned it. And it is yours.'

He also advised selling anything on the place that could be sold—'just in case', he put it, rather ominously. To set things going, he himself bought the two pigs and the six calves. It would be a help, he reckoned, though the price he paid was not particularly helpful.

Peter was down at the old place some time later, and he told his mother about the wages suit—after she had brought up the matter of rent once more. What happened then will never be very clear, but it must have been pretty terrible. Peter nearly ran home, and, with the barest of explanation to Rose, commenced to take the iron off the back room. He worked all night, and by next morning had nearly all the roof iron stacked in the lane that ran past the house. When the roof was off he took up the floor, and piled it up in the lane. Likewise, doors and windows and everything of value and use that had been fastened were unfastened and packed on the road. Peter, Rose, and the twins in the meantime slept in the shed. You see, Peter had discovered that his mother was a much greater bush lawyer than Rose's father. She had laid claim to everything of Peter's house. 'Talk to me of law, will you! I'll show you!' That accounted for the feverish haste.

However, Rose's father was not greatly surprised, and said things had worked out much as he had anticipated. They always did, he said. Also, he commended Peter greatly for his storing of the iron and timber on the road, and said it would take a hell of a lot of law to get them back again. 'You tricked her there, my boy, you tricked her there!'

He came along with a four-horse wagon, and carted

everything into his own place—for safety—and 'to give you a chance to look around'.

Then Peter looked round, but it doesn't seem that he saw much, for he lived on with his father-in-law and went into partnership with him, a very unequal partnership. It should have given him the chance of writing some really great poetry, but he never seemed to find the time to write poetry any more.

Without the roof, the walls weathered, and crumbled, and became picturesque. The roof, like a rakish hat on a fine old head, had always spoiled the look of those walls, and now they became beautiful and romantic in their misty-white under the full moon. A sapling or two grew up amid the ruins, and added greatly to the effect. Some said the ruins looked very sad—perhaps they did.

But they looked very beautiful, too!

SUBURBAN SOUVENIR
By HERMON GILL

WALTER said ah yes he could quite believe it would and he shook his head sadly and he looked for a place to put his cigarette ash because Mrs. Harcourt is rather particular about cigarette ash going on her carpet but he couldn't see an ashtray anywhere and he surreptitiously knocked it on to the floor and old Mrs. Ferguson said yes it did because he was a very sensitive man.

Because as old Mrs. Ferguson told Walter it was the principle of the thing that worried him he didn't care a bit about the money or anything like that it was the thought that people he had trusted could turn out in that way he said it almost broke his faith in human nature and then Mrs. Harcourt struck a chord on the piano and Harcourt started to sing when you are happy friend of mine and all your skies are blue.

And Harcourt worked on through his song to the bit about when one of us or both of us the long lone road must go let me be there let me be there there with you and old Mrs. Ferguson said but he had such a sweet nature that even that treatment couldn't altogether break his faith in his fellow-man and then Mrs. Harcourt struck a chord on the piano and Harcourt leapt into out of the night that covers me black as the pit from pole to pole with a fair amount of gusto.

Harcourt worked himself up a bit in that part about it matters not how strait the gate how charged with punishment the scroll I am the master of my fate I am the captain of my soul and old Mrs. Ferguson said ah well there you are we are as heaven made us and his was not the nature to bear malice he was one of nature's gentlemen if ever there was one.

Walter looked around rather anxiously then for an ashtray because his cigarette was burning very short but old Mrs. Ferguson appeared not to notice Walter's difficulty and she told Walter mind there had never been anything in writing but it had always been an understood thing that it would all go to him when the old lady died after all and then Mrs. Selby suddenly called out if you can keep your head when all about you are losing theirs and blaming it on you from beside the piano and Walter sank back with a silent sigh and tried to juggle his cigarette end so that it wouldn't burn his fingers.

And if ever you have tried to do that at a crowded

party when you're miles from an ashtray or the fireplace sitting beside old Mrs. Ferguson while Mrs. Selby recites 'If' you'll know how trying that can be and by the time Mrs. Selby reached yours is the earth and everything that's in it and which is more you'll be a man my son the cork tip of Walter's cigarette was smouldering and smelling evilly and Mrs. Harcourt saw it just in time to rush across with a full ashtray to catch the last of it but not in time to save Walter's fingers from being burned.

Mrs. Harcourt put the full ashtray on the arm of the couch beside Walter and old Mrs. Ferguson said he and his wife had made a home for the old lady when none of the others would be bothered with her and mind you she was fairly trying at times you know how old people get and naturally it tied them down a good deal and just then Beryl played a snappy sort of introduction on the piano and Burton burst in merrily with a sort of false Irish brogue supposin' oy talk tae yer fayther swoyte Mary said oy.

And as soon as Burton reached you'd better ask me and Beryl played the last crashing chord on the piano old Mrs. Ferguson said often they'd have to put off going to the pictures because they couldn't get anyone to come in and look after her while they were out you'd have thought that some of the others would have offered to have taken her for a few days now and again wouldn't you but no not on your life all they did and then Beryl played the piano again and Burton cast his mind back with a coy look and sang I remember meeting you in September '62 and he sang through to that was many years ago don't let anybody know and old Mrs. Ferguson said was to give advice and that cost them little enough.

There was a slight break in her story then because

Walter who was getting a bit cramped squashed up on the couch went to stretch his arm and inadvertently knocked the full ashtray off the couch's arm and scattered a lot of ash and cigarette ends and wisps of tobacco and stuff all over the carpet and although Harcourt said don't worry Old Man it keeps moths away and Mrs. Harcourt said it didn't matter at all Walter could see that it did matter quite a lot and there was a bit of bustling about with brushes and ashpans and things before Selby and a short fat man with a very loud voice started asking each other say watchman what of the night when the dews of the morning fall to Mrs. Harcourt's accompaniment.

And by the time the three of them were sort of racing neck and neck to the dawn of eternity lights on the gloom and night shall be no more old Mrs. Ferguson had got her second wind and she said and of course there was the financial side of it too because he and his wife never took a penny from the old lady and never asked for any financial assistance from the others not that they'd have got it if they had but it had been an understood thing that they would get the house and the furniture but there you are it just shows you and just then a tall thin gentleman with a drooping moustache who was a friend of Selby's started to pray the prayer that the Easterns do may the peace of Allah abide with you in a melancholy sort of hooting voice.

As the notes of the tall gentleman's final wish about the peace of Allah abiding with everyone died away old Mrs. Ferguson said that was where the deceit came in because although nothing definite had ever been arranged he and his wife had the moral right and yet he'd never blamed the old lady herself as he said after all her mind was failing and even though

K

she was very self-willed in many ways it would have been quite easy for anyone unscrupulous to have swayed her and then Beryl played some martial notes on the piano and the fat gentleman with the loud voice started to roar trumpeter what are you sounding now is it the call I'm seeking.

The questions and answers between the fat man and the trumpeter took quite a long time before the trumpeter said he was sounding the last reveille and then old Mrs. Ferguson said so after all they'd done for her they got nothing at all except a lot of nasty insinuations from other people who only came to the funeral for what they hoped to get out of it but that's the way of the world yet all he said was but then Mrs. Harcourt started to warble over the quiet hills slowly the shadows fall in one of those sort of wavy voices and at last she reached bird songs at eventide call me to you.

And then old Mrs. Ferguson said all he said was but before she could tell Walter what it was Mrs. Harcourt called come into the other room for supper everyone and Walter made good his escape.

So Walter still doesn't know who the gentleman was Mrs. Ferguson was telling him about or who did him for the house and furniture or what the old lady died of eventually or what the gentleman said about it finally. And what's more he doesn't want to know either. And neither do I.

THE PELICAN

By Cecil Mann

IT used to be one of the familiar sights to see Mr. Grigg (as he then was; he has moved up socially since) taking his regular Sunday stroll along the Twelve-mile Beach. A sight the inhabitants viewed with feelings between amusement and contempt.

The weather made no difference to Mr. Grigg; except in what he wore. On bright and sunny Sundays he dressed what there was of him in cream flannel trousers, black blazer with white pipings, panama hat and white pipe-clayed shoes. Not sand-shoes. Good leather. And stiff-collared white shirt, and black necktie.

Or else he would give his dark-blue serge, bowler and black shoes an airing. A high-cut white vest. A small black bow-tie. Long-linked gold watch-chain. Large gold ring on a left finger. Cane.

When rain came it fell at the Beach in a prodigious waste. It drove down in a heavy mass for days, some-times weeks on end. A thousandth part of it would have been more than ample for the few straggling pumpkin vines, the occasional pie-melons and chokos that constituted the inhabitants' gardens. It belted loudly on the red iron roofs scattered through the ti-trees and banksias. It came in from the open sea between the headlands at either end of the long curved beach like an advancing grey wall. It flogged the sea flat, belted the sloping sand smooth, filled the ti-tree swamp, swelled the weed- and swamp-stained acre of lake till sometimes it broke through the sand-silted block and emptied its brown wine-like water and its land-locked fish for a while into the sea.

Then Mr. Grigg took his Sunday stroll in rubber kneeboots, black oilskin, black sou'wester. He leant his meagre frame against the gale, trudging the hardened sand. Hands in the oilskin pockets. Hunched like a black pygmy. The lumps of rain struck him. They bumped from his shoulders up under his neck

and trickled down his chest-bone. For all his protective covering, he returned to his shop wet. He did
the same again the next Sunday, if it was raining
twice as hard.

Mr. Grigg never fished on Sundays. That there was
no church at the Beach made him all the more
meticulous in keeping the Sabbath, in his fashion,
holy. He compensated his soul with the thought that
you could commune there in the Almighty's own vast
cathedral, though its roof did leak rather badly at
times. As you went along communing, you might,
without desecration, spot out holes and channels in
the breakers that would be likely places for jewfish and
bream. Next night, the Sabbath over, you could be off
down the track through the ti-trees and she-oaks and
along the beach to cast out at the prospected spot,
marked by the gibbet silhouette of a banksia up on
the sandridge.

It was a local legend of Mr. Grigg that one Saturday
night he hooked a tremendous jewy. He had out a
brand new two hundred yards of No. 12. The jewy
made him use the lot of it. It drew him out into the
surf up to his waist. Not so good a fisherman, stones
heavier than Mr. Grigg, would have had no chance
with it. As it was, the struggle in the night took him
four miles along the beach. With the whole of the taut
line out, the fight lasted for over two hours. Then,
not having landed it by midnight, Mr. Grigg threw the
log-like cork after it and let it go. Rather than desecrate
the Sabbath. Anyway, that's how the tale went.

It wasn't that many of the others fished, or felt any
desire to fish, on Sundays. To them, fishing was something you did if you happened to want fish to eat or,
seasonally, when the big black-nose whiting or bream
were in. Only an occasional one or two, apart from

Mr. Grigg, even went out when the huge jewfish were known to be patrolling at night close in in the breakers. Mostly, indeed practically unanimously, they just preferred not to fish. But if there was any one day of the week when they might abandon their preference, or habitual laziness, it was Sunday. Then, perhaps with some visitors down from town, a few of them might wet a line.

They called Mr. Grigg Mr. Grigg. Friendly enough folk, they could have accepted Mr. Grigg going to church on Sundays, and some of the women might have gone, too, and the children been forced to go. It was just that Mr. Grigg's Sabbath abstinence set him apart. It made him superior. And the gap was not lessened by the fact that if there was one thing above all others positive about Mr. Grigg, it was that he was a regular crank on fishing.

Great red-shouldered jewfish that he could hardly lift. Bronzed-silver whiting; bream and tarwhine; and brown-backed, white-bellied sand flathead by the dozen. Caught and pulled, turning and leaping through the green-and-white swirl of breakers along the Beach by Mr. Grigg, and by Mr. Grigg given away gratis to any of the inhabitants who would eat fish, or sent by the mail-car up to town, to the hospital. With Mr. Grigg's compliments.

To Mr. Grigg, his discovery of fishing was practically a discovery of life itself. Two other discoveries went along with it.

One was that there were seven days in the week, instead of only one. Monday, Tuesday, Wednesday, Thursday, Friday, Saturday, Sunday—seven. Then start all over again: Monday, Tuesday—each a whole day, a whole twenty-four hours. Not a rush into the city inside the hot, screaming cylinder of an electric

train. Bacon department. Put on the white apron.
Sharpen the knife. Get busy. 'Thank you, madam.'
'A beautiful cut, madam.' 'A nice piece for boiling?
Yes, madam. Let me see now.' Take off the apron.
Join the crushing exodus. Rush home again. Read the
evening paper. Eat sausages. Put out the light in the
single room. Open the window. Sleep.

No. Complete days. Composed of time; of aged
hours; of early morning, later morning, noon, afternoon, evening, night. Days and nights. Some wet,
some windy, some sunny, some hot; pitch-black,
moon-flooded, starlit. Curve of open beach sweeping
its twelve miles from headland to headland. Gulls
winging over the whitecaps. Surf breaking on the sand.
Sun-haze dancing on the horizon. Pelicans floating
on the acre of swamp lake. Breaths of loose sand
puffed by the wind along the crests of the sandhills.
Fish.

Something to discover from the bacon department.

The other discovery had gall in it for Mr. Grigg.
He read the advertisement, made the great decision,
bought the grocery-and-residence shop (three unlined
weatherboard rooms in all) at the Beach. The previous
owner had amassed wealth there. Enough of it to go
to the south that Mr. Grigg came from and buy a pub
in salubrious surroundings. Paddington.

Mr. Grigg did not do so well. He made less than his
bacon department wages. The inhabitants did not do
anything so incredible as ostracizing Mr. Grigg. By no
means. They did not feel that way about him at all.
He could have dressed in purple tights and painted
his face ultramarine. He could even have built a
church. That would have been his affair. The
inhabitants would have been surprised, perhaps, but
would shortly have got used to it, and accepted it.

There was only the one shop, anyway. Grigg's; formerly McCarthy's.

The reason for Mr. Grigg's failure was the reason for McCarthy's wealth. It was not what was in the tins and jars on the sandy shelves. It was in what McCarthy kept under the counter. It was twenty-five miles up river to the town. The male inhabitants relied on McCarthy to make that immaterial to them. So did those who came down and lived in tents at Christmas and Easter.

It was a felon blow to Mr. Grigg. It led him to fishing. Fanatically. From then on—in old cabbage-tree hat, old coat, trousers rolled to the knees, bare-footed—he lived fish, talked fish and fished. Except on Sundays.

Some, perhaps—the dilettanti who wet a line about once a year, when on holidays, and wouldn't know a sergeant baker from a morwong—might not appreciate what that meant to Mr. Grigg. They wouldn't know the wild joy of standing or squatting alone at night on a windy beach, wet to the thighs from getting the heavy jew line well out over the breakers. They would be routed in one black engagement by the driven sand and salt peppering into their eyes and mouths and down their necks. They would shiver in the chill wet winter nights, and be tormented by blazing hearth-fires, warm beds and steaming food. They wouldn't know the obliteration from a line jerked suddenly taut by a terrific strength; the sizzling of it cutting through the fingers, the whishing of it through the water. Obliteration for anything up to an hour or more till the fifty-pounder was there, phosphorescent, thumping and leaping up on the beach.

What could they, the inhabitants or anyone else know of what went on in the mind of Mr. Grigg, taking his Sabbath stroll? If there is not one already, there should be a Saint Alfred in the exclusive heirarchy. Or there should have been. At least let it stand to his glory in the past tense. Let it stand to his glory, Lord, when he and they and the creatures of Thy making, yea even unto the misshapen, the toad-fish in the shallows, the pelicans on the beach, come up for the judgement.

The pelican Mr. Grigg saw on his Sabbath stroll squatted on the sand away ahead of him. As he approached, Sunday-neat in cream flannels, black blazer, panama, Mr. Grigg focused on the old fellow squatting there, great yellow beak pointed out to sea like a signpost. It surprised him, drawing nearer, that the big bird did not get up and float at first awkwardly, then superbly, away. Instead, with a display of confidence that at once touched Mr. Grigg, the old fellow got up on his short legs and came towards him. The big feet scarcely marked the sand; but a dragging wing-tip cut a thin line in it. A yard away, half-straightening the thick S-neck, the bird opened up his vast cavern of beak. In his throat he made a raucous, squawking sound. He spread out and flapped his good wing; clattered the long yellow slats of bill together like pieces of board.

Mr. Grigg looked down on the grotesque white body, fawn and brown down the wing-edges and over the abrupt square tail. The big bird squatted on his yellow webbed feet, looking up expectantly at Mr. Grigg with watery brown eyes.

'Hullo,' Mr. Grigg cried sympathetically. 'What's the matter with you now? Eh? Broke your wing, is that it? Somebody shot you, eh?'

The bird affirmed Mr. Grigg's deductions. He squawked more, flapped his good wing. Mr. Grigg put a friendly hand out to stroke him, but jerked it back as the hook on the end of the long beak nearly caught it. The bird shied off, snapping, backing away, half-falling over the dragging wing. The short white feathers on his neck came up like a dog's hackle.

It distressed Mr. Grigg. Kindliness rebuffed, he turned and began walking back along the beach. After him the pelican waddled, flapping the good wing to try to keep up, with the other drawing a crooked furrow over the damp sand.

The distance between Mr. Grigg and the waddling grotesque widened out. Mr. Grigg's brows puckered thoughtfully. Gradually, a thought, a turn of mind, an inspiration; fighting at first thinly, then strongly, for acceptance.

Mr. Grigg stopped, turned about, waited for the old fellow to catch up with him. The pelican came on awkwardly to within a few feet. The good wing flapped; cavernous beak opening and shutting.

'Yes, that's it,' said Mr. Grigg loudly. 'That's it, isn't it, eh? You're hungry, aren't you? You want a feed, don't you? Fish? Fish, eh? Fish,' shouted Mr. Grigg. 'Fish! FISH!'

Opening and clapping his beak, flapping his wing, the grotesque leered at him. It sat back on its hooked spurs watching him. The watery brown eyes glared malevolently. Mr. Grigg looked down on it in an ecstasy. He turned again on his heel and went in short, quickened steps along the beach, up the track through the ti-trees and she-oaks, into the shop.

In old trousers and grey flannel shirt, old cabbage-tree hat, bootless, he emerged again. A small gut line rolled round an empty bottle in one hand. In the other a lidless jam-tin half-filled with sand and sea-worms. Bait.

A quiet Sunday afternoon. The breakers falling lazily in slow crashes. Mr. Grigg with the surf washing round his shins. The light gut line over the shelf of sand. On the beach the old pelican a squatted, grotesque monument of Patience.

The thin line in Mr. Grigg's fingers jerked slightly. At the next jerk he hooked it. Trousers in a wet roll at his knees, barefoot, he backed through the shallow to the sand, pulling it in as he went.

The silver streak of whiting came skipping, gleaming through the water. The old bird, flapping and squawking down, nearly beat him to it. Mr. Grigg took the silver streak from the hook. He held it out to the bird, as if he was showing a bone to a dog. The flapping and guttural squawks taken as gratitude, he tossed the fish to the open beak.

The bird caught it deftly in the air. Juggled the still flipping fish between the slats of his bill so that it would pass down his throat head first, without the fins obstructing. Mr. Grigg watched entranced. He saw the moving length passing down and swelling out the old bird's throat.

He saw half a dozen more go the same way. Unawares, oblivious, Mr. Grigg had joined the company of the damned.

Alf Grigg, as they speak of him; Alf, as they speak to him; Old Featherlegs, as they not unkindly refer to him—that is, Mr. Grigg that was—has moved up all that way socially. He fishes on Sunday, like any other heathen. He fishes on any of the entire seven. The pelican follows him like a feathered dog. Lives with him; camps on the veranda of the shop. Squawks at strangers.

Often they sit there on the veranda together, thinking about fish. Otherwise the shop isn't much different from when it changed hands. There's still the same bell without a tongue standing on the counter. On the four sandy shelves a row of biscuit-tins, jars of lollies, half-pounds of tea, packets of self-raising flour, tins of camp-pie, boxes of hooks and lines and sinkers.

If the door's shut, it's no use knocking. They will be out along the beach, fishing. There's nothing for it, if you want, say, a drop of overproof rum to warm the cockles of your heart, or a bottle of beer to quench your thirst, but just sit down and wait till they come back.

GOING HOME
By Myra Morris

HE called the little girls inside and looked anxiously at their faces. There was dirt under the rosiness.

'I don't want to be cleaned up,' whined Julie, who was small for her three years and inclined to easy tears.

'You must,' he said firmly. 'Your mother's coming home to-day.'

He led the two into the bathroom, where the wind fluttered little whiskers of wood on the unlined walls, and washed their faces with the damp end of a roller-towel.

'And now you both keep clean,' he cautioned, tugging helplessly at the plaits of the elder girl. 'Don't lose your hair-ribbons, Kate, and do as Miss Bowden tells you.'

He sped them outside with a good-natured cuff, and started his prowl up and down the passage, peering into the rooms. The house was spotless. It smelled clean. He had worked till late the night before, and had hurried over milking so that he could get to the kitchen stove. The stove looked nice now—just as Marge liked it—shining as though it had been lacquered, the kettles scoured, and the ash in the pan no more than a delicate froth of rose and white like pink-sugared apple-snow. The same order prevailed in the crowded little dining-room, where he had evened up the crumbling bricks of the fireplace and raddled the hobs. The sideboard with its neat, crochet-edged runner was polished, and the chimney of the green-bowled lamp bright and thin like a bubble about to burst. He had put flowers in a vase on the table, and the stumpy sprays of yellow jasmine with their pointed terracotta buds seemed still to wear the imprint of his awkward fingers.

He stood for a moment nodding his satisfaction, a tall, stringy young man with a long face burnt to the colour of dust. His features were sensitively cut; his high forehead with the skin drawn tightly across, clean and worn as a stone worn by the sea; his grey eyes keen and a little perplexed as though the spectacle of life puzzled while it enchanted him.

Pulling a felt hat down over his thinning, dark hair, he went out into the yard, walking with the headlong, slightly pigeon-toed gait óf an active man. He could leave the place now with an easy mind. Miss Bowden, the obliging spinster from across the paddocks, would be here at any moment now to keep an eye on the kids. Already she had left the farm, and he could see her, a little square pepper-pot figure, weaving her way among the dead timber.

Without hurry he backed the tiny single-seater out of the shed, and waving to the children, who were scooping up leaves under the shaggy gum, drove past the side of the bare, weatherboard house towards the gate. At the culvert a red-faced man in a billowing shirt roared at him:

''Day, Joe! Goin' in for the missus?'

'That's right, Ted.' Joe lifted his hand from the wheel and gave a salute. It was the gesture of a man used to driving with a whip in his hand. 'Be back less than two hours.'

He wished regretfully as the wheels of the car fumbled for the crown of the road that he could have driven the gig instead. The deep mud-crusted ruts, the milky-yellow water lying in unsuspected seams and hollows, made steering difficult. But it was impossible to think of Marge driving home in the gig, sitting high up, exposed to the bitter winds from the plains, with a two-weeks-old baby in her arms. He was actually, now, at this moment, going into the township hospital for Marge and the nipper! The thought of it excited him, loosening in him a feeling of awe and pride. This was a fine and a good thing to be doing, to be bringing home his wife and child to the place he had made for them. He had done it before, twice, yet it seemed now as if he were doing it for the first time. He straightened up over the jerking steering-wheel, ducking his head as the car splashed and bumped through water, and a frail, dancing curtain of amber drops hung suspended between him and the sky. 'Poor Marge,' he thought, 'poor girl, it isn't much of a place.'

Sighing, he looked over the bleak, unaccented landscape. Bare paddocks tufted with winter-whitened grass and endless post-and-rail fences regular as printed staves of music; patches of young crop, unearthly green and tender, touched with quicksilver

where water flooded the hollows; at the side of the
road rusty mistletoe, bunched like old clothes on over-
hanging gums, and muddied grass and reeds; a farm
or two with ragged stacks and jumbled outhouses that
looked as if they would disintegrate with a touch. And
over all a sky faintly rose at the edges, colourless as
melting ice, floating textureless and formless as a
frosty breath.

He thought back to his place alongside the road.
Not as bad as some he had seen up north, but maybe
he could have done more. 'Stick it,' he had said in the
beginning. 'We've got to stick it.' He had been sticking
it now for ten years and was at last forgetting to trot
out the well-worn excuse for his failures—that he had
started on nothing. Ten years and there wasn't much
to show. The house had an unfinished look, with the
roof still unpainted, and the veranda only half-way
round. But he had worked hard enough, God knew,
putting the stubborn land into crop and pasture as far
down as Simpson's Corner, keeping his cows in good
fettle, and clearing the thick, dead timber from some
of the paddocks at the back of the house. With Ted
Simpson he had invested in a saw-bench and they
were now cutting the timber and stacking it ready for
carting. The sound of the saw biting into the resisting
wood, that harsh, clanging whine with its brazen bell-
like echo, soothed and gratified him, giving as it did an
impression of immense stir and activity. Ted might be
doing a bit of cutting this afternoon, he mused, thinking back to the figure who had hailed him at the
culvert. Immediately his mind became a prey to little
niggling worries. It was to be hoped that the children
would not go rambling into the back paddock seeking
sawdust from the pile. Ted, working with his young
son, was a careless beggar. Anything could happen to

kids. Those rusty nails bristling along the old fowl-house fence were a menace—rusty nails, tetanus. He remembered with a sudden shoot of dismay that he had forgotten to shut the little gate and the chooks would be in scraping all over the place. . . .

Swallowing nervously, he turned the car into a smoother patch of road where metal was hard under the wheels. He felt all of a sudden excited and up-lifted, aware of a grumbling discomfort in his belly. Nearly there now. Already he could see the tangle of roofs and posts and fences that made the township, the white bulk of the water-tower with its map-markings of rust, the new church wall lifting in all its defiance of raw, red brick, the glassy glitter of the hospital balcony.

He drew up in front of the big white hospital, the pride of the town, and looked at his watch. A painful shyness descended on him. He had visited Marge four times at the hospital, and on each occasion he had felt awkward and inadequate, knowing as he tiptoed down the corridors that the nurses laughed at him because he always blundered and lost his way. Sweat broke in beads on his face. He ran his fingers along the rough back of his neck. 'I'm early,' he thought with a feeling of relief. 'I'll slip down the street and have a haircut.'

Inside the hospital people sat about on wooden benches, waiting with long, patient faces. Nurses rustled past importantly, moving on ugly black-stockinged legs that did not seem to belong to them. Babies cried in the glass-doored nursery, their voices faint and far-away like the voices of magpies calling out of the grey void of early morning.

Marge waited, sitting on a chair in the little ward that held two beds. She was a big-boned, composed-looking young woman with a fuzz of sandy hair and colour in her cheeks that, lying close under the skin, constantly came and went. She was dressed in a faded brown cardigan and a tweed skirt with loose threads and a gaping placket. Her big feet were thrust into down-at-heel slippers.

A nurse bustled into the room, cheerful and managing.

'You leaving at once, Mrs. Anderson? Baby's all ready.'

'Yes, I fed him at two and they took him away.' Marge's voice was soft and unhurried, a little absent. 'I'll be able to have more of him now.'

'You won't want to be spoiling him,' scolded the nurse. 'Ach! you mothers! You want to keep to regular hours. And no taking him into bed, remember!'

She went out with a tread that set the bottles on the lockers jangling like little bells, and Marge and the grey-haired woman in the next bed exchanged a long, comfortable smile.

'What *they* know!' scoffed the woman with the grey hair. 'I've buried two and reared five, and all of them slept in bed with me. Nibble, nibble, nibble all night long like little mice, till they dropped off.'

'That's right,' said the younger woman reminiscently.

'Your man's late, isn't he, dear? Musta been kep'.'

'I don't mind waiting.'

Marge looked peacefully in front of her, her big, red hands folded on her lap. It was nice to be going home, but she had been happy in here with the days each one like the day before, sliding past in perfect, unbroken rhythm. Sleeping, washing, eating, feeding the baby, who was brought to her at stated intervals and whisked away again almost before she had had time to get used to the feel of him in her arms . . . sleeping again . . .

eating. . . . It would be different at home with everything to do. The work in the house, mending, washing, the napkins, the woollies that shrank and clotted together while you looked at them. Julie and Kate and poor old Joe eager to help, but clumsy, clumsy. . . .

Her thoughts ran on easily, comfortably. And then, there was Joe standing in front of her, straightening himself after an awkward kiss, looking sheepish, twirling his hat that had grease on the band, muttering breathless apologies. He was sorry he was late. He'd called in to Hogan's to have a haircut. The bloke had got him into the chair and kept him waiting, all bibbed-up, otherwise——

'It doesn't matter,' said Marge, and the quick red patched her smiling face and ran down into her furrowed neck. 'I'll tell nurse to bring baby. Have you brought my shoes?'

'Crumbs, no! I forgot them.' Joe stared at her slippered feet, contrite and wretched.

'Oh well . . . ' Her gaze absent and unfocused, like the gaze of a young kitten, slid past him as she rang the bell. 'Get my things out of that cupboard, and I'll want a warm top-shawl to put over him, and a rug over that. He's . . .'

It wasn't until he was in the car with the memory of the nurse's shrill patronizing laugh diminishing in his ears that Joe felt completely happy and at ease. He looked at Marge as she sat with her head tilted, her chin topping the fringe of woolly shawl. He felt tender towards Marge, in an obscure fashion grateful. He felt tender and grateful towards all women who went uncomplainingly down into the Valley of Shadow and brought life back with them. It was different with a man. A woman had the hard part—the burden of physical pain as well as anguish of mind. Look at Marge now! It was starting all over again for her—getting up to the baby at night, hanging over tubs eternally washing, coping with inevitable ailments, teething rashes, croup and the rest. Three children now at her heels! Three! And a mean little house and a lack of ready money. Pinching here, scraping there, making do. He was pierced by an anguish of pity for Marge, who said nothing, only stared steadily at the morsel of rubbery flesh visible between two folds of the shawl, while the car jolted over the ruts in the road.

Suddenly the girl straightened her sliding hat with a free hand and glanced bemusedly at Joe, only half-seeing him—his thin, sensitive face with its bony forehead, his narrow shoulders hunched over the wheel, his hands pocked with the tiny scabs of healing sores. Dear Joe, she thought vaguely. He's nice, he's good. . . . Some husbands . . . It will be nice to be home. . . . That new food in a tin. All nursing mothers should have some. I must get . . .

'Everything right at home?' she asked with an effort.

'Fine,' said Joe eagerly. He wanted to tell her in a rush. Women worried when they were away from home, imagined things. 'Great kids, Kate and Julie. Been gathering eggs. The white chooks have started to lay. I've knocked up some new roosts for them at the far end. . . .'

He talked on, but his voice faltered. She wasn't really listening. She was brooding, her mouth slightly open, her shallow brown eyes fixed as on some inner vision. She gave a tiny, contented laugh.

'I'm glad he's not a bottle baby like Julie was. Of course it'll mean giving him a feed at six—bringing him into bed——'

Joe grunted, dimly offended. The car dipped to a muddy creek, rose again. Wind moaned along the wires of Simpson's new fences. A cloud of white cockatoos lifted tremulously and broke like glistening sea-spray against the arch of sky. The car panted and wheezed over the last ruts. The house, small and bare and definite in outline like a model house in an agent's window, came into view.

As soon as they were inside the baby began to cry. Miss Bowden, loitering delicately, made clucking noises with her tongue, and Marge looked at her with a remote, chilled look.

'He'll be all right,' she said softly.

'Well, your cuppa tea's ready,' said Miss Bowden, preparing to depart. 'I've had mine. I'll be off now. Yes, it's a real nice baby and all.'

Joe went with her to the door and came back. Marge was putting the baby down in the cot. He was ready for her when she emerged from the bedroom, a child tugging at either hand. He waited on her humbly, drawing her chair close to the fire, putting a stool to her feet. He poured out her tea, stirring it anxiously. Good tea, wasn't it? Old Todd's best, Grade I Special. Not like that wish-wash at the hospital. And the fireplace? Did she notice the bricks he had evened up at the back? A nasty job.

'It's lovely,' said Marge, smiling. 'Yes, I noticed that at once.' She began to unplait Kate's tight, blonde plaits with practised fingers.

'And the flowers?' muttered Joe, clearing his throat and craning his thin neck. He spoke with a studied carelessness. 'That yellow jasmine stuff. Pretty. I put it in——'

'It's lovely,' said Marge, peering about vaguely. 'I noticed that too.'

But Joe's face had clouded. She hadn't really noticed it at all. She hadn't noticed anything. He was conscious of flatness. He smiled tiredly, listening to the little girl's piping prattle. The chooks had got out of the yard, and had scratched up mummy's seed-bed.

'Crumbs, I'm sorry, old girl, I left the gate open,' said Joe miserably. 'I thought of it afterwards.'

'It doesn't matter, love,' said Marge, screwing up her eyes. A few old seeds, she thought. What odds? It's round the sunny side of the house. I'll put the pram round there.

Joe clattered the dishes into the kitchen, wondering forlornly if Marge would notice the polished stove. Suddenly, from a point away at the back of the house, he heard the harsh, importunate whine of the saw. That would be old Ted with his gawky son. Damn! The sound went through him, plunging, cutting like a knife through quivering nerves and flesh and muscle. He had never noticed before how shattering the sound was, how inescapable. He went quickly into the dining-room.

'I'll stop that,' he said. 'At once.'

Marge was sitting with her knees wide, looking in front, smiling contentedly at nothing. Joe, looking at her, saw that she was miles away, inaccessible, absorbed, wrapped in a dream of her own making.

'Stop what?' she asked, in a blurred voice.

'The saw,' he said stupidly. 'It makes such a row. It'll wake the kid.'

'He won't hear,' she said, surprised. 'Anyhow, I don't mind. I really didn't hear it.'

Joe tiptoed out into the yard. It was funny Marge not minding the scraping saw—funny her not minding the scratching chooks. She had always made a row before. He looked appreciatively about him. The afternoon light was beginning to fail. The dead, silvery timber, the sheds, the shaggy gum-tree, the cows down by the bails, the white fowls pecking near the grassy border, seemed washed with a cold greyish-lilac, seemed melting, dissolving into that shadowy lilac, becoming part of it, inseparable from it. All at once everything that he saw seemed precious and significant. He wanted to gather every detail up and hold it fast. He could see now. Marge in there. She was temporarily removed from him, complete in herself, happy and serene, above and beyond the little irritations and obligations of outside life. She was shrouded, safe in her motherhood as in a cocoon.

'Wrapped in a dream,' he thought, as he moved through the lilac half-light, 'wrapped in a dream.'

DRY SPELL

By Marjorie Barnard

I walked because there was no reason for stopping, because it was more intolerable to stay still and because I wanted to reach the sea. I wanted to wade out into the water and perform a ritual act—like the Doge wedding Venice to the Adriatic, or William the Conqueror with his hands full of symbolic mud, or Cuchulain, or McDouall Stuart rushing into the Indian Ocean when he had crossed the Continent, or Cortez greeting the Pacific—but was that Pizarro, or was it somebody else altogether, Drake perhaps? My mind caught painfully on the doubt like a plane running on a knot in hardwood. It upset me. I began rubbing my hand across my chin again and listening to my footsteps. The things I had not been thinking came closer.

I was coming into the city along Anzac Parade. It was late and quiet. Occasionally a tram passed, an empty, illuminated box, leaping on the rails under a crackle of blue sparks. The trees were black and their leaves made a little dry sound like ghostly butter-pats. There were no soft rounded sounds in the night, only dry, brittle ones, and the pavement was gritty under my feet. My lips tasted of dust as they always did. The torrid street lamps were like sores on the night.

Walking alone at night always stimulated my imagination and now I was exalted as if with fever, but it was the city's fever, not mine. Images, like the empty, lit tram, ran through my mind and I was aware, with a febrile intensity, of my surroundings, immediate and remote.

It was the third waterless summer and the heat had come down like a steel shutter over the city. The winters between had been as bad, dry with a parching, unslaked cold, westerly winds that drove and drove, bringing such clarity to the air that a hill five miles away looked near enough to touch. The drought was in everything now, penetrating and changing life like blind roots at work upon a neglected pavement. The colours and quality of the world had been altered in the long months of desiccation. The pattern of existence was pulled awry.

Around the city there was a great fan of desolation. The sun had beaten the Emu Plains to a black-brown on which the isolated houses and the townships themselves drifted like flotsam on a dead sea. The mountains were not blue, but purple, a waterless ridge of rocks and shadows with the vegetation, except in the deepest seams of the valleys, mummified and black. Beyond again, the Bathurst Plains were like a petrified sea and very quiet, and farther west, in an eternity of their own, were the iron-hard, fissured Black Soil Plains. There was no green any-where. The stock had been driven away to agistment over the border long ago. Or had died. There was nothing even for the crows, who last year had had their saturnalia.

The country, with its endless aching death, pressed in on the city, the drought and the heat pressed on both. In the city and its environs its stamp was no less clear. The bush on the outskirts was more than half dead. Even the deep feeders, the blackbutts and their like, were dying. The life that was left was drawn in and banked down, muted and secret. The scrub was shabby and colourless. Fire had licked through it, leaving patches of black and sharp red-brown. Where there were houses wide fire-breaks had been cut as the only protection. Water could no longer be relied upon to combat the fires. These breaks were raw scars, even on the devastated country. They looked like the trail of vengeance. Orchards were long since dead and the trees fallen on the eroded ground. On the eastern slopes round Dural the orange-trees were burnt black. The flats that used to be vegetable gardens were bare, the last dried stalks blown away. Even Chinamen could make nothing grow.

In the wealthy suburbs of the North Shore and Vaucluse a change had taken place, too. It was as if the earth had been squeezed so that all the fine houses, that had nestled so comfortably in the contours and in the greenery, were forced up into the light. They bulged out, exposed, and the sun tore at them. The gardens that had embowered them were perished. Tinder-dry, fire had been through many of them, scorching walls and blistering away any plant that remained. Most of these houses were empty or inhabited, as if they were caves, by people who had come in from the stricken country. The owners had fled, not so much from present hardship, as from the nebulous threat of the future, the sense of being trapped in a doomed city. The shores of the harbour were lion-coloured or drab grey, sandhills showed a livid whiteness; only the water was alive and brilliant. And it was salt.

In the crowded districts there was less to perish, but light and air were equally abrasive, changing all surfaces, fading and nullifying all colour. There was no pleasure of touch left anywhere, for the dust was undefeatable. It pulled down pride and effort. The suburbs sagged under an intolerable burden.

I was perpetually aware of all this. It cumulated into a black wave which hung over me in threatening suspense. Nothing that I knew had escaped. From my windows I looked over the golf course, and that had taken, because it was defenceless, the clearest print of all. Its silvery green hills were stripped to pale brown and tawny purple. The earth was like starved, sagging flesh on an iron skeleton. Here and there a fire had run for a few yards before it had died for lack of tinder and left a black smear with a little edging of white ash. I used to think that the desert of Arizona looked like that. Now I know that heat and drought can bring even the gentlest country to it.

Yet this was consummation. Life was steep and furious, driven out beyond its own mediocrity at last, and I was glad to be carried on that wave towards an unalterable destiny.

There was a man walking in front of me whom I hadn't noticed before. When he passed a lamp I saw that he was a different shape from the pedestrians you'd expect to see about there. He was a swaggie all right, with his roll of old blue blanket across his shoulders and his quart-pot dangling from it. I overhauled him.

'Good night, mate.'

'Night, mate,' he answered as a bushman answers the gate-crashing townsman. He was an old-timer, might have been a fossicker, short and spare, with a wealth of grey whiskers and clothes subdued to use and wont as only a bushman's can be.

'Come far?' I asked him.

'Middlin' far.'

'Where's that?' I felt an insatiable curiosity.

'Back o' beyond.'

I'd seen hundreds like him, but here there was a sort of long-range persistence that was impressive. His gaunt and bristling dog at heel was cut out of the same stuff. My imagination took a leap.

'Did you ever do a perish on the Diamantina?'

'Aye, there and more places besides.'

'And now the track runs through the city?'

He didn't answer. So that was the way of it. I felt coldly sick. Looking back over my shoulder I saw that there were others, many of them, moving singly among the trees, all with the same intent, converging persistence. It would be the same on all the other highways. I took to the middle of the road and, almost, to my heels.

I reached Taylor Square ahead of them. The neon signs were sizzling and a few shop-windows still bulged with light on the indifferent night. There were hardly any people about in the narrow, crowded streets; at the bottom of the hill there were plenty, sitting on doorsteps, or on chairs dragged out on to the pavement. Children were playing languidly in the street because it was too hot to go to bed. There was a queue at the pump with buckets and kerosene tins and even jugs.

There was still water in the pipes, brownish stuff with a smell, but the pressure was so poor that it didn't reach the higher levels, so pumps had been put in where people could come and get it. The city hadn't been used to queues and they were changing the people's outlook. They made new channels for rumour, perhaps for thought.

So many things were different, and men's minds with them. Unemployment was general, either directly from scarcity or from its by-product of apathy. Idleness was everywhere and the people were differently distributed. Whole districts were almost depopulated, whilst others were overcrowded to suffocation. Practically all the food had to be brought in. Government was distributing it as a ration. There was enough and yet it didn't slake the public appetite. There was a sense of famine. Even those who were eating better than ever before felt it. The whole of our civilization was piled up like a pyre waiting for the fire to consume it.

The city seethed with rumours and with the promulgators of fantastic schemes, but every one was fatalistic about the drought. They didn't expect it to break, they even took an inverted pride in it. It at least relieved them of the responsibility of living their own lives. There was always a crowd at the General Post Office reading the bulletins that were posted hourly, but no one believed the jargon of lows, depressions and tropical disturbances, any more than they believed in the bona fides of the clouds that often blanketed the sky—as on this night—with their barren oppression. Yet nothing else mattered, all interest in outside events had been discarded as if it were the most obvious of luxuries. It was obvious that something must come sooner or later of this mass tension; but no one knew what. It was like a long thunderstorm that did not break. Apathy and exasperation were racing one another.

I followed the tram-line out of the hot and odorous streets. The open space beside the Blind Institute and the Domain beyond were crowded with people in search of air. They were quiet, bivouacked for the night, but never quite still. There was no grass to sit on, only dusty earth. The Botanic Gardens were the same, ruined between the drought and the trampling people. Authority had long ago given up the thankless task of conserving them.

I no longer wanted to get to the water. These febrile cravings died easily. I was just drifting. Did it matter what I did or where I went with those old-timers closing in? The narrow canyons of the city offered no relief. There was nothing for the mind to feed on but nostalgia. I remembered Macquarie Place and had a vision of it as it used to be, the three-cornered garden, the giant Port Jackson figs, dark against the pale, soaring buildings, the zinnias, the cushiony buffalo-grass, the statue, I forget its original, declaiming to the street, the anchor of the *Sirius* on a pedestal, Macquarie's obelisk in its bear-pit. . . . In the early days the officers and the higher officials lived round there. It was their compound, where the children romped in safety, and in the evening the regimental band played under those same trees, lovers counted the southern stars between the leaves and the gaiety of exiles flourished by candlelight. It was the outpost of something that had to fall, and it might be again. It was a goal, a place with significance in a meaningless desert, a spot where we might turn at last and resist invasion, the perishing men who came so quietly and surely through the dust. I hastened my steps like a hungry man who half remembers some forgotten fragment of food and hurries back to ransack his belongings once more. Down I went through narrow, twisting streets, between buildings glowing with heat but dead to light.

At first sight Macquarie Place did not seem to be greatly changed. The trees still stood and the lights showed the dark labyrinth of their leaves scarcely breached. It was, like all these places, crowded with people. I had the good fortune to find a seat on one of the benches. I was shaking with fatigue. All about me were points of light from cigarettes and a murmur of talking. Those crowds had their fits of talking and their fits of silence. I turned to my neighbour and was surprised to see that he was apparently in fancy dress: white breeches, a tail coat and a three-cornered hat. He was small and sharp, but fine, too. Before I could speak to him he addressed me:

'This is nothing new, sir, it happened before, and worse.'

'Indeed,' said I, not feeling comfortable.

'Not so much the drought—though that was bad enough, even the parrots were dropping dead out of the trees at Rose Hill—but the scarcity. You have no conception, sir, of what it was like then.'

'Was that long ago?' I asked, trembling.

'Some time ago. There was the same talk then of abandoning the settlement, but I didn't listen to it. I hope no one listens now. Of course, I've no authority these days. But if I could hang on surely you could. It was two and a half years before ships came from England that time. I'd grieve to see my work thrown away now.'

I got up hurriedly. 'Good night, Captain,' I said.

'Captain-General,' he corrected me.

A man buttonholed me. 'I've been to the Observatory every day, but no one will listen to me. In the Book of Revelations . . .'

I broke from him. I hoisted myself on to the pedestal and leaned against the anchor. That was something solid. Two men below me were quarrelling quietly. I tried to speak to them to tell them what would be happening to all of us soon. They both fell silent.

'That's right, mate,' said a man beside me whom I had not noticed. 'What we want's solidarity.'

I tried to see his face. 'Are you real?' I asked.

He laughed and called down to a friend: 'Here's a poor cove gone balmy.'

There was a roar of laughter and a screech came up. 'Don't laugh, you fools; repent.'

I sat trembling with rage. Let it happen to them, whatever it was. I wouldn't warn them.

Two men were talking over my head.

'There's a change coming.'

'I've heard that before.'

'It's true this time.'

'I don't hold with this metterology. It never did anything for us.'

'I don't either. I know this myself. Smell it, see? You listen, it'll begin any time.'

'I'll wait.'

'Feel that?'

'Nope.'

The country was coming to take its vengeance on

the city. Climax. Apotheosis. Then nothing. Come quickly. Come quickly. All ugliness, all corruption will be burned away.

'Feel that?'

'Something fell on my bald pate.'

'Rain.'

'Go on.'

'*Listen.*'

Silence fell. There was a crepitation among the leaves. Every one stood up, stock-still. I slid from the pedestal and stood with them. I felt the drops on my face. I was furious, nothing could hold me.

'No!' I shouted. It couldn't come now. It was too late. Our fate was on us. We were going up in fire, consummated. It was agony to turn back now with the end we had toiled so long to reach in sight.

There were people holding me. 'It isn't true!' I cried. 'It won't happen. No rain, ever.'

Someone forced me to my knees. There was a great silent ring of people round me. A match was struck and held in a cupped hand. I stared at the asphalt. Great black drops were falling on it, drying, disappearing, coming again, faster and faster, making a pattern like the leaves against the light, then coalescing and defacing it. I stared and stared. Out on the roads that pattern was tangling the feet of the perishing men, turning them back. Nothing would come of it now. Nothing would save us. We must take up the burden of remaking our world.

END OF AN IDOL
By Ernestine Hill

JACKADA saw him first—a puff of dust away on the plain across seven miles of glare. A small size in lubras, thin as a hairpin, stumbling up from the whip-spring well with a kerosene tin of water heavier than herself, it was remarkable that Jackada saw anything. One of her eyes slewed round south-west while the other gazed steadily north, and both were full of flies.

'Goldi-mun cummin'!' she shouted, and lifted her chin and pursed her lips to the distance.

The other blacks, sprawled in the shade of the meat-house, lazily followed the direction. Goldi-mun all right—some grey old prospector out of the ranges. The dust was low and steady and slow. No cattle-man ever travels donkeys. Sifting the sand through their long listless fingers, they made no move to tell white missus. Goldi-mun no matter, and Missus 'properly cranky longa that cookin''. Their voices drowsed away and they fell asleep.

The station roofs were a few white dots in the glaze of afternoon sun. The Boss was out with the stock-camp by some pandanus spring, and the Missus in the inferno of fire and hot iron that was the kitchen, brooding over her fate. No cook.

Out on the rim of beyond you cannot pick and choose your cooks, and any old passing bagman is welcome to take on the job, 'cooks, cuckoos and wilful murderers', clean and livery, or dirty and good-tempered, and the rest 'full-mooners'. Carozani Carlos de Blanco—he was the last one, eight months ago, a Castilian grandee who had forgotten Spanish. The one before that had been married in the Abbey by the Archbishop of Canterbury—or was it in St. Peter's by the Pope?—and the one before that was Pistol Bill, who spent all his spare time in the perilous recreation of firing at random targets through the kitchen window. Quaint old characters dreaming in age in a lonely country the adventures that in youth they missed. They can salt beef, and make yeast bread, and cook up hobble-gobble for the blacks, and so you are glad to have them—either that, or cook for the Boss, the blacks and the stock-camps yourself. That was her job for eight months now, and she was weary to death. No wonder they said it was no country for white women.

Sunset was smouldering in the ranges when the donkeys and the dust came in through the horse-paddock gate, and Missus, handing out the blacks their tea, was startled by a loud yacki of laughter. A fat little Sancho Panza in a cabbage-tree hat was standing up on his Dapple, rocketing round and round the poinciana tree. He slid down over the donkey's tail, turned a trim back somersault, and solemnly doffed the cabbage-tree in a sweeping theatrical bow.

'At your service, Missus!' he said. 'The Hidol of the Public.'

The lubras and piccaninnies shrieked and giggled, and Missus darkly scowled. Another full-mooner, the worst one yet.

'You can camp on the creek,' she called. 'Come up a bit later, and I'll cut off some dinner for you.'

The little man broke the tableau and smiled. His smile was reasonably sane.

'No offence, Missus!' he said. 'I always get the laughs, eh? Matchless Mirth-maker! Gusts of Gaiety! King of Comedy! See Billy Matthews in the Greatest Show on Earth. Meet the Hidol of the Public! You've heard of Hyland's Circus? That was my billing, Missus, in Hyland's Circus, an' I can show you them bills.'

'Mm. Well, we don't want any circus clowns here!' the Missus said dryly, and turned away.

'That's right! That's right. But you're lookin' for a cook. They told me at Bedford you was lookin' for a cook, so I threw on me packs an' come over. You won't beat my testaments, Missus—I been cook in every musterin' camp in the Territory in about ten years, and a white-tablecloth cook, you ask the boys.'

A bald, shiny little man, with a cockatoo crest of transparent white hair, and transparent twinkling eyes, he was normal enough close to, and his blue shirt was cleaner than most. The Missus sized him up. Bedford was two hundred miles away—a long spell with donkeys.

'What name did you say?'

'Billy Matthews.'

She had heard it. 'All right, Billy,' she said, 'I'll give you a try. You can take your swag to the men's huts—first room on the right. Have a wash and come up to the kitchen.'

He dragged his swag from the donkey, and threw it down in a little cloud of dust. Then his eye chanced to alight on her precious straggle of garden.

'Not carnations, Missus! Never them carnations in this country!'

A few spindly wisps and stalks, all joints and sinews, in the shelter of the hardy red cannas, had managed to survive. He went down on his hands and knees to make sure of them. The Missus was pleased. These exiles of a southern spring, under hostile suns and sands, had caused many a backache. She had said she would grow carnations, and she grew them, and never a visitor to see.

L

'Carnations.' The little bald man was lost in reverie. 'I haven't seen carnations in thirty-five years. By Jove, them things smell sweet! The bokays we used ta have of them when I was the Hidol of the Public!'

The Hidol of the Public he was from that moment on, to every wanderer of the track. When the mustering-camp rode in, they found him 'head serang' in the kitchen, 'running the gins around and gettin' work out of the whole jing-bang lot', the best of the wilful murderers the station had known. He could make a duff fit for a king, and put on dinner at Government House when the Missus was knocked out with the heat. She had time for her sewing-machine, and the homestead blossomed in new cretonnes, the lubras paraded in new dresses, colours all the week and white for Sundays. Bright smiles in dusky faces, they were willing slaves of 'ole Billy Hidol', a bubble of laughter and merry shrieks from morning till night at his antics and his childish japes.

That cheery waddling figure, white pants wrinkled above the elastic-side boots, round face beady with sweat, and likely as not a few black smudges for comedy, was a high spot in the melancholy sameness of the days. The men of the station liked him because he could put a crupper on a colt, and sit a buck over the wire fence. Once he rode out with the stock-camp, bringing a frying-pan and a mincer, if you please, to give them Number One Tucker out of the old salt beef, and on the way back he scattered a mob of cheeky-looking cattle-killers by the simple process of galloping down the gully standing up backwards on the horse. When the boys were out smoking on the back steps in the evening cool, he would give them the secret histories of the Greatest Show on Earth, the triumphs of the cities, the luck of the roads, and bring out the pile of old play-bills rolled up in his swag for years, with his own name as head-liner, Emperor of Mirth, Joey of Jollity, King of the Clowns.

Now and again when he was alone in the dull nights of do-nothing, when the mustering-camp was out, he strolled over to the blacks' camp to teach it new corroborees, all the dark eyes mesmerized and yacki ringing to the stars as he juggled a few knives and a tin plate in a red spotlight of camp-fire, bounced about with a paper tail on fire, and swung trapeze in the branches of the banyan tree. The piccaninnies worshipped him—whenever he went over to the store he was followed by a yelling mob of little Binghis, Jackada in the lead, all turning hand-springs and grinning at him wrong side up.

Yabber of the 'Hidol-corroboree' was passed on in fifteen languages till all the best black stock-boys of the big river, anxious to enlarge their dancing-corroboree, turned up at the station and asked for a job. He even charmed the myalls down from the ranges. The camp no longer whispered fearfully when 'bush black-fella' tracks were found in the morning, or when darker shadows than the trees flitted along the creek in the moonlight. 'No more cheeky-fella,' they reassured Missus. 'That-one been look-out longa Billy, I think. Him all right.' No one was speared in the station-camp that year, and the Boss heard about a good little mob of wild cattle out in country he had never been keen to ride.

But at the end of the second year the Hidol looked old and worn—the cocky crest hung dejected and limp, the twinkling eyes were pale and tired. He turned no more hand-springs and never made up with whitening and red ochre to startle the 'sing-about'.

He told the Missus he'd 'throw on the packs' because he 'couldn't get ahead with the work'.

'My brownie days are over,' he said. 'I reckon I've got white ants.'

The station decided he must go in to the hospital at Katherine to find out what the trouble was, and to rest there till after the wet. It was nearly a week's good riding, and he had to start at once to beat the rains. The Boss offered him horses, but no—he would go with his own donkeys. As a parting gesture, the Missus picked the last of that year's carnations. She pinned them to the Hidol's blue shirt.

'Now you get better, Bill,' she said, 'and come back soon. We'll be waiting for you after the wet.'

The blacks ran with him for four or five miles, as far as the river-crossing, and watched till the donkeys were a dust, and the dust gone.

The lone little cavalcade threaded the hills, cloud-shadows scudding before it; now and again a stony creek, a camp by a billabong at night; on through forests of bauhenia and silver box, winding down the gorges, then on across the buff-coloured downs, where the parrots were shimmering waves of light and the grey brolgas dancing. Once it passed a deserted out-camp, and once a lagoon of red lilies.

The rider saw none of these things. The breath of the withered carnations had drifted him back to the bitter-sweet of the past. . . . Linda, in her ballet skirt, riding, Madame Olinda, the World's Wonder Equestrienne, one hand to her painted lips and a chaplet of flowers in her hair, red-paper carnations.

. . .

The station blacks would never have known him now. The sun beat down on his cabbage-tree hat, his head was bent on his breast, and he was muttering

angrily, vindictively, the old forgotten words of the
sawdust ring in some poor little drama of that far-away
life. About him the glare of the rolling downs and the
heat-waves rolling. Linda was dead . . . long ago
dead . . . yet he pleaded with her, cursed her,
prayed to her as he rode.

It was nearing sundown on the third day that he
camped at Augusta Crown, that great white tent of a
quartzite hill that he had been watching for miles.
All through the breathless, menacing day he had
whipped on the donkeys through madmen's galleries
of ant-hills, the horrible half-formed effigies of a
crazed sculptor in the red desert sand. To his failing,
fever-addled mind they were faces, and alive—just as
in the old days, faces ringing him in. They were all
about him, smiling, beckoning, waiting for a show to
begin. He lay in the shade of a milkwood tree and
slept a little. It is not good that a man in fever should
travel those tracks alone.

The saffron-yellow sunset of the coming wet lay
over the plain when he wakened, Augusta Crown
shining above him, the Big Tent—those quartzite
walls swaying in the light, flimsy and unreal. The cry
of a rain-bird rang out like the long taut snap of a
whip.

The little man staggered up and stumbled forward.
He listened a moment and smiled to himself. Then
over and over he went in a mad whirl of hand-
springs, gambolling round, kissing his hand to the ant-
hills. He crowed like a cock and stood on his head,
spun like a top, turned catherine-wheels, then
bounced and bumped and pirouetted, running and
bowing in wide, crazy circles, and all the time holding
his sides in an eerie cackle of mirth. The clear whistles
of the bush birds at evening were as the clamour of a

crowd, and the gargoyle faces were closing in with the darkness, convulsed in a horrible silent laughter . . . one was a woman's, distorted and leering, a misshapen hand to its sagging lips, a chaplet of flowers in its hair.

He screamed and ran to destroy it, and tripped, and fell. Once, twice, he tried to rise, but the light was gone and the bush was quiet. He pillowed his head on his arm, there in the sand.

Riding in from Willeroo, the stockmen found him. In the goblin world of his own dreaming, in the ghostly shadow of that tented hill, the Hidol of the Public had taken the last call.

KAIJEK THE SONGMAN
By Xavier Herbert

KAIJEK THE SONGMAN and his lubra Ninyul came up the river, picking their way through wind-stricken cane-grass and palm-leaves and splintered limbs and boughs that littered the pad they were following. It was a still and misty morning, after a night of one of those violent south-east blows which clean up the wet monsoon. Mist hid the tops of the tall river timber and completely hid the swirling yellow stream. The day had dawned clear and cool; but now it was warming up again.

Sweat was trickling down Kaijek's broad gaunt face and through his curly raven beard, and down his long thin naked body from his armpits. He wore nothing but a loin-clout, a strip of dirty calico torn from a flour-bag and rigged on a waist-belt of woven hair. On his right shoulder he carried three spears and

a wommera; and from his left hung a long bag of
banyan-cord containing his big painted dijeridoo and
music-sticks. Fat little Ninyul, puffing at his heels,
bore the bulk of their belongings—swag balanced on
her curly head, big grass dillybag hanging from a
brow-strap down her back, tommy-axe and yam-
sticks in a sugar-bag slung on her left shoulder, and
fire-stick and billy in her right hand. She wore a
sarong made from an ancient blue silk dress.

Ninyul sniffed at the strong effluvium of her man.
Not that she objected to it. Indeed, she was as proud
of it as of his talent, of which she considered it an
expression. As her wide fleshy nostrils dilated, she
thought of how lesser songmen always came to him
during corroborees to have him rub them with his
sweat. And she glowed in recollection of the great
success he had made at the last gathering they had
attended—amongst the Marrawudda people on the
coast—with his latest song, 'The Pine Creek Races'.
Apart from the classics, corroboree-crowds liked
nothing better than a good skit in song on the ways
of the white man. But this pleasant recollection lasted
only for a moment. Ninyul became aware again of her
man's drooped shoulders and his frenzied gait; and
her anxiety for him in his struggle with his muse
returned. At full moon they were due to attend a great
initiation gathering amongst the Marratheil of the
Paperbarks. The moon was nearly full already; and
they were getting further from the Paperbarks every
day; and still Kaijek had not composed the song that
would be expected of him.

Kaijek was the most famous songman in the land.
His songs were known from the red mountains of the
Kimberley to the salt arms of the Gulf. Wherever they
went, Kaijek and Ninyul, who was always with him,

were warmly welcomed; for, though Kaijek's songs
always travelled ahead of him, he never failed to come
to a gathering with a new one. Not that Kaijek found
composing easy. Far from it! Often his muse would
elude him for moons. And so wretched would he
become in his impotence, and so ashamed, that—
pursued by Ninyul—he would fly from the faces of his
fellows, to range the wilderness like one of those
solitary ramping devil-doctors called the Moombas.

He was in the throes of that impotence now, while
he went crashing up the river through the tangle of
wrecked grass and trees. So he and Ninyul went on
and on, travelling at great speed, but heading nowhere. Wallabies heard them coming and fled
crashing and thudding from them. White cockatoos
in the river timber dropped down to pry at them, and
wheeled back shrieking into the mist. And on and on
—till suddenly they were stopped in their tracks by a
burst of uproarious dog-barking in the mist ahead.

Kaijek, staring ahead, heard the click of Ninyul's
tongue, and turned to her. She gave the sign 'white
man', then pointed with her lips to the left. Kaijek
looked and saw the stumps of a couple of saplings of
size such as no blackfellow ever would fell to make a
camp. Ninyul was already aware of the likelihood of a
white man's presence in the neighbourhood, because
some little distance back she had observed fresh
prints of shod horses, and just before the dog barked
had fancied she heard a horse-bell. Kaijek had seen
and heard nothing consciously for miles. He turned
and looked ahead again.

Then the dog appeared, a little red kelpie. When he
saw them he yelped, turned tail and disappeared,
yapping shrilly. They heard a white man yell at him.
Still he yapped. They judged the distance. For a

moment they stood. Ninyul glanced into the mist to the left, thinking of wheeling round that way to avoid what lay ahead. Then Kaijek turned to her again and hissed, 'Inta jah—tobacca!'

She nodded. They had been without tobacco for a long while. Kaijek had often moaned in his despair that if he had only a finger of tobacco he might find his song.

They went ahead cautiously. A score of paces brought them into dim view of a camp. There was a tent, a bark-roofed skillion, a bark-covered fireplace, a springcart, and pieces of mining gear. Kaijek and Ninyul knew what the gear was for, because they had often worked for prospectors. There was only one white man, and no sign of blacks. The white man was sitting on a box in the skillion, kneading a damper in a prospecting-dish between his feet, and looking into the mist in their direction. His dog was crouched before him, silent now, but tense.

Kaijek gave his spears and bag to Ninyul, but retained the wommera. Ninyul slipped behind a tree. Kaijek went on slowly. The white man soon saw him, stared hard at him with bulging blue eyes that bade him anything but welcome. Kaijek stopped at the fireplace. He knew the man slightly. He had seen him working a tin show in the Kingarri country, and had heard blacks describe him as a moody and often violent fellow. He was Andy Gant, a man of fifty or so, stout and stocky, with a big red bristly face and sandy greying hair and a long gingery unkempt moustache.

Andy Gant was in a particularly bad mood just then. The heavy humidity had upset his liver and brought out his prickly heat; which was why he was doing camp chores at that time of day, instead of digging gravel from the bench behind the camp and lumping it down to the sluice-box. To slave at digging that hard-packed gravel and washing out the lousy bit of gold it yielded was heart-breaking at any time, and too much to bear with a lumpy liver and fiery itch. He had slaved at that mean bench-placer throughout the wet, and had not won enough gold from it to pay for tucker, although the indications were that there was rich gold thereabouts. And most of the time he had been alone, deserted by the couple of blacks he had brought with him. He was just about ready now to shoot any nigger on sight.

Kaijek spat in the fire to show his friendliness, then grinned and said, 'Goottay, boss!' And he stroked his beard and lifted his right foot and placed it against his left thigh just above the knee, and propped himself up with the wommera.

For answer Andy raised a broken lip and showed big yellow teeth. Then he gave attention to his damper.

Kaijek coughed, spat again, then said, 'Eh, boss— me wuk longa you, eh?'

Andy's face darkened. He kneaded vigorously.

A pause, during which Kaijek coveted the pipe and plug of tobacco on the sapling-legged table at Andy's back. Then Kaijek said, 'Me prop'ly goot wukker, boss. Get up be-fore deelight, wuk like plutty-ell——'

Andy could contain himself no longer. With eyes ablaze he leapt to his feet and roared, 'Git to jiggery out of it, you stinkin' rottin' black sumpen, before I put a bullet through you.'

And his dog joined in with him, yapping furiously and dancing about.

'Wha' nim?' cried Kaijek, dropping his leg.

Andy grabbed a pick-handle with a doughy hand, and shouted, 'I'll show you what name, you beggin''

son of a sheeter—I'll show you what name—the ghost
I will!' And he rushed.

'Eh, look out!' yelled Kaijek, and turned and fled
back to Ninyul with the dog snapping at his heels.
Ninyul bowled the dog over with a stick. Then
together they snatched up their belongings and bolted
back along the track.

They stopped at the sapling stumps. 'Marjidi
naijil!' grunted Kaijek, and spat over his shoulder to
show his contempt. Then he pointed with lips to the
left, and set off in that direction. But though they were
not seen as they skirted the camp, and though they
went warily, their going was followed every step of the
way in imagination by Andy's dog yapping at his
master's side.

They had gone no more than fifty paces past the
camp, and were still at the foot of the flood-bench,
when they came upon a river-gum that had been
uprooted in the night. Kaijek paused to look among
the broken roots for bardies, and saw gold gleaming in
a lump of quartzy gravel. He knew gold well, but had
no more idea of its value than any average bush
blackfellow. He gave his spears to Ninyul, and fished
out the lump of gravel and freed the gold. It was a
nugget of about two ounces on a piece of quartz.
Kaijek picked it clean, spat on it, rubbed it on his
thigh, weighed it, then looked at Ninyul and said
with a grin, 'Kudjing-gah—tobacca!'

They turned back, heading straight for the camp.
The dog knew they were coming, and barked blue
murder. Andy, now at the fireplace setting his damper
in the camp-oven, rose up and peered into the mist
again; and when Kaijek appeared he let out a stream
of invective and grabbed up the pick-handle and
rushed.

'No more—no more!' yelled Kaijek, and held out the nugget in his palm.

Andy had the handle raised to hurl it at him. He saw the gold. But his dog was flying at Kaijek.

'Goold—goold!' yelled Kaijek, and flung it at Andy's feet, and made a swing at the dog with his wommera.

Andy snatched up the nugget, goggled at it, then looked up at Kaijek fighting with the dog, and rushed in with the handle to put the dog to flight. 'Where— where'd you find it?' he gasped.

Kaijek pointed with his lips and replied, 'Close-up behind.'

'Then show me,' gasped Andy. 'Show me!' And his voice rose shrill. ' Quick—where is it? Show me! '

Kaijek knew the symptoms of the fever. He turned and led the way with a rush.

Andy fairly flung himself at the roots. In a moment he had another nugget of an ounce or more, and then found one as big as a goose-egg. He turned his jerking face to Kaijek and cried, 'Go longa camp. Gettim pick an' shovel. An' the axe. Quick, quick!'

Kaijek moved to obey, then turned and said, 'Me hungry longa tobacca, boss.'

'Tobacca there longa camp.'

'No-more gottim pipe, boss.'

'Pipe there, too,' yelled Andy. 'Take it. Take anything you like. But be quick!'

Kaijek flew. Ninyul, in the background, set down the belongings and followed him. It was she who took the things to Andy. Kaijek stopped in the camp to chop up tobacco and fill Andy's pipe; and when he went to the fireplace to light the pipe he swigged a quart of cold stewed tea he found there. Then he strolled back to the tree, puffing luxuriously.

Andy now had a good dozen ounces of gold on a rock beside him, and was chopping off roots with the energy of a raving madman. And it was the eyes of a madman he turned on Kaijek when at length he paused for breath. He lowered the axe, and stepped up to Kaijek, and laid a great wet hairy hand on his slim black shoulder, and gurgled lovingly in his face, 'Thank you, brother, thank you! It's what I've been lookin' for all me flamin' life. An' I owe it all to you. Yes, to you who I nearly druv away.' He shook Kaijek till he rocked. 'I won't forget it,' he went on; and now he was near to tears. 'My oath I won't! I'll look after you, brother, don't you worry. I'll pay you the biggest wages a nigger ever got. I'll pay you bigger'n white man's wages. Oh, ghost, I love you! I'll buy you everything you ever want. Gawd bless you!' And with that he flung himself back at the roots.

For a while Kaijek watched him. Then he said, 'Eh, boss, me two-fella lubra hungry longa tucker.'

Andy stopped chopping and gasped at him, 'Plenty tucker longa camp. Take the lot. Take the rintin' jiggerin' lot! And when you're comin' back bring another pick an' shovel, an' a dish. There's damper in the oven. Eat it! Eat anything you flamin' well want to, brother. Everything I got is yours!'

Kaijek turned away, and signed to Ninyul, who picked up the belongings and followed him to the camp.

They sat by the fireplace, gorging bully-beef and hot damper and treacle, and swilling syrupy tea, while the racket of Andy's joyous labouring went on in the distance. Then they sat taking turn about with the pipe. Twice Andy yelled to them to come see fresh treasures he had unearthed. The first call Kaijek answered. Ninyul answered the second, because Kaijek, the artist, staring fixedly at the fire and humming to himself, did not hear it. Then suddenly Kaijek leapt up and smacked his rump and danced a few steps and began to sing:

> *O munnijurra karjin jai, ee minni kinni goold,*
> *Wah narra akinyinya koori, mungawaddi yu . . .*

He swung on Ninyul, whose eyes were shining and lips aquiver. For a moment he stared at her. Then he began to clap his hands and stamp a foot.

Kaijek stopped, turned panting to Ninyul. She leapt and cried joyously, 'Yakkarai!'

Then Andy's voice rang out through the thinning mist, 'Eh, brother—come here! Come quick! Come quick an' see what the angels 've planted for you an' me. O Gawd!' He ended with a sob.

Kaijek looked towards him for a while. Then he turned back to Ninyul and made a sign. She went to their belongings. He followed her, and gathered up his stuff and shouldered it, then led the way down the river again, heading full speed for the gathering in the Paperbarks.

FEAR

By H. Drake-Brockman

THE woman stood in the doorway of her wood-and-iron house and looked across to the big shed. If anything, the shed appeared rather better finished than the house. But they were neither of them much; the buildings had only been there a year or two—set back a little from the creek, where the river-gums, as befitted the only trees for miles, smirked at their reflections in a dark pool—set back right on the edge of the ranges, on the very rim of civilization.

The slanting afternoon sun made the spiky, prickly tufts of spinifex grass look soft, luxurious; then spent its golden virtue in a riot of rainbow colour over on the ironstone ridge. And the dry, aromatic smell of an uninhabited land rose fragrant to the nostrils.

Behind the house, in the brush lean-to serving as kitchen—it was cooler that way and kept the flies from the house—the woman could hear Edie and Sam at play with pots and cans. She would have to stop them —too costly and difficult to get if small hands should do damage. And they'd be getting into the store-cupboard next—Sam was a terror for sugar, just like the natives! Baby would be awake in a few minutes, too; he was regular as a clock for his feed.

Yet she continued to stand there, staring across at the shed. She was feeling restless; had she not been a woman of great sense and fortitude, she would have called herself nervous.

The sunlight streamed without mercy on her well-worn print dress with its boned bodice and yards of skirt; but it caressed lightly a young face long since drained of colour, tanned to a golden brown. The light had drawn early lines round a pair of blue eyes, too; she was for ever running out, hatless, into the glare after the children.

All round about the few scattered buildings roamed her blue eyes. Except for little noises from the children, and the caw-cawing of crows sailing over the killing pen, an unearthly silence wrapped the place. Not a native in sight. The kitchen gins had padded off to their noon camp the moment washing-up was over. Most afternoons she could stand and listen to the tapping of sticks or a drowsy corroboree chant. But to-day everything was silent. She imagined it must have been the silence that had brought her out.

Where were little Johnnie, and that Lloyd?

She didn't like Lloyd. She had told John so, many a time. But her husband just said men were difficult to get; Lloyd was all right, a good stockman and all that. But she didn't trust the fellow; he was altogether too rough on the natives. John himself could be brutal enough at times, but he was always just; the boys respected the boss, liked him—his kind of brutality was their own, and seen only when the isolation of the place rendered a firm hand advisable. But that Lloyd! She could never forget seeing him set the dogs on to the gins one day, so the poor wretches ran screaming to the trees and scaled them like cats. Horrible, it had been. And Lloyd had laughed fit to kill himself. Pity he hadn't! She had told John. That time he had spoken to the man, said such a thing must not happen again. And it hadn't.

All the same, she did wish it had not been necessary for John to go into the port to meet their first mob of sheep, to leave her like this, alone with the children and Lloyd.

The man she was thinking about came suddenly round the shed, little Johnnie at his heels. The small boy staggered along under the weight of a saddle; the man carried a knot of twine. The mother's anger rose. Just like him! There they had seated themselves, backs to the shed, and Lloyd was proceeding to mend a rent in the leather. She would call Johnnie, she decided, get him to mind the others. She hated the way he was for ever trailing after Lloyd. But what could you expect? A little fellow of seven loved to be out with the men, and the sooner a child learned to fend for himself in this country the better.

Her lips parted for a shout which congealed to a strangled intake of breath.

Once again round the corner came a figure, a painted buck. Red and yellow ochre and a white lime pattern on his body made him look like a walking skeleton. Quicker than thought the long shaft of the spear already quivering in his wommera flew out. It missed the little boy by inches and buried itself, still quivering, in the man's outstretched arm. Before ever Lloyd yelled, the native was gone.

The woman ran across the hard earth, her tanned face livid, yellow. The child flew to meet her. The man lay picking at the spear hanging from his arm. His eyes twisted, terrified.

But there was nothing to see. Everything was silent, except for the short sobs of the boy and the cawing of the crows.

She left the four children with Lloyd in the front room while she went alone to the kitchen for hot water. Johnnie seemed calm enough now, only interested, like the others, in the barb stuck in Lloyd's arm, and keen to watch the blood oozing out. 'It was Billycan, that was,' the boy kept repeating excitedly. 'Why ever should old Billy do that?'

Lloyd said nothing. He was white and trembling. The woman, as she fetched the water, decided she would have to give him a little of the whisky she kept, hidden, just in case. Her eyes raked the plain and slid along the creek-bed. She wanted to keep her mind busy with observation, but there was nothing worth observing. Still only the silent countryside. She could sweep the horizon right round and see nothing. She found herself thinking that the gins wouldn't be coming up now—probably the camp was deserted; they had cleared to the hills. She couldn't expect John for another couple of days, either. Hastily she dragged her mind from such thoughts and ran back to the house.

She had already broken the shaft from the barb— only about a foot stuck out of Lloyd's arm now.

'It'll hurt,' she said to him. 'I'll have to cut it out.' He whined.

'I'll give you something first,' she said and, going to the bedroom, came back with a tot in an old pannikin. 'There'll be another when it's over,' she said.

She sent the children away—told them to keep baby quiet; he was wide awake now and would begin fretting soon. Then she ripped up a sheet.

She hated touching the man. And he shrank beneath her gentle hands, whined again, begged more whisky. His beady dark eyes, set in a face dirty with half-grown beard, grew scared and shifty.

The woman said: 'It's got to be done, Lloyd. Don't be a fool.' And she did it. A bloody job. But at last it was finished, the wound bound, most of the mess cleared away. Lloyd had another tot. Then demanded the lot. Said he needed it.

'No,' she said.

'Yes, missus. You make no mistake about it. I'm having that whisky and then—well, I'm scooting.'

'Scooting?' she repeated blankly, her mind with the children.

'Scooting. Going. Clearing out. That's plain, ain't it? I'm not stopping here for no more blanky niggers to run spears through me! I'm off into the town, I am. The boss left one moke in the horse-yard, and that's mine. Or soon will be. I'm off. I'll tell 'em to hurry on out here, if you like.'

She flared. 'Thank you! Call yourself a man, do you?'

'Hell to you! I'm going. Anyway, you're all right, missus. The abos ain't no call to touch you. Didn't you reckon they would all be gone?'

'Yes. But if it *was* all right, they would still be here. They mean trouble when they go.'

'Well, I tell you I'm not staying, anyhow.'

She noticed he was still trembling. 'Go, then,' she flung at him. 'You're no use as you are!' So that he would not discover her fear, she turned aside.

Too late she realized he was banging the door behind him and that the whisky bottle was under his arm. Like a fool she had let him take it!

She fought down her fears, and with a smiling face went in to the children. But Edie said, as she was pushed aside from the baby, 'Oh, Mum, how cold your hands are!'

Johnnie immediately wanted to go outside, but she forbade him. They had to stay and play quietly while she nursed baby. And as she sat there, on the low chair her husband had made, her mind flew back and forth like one of the ever-hovering crows.

Presently the beat of a horse's hoofs hammered the silence.

'Mum,' cried Johnnie from the window, 'where's Lloyd going?'

'Just a message for me,' she answered tranquilly; but, sharp and bitter, her mind recalled the chance-heard remark of another man, an epithet applied to Lloyd. 'It's right, too,' she thought. '"Not got the pluck of a louse", he said. That's just what Lloyd is—vermin. No good in him.'

All the afternoon nothing stirred outside. The children grumbled at having to stay with their mother; they wanted to go down to the camp and play with the blacks. At sundown the woman fed them well, and put on what warm clothes they possessed. The nights grew cold outside. Then she made up a packet of food and filled three water-bags. She went into the bedroom, returned wearing a coat; in the secrecy of her pocket her fingers closed on the butt of a revolver her husband had given her when first they sailed north.

Already it had grown murky outside, with the swift falling of the Australian night.

'Come, children,' she said, 'we're going walkabout to-night. It will be fun to camp out in the spinifex.'

She could not repress a shudder. Often enough she had groaned over her rough little home. Yet how cosy it looked now, and safe! Filled with things she had herself fashioned from bits and ends, just to make it bright. She lit the lamp, set it on the table, and drew the curtains.

She picked up the baby. As she went out, followed by the children carrying the water-bags, she wondered if she was being a fool—subjecting them to unnecessary exposure. Well, in that case they could return in the morning. But she felt she couldn't risk the night; the natives might come after Lloyd again; they might come after the stores; that one act of violence might have gone to their heads. She did not want to think the childlike people she had so often looked after would set out to harm her children or herself; but she had to remember that two years ago they had not ever seen a white man.

She did not make the children walk far: if the worst befell they would have many miles to go. Just a little

way on towards the distant settlement she took them;
then, hiding snug behind an outcrop of rocks, she
settled them down. Even though it was pitch-black
by now, she knew that she was still within sight of the
homestead.

Sam and Edie fell asleep. 'Mum,' whispered
Johnnie, 'are you frightened of the abos? Don't be
scared, Mum, I'll look after you. Why did old Billycan
do that to Lloyd, Mum?'

'I'm not frightened,' she replied. How frightened
she was! 'But I think they might go a bit mad
to-night. . . . Lloyd was a rough, bad man, son,
that's why.'

An age she crouched there, it seemed to the woman.
Even Johnnie prattled himself to sleep. She began to
call herself a silly, nervous creature.

A tongue of flame leapt up in the darkness. To the
woman it seemed to leap through her own veins. The
shed! They had fired the shed!

Instantly with the light came sounds. The sharp,
staccato barking of dogs, shrill native voices, yells,
bursts of song. As the light gained she could distinguish figures leaping like black imps in the blaze of
a second fire. That was the house! She knew now that
the storeroom had been raided; she could see black
naked figures posturing about, throwing things to each
other.

The noise increased. She shook the children. Time
to move. As long as the natives feasted and played with
the fire she was safe; she still did not want to think
they would hurt her—but they had burned her home.
Guilty consciences wrought terrible crimes. They
could track her so easily had they a mind.

She looked at the heavens, took a bearing south
by the Cross and the cold sparkling Pointers, and

stumbled off, the sleepy children dragging at her heels. There would be a moon later, she remembered with thankfulness, after Sam had been picked up and the place kissed five times—she had to take his water-bag, along with the baby, then. Yet she stumbled on, resolute, cheerful with the children.

At last the moon rose, but its fading brilliance only unleashed her long-held fear. The country lay spread about like a desert peopled with terror, a void filled by shadows having no substance. Cold, cruel, impersonal, rejecting the soft alien woman and her brood.

The baby wakened, began to kick and struggle. Her whispers and the thin cries of the children seemed to reverberate like a laugh echoing beneath a church dome. She offered no comfort when Sam and Edie started to complain. She was sharp now. She gave the baby to Johnnie, and he staggered along as best he might, while the mother took Sam pick-a-back. She found the child's weight did nothing to deaden the nausea threatening to engulf her, the sickness of fear.

At length the keen edge of sensation dulled. She no longer looked at every shadow with a cold thrill of rigid expectancy; she no longer strained her ears for fancied footfalls.

She grew harsh with the children. A slave-driver. Even Johnnie sobbed at her rough words. And he was being so good! 'Don't fret, Mum,' he kept on saying. 'They wouldn't hurt us. Billycan's a mate of mine—they wouldn't hurt us.'

The night was without end; the country without end. Did there exist, anywhere in this grey and silver emptiness, human creatures other than black devils: were there houses, helping hands?

Dawn at last—and an unbearable radiance in the

skies. A hard, rough land; and a sun gaining hourly in strength. A short sleep for the children. A drink of water and a piece of bread. Then up and on.

The woman felt safe from the natives now. She could reckon they would not attack until night fell again, if they were after her. That was what the men always said, anyhow. But if John were not already on the way out! The ghastly sickness swept back—they would all perish long before little legs could reach the settlement.

She was too tired to think for long. It took all her energy to watch. Up and on, then; up and on; through heat, with flies clinging and children crying. Hotter and hotter and hotter.

They had come on to the track—faint wheel-marks across the baked earth—soon after sunrise. It was Johnnie who spotted his father. The woman was trudging along with her eyes on the ground; she was carrying both Sam and the baby now. Breathing burnt her chest. Yet not until she looked into her husband's face did she realize *how* she must look. Haggard, livid, fallen-in, his face was. He had been riding, with two others, most of the night. That miserable Lloyd must have passed them, after all!

'Anna,' was all her husband could say for a bit. 'My God! Anna!'

The evil wrought by Lloyd was over, the woman told herself; but as she sobbed out her tale she knew it had only just begun. The other men were petting and soothing the children; Johnnie was boasting of all he'd done, telling them Billycan was a mate of his. Her husband's hand on her wrist felt safe, firm, tender.

'We'll take you into town, dearest,' he said. 'Then we'll come back and teach those black devils a lesson.'

'Lloyd!' she murmured.

'He'll have to leave the North, I reckon,' struck in one of the men.

'It was all his fault,' she repeated. But she knew it was no use arguing. The work of years had been destroyed; probably half their cattle had been speared now, too. What devils fear made of men, whether black or white—an hour ago she had been inhuman herself! But now, as she lifted heavy eyes to her husband's grim mask, she felt sorry for the natives.

'TELL US ABOUT THE TURKEY, JO . . .'

By ALAN MARSHALL

HE came walking through the rusty grasses and sea-weedish plants that fringe Lake Corangamite. Behind him strode his brother.

He was very fair. His hair was a pale gold and when he scratched his head the parted hairs revealed the pink skin of his scalp. His eyes were very blue. He was freckled. His nose was tipped upward. I liked him tremendously. I judged him to be about four and a half years old and his brother twice that age.

They wore blue overalls and carried them jauntily. The clean wind came across the water and fluttered the material against their legs. Their air was one of independence and release from authority.

They scared the two plovers I had been watching. The birds lifted with startled cries and banked against the wind. They cut across large clouds patched with blue and sped away, flapping low over the water.

The two boys and I exchanged greetings while we

looked each other over. I think they liked me. The little one asked me several personal questions. He wanted to know what I was doing there, why I was wearing a green shirt, where was my mother? I gave him the information with the respect due to another seeker after knowledge. I then asked him a question and thus learned of the dangers and disasters that had beset his path.

'How did you get that cut on your head?' I asked. In the centre of his forehead a pink scar divided his freckles.

The little boy looked quickly at his brother. The brother answered for him. The little boy expected and conceded this. He looked at the brother expectantly and, as the brother spoke, the little boy's eyes shone, his lips parted, as one who listens to a thrilling story.

'He fell off a babies' chair when he was little,' said the brother. 'He hit his head on a shovel and bled over it.'

'Ye-e-s,' faltered the little boy, awed by the picture, and in his eyes was excitement and the thrill of danger passed. He looked across the flat water, wrapt in the thought of the chair and the shovel and the blood.

'A cow kicked him once,' said the brother.

'A cow!' I exclaimed.

'Yes,' he said.

'Go on, Jo,' said the little boy eagerly, standing before him and looking up into his face.

'He tried to leg-rope it,' Jo explained, 'and the cow let out and got him in the stomach.'

'In the stomach,' emphasized the little boy, turning quickly to me and nodding his head.

'Gee!' I exclaimed.

'Gee!' echoed the little boy.

'It winded him,' said Jo.

'I was winded,' said the little boy slowly, as if in doubt. 'What's winded, Jo?'

'He couldn't breathe properly,' Jo addressed me.

'I couldn't breathe a bit,' said the little boy.

'That was bad,' I said.

'Yes, it was bad, wasn't it, Jo?' said the little boy.

'Yes,' said Jo.

Jo looked intently at the little boy as if searching for scars of other conflicts.

'A ladder fell on him once,' he said.

The little boy looked quickly at my face to see if I was impressed. The statement had impressed him very much.

'No?' said I unbelievingly.

'Will I show him, Jo?' asked the little boy eagerly.

'Yes,' said Jo.

The little boy, after giving me a quick glance of satisfaction, bent and placed his hands on his knees. Jo lifted the back of his brother's shirt collar and peered into the warm shadow between his back and the cotton material.

'You can see it,' he said uncertainly, searching the white skin for its whereabouts.

The little boy twisted his arm behind his back and strove to touch a spot on one of his shoulders.

'It's there, Jo. Can you see it, Jo?'

'Yes. That's it,' said Jo. 'You come here and see.' He looked at me. 'Don't move, Jimmy.'

'Jo's found it,' announced Jimmy, his head twisted to face me.

I rose from my seat on a pitted rock nestling in grass and stepped over to them. I bent and looked beneath the lifted collar. On the white skin of his shoulder was the smooth ridge of a small scar.

'Yes. It's there all right,' I said. 'I'll bet you cried when you got that.'

The little boy turned to Jo. 'Did I cry, Jo?'

'A bit,' said Jo.

'I never do cry much, do I, Jo?'

'No,' said Jo.

'How did it happen?' I asked.

'The ladder had hooks in it . . . ' commenced Jo.

'Had hooks in it,' emphasized the little boy, nodding at me.

'And he pulled it down on top of him,' continued Jo.

'Oo!' said the little boy excitedly, clasping his hands and holding them between his knees while he stamped his feet. 'Oo-o-o!'

'It knocked him rotten,' said Jo.

'I was knocked rotten,' declared the little boy slowly, as if revealing the fact to himself for the first time.

There was a pause while the little boy enjoyed his thoughts.

'It's a nice day, isn't it?' Jo sought new contacts with me.

'Yes,' said I.

The little boy stood in front of his brother entreating him with his eyes.

'What else was I in, Jo?' he pleaded.

Jo pondered, looking at the ground and nibbling his thumb.

'You was in nothin' else,' he said, finally.

'Aw, Jo!' The little boy was distressed at the finality of the statement. He bent suddenly and pulled up the leg of his overalls. He searched his bare leg for marks of violence.

'What's that, Jo?' He pointed to a faint mark on his knee.

'That's nothin',' said Jo. Jo wanted to talk about ferrets. 'You know, ferrets . . . ' he began.

'It looks like something,' I said, looking closely at the mark.

Jo leant forward and examined it. The little boy, clutching the crumpled leg of his trousers, looked from my face to his brother's and back again, anxiously waiting a decision.

Jo made a closer examination, rubbing the mark with his finger. The little boy followed Jo's investigation with an expectant attention.

'You mighta had a burn once. I don't know.'

'I wish I did have a burn, Jo,' said the little boy. It was a plea for a commitment from Jo, but Jo was a stickler for truth.

'I can't remember you being burnt,' he said. 'Mum'd know.'

'Perhaps you can think of another exciting thing,' I suggested.

'Yes,' said the little boy eagerly. He came over and took my hand so that we might await together the result of Jo's cogitation. He looked up at me and said, 'Isn't Jo good?'

'Very good,' I said.

'He knows about me and everything.'

'Yes,' I said.

There was a faint 'yoo-hoo!' from behind us. We all turned. A little girl came running through the rocks in the barrier that guarded the lake from the cultivated lands. She had thin legs and wore long, black stockings. One had come loose from its garter, and, as she ran, she bent and pulled and strove to push its top beneath the elastic band. Her gait was thus a series of hops and unequal strides.

She called her brothers' names as she ran, and in her voice was the note of the bearer-of-news.

'Dad must be home,' said Jo.

But the little boy was resentful of this intrusion. 'What does she want?' he said sourly.

The little girl had reached a flat stretch of grass and her speed increased. Her short hair fluttered in the wind of her running.

She waved a hand. 'We have a baby sister!' she yelled.

'Aw, pooh!' exclaimed the little boy.

He turned and tugged at Jo's arm. 'Have you thought of anything exciting yet, Jo?' His face lit to a sudden recollection. 'Tell him how I got chased by the turkey,' he cried.

BLOW CARSON, I SAY
By Alan Marshall

WHEN night came I heard him again. I swore and lit my pipe, then walked to the door of the hut and looked towards the river. The red gums that fringed its banks made twisted scrolls on the sky's edge. The stars were coming out and I could smell the breath of the lignum and reeds that spread back from the river in a protecting barricade of shadowy growth. Plovers cried across the sky. I listened, but he was silent. I waited a few minutes, then went back into the hut. Surely he won't cross the river again, I thought.

He was an old scrub bull, a brindle with snaily horns who roamed the timbered hills beyond the Murray. I had one of Carson's shorthorns running with my herd, and though I paid only a tenner for him Carson said he was a champion. 'He's a champion, I'm telling you,' he used always to say. The old scrub bull used to spend a lot of time trumpeting challenges across the river, but I did not think he would swim across again to fight it out.

I had driven him back a week before, and that morning I gave him Larry Dooley across the bend after I had found the two facing each other in a clearing.

I drove him through the reed beds at a gallop. Near the river the water became deeper and I drew rein. He slowed down then and began to bellow. I cracked the stock-whip and yelled at him. He moved forward, a low, sullen rumble coming from his throat.

He was a big bull and he sank deep in the mud. He plunged violently as his hind-legs failed to find a solid footing. A spray of muddy water shot above the reeds and splashed against his sides. A frightened water-hen shot from a clump of lignum and hurtled across the river with its feet scratching furrows on the smooth water. The bull suddenly slid into deep water between the submerged river banks. It curved in a tumbling roll around his chest. He lifted his head till the level plane of forehead and nose was parallel with the surface and struck out for the other bank. I watched him wade ashore with water streaming down his flanks and mixing with the mud clinging to his legs.

Next morning I saddled up and rode along a pad skirting the reeds. Even then it must have been touching a hundred. Just above the ground the air shimmered in waves and in the distance cattle had the appearance of being submerged in water.

I heard the old bull trumpeting across the river. He lowed menacingly, then sucked in his breath in a high-pitched challenge. I rode towards the bend and saw

him standing on the opposite bank. He was silent now
and stood with his head rigidly still, the muzzle pulled
in towards his neck. His tail was held away from his
hindquarters. His stillness was an alive and ominous
thing.

On my side of the river billows of dust were rising
from beyond the reeds beside which I had reined my
horse. The young shorthorn was expressing defiance
of the old bull's challenge by savagely pawing the
brown earth and tossing the dust into the air. It fell
upon his shoulders and spilled to the torn ground. He
buried his short horns into the soil and flung lumps of
grass and earth above his head.

I was proud of that bull. Carson said he was a
champion. 'He'll improve your herd out of sight,' he
had said. But this day I had no sympathy for him in
his quarrel. I suddenly felt sorry for the old campaigner
who was fast losing his right to the country he had
ruled over for so long. Where he had wandered without hindrance, barbed-wire fences now barred his way.
Men were pushing their way farther and farther into
the hills that sheltered him. One by one the sleek cows
that had borne his progeny were rounded into cattle-
yards. Milling and crushing against each other, their
lifted heads supported by the flanks of those snorting
in front of them, they surged forward to escape the
savage attacks of wall-eyed heelers. They blundered
forward in droves, urged by shouting men along the
stock route that led to the railhead and to trucks dirty
with the smoke of cities. The old bull's hocks still bore
the teeth scars of dogs. The calloused ridge of a stock-
whip cut slashed his flank. Carson had told me of the
furious charge that shattered a six-foot post-and-rail
fence and earned him the freedom he alone enjoyed.

He had warned me about him, too. 'Don't let him

get with your herd. He'll ruin your stock. Now, my bull, he's a champion——'

I tied the horse to a yellowjack and crept towards the river. I crouched behind a log and watched the old warrior slide stiff-legged down the dusty bank. He waded through the shallow water, then, snorting, launched himself forward.

My champion waited for the challenger. He moved his hindquarters, using his firmly placed front legs to pivot on so that he faced the old bull as he clambered up the bank. The old chap shuffled sideways towards him. The shorthorn changed his position so that he stood at right angles to the older bull's approach. Both their heads were drawn sharp down. When the scrubber was within a few yards of the youngster he stopped. They both stood very still, their small, black eyes gleaming with a cold, calculating fury.

'My champion shorthorn,' I kept saying to myself. 'Don't be a fool. Carson says he's a champion, but if he gets one good rip he won't be worth two bob. Hop in and stop them.' But then I thought of the old fellow's horns. He couldn't do any harm with snaily horns like that, and, anyway, the shorthorn had youth on his side.

He had youth all right, and the impetuous courage of youth. He suddenly lowered his head and, whipping into position, drove for the old bull's shoulder, but, quick as a dingo, the veteran leapt round and met the powerful head of the champion with his own.

Head to head they dug their hooves into the ground and struggled to force each other back. With enormous shoulders bulged with straining muscle they pivoted around their locked heads, tearing the earth for a foothold, each striving for a quick, evasive leap sideways that would leave him free to drive a rip to the other's shoulder. I was shaking a little as if it were friends of mine that fought together. I repeated softly to myself: 'Carson says he's a champion. Carson says he's a champion '—and then, 'You old beauty,' I cried.

The old bull had made a savage lunge forward. He drove the youngster back with a swift rush. The shorthorn bellowed with surprise and rage. He leaped sideways, evaded a side toss that the old chap aimed at his shoulder, then hurled himself at the other's exposed side. One of his shining horns slid into the thick flesh behind the warrior's shoulder and he tossed his head, tearing his horn through flesh and muscle and then wrenching it free in a savage twist.

The red blood gushed down the scrubber's brindle hide. It stained the champion's horn with crimson and trickled among the close-curled hair between his eyes. I had expected a roar of pain from the old chap, but, save for a deep grunt when the horn sank home, he was silent. He twisted away in a quick leap and turned to face a rush from the champion. The impetus of the drive forced him back. His hindquarter scraped across the jagged end of a broken limb projecting from a stump. He bellowed with rage and stayed his backward run with a convulsive thrust of his back legs that scattered the dry leaves and sticks behind him. Step by step he forced the champion back.

Suddenly, with the skill learned in a hundred fights, the old bull gave ground in a leap backwards. The shorthorn, freed from pressure, blundered forward to lock horns again. But the old bull was not there. He had whirled to one side and, bellowing savagely, he now drove his lowered head at the other's side. His thick-boned crown slid beneath the young bull's body. He reefed his powerful neck upwards, lifting the shorthorn from his feet and throwing him floundering

M

to the ground, and then drove in again, sinking to his knees the better to bury his snaily horns in the other's soft body.

The champion bellowed and kicked in anguish. He rolled, half rose, fell again. Strands of tenuous saliva blew from his mouth. The silver threads clung like cobwebs to the old bull's head. The old scrubber crushed his plated head against the champion's ribs, shaking it to and fro in a savage mutilating of his fallen antagonist. The shorthorn rolled clear and, springing to his feet, fled, with the old bull in pursuit.

The scrubber did not chase him far. He stopped and pawed at the earth, tossing lumps of soil shoulder high and lowing triumphantly. I made a bee-line for my horse.

'Back over the river he goes,' I said; but when I returned I reined the horse and looked at him. He was grazing quietly amongst several of my best heifers.

I swung my stock-whip, then slowly looped it again.

'The shorthorn may be a champion,' I said to myself, 'but so is this fellow. Blow Carson, I say.'

I turned my horse and made for the hut, and I felt better somehow.

THE NIGHTSHIFT
By John Morrison

Eight o'clock on a winter's evening.

Two men sit on the open section of a tramcar speeding northwards along St. Kilda Road. Two stevedores going to Yarraville—nightshift—'down on the sugar'.

One—old, and muffled to the ears in a thick overcoat —sits bolt upright, his tired eyes fixed on the far end of the car with that expression of calm detachment characteristic of the pipe-smoker. His companion, a much younger man, leans forward with hands clasped between his knees, as if enjoying the passing pageant of the famous road.

'It'll be cold on deck, Joe,' remarks the young man. 'It will that, Dick,' replies Joe. And they both fall silent again.

At Toorak Road a few passengers alight. A far greater number crowd aboard. Mostly young people going to dances and theatres. Smoothly groomed heads and white bow-ties. Collins Street coiffures and pencilled eyebrows and rouged lips. Creases and polished pumps. Silk frocks and bolero jackets. They fill the tram right out to the running-boards. The air becomes heavily scented.

The young wharfie, mindful of past rebuffs, keeps his seat. He can still see the road, but within twelve inches of his face a remarkably small hand is holding a pink silk dress clear of the floor. He finds it a far more interesting study than the road. Reflects that he could enclose it completely and quite comfortably within his own big fist. Little white knuckles, the fingers of a schoolgirl, painted nails—like miniature rose-petals. He sniffs gently and appreciatively. Violets. His gaze moves a little higher to where the wrist—a wrist that he could easily put thumb and forefinger around—vanishes into the sleeve of the bolero. Higher still. Violets again. Real flowers this time, to go with the perfume. From where he's sitting, a cluster of purple on a pale cheek. She's talking to a young fellow standing with her; her smile is a flicker of dark eyelashes and a flash of white teeth.

Dick finds himself contrasting his own immediate future with that of the girl's escort. Yarraville and the Trocadero. Sugar-berth and dance-floor. His eyes fall again to the little white hand so near his lips, and he sits back with an exclamation of contempt as he catches himself wondering what she would do if he suddenly kissed it. Sissy!

Old Joe's thoughts also must have been reacting to the impact of silks and perfumes.

'The way they get themselves up now,' he hisses into Dick's ear, 'you can't tell which is backside and which is breakfast.'

Dick eyes him with mild resentment. 'What's wrong with them? They look good to me.'

Joe snorts his disagreement, and the subject drops. Dick is only amused. He understands Joe. The old man had showed no disapproval of similar passengers who joined the tram at Alma Road and in Elsternwick. It's the name: 'Toorak'. It symbolizes something. Poor old Joe! Too much courage and not enough brain. Staunch as ever, but made bitter and pig-headed with the accumulation of years. Weary of 'The Struggle'. Left behind. A trifle contemptuous of the young bloods carrying the fight through its final stages. A grand mate, though. And a good hatchman. That means a lot on a sugar job. With the great bulk of the old stevedore at his elbow, and the little white hand before his face, Dick is sensitive of contact with two worlds. Shoddy and silk. Strong tobacco and a whiff of violets. Yesterday and To-morrow.

Flinders Street—Swanston Street intersection. They get off and push through the pleasure-seeking crowd on the wide pavement under the clocks. Another tram. Contrast again. Few passengers this time. One feels the cold more. Swift transition from one environment

to another. Swanston Street to Spencer Street. Play to
work. Light to darkness. No more silks and perfumes.
Shadowy streets almost deserted. Groups of men,
heavily wrapped against the cold, tramping away
under the frowning viaduct.

'It'll be a fair bitch on deck,' says Joe, quite
unconscious of his lack of originality.

'Yes, you can have it all on your own.'

No offence intended; none taken. They walk in
silence. Joe isn't the talking kind. Dick is, but the little
white hand and the glimpse of violets on a pale cheek
has set in motion a train of thought that makes him
irritable. He keeps thinking: 'Cats never work, and
even horses rest at night!'

Number Six Berth, River. Passing up the ramp
between the sheds they come out on to the wharf.
Other men are already there. Deep voices, and the
stamping of heavy boots on wood. The mist is thick
on the river, almost a fog. Against the bilious glow of
the few lights over on south side dark figures converge
on one point, then vanish one at a time over the edge
of the wharf.

Dick and Joe join their mates on the floating
landing-stage. Rough greetings are exchanged.

'How are you, Joe?'

'What the hell's that got to do with you?'

'You old nark! Got a needle on the hip?'

'I don't need no needle. How's the missus,
Sammy?'

'Bit better, Joe. She was up a bit to-day.'

'Line up there!—here she comes.'

As the little red light appears on the river the men
crowd the edge of the landing-stage, each anxious to
get a seat in the cabin on such a night. The water is
very black and still, and the launch moves in with

hardly a ripple. The night is full of sounds. Little sounds, like the rattle of winches at the distant timber berths; big sounds, like the crash of the coal-grabs opposite the gasworks. All have the quality of a peculiar hollowness, so that one still senses the over-whelming silence on which they impinge. In some strange way sound never quite destroys the portentous hush which goes with fog. Dick feels it as he follows old Joe over the gunwale and gropes his way through the cabin to the bows.

'It's quiet to-night, Joe. Can't be many ships working.'

'Quiet be damned. There's four working on north side. Where the hell're you going, anyway?'

'I'm going to sit outside.'

'You can sit on your own, then. This ain't no Studley Park tour.'

Dick doesn't mind that; all the same he isn't left alone. Other men are forced out beside him as the cabin fills. He finds it hard to dodge conversation. Racing. Football. Now if it was politics. . . . The Struggle! Just a humour, of course. He has no fixed antipathies to nightwork, the waterfront, or his mates. Nightwork means good money; three pounds a shift. A real saver sometimes. Many a time he's stood idle for days, then picked up a single night—enough to keep landlord and tradesmen quiet, at least. Two hours less work than the dayshift, too. Nevertheless it's all wrong. Surely to Christ the work of the world could be carried on in daylight. So much waste and idleness during the day, and toil at night. Only owls, rats, and men work at night.

'What's wrong, Dick? You're not saying much.'

'Just a bit dopey, Bluey. Not enough shut-eye.'

Damn them!—why can't they mind their own business?

The launch travels smoothly and swiftly. Quite safe. The mist is thickening, but there's a bit of light on the river here from the ships working on north side. Small ships, as ships go, but monstrous seen from the passing launch. Beautiful in a way of their own, too, with the clusters of lights hanging from masts and derricks. Little cities of industry resting on towering black cliffs. One can't tell where the black hulls join the black water.

Nameless bows, but still familiar to the critical stevedores.

'That's the *Bundaleera*. Good job. She worked the week-end.'

'The *Era*. She'll finish to-night.'

'The *Montoro*. They say there's only one night in her.'

Strange twentieth-century code of values. A collier which works Sundays is a good ship; a deep-water liner which works only one night is a bad ship.

'They can stick their Sunday work for mine!' Joe's voice.

'I suppose you get more out of the collection-box, you bloody old criminal!'

'That's all right. I only been to church twice in my life. The first time they tried to drown me, and the second time they married me to a crazy woman.'

Dick smiles to himself. A smile of affection for the old warrior. Joe's a good Christian, whether he knows it or not. There's a word for him: 'Nature's Gentleman'. A hard doer and a bit of a pagan, that's all. Three convictions: one for stealing firewood during the depression, one for punching a policeman during the '28 strike, and one for travelling on an expired railway ticket—also during the depression. Across one

cheek the scar of a wound received on Gallipoli. A
limp in his right leg from an old waterfront accident.
'Screwy' arms and shoulders from too much freezer
work in the days when every possible job had to be
stood up for. 'Sailor Joe'. Dick loves him as any
healthy youth can love a seasoned guide and mentor.
They work together, ship after ship. They travel
together, live near each other.

With a mutter of deep voices the launch chugs its
way across the Swinging Basin. The mist continues to
thicken. South side is just visible. Haloes of brassy
yellow around lonely lights. Dismal rigging of idle
coal lighters—grimy relics of the white wings of other
days. North side can be heard but not seen. Beyond
the veil ageing winches clatter at the coal berths and
railway trucks crash against each other in Dudley
Street yards. A man's voice hailing another comes
across the water with extraordinary distinctness.

A few minutes later everything vanishes and the
speed of the launch drops to a walking pace. Real fog
now. Dick's eyes have been fixed on the ridge of water
standing out from the bows. Twice since leaving
Number Six it has fallen in height; now it is but a
ripple. Voices in the cabin are still cursing the cold,
speculating lightly on the chances of reaching shore in
the event of a collision. Dick wishes they'd all shut up.
He's cold himself, but some of his irritation has gone.
Here again is beauty—of a kind, like ships working at
night, and the little white hand. Just three feet away
the sooty water flows slowly past. It's easy to imagine
that only the water moves, that the launch is motionless, a boatload of men resting in the perpetual night
of a black river. To port, south side has ceased to
exist; to starboard, north side is only the distant
clamour of a lost world.

Nine o'clock.

The green navigation light of Coode Island.

Only the light. A bleary green eye, neither suspended nor supported. Green eye and grey fog. They pass fairly close. Too close, they realize, as the launch swings sharply off to port. New sounds come out of the night. Sounds of a working ship. Dead ahead, and not far away. Yarraville. Conversation, which has languished, flickers into life again.

'What the hell's that?'

'Don't tell me it ain't nine o'clock yet!'

'Just turned. Maybe there's rockboat in.'

'There is. They picked up for her this morning.'

'We won't be long now—thank Christ! I'm as cold as a frog.'

'Listen to the dayshift howl when we pull in. It'll be ten o'clock when they get up the river.'

In two places, one on each bow, the fog changes colour. Two glowing caves open up, as if a giant had puffed holes in a drop-curtain. And in each cave the imposing superstructure of a ship materializes with all the bewildering play of light and shadow characteristic of ships at night. Rockboat and sugarboat. The *Trienza* and the *Mildura*. The comparatively graceful lines of the bigger ship don't interest the approaching stevedores. Their eyes are all on the *Mildura*, their minds all grappling with one question: how many nights?

'By God, she's low!'

'She's got a gutsful all right.'

'Three or four nights—you beaut!'

Under a barrage of jeers and greetings from the dayshift the launch noses in to the high wharf.

'You were a long time coming!'

'What're you growling at? You're getting paid for waiting.'

'Ho there, Bluey, you old scoundrel!'

'How are you, Jim? Left a good floor for us?'

'Good enough for you, anyhow. She ain't a bad job.'

'How many brands?'

'Five in Number Two. Grab the port-for'ard corner if you're down there. You'll get a good run till supper. Two brands.'

'Good on you, son!'

The nightshift swarms up the face of the wharf, cursing a Harbour Trust which provides neither ladder nor landing-stage. Dick is last up, for no other reason than that Joe is second last. The strain imposed on the old man to reach the top angers his young mate. Damn their hides! All ugliness again. A man can never get away from it for long. The strange charm of the fog-bound river has gone. The black beams of the wharf, with the shrouded men clinging to them like monstrous beetles, symbolize all the galling dreariness of the ten hours just beginning. Symbolism also in the tremendous loom of the coal-gantry. Toiling upwards, always toiling upwards, with just a little glimpse of beauty now and then, like the mist, and the little white hand, and the ridge of black water streaming away from the bows of the launch.

'Shake it up, old-timer!' someone cries from above.

Joe's big boots are just above Dick's head. One of them is lifted on to the next beam. He waits for the other to move, but the old man is still feeling for a higher grip for his hands. Dick's own fingers are getting numb. The beams are covered with wet coal-dust and icy cold. At either side the dayshift men are swarming down. Noise, confusion, and black shapes everywhere.

A sudden anxiety seizes Dick as Joe's higher foot comes down again to the beam it has just left.

'On top there!' he yells. 'Help this man up!'

Too late. Even as he moves to one side and reaches upwards in an endeavour to get alongside his mate the old man's tired fingers give in. A big clumsy bundle hurtles down, strikes the gunwale of the launch with a sickening thud, and rolls over the side before anyone can lay a hand on it.

An hour later another launch noses away into the fog. Only two men. Both are within the cabin, one standing behind the little steering wheel, the other crouched near the open doorway with eyes fixed on the grey pall beyond the bows. Coode Island is astern before the boatman speaks.

'He was your mate?'

'Yes, he was my mate.'

'You got him out pretty quick.'

'Not quick enough. He hit the launch before he went into the water, you know.'

After a minute's silence. 'Does the buck know you've left?'

'I'm not worried. I wouldn't work to-night, not for King George. And somebody's got to tell his old woman.'

'I'm going right up to Number Two. Will that do you?'

'Yes, anywhere.'

Anywhere indeed. And the further and slower the better.

Not so much different from an hour ago. Mist, black water, and the crash of trucks over in the railway yards. But no men. One of them embarked now on a longer journey than he ever dreamed of. And in a few minutes there will be lights, and more lights. And voices, and the faces of many people. And not one of them will know a thing of what has happened. Princes Bridge, and the bustle of the great intersection. Trams, and St. Kilda Road. And the big cars rolling along beneath the naked elms. The other world— violets—and the little white hand.

The little white hand. Funny. She'll be dancing somewhere now, and the grand old man with whom she very nearly rubbed shoulders——

'What was that?' asks the boatman.

Dick is startled to find he has spoken aloud.

'We don't know much about each other, do we?' he says without hesitation.

'What d'you mean?'

'Oh, nothing. . . .'

HARVEST
By John K. Ewers

ALL day they had been working against time to finish the second haystack. To-morrow Larry was leaving to go into camp. But it wasn't only the thought of his leaving that spurred them on. Along the northern rim of the sky thunderclouds lay like piles of new-shorn wool. Mac had seen them when they went out for the first load and he didn't like the look of them.

'If the rain beats us,' he said, 'we'll have to pull the whole blamed stack down and build her again.'

He didn't fancy the idea of rebuilding the stack with only Mary to help him. Mary was twenty-five, stronger than most women and as useful as most men, but there was no one like Larry for building haystacks. People going along the road used to stop to admire the haystacks at Coorabbin, but it was all Larry's doing. Mac couldn't build a straight side to save himself. So they kept hard at it, pausing only to scald their throats with hot tea the missus brought down from the house each time they came in with a load.

Mac was sorry Larry was leaving, but the kid was breaking his neck to get into the Army. When he had put in his papers six months before the military had ordered him to stay and help with the seeding, because the district was short of men. Mac had shared him round among the neighbours. But the last mail had brought his call-up, he had to report on Monday. Mac wondered when he'd get another man as good as Larry.

The only one who seemed glad Larry was going was the missus. She liked him all right. They all did. But she was glad he was going, all the same. Mac knew why. He was the only one who did know, but that didn't make him see eye to eye with her in the matter.

Mary had been two years old when Mac married her mother. Everyone in the district, including Mary, thought he was her father. For himself, he had no objections to a ready-made family, and he never thought of Mary as anything but his own daughter. If there'd been other youngsters it might have been different, but there weren't, and he and the missus were happy enough watching Mary grow up.

But as the girl grew older he could see the old fear coming back. He knew the missus didn't want it to happen to Mary the way it had to her. Neither did he, for that matter, although he couldn't help thinking that it hadn't turned out so badly for either of them, and he didn't like the way the missus kept Mary away from the company of the young chaps in the district. There were plenty of them, decent, hard-working lads, or there had been before the war started, but the missus never made any of them welcome at Coorabbin. Mac had told her she was cranky and just looking for trouble, but it made no difference.

She hadn't wanted Mary to go out in the paddock with Larry that morning, but Mac said, 'I want her out there, and she's going.'

So Mary went, but each time they brought in a load the missus was there with tea, and when they had drunk it she grabbed a fork and worked on the stack alongside Mary and Larry.

After lunch the clouds began to move up the sky.

'We're gonner get it, all right,' said Mac between sheaves.

Larry paused long enough to take a quick glance behind him. 'Oh, I dunno. Just a dry thunderstorm, I think.'

Mac wasn't convinced. 'Let's have 'em a bit quicker,' he said.

Larry responded at once and Mary tried to follow, but her arms were live coals of pain about the wrists and there was a dull ache between her shoulder-blades.

'Take it easy, Mary,' Larry said. 'I'll do the hurrying.'

She smiled gratefully at him, but she tried to keep pace and to toss sheaf for sheaf, to maintain the rhythm of bending and lifting and heaving.

When the wagon moved off, Mary paused a moment, leaning on the handle of her fork. Larry came over to her. 'You oughtn't to go so hard,' he said.

'I like it, really, but I s'pose I'm not used to it.'

'Anyhow, it's nice working alongside a good mate,' said Larry. 'Let's carry your fork.'

He put the two forks across one shoulder and walked beside her, his free arm brushing against hers as they trudged behind the wagon. Somehow, she didn't feel so tired when they walked together like that.

The sky was completely overcast now and the air so still that the scrawny gums by the house-paddock seemed like a dark frieze cut out of stiff paper. Lightning played about the horizon as they passed the sheaves from one to another, Larry high up on the crest of the stack, a dim figure in the half-light.

When the last sheaf was in place Larry climbed down the ladder. The others were waiting for him. It was dark in the shadows of the haystack, but they felt good to think it was finished.

'Well, we beat it,' Larry said. 'You go off an' I'll fix the horses. An', missus, I'm hungry enough to eat one.'

Mac was glad of the chance to trudge off. He could remember the time when after a day like this he'd have cleaned himself up and driven ten miles and danced till his stiff collar was a limp rag. But he couldn't do it now. And how he was going to manage without Larry was more than he could tell. But the missus hung about uncertainly.

'Coming, Mary?' she asked.

Mary was already among the horses. 'I'll just help Larry feed up, Mum,' she said.

'All right, but don't be long.'

Larry grinned at Mary over the leaders' backs. Her fingers moved as expertly as his, then she smacked each one on the rump in turn and sent them trotting off to the troughs.

In the dark of the stables she found a hurricane lantern and held it up for him to light. The glow of the match fell upon their faces, close together, as Larry lit the wick.

'I wish I wasn't going now. I like working for your dad. He's a good boss.'

'He'll be sorry to lose you.'

'It's been sort of home to me,' he said.

The leading horses were coming back, plodding resolutely into the stableyard, with an occasional expectant whinny. Larry hung the lantern on a nail by the door of the chaff-house and they filled the tins, side by side. The horses snuffled eagerly into the chaff and presently there was a steady, contented munching. When Mary had finished filling her half of the mangers she flung her empty tin back where she had got it, and leaned against a dusty, cobwebby upright waiting for Larry.

He would miss all this, she thought, and at night—his little room was just around the corner—the sound of the horses munching, the stamp of their hoofs, an occasional whinny; and she knew that after he had gone she would never be able to go near the stables without thinking about him.

His voice beside her made her jump a little.

'Tired?'

She shook her head, although every bone in her body was aching.

Larry lifted the lantern to her face. 'Mary! You're crying!' he said softly.

'No.' She turned away and brushed her eyes with the back of her hand. Larry was close behind her. She could feel the warmth of his body and his breath on the back of her neck.

'Mary!' he said. One hand stole about her. 'Mary, I don't want to go. I didn't know you felt like this. I didn't know how you felt. Your mum was always keeping us apart, and I thought perhaps there were reasons.'

'What reasons, Larry?'

'Someone else, perhaps. Or that I wasn't good enough. That was why I wanted to go. If I could have gone six months ago . . . but it's been hell staying on and seeing you.'

'Oh, Larry!' She turned quickly and flung both hands around him.

Back at the house, the missus was in a fidget all the time she was getting the tea. Every now and then she stopped and listened. Twice she went to the door and peered out in the darkness. The day had been so sharp, so like that day before Tom had gone away. She could feel it all over again. Tom and she alone behind the haystack the last night of his last leave. She had not told him in any of her letters. He had written 'When I come home we'll get married.' Two days before Mary was born she heard that he had been killed in action. It was all so like this day and she was afraid. She couldn't stand it any longer. She turned to where Mac was sitting reading a paper. 'They're not coming. Won't you go and see what's keeping them?'

Mac looked up irritably. 'Oh, leave 'em alone. They're not children, either of them.'

She had an answer on the tip of her tongue, but at that moment the rain came. It came with only a few warning drops, then a solid deafening roar on the iron roof. The missus hurried to the door. Outside, a blinding wall of water obliterated the dim outlines of even the nearest tree. A wind that had sprung mysteriously from nowhere wailed under the eaves.

There was despair in her eyes when she turned to her husband. 'They can't come now,' she said.

He looked up cheerfully. 'They'll be over presently.

My, listen to that rain! Mighty lucky we got that stack finished in time.'

But to her there was no time, no present, no past; only men leaving and women left, through all the changeless ages.

HE WALKS HOME WITH HIS WIFE
By DON EDWARDS

PERHAPS she won't come at all, you think, and your high spirits go as the last passengers walk briskly from the station and the electric train rattles over the far roadway. Perhaps it would be as well if she didn't come, you think, then; but you have seen three trains arrive, you don't expect her till the next, and you don't mind waiting.

That is the most surprising thought—you don't mind waiting. Standing there beneath the awning you recapture the feeling of elation you used to have a few years ago when you waited like this for her. A few years ago; and the contrast of then and now suddenly drives away your elation. For a moment you almost decide to give up the idea and leave, but you look at the brown-paper parcel clutched in your hand and you decide to stay.

She should be on this train. Eagerly you stand there peering at the hurrying passengers who emerge from the dark doorway on to the street that glows with late-afternoon sun. You see her, and the sight of her drives your pretty prepared speech right out of your head. You start forward, then step back on to the pavement and stand there watching her walk away from you.

This is the time for which you planned, and now you are doing nothing. It is absurd that you should be like this about meeting your wife. If you don't do something about it soon she will be round the corner and out of sight. You hurry after her.

It might be as well to make it appear as if the meeting is an accident. That is quite a good idea. If you hurry down that side street you can meet her farther along.

Nearing the main street you walk more slowly and wonder whether you have succeeded in getting ahead of her. You look up the street and draw back as you see her coming.

'Hallo, Claire!' Timing it nicely, you walk out from the side street and express surprise at meeting your wife like this. What a coincidence!

'Hallo!' she says, and her eyes tell you that your stratagem has not deceived her. You never could deceive her anyway, Perhaps that is why it all ended in such a mess.

You are standing waiting for her to make it easier for you and knowing that she won't. She stands there beside you silently, keenly.

'I suppose you are still with your people, Claire?' you say casually, not as casually as you would like.

'Yes,' she says abruptly.

'Still in the same job?' you ask, and after she has answered you almost spoil things by nearly saying, 'How about us trying to knock along together again?'

She glances at you quickly, and in that glance is an answer in no uncertain terms to the question you nearly asked. You try to think of something else to say. She remains quiet and doesn't help you. In your confusion you nearly ask her the question that you have been waiting to ask for a year; the question that you

intend to ask soon. But no. Later, when you have seen
how things are, and when you have seen the boy. So,
'How is David?' you ask.

'Very well.' She is more on her guard than ever.
You sense her drawing away, her attitude of defence.
Just 'Very well' and no more. She could at least have
told you something about him, how he looks, if he
asks about you at all.

A hot anger works in you as you stand there. You
feel like grasping her arm and saying to her: 'He is
my son, understand that. He is my son, too.' Instead,
you shift the parcel from one hand to the other and
remark that it is a wonder she doesn't go home by
bus.

She says that it is barely a mile and the exercise
does her good, so she always walks.

Then you ask: 'Can I walk home with you, Claire?'
She glances at you and at the parcel, and in an offhand
sort of way answers: 'Please yourself, I don't mind.'

You set off beside your wife, looking in at the shop-
windows, at the passing people, anywhere but at her.
Nothing is said. You realize that you both have only
one interest in common, your son. You want to talk
about David, but you won't mention his name, and
she knows that you want to talk of him, so she won't
mention him either. When you ask a question she
answers briefly and sharply. Why should you consider
her any longer? Do you owe her anything? You are a
fool.

These thoughts go through your mind over and
over as you walk beside her.

You cross the street, and as you step up beside her
you look straight into a shop-window and see a small
cowboy outfit. Leather chaps, holster, pistol, sombrero,
placed among other toys and coloured ribbons, for it

is getting close to Christmas. 'Do you mind waiting a minute, Claire?' you ask, and you go into the shop.

The man has to take the outfit from the window. From the shop you see Claire watching him. Soon you are back at her side with another parcel under your arm. 'You don't forget birthdays, do you?' she says. She smiles at you. 'Not my son's,' you answer. She asks you if the other parcel you have is for David, too, and you tell her that it is.

After that you both seem to find it easier to talk to each other. You ask her questions about David, and she answers them readily. Strangely enough, though, you find it harder to ask the important question than when she was cool, distant, suspicious, almost bitter. You have come to ask for your son; to say to her: 'Claire, I want my son. He is as much mine as yours. I know when we separated I said you could have him, but I didn't know what I was giving up. He has been yours for four years. I want him now.' That is what you have come to say, but you haven't said it yet, and now that she is more friendly you can't say it.

So you decide to postpone asking the question till you are ready to go. Meanwhile, you walk homewards with Claire and she talks about your son, and the enthusiasm in her voice and the hope in her eyes make you hate yourself and your purpose. But only for a time. You harden your heart by thinking back to the way she messed things up for you. You even wonder whether she might not have sensed your purpose and be adopting this method of defeating it.

In the distance, on the other side of the street, you can see her home. You wonder if David will be pleased to see you or whether she has turned him against you. You would never forgive her for that. Yes, perhaps it is as well you have come for your son.

Just then you see him in a sweater and long trousers, playing on the front lawn with two boys not much bigger than himself. He looks from the terraced lawn across the street. Your wife waves her hand.

With a shout he rushes through the gate and across the footpath. You see the car sweeping along the road, but your son's quick movement takes you by surprise. Your wife beside you gasps, and you suddenly spring forward as your son runs into the street. With blaring horn the car rushes past. Then, you see him running towards you.

Claire is on her knees with her arms about David kissing him, holding him as if she would never let him go again. She is crying. You stand there rather awkwardly. You are angry with her for beckoning to him, for not teaching him to be more careful when crossing the street. But your anger soon goes and you realize that it was only caused by relief.

Your wife turns toward you holding David's hand. 'Go and speak to your daddy,' she says. You are delighted that she refers to you in that way. 'Hallo, Dad!' your son shouts and rushes to you. Leaning down, you shake his hand.

You wish him many happy returns of his birthday and hand him his presents. He sits down on the kerb and pulls away the brown paper. Soon he has the cowboy suit on his knees. Proudly you watch his pleasure and enthusiasm. Without waiting to unfold the other parcel, he rushes back across the street. You watch him running with the sombrero on his head. You hear him call to the other boys. Your wife is watching him, too. 'I don't know what I would do without him,' she says.

You remember how your wife clutched him a few

minutes ago, how she looked after him just now. So
you turn to her and say: 'I must go now, Claire.'

She doesn't ask you to come inside. She seems to
have fallen back into her defensive attitude again.
'He's a great little boy,' you add. 'Some day I'd like
to have him for a day.'

'Yes,' she says. 'Good-bye then.'

You set off along the way you came.

THE ENTHUSIASTIC PRISONER
By E. O. Schlunke

HENRY HOLDEN decided to get an Italian prisoner
of war after he had seen several at work on Esmond's
farm. Esmond was building a shed, and it was
beautiful to see how they ran to get the things he
needed, how they rushed to carry anything he picked
up, and how they seemed to take it for granted that
they were there to do all the heavy work while the boss
gave the orders.

When the captain in charge of the P.W.C.C. had a
preliminary look over Henry's place he tactlessly
asked him if he was an invalid; he saw so few signs of
work being done and so many of neglect. He wasn't at
all keen on letting Henry have a P.W.; he didn't think
he was the type to handle them successfully, but, on
the other hand, he was eager to get his 'hundred'.

When the P.W. arrived, Henry was decidedly
disappointed with him at first sight. He did not look
obliging and polite; he didn't even look like an
Italian. He had a tremendous amount of fuzzy brown
hair; his eyebrows were so large and dense they nearly

surrounded his eyes, and thick hair grew all round his
neck and jutted out of his ears. His small, bright eyes
glinted sharply from among all the hair; not at all
like the large, soft and servile eyes of the Italians at
Esmond's. In fact he reminded Henry of a big brown
bear, with his air of having great physical strength and
tremendous determination. When the military truck
drove away Henry had an uncomfortable feeling of
having let himself in for something.

He directed Pietro to his room, and while he was
settling in, tried hurriedly to work out a plan of what
to do with him. There was, of course, plenty of work
to do, but it wasn't so easy to start a man who didn't
understand English, or know Australian farms. In a
few minutes Pietro appeared.

'Worrk,' he said, briefly and determinedly.

Henry abandoned his half-formed plan to let him
have the first half of the day off to get settled. Getting
quite panicky, he thought of a number of jobs, only
to realize he didn't have the necessary materials. In
desperation he decided to repair a fence. He pointed
to the fence, and to some tools and tried to explain to
Pietro.

'Unnerstan, reparare,' said Pietro.

Pietro picked up the shovel and pick, and started
hunting for a 'leva'. Henry soon realized that he
meant a crowbar, but he couldn't remember where
his was. Pietro looked at him in astonished reproval.
When they started off, Pietro carrying all the heavy
tools while Henry carried the wire strainer, Henry
felt better, though he was sure that Esmond's men
would have offered to carry the wire strainer too.

They did little good with the fence although
Pietro was obviously eager to work. It really needed a
lot of new posts and wires, and Henry had neither.

They tightened what wires were there and braced and stayed some of the key posts in a makeshift manner. Pietro liked the wire strainer, apparently he had never seen one before and he was greatly intrigued with the way it worked.

'Very ni, very ni,' he said.

But when they were going home for dinner he glanced disapprovingly at the propped-up posts.

'No good, no good,' he said.

Henry usually had a nap after dinner, which lasted well into the afternoon if the day happened to be warm. But Pietro apparently didn't know about 'dinner hours'. He waited outside the door for a while, then knocked and said, quite politely but very firmly, 'Worrk'.

Henry went out and remembered the wood-heap. It cheered him immensely. He had recently brought in a load and it would take Pietro several days to chop it up. It would be a great stand-by. Pietro could work there all the afternoon. He lay down while Pietro chopped with great vigour, but he could not sleep or even relax properly because of his problem. His wife and children, too, kept asking him questions about Pietro; they were rather awed by him.

He heard the rumble of the wheelbarrow on the veranda several times, and sounds of cut wood being tipped out. Then Pietro knocked on the door. He pointed to a great pile of wood and said, 'Sufficiente?'

'No, not sufficient,' said Henry, 'chop more.'

Pietro looked at him with a blank expression.

'No unnerstan,' he said, and before Henry could work out another way of expressing himself, he inquired, 'Sufficiente one day? Two day? Tre day?'

'Tre day,' Henry admitted reluctantly.

Pietro smiled broadly and looked surprisingly

pleasant as he did so. 'Plenty sufficiente,' he said, closing the argument.

Henry went and got his hat. He could hear the wind banging a loose sheet of iron on the roof of the machinery shed. They would begin by nailing it down. But when they got on the roof Pietro discovered that half the sheets were loose. Henry gave him nails and directed him to fasten down the flapping sheets. But Pietro was hunting round for causes. He discovered that the rafters were rotting, and demonstrated it by giving one a hard hit with the hammer. It split from end to end, and a couple of sheets immediately blew off the roof.

They spent the afternoon cutting trees in the scrub and trimming them for rafters, though nothing was farther from Henry's intention and inclination. He cut down a few little trees while Pietro cut a lot of big ones. Pietro always took the heavier end when they loaded the rails, but even so Henry became exhausted. Round about four o'clock he decided to go home.

'Sufficient,' he said.

Pietro consulted a diagram he had made.

'No sufficiente,' he said. 'Encora four.'

They went on working.

At tea that night Pietro met all the family. There was a flapper daughter, three younger boys, and a baby. He was particularly interested in the baby. He made some queer foreign noises at it, and to everyone's surprise it showed unmistakable signs of affection for him. He asked Mrs. Holden if it was breast-fed, and when she told him, in some confusion, that it was not, he wanted to know why. Then he gave her detailed and intimate directions, mainly by signs, about how to ensure an abundant flow for the next baby. The flapper daughter half smothered a lot of embarrassed giggles, and the boys nearly 'busted' trying not to laugh. Henry felt that he ought to reprimand Pietro for his indelicacy, but didn't know how he could make him understand.

The next day Henry felt stiff and sore. He decided to relax, but Pietro kept calling him on to the roof; sometimes for advice, but mostly to help him in fitting rafters which were too big to be 'poseeble solo'.

They finished re-roofing the shed by the week-end. Pietro wanted to know if they would cut some fence-posts next week to repair the fences. Henry thought of how he would suffer if he had to work on the other end of a crosscut-saw with a tireless bear like Pietro. He said, 'No, some other work.'

But he didn't like the way Pietro looked at him, so he decided to hide the crosscut-saw.

On Sunday Esmond's Italians came to visit Pietro. They must have told him all about what was going on at their place, because on Monday morning Pietro wanted to know why Henry was not preparing his soil for his crops, like Mr. Esmond. Henry looked a bit guilty, then he tried to explain that he used different methods from Esmond's. Pietro was not satisfied.

'Mr. Esmond good resultare? No good resultare?'

Henry had to admit that Esmond's results were good. He also had to confess that his own results were often bad.

'Provare similar Mr. Esmond,' Pietro suggested enthusiastically. 'Poseeble very good oat, very good weet.'

'Tractor broken,' said Henry. He was always over-whelmed by a feeling of hopeless apathy in the autumn, and he couldn't face the strain of all the preparations necessary for his worn-out plant.

'Me look?' asked Pietro, and was off before Henry could say anything to the contrary.

Pietro had a thorough look over the tractor and scarifier. He made a list of all the new parts needed, which he laboriously translated into English with the help of his little dictionary. He explained that he was not a mechanic, but he had had a lot of experience with military vehicles. He suggested that Henry go to town and get the necessary parts, and Henry went, glad to get away from the responsibility of Pietro for an afternoon.

While Henry was away Pietro 'polished' the toolshed and the farmyard. When Henry came home, rather late in the evening, and somewhat the worse for wine, he thought he had come to the wrong farm until Pietro came out of his room and carried his parcels for him. He was in an exalted mood and gave Pietro an orange for his services. But Pietro spoiled the effect by telling him of several things he had forgotten to bring.

At the table that night Pietro objected to Mrs. Holden giving the baby honey to stop it crying.

'No good, 'oni, no good,' he said.

But she continued to exercise the lawful rights of a mother. Suddenly the baby vomited. Pietro made an angry noise, jumped up and put the honey away in the cupboard.

'No good, no good,' he said, so emphatically that she was startled and impressed.

Henry found that he couldn't tell Pietro much about overhauling farm machines. He stood by to tell him where tools, parts and materials were kept; frequently he found it easier to get them than to explain; sometimes when Pietro was held up and impatient Henry found himself running just like one of Esmond's

Italians, until he remembered his dignity as a 'padrone'. They had an auspicious rain when everything was ready, and Henry's land was never worked into better condition.

The tractor ran very well. Pietro assumed a jealous control of it and appeared to be very happy on it no matter how long he worked. The arrangement suited Henry extremely well. He felt free for the first time since his prisoner arrived. He had plenty of time to turn over all the vague plans he had in his head.

When Pietro finished working the land he suggested again that they cut some fence posts. But Henry was ready with his own plan. Pietro was to paint the house. Pietro agreed heartily; the house certainly needed painting. They went to have a good look at the walls. Not only had the paint peeled off, but much of the plaster was cracked and loose.

'No good paint,' said Pietro. 'Prima plaster.'

But the thought of all the work and expense involved in plastering horrified Henry. He said authoritatively, 'Paint sufficient'. And he got a trowel and demonstrated how the rough plaster could be smoothed off sufficiently. He handed the trowel to Pietro, who made what appeared to be a similar movement. But the result was vastly different, at least a wheelbarrow-load of plaster fell off the wall.

'Plenty similar,' he said, and knocked off another square yard with a flick of his wrist. Henry gave in.

Henry was kept very busy mixing the plaster and carrying it to Pietro. It had to be mixed in small lots and applied immediately, Pietro said, otherwise it would fall off just like the previous coat.

When it was finished Henry brought out the paint. Pietro was very interested in the 'colore'. But when he discovered that it was to be a drab, uniform stone-colour all his eagerness vanished.

'No good, no good,' he said, 'similar dirt.'

He wouldn't take the brush when Henry offered it to him.

'Brush no good,' he said. 'Troppo old.'

Henry tried the brush and had to admit it was worn out. He decided to go to town and get a new one. Pietro wanted to go too; to get his hair cut. Henry left him at the Control Centre and went to do his shopping. When he walked into the general store, where he did most of his business, he had an uneasy feeling that he was being followed. He turned and saw Pietro carrying the two big tins of stone-coloured paint. He had that brown-bear look about him which Henry hadn't liked the first time he saw him.

The manager of the hardware came up to them. He saw by the look in Henry's eye that he wasn't sure of himself, so he turned to Pietro, who appeared to know exactly what he wanted. Pietro held up the tins.

'Colore no good,' he said.

The manager remembered having advised Henry against a uniform drab colour, and immediately set out to help Pietro. He quite ignored Henry's somewhat indistinct, 'No, it's all right. I'll keep it.'

He showed Pietro a colour card and he selected a very light cream, a bright blue and a black.

'One big crema, one little blue, one little little nero,' he said.

The manager was, as he would have said, intrigued. He tried to discover what design Pietro had in mind, and Pietro demonstrated as best he could, attracting a lot of attention from other shoppers, who began to gather round. Henry became most uncomfortable.

'I won't have it at any price,' he protested, 'everyone who goes past will die laughing.'

'Ah, garn!' said a big voice from the back. 'Let him have a go. It couldn't look any worse than it's looked for the last twenty years.'

Then a couple of ladies joined in.

'How interesting!' said one. 'The Italians are so artistic, aren't they?'

The other one said, 'I remember seeing the adorable Italian cottages painted just like that; you must let us come and see it, Mr. Holden.' She happened to be the wife of Henry's long-suffering mortgagee, and her word carried some weight with him. Quite a number of others voiced favourable opinions before Henry and Pietro carried out their cream, blue and black paint.

Pietro took endless pains over the painting, and all the time he was at it Henry felt resentful, despite the fact that many people came and admired it. He comforted himself by compiling a long list of heavy jobs Pietro would have to do when he was finished. He had the interpreter prepare a translation so that there would be no 'no unnerstan' business, and when at length the house was finished he gave Pietro a week's programme, consisting mainly of firewood carting and post-hole digging.

But that day it rained; a splendid soaking rain, and during the night it cleared. Henry was wakened early in the morning by the roar of the tractor starting. He was puzzled and rather annoyed; Pietro was up to something. Then he realized that Pietro had taken it upon himself to make the all-important decision of the year—that the time was right to start sowing the wheat.

Henry thought with some indignation of the programme he had given Pietro, but he also realized that it was much more important to get the wheat sown while the soil was moist. He lay thinking for a long time of ways in which he could reassert himself, and all the time he heard the noise of Pietro's preparations. He stayed there because he always hated the worry of working out the proportions of wheat and fertilizer, and adjusting the machines accordingly, and all the other important details necessary for a successful sowing season. When he finally went out, Pietro hurried up to him, his face aglow with enthusiasm.

'Oh, rain very nice,' he said. 'Terra very nice. Poseeble very good weet this year, similar Mr. Esmond.'

He pointed to the tractor hitched to the sowing combine and the farm cart loaded with supplies of seed, fertilizer and tractor fuel.

'After brekfus me take trattore and wheat machine. You bring carro; allora we commence before Guiseppe and Leonardo on farm Mr. Esmond.'

'O.K., Pietro,' said Henry.

SEED AMONG THORNS
By DOROTHY SANDERS

WHEN I was young my friend Jane took me to her home out in the limestone country. It was my first holiday in the farmlands and I went with mixed feelings.

I liked Jane immensely but I was not sure that a whole fortnight of her in the country wouldn't be too much for me. At that time I was much engrossed with my many friends. I loved a gay life just as the other

girls in the city did, and I was always full of my
exploits with the opposite sex. Heaven knows, they
were unbelievably innocent, though at the time I
thought I was a devil of a lass.

In those days it was quite a journey to go the sixty-
odd miles by slow train and then drive three miles by
buggy. I remember that the first time I went to
Minanoo we arrived at night-time. Jane's family had
had their dinner and had kept ours in the kitchen
oven.

My first real impression of the old homestead was
of the enormous kitchen, that was built like a lean-to
off the more solid edifice of stone. At the far end of the
kitchen a big range glowed with the dying fire and
the oven stood open with our dinners in it on a
shelf.

Jake, the eldest brother, managed the estate, and I
noticed at once that the others treated him with
deference. I did not see anything in him that night
that made him seem so very different from any other
man, except that he was quiet and reserved and held
this astonishing sway over his family.

The day after my arrival I found that no one in the
family—and it was a big one—had time to treat me as
a visitor.

This puzzled me. Not that there was so much work,
but that they should all do it so thoroughly and
willingly. If it had been my family we would have
argued and perhaps been disagreeable about it. And
I was even more astonished when I found that every
major domestic problem was referred to Jake, and
that he always gave a quiet decision without consult-
ing any of them, and that no one dreamed of disputing
the decision. This was a strange phenomenon to
me.

N

In all other respects that holiday was a typical farm holiday. I went riding, though I wasn't much of a horsewoman. I helped move sheep from one paddock to another. I watched the dipping. I went into town for the mail. I sang with the others round the piano in our after-dinner sing-song and I played bridge nearly every night.

It was all so quiet and serene. I began to like it, terribly. The country smelled so good, the fresh-baked bread tasted better than any I had ever eaten. Though I thought that Jake was very nice and his manners charming, I couldn't help thinking it was rather a joke that he lorded it over the others so easily and so unobtrusively.

When I went home I hoped that Jane would ask me back to Minanoo again.

City life was the same as ever. There were more males to be slain with a look, and an endless stream of dances, sports afternoons and teas. I nearly forgot the family in the farmlands.

However, before Jane's next holidays I had a series of bad bronchial attacks and was very ill. When I recovered I hadn't the energy or the heart for the gaiety of the town and I remembered how lovely it had been at Minanoo. I wrote and asked Jane's family if I could come and visit them.

In due course there came a welcoming letter, though I felt sure that Jake's permission had been asked before they despatched it. The thought made me giggle.

When I arrived at Minanoo it was again evening and everyone came into the kitchen to greet me. That is, everyone except Jake. I asked where he was.

'Oh, he's gone over the limestone to the round-up at the coast,' someone said. 'He ought to be back to-morrow.'

Somehow I was disappointed. But to-morrow was another day, I thought, and if he doesn't come then he will surely come the day after. I put on a very gay turn for the family that night.

It was odd how I kept going out on to the front veranda and watching over the hills to the place where the feed grew in thick green swards. That was where the limestone started and it was beyond it that the track led to the coast.

Down the creek-bed below the homestead the horses were feeding, and over a little to the right I could see the red roof of the Parker home. Jas Parker was away with Jake too. Once when I heard the dogs barking over there I wondered if Jas had come home.

'Maybe they'll come through the Five-Mile and up the back road to Parkes,' said Jane's sister. After that, each time I went out on to the veranda I found myself looking in that direction.

I watched all that day for him, and when sundown came at last, and dinner was ready, I could hardly keep the disappointment from my face.

We had finished dinner when Bill sat up stiffly in his chair.

'Listen!' he said.

There was silence and we all listened. At first I could hear nothing, but presently over the soft night air came the thud, thud of hoofs up the hill from the creek. Clip-clop, went my heart happily. Everyone looked at one another and smiled.

I did everything I could to try to help the family and take my place with them. But somehow it was not a success. My pretty dresses were out of place and they joked about my efforts at cooking. And I was proud and their jokes hurt me, so I covered up my feelings by being gay.

And I loved Jake and I covered up that, too, by being clever to him in a smart, towny way. Suddenly the whole atmosphere had changed and they were bewildered by it. So was I, and I did not know where I was wrong or how to rectify it.

When I was going home I wanted to cry every yard of the buggy ride into the station. I was afraid that I would never be invited to Minanoo again.

Well, all that happened a long time ago.

The years after my visits to Minanoo slipped by. I still had a gay time in the city. I went to dances and balls and had flirtations—some more serious than others. But in my heart I hankered after Jake.

The time came when I knew it was no good wishing for ever. My family began to say . . . 'Aren't you ever going to marry?'

So I married John. I was fond of him and he was a good matrimonial bet, but there wasn't any ecstasy about it when we announced our engagement.

We were a good pair and in years I grew to love him. We had two beautiful children and I stopped giggling and being too gay and too flamboyant. I grew a little plump and John became iron-grey over the temples. Rather distinguished, I used to think. We had a pleasant and a full life and I was contented in a happy, restful way that I had never known in my girlhood. I smiled rather whimsically at myself and my old love for Jake. I often wondered if he had really disliked me.

Then one day I met Jane again. She had married, too, but had more arrows to her quiver than I. No fewer than four. When we met she was making arrangements to take the children to the old homestead for a holiday.

'Why not come for the day?' she asked. 'I'm

leaving the children there and returning in the evening. Jake's married, you know. He still lives at Minanoo, though you will find it much altered. I'd love you to come.'

'And I would like to come,' I said. 'I'd like to come for old times' sake.'

We left the city the next morning. In less than no time we were out on a beautifully made main road passing through vineyards on the slopes of the hills.

'Rather different from the old days,' I said to Jane at the wheel. 'Remember the train that stopped for breath at every siding?'

We laughed. Those days were gone for ever. To-day was the day of good roads and fast cars. Minanoo was hardly in the country at all. We'd be there in no time.

When we came to the village we turned off the main road to the old familiar track that wound along the creek-bed. It at least was not different. Fewer ruts, perhaps, but the straggling river gums on either side stood as they had stood years before.

When we crossed the creek, there stood Minanoo, with the same old wattle leaning over the gate. But the wooden gate was replaced by a wrought-iron one and there were brick pillars to the veranda. As to Minanoo itself—well, it was modernized, but underneath the veneer it seemed the same to me and best of all there was the big kitchen.

Jake's wife was just removing a tray of coffee-rolls for our morning coffee. She was small and quiet and pleasing; essentially right, she looked.

'Jake's out at the Five-Mile,' she said. 'He won't be back till this evening. You two will stay for dinner, won't you?'

Oddly enough I rather hung on Jane's answer. I

hoped that she would say 'yes'. When she accepted the invitation I was glad.

We had had dinner and were smoking cigarettes on the front veranda. The night was gentle and full of the soft noise of the creek and of the bull frogs croaking in its bed. On the air the scent of the wattle hung heavily. The sky was brilliantly starred. Over the turf came the clip-clop of horse's hoofs.

'That is Jake now,' said his wife. 'How fortunate that he is able to catch you.'

I listened to the crescendo of thudding as the horse's hoofs passed the house and my heart was loudly keeping time to the beat. Fifteen years had disappeared as if they had never been and I was a young and lovesick girl waiting on the veranda of Minanoo for the sound of a horseman coming home.

I heard the horse going round to the stables and presently the crunch of Jake's boots on the path and his foot on the steps. His shadow loomed up out of the night, giving the illusion that he was taller than he was, as he came into the half-light of the veranda. Involuntarily I had risen from my chair and, walking over to the railing, I threw my cigarette into the night.

We stood for the fraction of a second and looked at one another through the haze of smoke. In that moment we looked into one another's eyes and saw through the screen of placid, orderly happiness we had made of our lives.

Jake took a cigarette from Jane and lit it. He came over to the veranda rail and stood beside me, but we said nothing.

The brilliant stars patterning the black velvet of night looked down upon us. I knew that this time I must go from Minanoo for ever.

DUST
By Gavin Casey

A FEATHERY tower of dust was dancing over the
housetops towards the hospital buildings, swaying and
leaning, and scurrying across open spaces so fast that
it sometimes left its top trailing away behind it. After
the manner of inland willy-willies, it picked up light
things that lay in its path and tossed them high,
swooped through open doors, leaving a red trail
wherever it went.

From the laboratory veranda a dozen men watched
its erratic progress and eventual dissolution as they
waited.

The red, honest dirt of the surface soil that was
swept about by the wind, thought Parker, visible and
avoidable, quite unlike the stale, still, malicious
menace that polluted the atmosphere of far underground.

'Marvellous what them things'll shift if they git
right under it,' said Big Joe.

'I seen one take the roof off my front veranda an'
land it in th' chookyard at the back,' said old
Penberthy, who was squarely built and had inherited
thick, strong limbs from many generations of mining
ancestors.

The morning was bright and warm, and normally
Parker and the others would have been far below the
sunlight, underground. Parker wished he was. He
leaned, with his elbows on the rail, smoking and
watching the dumps away on the other side of the
town.

His breathing was heavy, sometimes catching and
whistling softly in some mysterious passage behind

his chest. He felt tired and listless. The long row of glittering, curtainless windows of the laboratory depressed him, because he always thought of the 'tickets' that were made out, signed, recorded and filed away behind them as 'death warrants'. The ordeal of waiting for the doctors to open the doors, and then for his turn to go in and be subjected to the tests and examinations that might mean the end of everything, shattered his nerves, as it always did.

'Y' git miner's complaint jist as easy on th' surface as y' do down below,' someone was saying. ''Specially in th' mill.'

'We all git it at the office every third an' seventeenth,' came the voice of young Pope. 'Not enough money!'

Parker shivered.

It was a hell of a subject to joke about, he thought indignantly. The kid was too young to know any better, had probably never seen a man with 'dust'. But old Penberthy and Big Joe—they should know.

Pictures out of the past floated on the heat haze that shimmered over the red earth in front of Parker. His old dad, just before he passed out, when Parker himself was just a little shaver. Still on the right side of fifty the old boy had been, but there had been only nine stone left of his original fourteen. The lungs rotted out of him, so that every movement was heavy labour. Bleached, papery claws of hands that had seemed natural enough to the boy. Now he could well imagine the kind of fists the old man had had before the dust got him. He looked at his own big, hard paws, clutching the rail in the sunshine.

Of course things had changed, he tried to reassure

himself. In his dad's time a man had just kept going in ill-ventilated depths until he could work no longer, and then it had been too late to do much for him. To avoid that sort of thing was the purpose of the laboratory, the periodical examination of all mine employees, the whole system of first tickets and second tickets and pensions. Venturis down below and water everywhere to keep the dust down.

But some men still went out. Give it time enough to do its work and the dust still defied science.

When the big doors at last clashed open the pumping of Parker's heart and lungs forced a wheezy whistle between his teeth that terrified him.

Treading the jarrah boards heavily, Big Joe went in, and Parker glimpsed a dancing muscle behind the giant's jaw that seemed to tell of nervous tenseness. Even in Pope's eyes there seemed to be the shadow of a vague, unspoken fear. Parker felt for a moment very much one with his comrades, held together by fear and hatred of the life they lived.

Why had he given all those years since the war to toil in the deep levels? Why must he continue there, breathing stagnant death? Why could he laugh at risks to life and limb in the months that fled between each laboratory inspection, and yet inevitably find himself quailing before the memory of his old dad, in agony and fear each time the day for his examination drew closer? Was he all his life to tremble at the after-effects of a stubborn cold, imagining a warning of disease in every speck of phlegm?

By the time Big Joe came tramping out and young Pope went in Parker felt elated and wanted to laugh at them both. The dust would get them sooner or later. It was only a matter of time.

But he, Parker, was stepping out of it all, just like that. Right now he was going to set out for town with Big Joe, have a drink and say good-bye to the mines for ever. Chuckles bubbled in his throat and then there whistled through them a tiny, sobbing intake of breath, sucked through some obstruction by labouring lungs. Parker put down the hat he had grabbed and stayed where he was.

'Well, that's that!' said Big Joe, tightening his belt. 'Y' don't look too good, Tom.'

'I'm all right,' Parker managed. 'Got a bit of a cold.'

When the other had gone he prayed wordlessly as he leaned against the veranda rail in the sunshine. He would leave the mines, but first he must know, be sure that the wheezing in his lungs was only the aftermath of the cold that had gripped him earlier in the year. He could not go now. He must have the verdict, and then he would be through with underground.

When his turn came he tensed himself to go through with it. To the X-ray operator he even tried to voice the customary jocular comment on the coldness of the plate against his bare chest, but it stuck in his throat. The doctors he knew from many previous visits, and he wanted to ask questions, but dared not.

'You're heavier,' announced the last of them amiably as Parker dressed himself. 'Six-seven pounds on since the last card was filled in.'

Parker took courage from the fact.

'When'll a man know if he's come through all right?' He tried to make his tones unconcerned and casual, though blood seemed to be pumping hard against his eardrums.

'I won't see the plates for a day or two,' said the doctor, 'but I'd bet on you without seeing them. You're as fit as a fiddle, Parker, and we certainly won't be using any ink making out a ticket for you this time.'

His surroundings turned momentarily black. Light-hearted and faint with relief he scrambled into his clothes, and when he reached the sun-warmed outer air he sucked it in in appreciative gulps. Bright skies looked good, and the subdued thunder of the mines was a pleasant drone that sang of toil and prosperity.

'Well,' he said to old Penberthy, 'that's over for another six months! I'll hang around until they're through with you and we'll have one at th' corner.'

'If they're ever through,' grumbled Penberthy irritably. 'They muck about enough, don't they? Doesn't matter t' these wages fellers t' miss half a shift, but you an' me ought t' be pushin' th' winze down right now, Tom. They ought t' let a man make a time fer this that suits him.'

'Aw, we should worry,' said Parker gaily. 'It'll be a good pay fer us without this mornin', anyway. An' Doolan was tellin' me that when we got her finished he wants one on th' Fifteen. We can make a bit down there.'

'Th' Fifteen?' said Penberthy. ''S unhealthy on th' Fifteen. Dunno as I altogether like th' Fifteen.'

'Aw, bunk!' said Parker. 'The unhealthy places is where th' money is.'

TWO WOMEN
By A. C. Headley

NINETEEN hundred and forty-one. . . . It was cold in the kitchen and the woman was conscious of the vague discomfort of it in her body. Outside in the small square of sun in the back-yard she could see her husband, and the sight aroused in her the small sense of anger that was directed as much against herself as against him. She was a small woman. Her face was thin, and pinched in under the cheek-bones, so that there were two blobs of bone-stretched skin. Her hair was untidy and she wore an old tattered cardigan that had once belonged to her husband. When she moved the soles of her slippers made flapping noises on the bare boards of the floor. Looking through the window she was conscious that it was dirty and also that she didn't care.

She was aroused suddenly by the sound of the baby's whimper, and with a queer spiteful satisfaction she went to the door. 'You better come an' look after the kid,' she called. 'I got work to do.'

He looked disgusted, but he got up and came into the house. 'If you'd leave the kid alone,' he said, 'it'd go off again. That's the trouble with you women—always findin' things to do.'

She looked at him and the little quirk of anger got up in her again. 'It'd be better,' she said, 'if you'd find somethin' to do instead of sittin' on your backside all day. It'd suit you better to be out lookin' for a job.'

He said nothing. The baby in the back room was getting louder in its protestations, and he went into the room and brought it out. In his arms the sobs started to ease off. Without looking at his wife he returned to his spot in the sun. Behind him her thin voice told him to keep something over its head.

The woman went back to scrubbing a pan in the greasy cool water in the dish. She was thinking about it, thinking about being married and having a baby. They were thoughts like the squalid narrowness of the

kitchen, of floors without lino, of a mattress bulky with
lumps that were hard against your body.

'You said you was gonner do the bed out,' she
called.

He blinked in the sun and looked along the yard
towards her. 'I'll 'ave a go at it to-morrow,' he said.

'What's wrong with to-day?'

He grinned. 'I gotter see a coupla blokes. It might
mean that I'll get a chance of makin' some dough.'

'If it's work,' she said, 'you wouldn't know what it
was.'

She watched the way he puffed his eyes together.

'Listen,' he said, 'don't go takin' that attitude. If
there was any work I'd be in for it like a shot.'

He meant it then. He always meant it, but it
always made her think about the job at the glassworks that he had thrown up because it was too
hard. It had been a long time since that glassworks
job, a long time on the dole. She looked at him now,
noticing the thickness of unshaven beard on his face.
There was nothing much she could do about things.
She could nag, but he always came back with the
indisputable fact that if there wasn't any work you
couldn't get it.

'Where's the dough comin' from?' she said.

'One of Tommy Raven's runners has knocked it off,'
he said, 'and he's give me the connexion. I get two bob
in the quid, an' there oughter be a few quid in it.
Tommy was tellin' me——'

'And did he tell y' what'd 'appen if y' got caught?'
she wanted to know.

He winked. 'I won't be gettin' caught,' he said. 'I
got me 'ead screwed on the right way. Tommy was
tellin' me the other bloke used t' take in between two
an' three quid in bets every race.'

Almost without thinking she was working it out. So many shillings for the day. With eight races, even at two quid a race, that was thirty-two bob, and there were two race meetings a week. In that moment she began to think of the things that the money would buy. 'You gotter be careful,' she said, 'that you don't get caught.'

All the afternoon she was thinking about him, thinking of him being caught and sent to jail. Then when an hour had passed since the last race and he had not come home she was conscious of a growing sense of dread. It was a peculiar feeling. In it there was no feeling for her husband, only the fear of being alone. For the first time she came to the realization that he was a buffer against the awkward things of the day—the thought of the landlord and the order man. There was nothing he did about those things, but there was always the feeling that he was in them with her and that the chief responsibility was his. Sitting in the darkness she thought about it. The feeling of not being alone; it was the one thing she had got out of marriage. A dozen times she got up from her chair and went to the door to peer along the darkened street.

At seven o'clock he came, thick and heavy with beer. She was angry suddenly at the sight of him, and when he came into the house and blinked stupidly in the light she swore at him. 'Where the 'ell you been? I been worryin' me soulcase out.'

He grinned foolishly. 'I been all right.'

'I been waitin' all this time for y' t' come 'ome. I don't s'pose that means anythin' when y' get in a pub with y'r friends. I'm the one that 'as to do all the worryin'.'

He sat down heavily on the side of a chair. 'I 'ad a

good day,' he said, 'over two quid.' He pulled a handful of silver from his pocket.

She looked at the pile of it on the table. It was the rent and the order man, and a new pair of shoes. She scooped it up from the table while her husband grinned stupidly.

'An' there's more where that come from,' he said thickly. 'Two days a week an' I'm makin' more'n if I was on full time.'

Already she had almost forgotten the anxiety of waiting for him and the fear of being left alone. It was funny how the thought of those two pounds made everything different. It was funny the number of things you could think of that wanted buying, and it was funny how inadequate two pounds were when you had two pounds. 'You better git t' bed,' she said. 'You've 'ad a couple too many.'

After that there were Wednesday afternoons and Saturday afternoons when she was worried because he was late coming home, but it wasn't the same as that first afternoon of waiting. The money had changed things. It was a relief from waiting for the scrimped to-morrows, or wondering whether the dole would last the week. It gave her the feeling of being alive. It was good to go into town and do a bit of shopping.

And then there came a day when he didn't come home. It took a long time in coming, but it came.

At eight o'clock they sent a man from the police station to tell her about it, and she went down to see him. He was frightened; she could see it in the look of him. All he could talk about was getting the money to get him out.

'It's a fiver for the bail,' he said. 'You could get it off the old man. Tell 'im that y' want it for y'self.'

It was funny talking to him through the little half-circle cut into the door. At the back of him she could see the white walls of the cell, and there was the sound of a drunk swearing. 'I'll see,' she said. 'I'll see what dad says.' But she was thinking of the few pounds she had managed to save.

She walked back to the house very slowly. In some way or other she had lost that feeling of being alone. There were other things to be thought about. Now that he had been caught she knew that he was finished with the betting. It was almost like the end of that one week at the glassworks. After the few pounds every week it was hard thinking back to the dole, worrying about the rent and the order man. That was what it meant. When he came out he'd go back to sitting in the sun in the back-yard, and he'd get angry every time she nagged him about getting a job. She was suddenly conscious of the hurt of having to live that way again.

Her mind was filled with those thoughts about the dole and she was worrying about to-morrow. Suddenly she was thinking of a job for herself. They were always wanting women at the jam factory and they paid good wages. She could always leave the baby with her mother. It was a chance to stay clear and to live.

The whole thing was growing into a pleasant thought in her mind. When he came out of jail he would have to have a job before she would even consider going back to him. Meanwhile she'd be working and having money to spend and money to pay her debts. She was conscious of a sudden swift feeling of happiness. It was almost as if she had been waiting for her husband to get caught and sent to jail. It was an opportunity to start life again.

When she got back to the house she sat for a long time in the darkness thinking about it. Then suddenly, before she quite knew how it had happened, she had taken the money from the place where she kept it and was looking at it. 'It's a fiver for the bail.' She thought of him in the little half-circle cut into the cell door, and it gave her a queer kind of sickness in the stomach. With the baby in her arms and the money in her pocket she got up and went back to the police station. 'I've come to pay me husband's bail,' she said, and while she was saying it she was thinking of the things she was buying for herself. She was thinking of watching the landlord and the order man from behind the yellow dusty curtains in the front room.

Nineteen hundred and thirty-four. . . .

It was good having a boy. It was good having Sid. She remembered the time when she had met him at one of the shilling dances. It was funny how she had known that he was different from the rest of them even then. The first night he had taken her home he had stood there at the front gate not knowing what to say. And then soon they were talking about getting married, and more than anything she wanted to be married to Sid. There had been other boys, but Sid was different. Sid was someone you could rely on. They were happy, and that was the way they were going to stay.

At the wedding her mother had cried, and it had made her want to cry. To hear the minister reading was something tremendous in her heart. Beside her she knew that Sid was pale with nervousness, and she felt strangely comforting. When it was over he had kissed her shyly and she had known that she was going to be safe with Sid. She would always be safe with Sid.

'I've come to pay me husband's bail,' she said. 'His name's Dennett—Sid Dennett.'

On the way back to the house he was excited with telling her about it. She was glad when at last they came to the front gate in the darkened street. She led the way into the house and he switched on the light.

'Everythin' will be orright,' he said. 'I can use the bail money fer the deposit, an' I'll get time to pay. Then all y' gotter do is write to the Minister of Justice, an' he breaks it down to a fiver, an' that's all y' gotter pay.'

She was thinking of the job in the jam factory, and of having money. She was thinking of him sitting in the sun in the back-yard. She rose suddenly with the baby hoisted in one arm. The next moment she had slapped him across the face with the back of her hand.

He stood looking after her as she turned and went into the darkened bedroom. 'Women,' he thought, 'bloody women.'

NO ONE SPOKE
By RUSSELL J. OAKES

HE had six wounded men to load into the transport plane on the kunai strip and four boongs to help him. In five minutes' time the plane would take off, rush away from the coast, unarmed, unescorted, up—up— towards the highest peaks of the tropic ranges until the air turned bitterly cold and a valley appeared between two massive mountains. This would be the Gap.

Early in 1942 the Japanese planes had flown through

or over that Gap, taking their bombs to Moresby, but now in late November it was no longer safe for them.

The transports that made their unescorted flights every morning before the rain would dash for the Gap on the homeward trip like rabbits running for their warren. There would be no glorious sweep into the vault of the sky. There would be a quick take-off from the kunai, a furtive rush over the coastland trees at a height of a hundred feet or so, then a grim climb upwards to where the mountains trespassed on the realm of birds and aeroplanes, a great roaring as the plane fought the upper currents in that confined, dangerous valley twelve thousand feet above the sea. Once through the Gap and there was an easy glide down to the southern dromes of the island. It was quite simple—if no Zeros came; and if Zeros did come, a lot would depend on how busy our own fighters were. They might be overhead patrolling the sky, or they might be out at sea 'sweating' on the enemy; but for the transports there was always that threat in the stretch from the coast to the Gap.

All this was running through the medical orderly's mind as he loaded the plane. The first patient, a burly infantry private with nothing worse than a cracked fibula, was making himself a nuisance. Why did he always want water when you had your hands full? Why was it his bandages always began to slip when you were lifting someone else on to a stretcher? Now he was yelling because one bandage was too tight. The harassed orderly paused and snapped irritably:

'Aw, stop moaning, you! I've got an officer and four more to put on board yet. I'm not an octopus.' The sudden indignant outburst from the docile-looking figure shocked the surly private to injured silence.

'That's the way to talk,' a cheerful young sergeant piped up. 'You tell him where he gets off, Pills. We'll find him a nice little A.M.W.A.S. to hold his hand when we get to Moresby.'

The cheerful young sergeant was loaded in on the opposite side of the cabin, but the private was too absorbed in self-commiseration to notice that the sergeant's cheeriness was forced and that his right foot was missing from his ankle down. The captain was on a third stretcher. He was much older than the others, a tall lean man with a moustache; and whenever anyone spoke he turned quietly and earnestly to listen, but he did not speak except to thank the orderly if he helped him. He had shrapnel in his chest. The fourth man was a gunner, a bulldozer of a man, quite capable of suffering his own injuries and those of others, too, if necessary. He was a physical king, lamed by a broken leg. The gunner was followed by a little engineer, amusing because of his loquacity and lack of stature. He had had a bullet taken from somewhere under his ribs. He and the cheery sergeant exchanged badinage across the cabin and provoked responsive smiles from everyone save the burly private. The sixth case was another infantryman, too sick to speak. He lay at full length, hands curling, one arm across his forehead, his face bloodless. A bullet had gone through his chest, missing the lung, but he seemed to have lost a lot of blood. Probably he had lain for a long time before being found. He had no interest in the drome or the plane or the other wounded. He was too busy hanging on to consciousness.

The stretchers were put two by two along the cabin and the orderly was about to follow them when a native voice said, 'One more come, taubada.'

Four A.A.M.C. privates came through the kunai

bearing another stretcher. The man in charge was apologetic.

'He's got to go south. Intelligence want him.'

An excited chatter broke out among the natives who stood around. One stepped forward and spat towards the stretcher, muttering, 'Deka!' (Bad!) The good-humoured badinage passing between the sergeant and the little engineer stopped abruptly. All eyes went to the seventh stretcher, save those of the very sick infantryman. He continued to stare at the cabin roof, unheeding. The bearers loaded in the seventh stretcher, setting it at the aft end well away from the others. The surly infantryman with the cracked fibula and the hairy arms sat up violently.

'Here, take me out of this,' he yelled at the orderly. 'I won't ride in no plane with no dirty yellow——'

'Shut up!' growled the gunner, with such ferocity that the other stopped in mid-sentence, shocked to silence, yet the gunner's eyes were smouldering, too, as he looked at the wounded Japanese. The Japanese looked back at them through his spectacles, and, exhausted though he was, he sneered. The doors of the transport closed like the doors of a bank vault, shutting out the jungle world. The medical orderly sat on the steel floor midway between the Japanese and the other stretchers. It was stifling in the cabin and the grin on the Jap's face was devilish.

No one spoke.

The transport taxied slowly along the drome, then, revving on one engine, swung around to face down the strip. Both engines howled and a gale whipped back from the plane and set the tall kunai grass swaying and reeling in the oppressive midday air. Soldiers near by clutched at their battered hats. Some natives laughed, leaning on the wind, letting it tear at their hair and their scanty garments. The transport moved over the brown earth. The kunai rushed by faster until, from the ports of the plane, it looked like wainscoting. Clamorously the engines howled their commands to the bulky machine. Grim battle gripped it as it lifted and soared above the trees. In widening sweeps it climbed. To the north was the sea. Below and running southward was the swampy coastal strip giving place to undulant country, then to hills and finally to the ranges.

The Japanese lay quiet, in a hunched position, hands crossed on his chest, his cheeks sunken and his face monkey-like. His chest was swathed in bandages that were dyed fresh yellow by antiseptic. His eyes never left the others and in spite of his pain his lips never stopped sneering.

The medical orderly could not have been more than twenty years of age. He had a young, ingenuous but very earnest face. He was extremely thin but neat and clean. He could see the eyes of the others wandering to the enemy private at the aft end of the cabin and he could read their thoughts.

'That surly bloke would shove him out of the plane,' he mused, 'and he'd do nasty things to him first. The cheery sergeant would shoot him and think nothing more of it. The little ear-bashing engineer would take him along and hand him over as a matter of routine. The gunner would strangle him with his bare hands, but he'd do it for the sake of his wife and kids. The captain joker—? Well, he's got me beat. Quiet and reserved. I reckon he'd be all right. Wonder how these blokes behave when they're up against it?'

The sixth man was too sick to enter into consideration. He was staring at the roof and now and then he would swallow hard and close his eyes. Nothing more.

The plane climbed with the country, lifting steadily until the river was a white thread in its mountainous course. They travelled very fast and low over the trees for some miles, then the ranges forced them high. The sky was a vast vat of glaring blue without a sign of the clouds that would roll over and deluge the country within another couple of hours. The cabin resounded to the noise of the engines. Through the small round ports the outspread wings could be seen. The oppressive air in the cabin had been swept away by the cold air of altitude. In that there was always danger. You took wounded, shocked men with their resistance lowered, and you lifted them from the humid, tropic coastline into air as cold and keen as winter's.

The orderly felt his way around the cabin, putting an extra blanket on each man, including the Japanese, and pushing a hot-water bottle to the feet of the very sick boy, who took little notice of the ministration. This done, the orderly was returning to his place when he stopped beside the gunner to look out of a port. Far away, behind them, towards the sea, he saw three small black objects hurtling towards the ranges. He examined them anxiously, unable to hear anything save the routine drumming of their own engines. Uneasy, he drew back and found the gunner's steady grey eyes looking at him. There was no need to speak. The gunner knew. The orderly went back to his place but he and the gunner had joined hands in a pact of silence: the anxious, ingenuous little orderly and the stalwart giant.

The seconds thundered away in the confined space of the cabin. The transport was climbing, climbing—

always towards the Gap. Their speed had increased considerably so that the framework of the plane trembled and the engines seemed as though they would whirl right off the wings.

The rabbit was running for its burrow.

The orderly looked around at the unsuspecting patients, trying to gauge how they would behave when they knew. The surly, hairy private; the weary but cheerful sergeant; the strangely quiet captain; the little engineer; the semi-conscious boy, and, lastly, the Japanese. The orderly remembered something he had learned years before in Western Australia, in the drowsy summer days at Northam; something in a lecture that he had not paid much attention to at the time, because he had been thinking of the dip they would have in the cool Avon River immediately the lecture was over. War had seemed so far away, then, on that drowsy summer day beside the hayfield, just as peace seemed far away now.

'If ever you find yourself in a spot of bother, with patients, remember, you have to do more than stop hæmorrhage and splint fractures. You have to stop the flow of arterial fear and splint the mind that cracks.'

On the ground, where a man could occupy his frightened mind with work, that had not been so hard; but what about when he was sitting in the sky waiting for things to crack open?

The first intimation the others had was when a dark shadow swept by a port and a crackling of machine-gun fire assaulted the air outside. Everyone listened, startled. The hairy private looked horrified and shouted something that no one understood above the engines' roar. Then came the first lurch. It came without warning, a sudden, sickening wrench as the

clumsy transport changed speed and banked. The
stretchers, unimpeded, rushed together, shrieking on
the metal floor, and jammed themselves against the
starboard side, throwing all their weight on that side.
The orderly went with them, turning head over heels
in a ridiculous fashion and ending on his back with
his feet against the wall. Someone uttered an uncon-
trollable howl of agony that rose above the roar, but
the orderly could not tell who it was. With his mind
thundering fear inside him, he began to push the
stretchers back into position. It gave him something
to do and he was grateful. He went from one to
another, checking bandages, lifting the men back on
their stretchers. He was not a big boy and his thin
arms were hardly equal to it, especially when he
found he had to lift the gunner—fourteen stone of
him.

The surly private was dead scared, now, so scared
that his mouth was drooping open. He tried to
disguise it as pain by moaning more than was
necessary, and he had to moan loudly so he would be
heard. The engineer was more excited than scared—
excited and surprised. The officer did not seem to have
suffered any ill-effects and he nodded and smiled
reassuringly when the orderly came to him. There was
sweat on the gunner's forehead and little quivers of
pain ran over his face in spite of his efforts to hide
them. The sergeant was lying very still, keeping his
eyes tight closed, nevertheless tears were forcing
their way between his lids, tears of pain because he
had rolled on the foot that wasn't there.

Outside the transport, the engines of the fighters
could be heard weaving a drowsy sound in the sun.
They seemed to be circling up over the transport,
making ready for a dive. The orderly drew a syringe

from his kit and a small bottle with a rubber cap and, plunging the needle through the rubber, he inverted the bottle and drew morphia into the syringe. Another little bottle held spirits and, wetting a swab of cotton wool, he steadied himself over the steel floor and knelt by the sergeant's side. Two strokes with the cotton wool and the sergeant's arm was ready for the needle, but as the orderly bent forward with the syringe he happened to look into the boy's face. The expression he saw was one of utter horror. The sergeant might have spoken but it would have been useless to do so, so that dreadful questioning in his eyes was his only eloquence. Morphia—oblivion— and outside, the Zeros, diving out of the sun. If the transport was shot down and he had had morphia, he would not *know*.

Startled, the orderly hesitated in face of this ghastly appeal. Then, grimly closing his lips, he put away the syringe unused. The sergeant's expression changed. Gone the horror, and instead, behind his pain, gratitude.

Out in the glaring sky a Zero started its Banzai run. They could not see it but they heard it coming, sounding like an outsize in motor-bicycles travelling very fast along a concrete road. Terror gripped the surly private and he yelled again, but no one took any notice of him. The Zero rushed over them so close that they could have sworn it had touched them as it passed. The transport nosed up sharply and instantly the stretchers slithered aft. The wounded men were ready, this time, and saved themselves by bracing their hands on the floor or against the cabin sides. The Japanese was unable to do so. His stretcher thudded against the far end of the cabin. Pain contorted his features. He closed his eyes and rolled his gums until his teeth showed, but then he regained control.

A transport carried no cannon and there was nothing to do but take evasive action and pray for some clouds. Another Zero dived in attack. The lazy clatter of its machine-gun sounded and hammers beat a tattoo on the hull of the transport. Then it, too, swooped away. The orderly wanted to do something to 'stop the flow of arterial fear', but he felt helpless against what appeared to be inevitable.

Then another sound came through the sky from the direction of the Gap. It was a high-pitched whine, scarcely distinguishable above the transport's roar. The machine came into view, hurtling by like some monstrosity from a futuristic world. The orderly gasped and tried to yell the news to the wounded, but they did not hear him, only saw his mouth move. The new arrival resembled two slender plane bodies joined by the one set of wings and tail and the twin fuselages put its identity beyond question. The P38. The Lockheed Lightning. The Gutless Wonder.

In a matter of seconds it had joined issue with the Zeros, charging, diving, climbing, weaving its high-pitched scream in and out through the heavy rattle of the Japanese fighters. Smoothly, easily, it rode the upper air, square and dark against the sky, so that the Zeros, though there were three of them, found themselves fully occupied in defending themselves. Wild hope rushed in through the ports and filled the cabin. The Japanese was alone unmoved, still lying on his stretcher, sneering at them all. The heavy transport charged on towards the Gap, while the fighters gradually fell astern in their defensive and offensive manœuvres. The transport's engines became more clamorous as they attacked the air currents that poured through the Gap. The ravines' below and on either side threw back their defiance, magnified a thousand times over. The sky was one great mechanical howl, while the wings of the plane thrummed and throbbed like strings of a musical instrument.

This was the Gap. This was safety. The rabbit leaped for the entrance to its warren and gained it.

The orderly rose, staggering as the transport rolled, crossed to the sergeant and again took out the hypodermic syringe. This time the sergeant's face was serene. The orderly injected the morphia and rose to go back to his place. As he did so, he leaned a hand against the cabin side and looked out through the round port nearest him. He could see the world spread out below with its ranges upon ranges falling away to the coast, a world of green broken only by the turbulent, frothy white of a torrent hurtling down the heights to become one of the northern rivers. All this was below him, but up in the sky, behind them, he saw the four planes. Three were the stumpy little machines and they were headed away towards the sea. The fourth was the twin-fuselaged Gutless Wonder: it was spiralling down slowly, thin wreaths of smoke ribboning up from it—and something white, that might have been a parachute, was caught on the tail. It went down and down in the sunshine, twisting slowly, smoking, catching the sun—falling, falling towards the far away jungle trees that looked like dark green cauliflowers.

The little thin orderly felt a stone in his throat and he had to shut his lips quickly so that his eyes would stay dry.

He went back across the rocking steel floor and put away his syringe. Then he sat down in his place and, as he did so, he was aware of the wounded Japanese looking across at him through his spectacles, still sneering.

The transport roared on its way through the Gap, battling with the air currents of the ravine.

No one spoke.

THE BLEEDING OF IRISH O'BANION

By James Sweeney

There is a meeting of the 69th Brigade Boxing Association and me and Brannigan are appointed a sub-committee to procure a heavyweight.

It is the first time me and Brannigan have been vested with committee status, but the honour of the A.I.F. is at stake and the Amenities Officer is a man with a shrewd turn of mind and an eye for intelligent men like me and Brannigan.

So we start the search for a heavyweight—as tough as the Ninth Division and as thick in the hide as a Queen Street Commando. For in two weeks' time the 69th Brigade is to swap punches with the United States Army and the heavyweight is top of the bill against a killer by the name of Big Joe De Bashio from Brooklyn—Purple Heart and Bar.

For six months the 69th Brigade had been punching the innards out of the United States Army in every division but the heavy, and me and Brannigan and the Amenities Officer do not like this state of affairs. And we do not particularly like anyone by the name of Big Joe De Bashio, ever since the time at Fort Capuzzo when the Ities bust Padre Sullivan's harmonium with a lump of high explosive.

So we go to the details depot next day and watch the new recruits coming in, and there is nothing that looks like a sleeping draught for Big Joe De Bashio until we come to the Salvo hut where there is a big joker sitting on a form drinking coffee and eating biscuits.

There is nothing unusual in a man eating biscuits and coffee in the Salvo hut but it is most unusual to see a man biting the packet on the end and putting the greaseproof wrapping down the hatch along with the coffee and biscuits.

So me and Brannigan slip up alongside and ask him the strong of the greaseproof diet.

'I'm hungry,' he says.

This joker is as big in the frame as any I've seen in the A.I.F. and I've seen 'em as broad as the Myer Emporium, which is as broad as they come.

Sticking out from each side of his head are the unmistakable hall-marks of pugilism, and on his face there's a map of Ireland with the harp that once through Tara's halls running down the middle where his nostrils ought to be.

We size him up for a while and Brannigan asks him where he's heading. 'Old and Bold,' he says, 'but I'd sooner be in the line.'

Brannigan says it's a shame for such a big strong man to be in the Old and Bold and suggests that maybe if we ring the adjutant we can fix him up on the hygiene on the 69th Brigade, which is working under establishment on account of the flies.

So we get in touch with the adjutant and by the careful manipulation of service channels we get the Frankenstein taken on strength.

He's a joker by the name of Irish O'Banion with a record of ninety-nine fights and ninety-eight defeats and the only time he took a decision was against a has-been from Hobart with a fatty heart and three floating ribs.

Brannigan says his record is not impressive but he reckons that Irish has the makings and the marks and he tells Irish that if he's willing to have a crack at Big Joe De Bashio, me and Brannigan would be willing to train him.

Irish is not too keen about the proposition for a while but me and Brannigan get to work on him. And we tell him about the fighting tradition of the A.I.F. and all about the shame that has come upon us since Big Joe De Bashio from Brooklyn has been dishing out the punishment.

The Irish gets full of emotion and tradition and says he'll have a go. 'Me record don't look good on paper,' he says, 'but there's one record I've held in ninety-nine fights that makes a man feel proud. I've been beat,' he says, 'but I ain't been bled.'

Next day we put Irish O'Banion into strict training and line up a few sparring partners. He wades into them like a fifty-ton bulldozer and after belting two of them all over the ring, he takes the remainder on three at a time just to show me and Brannigan that he's not averse to a bit of punishment either.

For the next seven days we keep him in strict training and we fill him up with more vitamins than you read about in a cookery book.

He's just oozing vitality on the night of the fight.

Me and Brannigan win twenty quid and ten cartons of Lucky Strikes on the preliminaries, and we set the lot on Irish O'Banion for a clean up.

The Yanks are setting all they can on Big Joe De Bashio and I feel sorry for the Yanks, especially Big Joe De Bashio who is going to remember Irish

O'Banion in the years to come when Pearl Harbour is ordinary history.

Irish lumbers into the ring with me and Brannigan at his side, a shamrock on his pants and kangaroos on his singlet front and back.

Then Big Joe De Bashio makes his entrance and he's covered in stars and stripes and the band plays *The Star-spangled Banner*.

Me and Brannigan do not mind this display of patriotism but we look at Irish and his discomfort at the sight of stars so early in the piece is plainly inscribed on his honest face.

The gong goes and the battle is commenced.

Throughout the first round Irish is back-moving. Occasionally he makes a forward move into Big Joe De Bashio's glove and on the whole me and Brannigan get the impression that Irish is not making too much progress.

In the interval between the first and second round Brannigan gives Irish a pep talk and tells him that apart from a good left, a good right and first-class footwork, Big Joe has nothing on Irish O'Banion, which inclines me to believe that Joe De Bashio has plenty.

When they shape up for the second Irish is immediately in distress. Big Joe cuts loose and plasters Irish with everything except the buckets, but Irish is standing up to it and says when he comes back to his corner, 'Me and London can take it.'

And I get the impression that London must be taking a hell of a lacing.

No sooner does the gong go for the third than Irish walks into a haymaker—a rip-snorting tank-buster that Big Joe has been saving up for a secret weapon.

Irish collects it fair on his honest Irish harp and the rich red blood of the O'Banions flows down to the boards like the very River Shannon itself in flood.

Irish is standing still in the centre of the ring. The Yanks are screaming for the kill and Brannigan goes to ring up the ambulance. And all the while Big Joe De Bashio is inflicting more terrible and merciless punishment on Irish O'Banion than a formation of Heinkels, and Irish is taking it like London.

But I start praying for a miracle and the call goes through. Irish leaps into Big Joe with all the ferocity of his martyred ancestors and for the next half-minute Big Joe is taking more punishment than the Japanese Navy.

A few seconds later Big Joe De Bashio is lying in the middle of the ring and he is knocked so cold he will keep for a month.

The referee raises the hand of Irish O'Banion in victory and we get him out of the ring and into the dressing-room before the referee can change his mind.

And on the couch lies Irish and a flood of tears streams down his battered face.

'What are you whingeing for?' says Brannigan. 'You beat him, didn't you?'

'Yeah,' says Irish, 'I beat him all right. I beat him, but he bled me.'

o

YOU GO,
FLORENCE NIGHTINGALE!

By Dal Stivens

I

IN the ladies' toilet at the Trocadero this night Merle, sixteen, who worked behind the stocking counter at Snow's during the day, powdered her nose and put more lipstick on her lips. She wore a bright pink taffeta evening frock and had flung her brown top-coat, with the sleeves hanging loose, over her shoulders. Her brown hair was done in tight curls and her full lips were heavily painted. She had a turned-up nose.

At the next basin her friend Shirley, from the same store, was also powdering her nose. She wore a blue evening frock with a shoulder spray of artificial flowers. She was a blonde with heavy cheek-bones.

Wiping her lips with a make-up handkerchief, Shirley said:

'I dunno what's got into you to-night. You've never been like this before. You've dumped plenty of fellows before.'

'It kind of seems mean. They're lonely,' Merle said.

'That's their worry. You ain't been this way before. I've seen you dump plenty this way before.'

'We've got to go back,' Merle said. 'We've been here too long.'

'You're getting soft. Don't tell me you're getting soft at last.'

'No,' Merle said. 'I'm not getting soft but it does seem mean to talk to fellows and have a dance with them and then ask them to wait and not come back.'

'You've done it before, Merle. You stay the way you are and get all you can out of men.' Shirley shut her handbag up with a snap, fluffed out a curl. 'All of them only want one thing. You want to make them pay. These kids haven't got any money.'

'I'm going back to them,' Merle said. 'I'll tell them you got sick.'

'You tell them what you like. I'm not going to spend the evening with two kids of sailors without any dough.'

Merle walked five steps away and turned back, looking to her friend.

'Come back, Shirley. They mightn't be so bad.'

'You go to hell,' Shirley said. 'You do what you like. Dumping me like this for a couple of dumb sailors. I dunno what's got into you.'

'I'm sorry, Shirley.'

'You're a bloody fool. I dunno why we let them pick us up in the first place.'

'The fair one seems kind of nice.'

'Listen, Merle, they're nicer when they've got some dough. Let's dump them and pick up a couple who'll give us a good time—like the two what took us to Prince's. My, didn't we get a skinful. You did too.' Shaking her head, 'I dunno what's come over you.'

'I'm sorry.'

'Letting me down like this. You said you wanted a good time to-night.'

'I'm sorry, Shirley. Honest I am. I'm going back —you come too.'

'Not on your bloody life. You go, Florence Nightingale.'

Merle went slowly out of the ladies' toilet and through the girls standing around waiting for men to come up and dance with them. Many girls wore evening dress. Some were A.W.A.S. and W.A.A.A.F. Men stood around alone and in pairs and looked the girls over. Most of them were servicemen. Along the wall men and girls had teamed up and were sitting at tables. The two Australian sailors were waiting and smiled when they saw her.

'Hallo,' the one with the fair curly hair said. He looked about nineteen. 'Where's your friend?'

'She's going home,' said Merle. 'She isn't well.'

'That's bad luck,' the dark sailor who looked a little older than the other said. 'Can we take her home?'

Merle sat down alongside the sailor with curly hair. 'No,' she said. 'Shirley will be all right. Don't worry about her.'

'She mightn't be all right,' the fair sailor said. 'We'd better take her home. You go and fetch her.'

'Don't worry about her. Please.'

'All right.'

The orchestra began to play and the fair sailor stood up and asked Merle to dance. She half got up and then sat down.

'You ought to look around for two other girls,' she said.

'Don't you want to dance with me?'

'Yes. But it's no fun for you two. You want two girls.'

'Let's dance,' he said, and walked close to her. She got up. As they went off the dark-haired sailor laughed and waved to them. Then he stood up and left the table.

'Jack will be O.K.,' the fair sailor told Merle, 'I'm glad you didn't get sick. My name is Bill. What's yours?'

'Merle.'

'I like it.'

He started to say something else and then stopped. Merle looked at him, smiled and pressed his hand.

'You're shy,' she said.

His face went red.

'Yes.'

They danced three more dances. Then they went and found a vacant table and sat down. A girl in a green frock came out and crooned *Concerto for Two*. A yellow spotlight played on the girl. She mouthed her red lips at the mike and once she stood on her toes and leaned over it. She sang two other numbers.

II

'Let's go to a night club.'

'Haven't you got any in Perth?'

'Not like the ones in Sydney. I want to see one.'

'You don't want to waste your money. It's all right here.'

'It's hot,' the boy said.

'Let's go outside.'

They pushed through the glass doors and went down the steps to George Street. The street was browned-out and they couldn't see clearly for a minute. After the dance floor the street seemed quiet. They saw the dark Town Hall tower with the grey-white faces of the clock. The hooded headlights of a taxi coming over a small swelling in the street flashed brightly and then blinked back to a little glow.

Merle led the way into Park Street, looking back once over her shoulder to peer into an unlit frock window; servicemen were waiting for girls at the entrance to Hyde Park. They found a seat under a wattle tree. There were other couples around them in the darkness; on the right a girl laughed suddenly and loudly; ahead a man lit two cigarettes and the match lit up cheeks, nose and eyes. A tram whined along Elizabeth Street and its pole struck out blue sparks as though from an emery wheel.

'Tell me,' Merle said, 'was it very bad—up there?'

'It was very bad. The Japs gave us everything they had. They sent bombers and tried to sink us. They seemed to come from everywhere.'

'Couldn't you do anything?'

'We tried all we could. There were too many of them. I don't want to talk about it. There were too many of them.'

In the dark a girl giggled. Arm in arm, a soldier and a girl walked through the dim cone of a browned-out light.

'I don't want to talk about it,' the boy said, loudly this time. 'Please don't ask me.'

Merle put her hand on his.

'No, we won't talk of it,' she said. 'Let's talk about something else.'

'I don't want to talk now,' the boy said. 'Please don't take it the wrong way. I want to get drunk. You take me to a night club.'

'Getting drunk won't do you any good. Let's go back to the Troc.'

'I want to get drunk,' the boy said. 'I'm on leave. You be a sport and take me to a night club. I've got plenty of dough.'

'All right, Bill,' Merle said. 'If you want to go so badly.' She stood and chattered at him gaily. 'Let's have some fun. You have all the fun you can. Kiss me again, please. Suppose we both get drunk?'

III

The fat waiter, who was going bald and who had dandruff flakes on the shoulders of his black jacket, said:

'Another two bottles of gin, sir?'

'Yes,' the boy said. 'Two more.'

The waiter smiled, picked up two empty bottles from the table, gave his jacket a tug and went away. On the platform one of the band tipped his saxophone up to drain it and the 'cellist spun his instrument on its point. At the next table a girl leaned her head on the shoulder of an A.I.F. private.

'Where'll we go to-morrow night?' the boy asked.

'Anywhere you like, Bill. Anywhere.'

He passed her a packet of Turf.

'Am I very drunk?'

'No, you're just nice. Nice and happy.'

The band started to play and he said:

'Let's dance.'

'Yes.'

The waiter came along with the gin, put them down, smiled and waited to be paid. Someone threw a switch and the lights dimmed. The night club was decorated after the style of a ship's interior, and the globes were set in imitation ships' lanterns.

A girl in pink in front of the band threw streamers over the dancers.

One streamer fell across them and Merle caught it.

'See, I'm a maypole dancer,' she said. Then she began to laugh. She went on laughing and he half-let his arms fall and looked at her.

'No,' she said. 'I'm not a maypole dancer. I'm Florence Nightingale.'

'Florence who?'

'Florence Nightingale. You know, the one with the lamp. I'm Florence Nightingale.'

'I remember. She was a nurse.'

'I'm her,' Merle said. 'She carried a lamp.'

'Do you want a lamp?'

'I'd look good with a lamp. I'm Florence Nightingale.'

He stopped dancing abruptly. He climbed on to a table and reached up for the lantern.

'Don't,' she said. 'Please, Bill, don't. You can't do that.'

'You said you wanted a lamp.'

The fat waiter came running up.

'Do you want anything, sir?'

'The lady wants to be Florence Nightingale,' the boy said. 'She wants a lamp.'

IV

It did not seem long after that before they were in a taxi on the way to her home at Glebe. He had hailed the taxi, walking drunkenly into its headlights and the driver had braked sharply, the taxi's tyres searing the asphalt.

He leaned heavily against her in the back seat and she put her arms round him. The taxi went on smoothly and the black silk of George Street was wound softly and swiftly on the wheels. A No Parking sign swam before her eyes, dipped and disappeared. She felt sleepy and happy. She snuggled close to him. He stirred then.

'I'm very young,' he said. He furrowed his forehead, trying to open his eyes.

'I'm very young,' he said again. He sat up suddenly, with his body tense and his teeth tight together. 'I'm too young!' he burst out. 'You say I'm too young, darling.'

Merle couldn't say anything. She found she was crying. She put her arms around him and drew him tightly to her.

THE MAN WHO BOWLED VICTOR TRUMPER
By Dal Stivens

'EVER hear how I bowled Victor Trumper for a duck?' he asked.

'No,' I said.

'He was a beautiful bat,' he said. 'He had wrists like steel and he moved like a panther. The ball sped from his bat as though fired by a cannon.'

The three of us were sitting on the veranda of the pub at Yerranderie in the Burragorang Valley in the late afternoon. The sun fell full on the fourteen-hundred-foot sandstone cliff behind us but the rest of the valley was already dark. A road ran past the pub and the wheel-tracks were eighteen inches deep in the hard summer-baked road.

'There was a batsman for you,' he said.

He was a big fat man with a chin like a cucumber. He had worked in the silver mines at Yerranderie. The last had closed in 1928 and for a time he had worked in the coal mines further up the valley and then had retired on a pension and a half an inch of good lung left.

'Dust in my lungs,' he said. 'All my own fault. The money was good. Do you know, if I tried to run a hundred yards I'd drop dead.'

The second man was another retired miner but he had all his lungs. He had a broken nose and had lost the forefinger and thumb of his right hand.

Before they became miners, they said, they had tried their hand at many jobs in the bush.

'Ever hear how I fought Les Darcy?' the big fat man asked.

'No,' I said.

'He was the best fighter we have ever had in Australia. He was poetry in action. He had a left that moved like quicksilver.'

'He was a great fighter,' I said.

'He was like a Greek god,' said the fat man reverently.

We sat watching the sun go down. Just before it dipped down beside the mountain it got larger and we could look straight at it. In no time it had gone.

'Ever hear how I got Victor Trumper?'

'No,' I said. 'Where did it happen?'

'It was in a match up at Bourke. Tibby Cotter was in the same team. There was a man for you. His fastest ball was like a thunderbolt. He was a bowler and a half.'

'Yes,' I said.

'You could hardly see the ball after it left his hand. They put two lots of matting down when he came to Bourke so he wouldn't kill anyone.'

'I never saw him,' I said, 'but my father says he was very fast.'

'Fast!' says the fat man. 'He was so fast you never knew anything until you heard your wicket crash.

In Bourke he split seven stumps and we had to borrow the school kids' set.'

It got cold and we went into the bar and ordered three rums which we drank with milk. The miner who had all his lungs said:

'I saw Tibby Cotter at the Sydney Cricket Ground and the English were scared of him.'

'He was like a tiger as he bounded up to bowl,' said the big fat man.

'He had even Ranji bluffed,' said the other miner. 'Indians have special eyesight but it wasn't enough to play Tibby.'

We all drank together and ordered again. It was my shout.

'Ever hear about the time I fought Les Darcy?' the big fat man asked me.

'No,' I said.

'There wasn't a man in his weight to touch him,' said the miner who had all his lungs. 'When he moved his arm you could see the muscles ripple across his back.'

'When he hit them you could hear the crack in the back row of the Stadium,' said the fat man.

'They poisoned him in America,' said the other miner.

'Never gave him a chance,' said the fat man.

'Poisoned him like a dog,' said the other.

'It was the only way they could beat him,' said the fat man. 'There wasn't a man at his weight that could live in the same ring as Les Darcy.'

The barmaid filled our glasses up again and we drank a silent toast. Two men came in. One was carrying a hurricane lantern. The fat man said the two men always came in at night for a drink and that the tall man in the raincoat was the caretaker at one of the derelict mines.

'Ever hear about the kelpie bitch I had once?' said the fat man. 'She was as intelligent and wide awake as you are. She almost talked. It was when I was droving.'

The fat miner paid this time.

'There isn't a dog in the bush to touch a kelpie for brains,' said the miner with the broken nose.

'Kelpies can do almost anything but talk,' said the fat man.

'Yes,' I said. 'I have never had one but I have heard my father talk of one that was wonderful for working sheep.'

'All kelpies are beautiful to watch working sheep but the best was a little bitch I had at Bourke,' said the fat man. 'Ever hear how I bowled Victor Trumper for a duck?'

'No,' I said. 'But what about this kelpie?'

'I could have got forty quid for her any time for the asking,' said the fat miner. 'I could talk about her all day. Ever hear about the time I forgot the milk for her pups? Sold each of the pups later for a tenner.'

'You can always get a tenner for a good kelpie pup,' said the miner who had all his lungs.

'What happened when you forgot the pups' milk?' I said.

'It was in the bucket,' the fat miner said, 'and the pups couldn't reach it. I went into the kitchen and the bitch was dipping her tail in the milk bucket and then lowering it to the pups. You can believe that or not, as you like.'

'I believe you,' I said.

'I don't,' said the other miner.

'What, you don't believe me!' cried the fat miner, turning to the other. 'Don't you believe I bowled Victor Trumper for a duck? Don't you believe I fought Les Darcy? Don't you believe a kelpie could do that?'

'I believe you bowled Victor Trumper for a duck,' said the other. 'I believe you fought Les Darcy. I believe a kelpie would do that.'

The fat miner said: 'You had me worried for a minute. I thought you didn't believe I had a kelpie like that.'

'That's it,' said the miner who had all his lungs. 'I don't believe you had a kelpie like that.'

'You tell me who had a kelpie like that if I didn't,' the fat miner said.

'I'll tell you,' said the miner with the broken nose. 'You never had a kelpie like that but I did. You've heard me talk about that little bitch many times.'

They started getting mad with each other then so I said:

'How did you get Victor Trumper for a duck?'

'There was a batsman for you,' said the fat man. 'He used a bat like a sword and he danced down the wicket like a panther.'

THE THREE JOLLY FOXES
By Douglas Stewart

AT the hour of seven on a fine June morning, two handsome glossy foxes are hurrying towards the store and teashop on Fat Chow Creek. The one who is closest is carrying no rabbit in his mouth; and that is a pity, for the great red fellow, trotting from the tea-tree to the golden rushes by the creek, ears up, plumy brush waving—a rabbit in his mouth would make him the perfect picture of a fox on the hunt in the morning.

As for Mr. Hardcastle, his big, knuckly hands gripping the steering wheel of his shiny red car—he's got his rabbit all right, and you can almost see her in his mouth; the new Mrs. Hardcastle—brand-new; only last night—snuggling beside him in her cony-seal coat. The tip of her small nose twitches.

'You're cold!' shouts Mr. Hardcastle. You can tell he's a fox by the bark of his laughter. 'You're cold.' (Bark! Bark! Bark!)

'Oh, no,' she says, archly, sarcastically. She laughs, too, very loud and shrill and high, like a tremendous and surprising bell; the pealing of wedding bells.

'Hey, yes you are, you're cold. It's too early in the morning for you. Ha, we'll make a man of you yet.'

'You wouldn't want to do that.'

'Ha, that's right!' Mr. Hardcastle barks and barks. 'But you *are* cold. I'll warm you up. I'll stop the car and warm you up.'

'You'd better drive on. Besides, I'm not a bit cold. Really I'm not. I love this south coast in the morning. The mountains with the sun on them; and the sea that delicate, delicate blue; and the foam. It's a wonderful place—for a honeymoon.'

'Honeymoon! Ha!' The big fox barks. His hair is silver, there is a bald patch on top, his eyes are grey and small; the character of his face is in his large, fleshy nose and his mouth, which sets firmly, even savagely, as he steers the big car round a bend. He makes it lurch round the corners.

'Just to be driving along,' says the rabbit. She smiles up at him, so that her frizzy hair and her horn-rimmed glasses seem to disappear, and all he can see are her red, red lips and her enormous false teeth. 'And a whole week of it,' she says. 'A whole week to Melbourne.'

'If I can find that Middleton scoundrel in Melbourne I'll prosecute the brute,' he says. 'He took us down. Deliberately. We supply him with the goods —two years ago—and that's the last we hear of him. I'll get him and I'll send him to jail.' Mr. Hardcastle has a factory.

'Oh,' says the new Mrs. Hardcastle, 'don't let us think about business. This is too heavenly.'

But the fox—the other red fox in the rushes—is certainly thinking about business.

He knows it is heavenly, all right. The sun is warm on his back; the creek before him glitters; he can smell the salt sea, the tidal mud, the crabs; he can see a black-and-white bird, a pee-wee, that runs along the path between the rushes. But he cannot catch that pee-wee. And if he could it would not be much for a fox's breakfast. To run from dawn to seven o'clock, to hunt from dawn to seven o'clock, to hunt and sniff and hunt and sniff all the way from the rocky bush to within sight of Joe Packet's store and teashop by the bridge on Fat Chow Creek, to watch the mist lift and the dew dry and the seagulls go over in a clear, shiny light, to have the scent of shellfish and birds and vegetation in your nostrils—all this is to make hunger grow immense, a madness.

And if it is a madness to sneak right to the edge of the rushes where, along the line of his withered corn, Joe Packet has set his rabbit-traps—then let it be madness. But nobody sings or shouts in Joe Packet's store and tearooms, no smoke yet curls from the chimney. Joe Packet and Mrs. Packet lie snug abed while the fox is at their rabbit-traps.

Yet it might, indeed, be a mad fox who thinks he can catch Joe Packet asleep. Joe is like a fox, too; he lies snug with his vixen in the warm burrow of the bed, but all night long he leaves his mouth out in the paddock to catch the rabbits; his spare mouth, his dozen spare mouths, all gaping, waiting, with sharp steel teeth. Joe Packet has caught two rabbits while he sleeps. Broken, they lie in his spare steel mouths —fast shut these mouths are. How warm, how appetizing they smell! How inviting is the thought of pink flesh under that soft grey fur! The red fox lolls his tongue. He whines with pleasure.

He takes a little run round the rabbits, partly for joy, partly to make sure Joe Packet is not about. Not a sign of him; only, on the steel mouths, a little rank smell of Joe Packet where he has touched them last night; to cover a yawn, it might be.

Fox, fox, Joe Packet never yawns. Look out, red fox!

Yes, yelp! But yelp too late, you mad red dog of the mountains. Joe Packet is a lucky man, he has caught a fox in his trap.

Joe Packet stirs in his bed. Time for a cup of tea. And the store and the tearooms to open. Someone might be coming along the road. A fine day for business.

And then, too, a fine day to take a little walk round the traps while the wife lights the fire and cooks the breakfast. A black woman in the mornings! But a blue day outside. Joe Packet in his blue dungarees, his hard, big belly rolling over the narrow black belt; his open grey shirt showing the dark hair on his chest; dark hair turning grey.

The square head of Joe Packet, usually hunched forward, now thrown back as he snuffs the salty air. The feet of Joe Packet, in the unlaced, torn, dirty, comfortable, rubber-soled sandshoes, travelling lightly over Fat Chow bridge. Grunt as he climbs through the fence.

Stealthily along the corn, as if the dead rabbits could run away out of his mouths. Ho! And a high, whinnying laugh.

A fox, a fox in the trap! Before he can bite his leg off. A stick, a stick, a cudgel. The red fox spins and dances.

Joe Packet, a heavy man, light on his feet, darting about the cornfield and the rushes, hunting for a cudgel—he hardly notices the big red car crossing the bridge.

Burly man, tall skinny girl, Mr. and Mrs. Hardcastle alight from the car at the tearooms. Ah, Joe Packet sees them.

Thud goes the stick on the fox. 'Tourists!' says Joe. 'My lucky day to-day!'

Mr. Hardcastle is as hungry as the fox was, but nobody is going to hit him on the head with a cudgel. Not if he knows it.

'Come on now. Quick, quick, quick!' he says to Joe Packet's wife. 'A cup of tea before we start. Then bacon and eggs for two.'

'Oh,' says Mrs. Hardcastle. 'Just a piece of toast. Just a *wafer*.'

'Bacon and eggs for two!' shouts Mr. Hardcastle. 'Now, quick about it, old dear.'

'Certainly,' says Joe Packet's wife.

The honeymoon couple are alone. They are among fragile cane chairs, and glass-topped tables and vases of paper roses. A wall of windows shows between creamy curtains the distant blue of the sea and a section of the white-painted railing of the bridge. Shafts of sunlight enter. Almost, a faint, subsiding rattle is heard as Mr. Hardcastle's jollity ceases to crash about the glassy room. The floor quakes as Joe Packet's wife goes about her business.

'They'd do pretty well here,' says Mr. Hardcastle confidentially. 'Cheap. No rent. Grow your own vegetables. Pluck your own fowls. Pluck the tourists.'

'Really?' says Mrs. Hardcastle. 'So far from any-where—I wouldn't have thought. But of course you'd know.'

Is she mocking him when she flatters, or does she really respect it so much—his business ability? Mr. Hardcastle's eyes narrow. His mouth takes on that savage, down-curving line that shows when he is heaving the car round a bend. 'Of course they'd do well!' he shouts.

'A peculiar woman, isn't she?' says Mrs. Hardcastle. 'So dark and slinking. She gives me a creepy feeling. That long, snooping nose, those jet-black eyes. She's the sort of woman who'd have lain in wait for travellers in the old days—an innkeeper's wife—and murdered them in their beds.' Mrs. Hardcastle's large eyes blink behind the horn-rimmed glasses. She thrusts her hands into her frizzy hair and drags forward a black curl of it, as if she is the villain in a melodrama throwing his cloak over his features. 'Like some cold, slinking animal. I'm sure she'd like to murder us.'

'Stuff!' roars Mr. Hardcastle. He has noticed his wife's tendency to romanticize. It might become worse.

Joe Packet's wife brings in tea and toast. She points her long nose at the tourists. 'Joe's caught a fox. He's out there now with the skin.'

'Now, what's that worth?' says Mr. Hardcastle quickly.

'A fox. The skin of a fox. Oh, I must see it!' cries Mrs. Hardcastle. 'Where is it? Can I see it? Where?'

'On the garage door,' says Mrs. Packet. 'He's nailing it up to dry.'

'To think,' says Mrs. Hardcastle dramatically, pausing in the doorway, 'to think that at this very hour I would have been arriving at the office and taking the cover off my typewriter; and here—down the south coast—on the way to Melbourne—and the lovely skin of a fox!' She rushes out.

'She's excited, isn't she?' says Joe Packet's lean dark wife. 'Just like a girl.'

'My dear lady,' says Mr. Hardcastle very winningly, 'how much you could excite me by bringing me my bacon and eggs.' He pushes a whole finger of toast into his mouth, and the butter runs down his fingers. He sucks them. 'Ah!'

'Just like a girl, eh?' he thinks as Joe Packet's wife retires to the kitchen. 'Ha! Last night!' (He barks.) Yes, like a girl. And not as if—well, she'd been his secretary for ten years. Secretary, you could call it. And still like a girl; kittenish, excited; rolling her big eyes behind the glasses, twitching her nose, smiling with her huge white teeth. A girl, a kitten, a rabbit.

Mr. Hardcastle's rabbit is forty years old. Why marry her, then? And after ten years. Well, we grow old. Time, loneliness and—the dark thing. A widower in a dark house. And then, she wanted it so much. On the shelf; spinsterish; really, a little bit dotty; damn' nearly, anyhow. Why not please her? A house, money, a cony-seal coat, a car, a wedding, a honeymoon on the south coast; and a man—ha, yes, a man! —how much he could give his little rabbit.

Joe Packet's dark-eyed wife brings him his bacon

and eggs. 'I'll keep the lady's warm for her,' she said. 'Are you sure she really wants it?'

'Of course she wants it,' says Mr. Hardcastle roughly. 'Fill her out. Do her good. A leaf of lettuce in a back room in Darlinghurst, that's what these girls live on.'

Mrs. Hardcastle's knees are too bony, he thinks. Ah, well, she shall eat. Not really a girl, not trim and tight and bouncy; but there you are.

'How would I look with a girl?' he asks Joe Packet's wife. 'An old codger like me!'

'I'm sure you'd look very well with a girl, sir,' says the sallow-faced woman diplomatically.

'Ha!' he says scornfully. 'Run you down into the grave and then make off with your money. You don't catch me like that.'

Mrs. Hardcastle comes flying in.

'Oh!' she cries, 'it's horrible. He's got it all pegged out on the wall, crucified. The inside of the skin showing. Ugh, slimy. And the head's lolling forward, it looks alive. And it's grinning. There on the wall, grinning.' Her frizzy hair seems to be springing up and down with alarm.

'Ha!' says Mr. Hardcastle. 'I must have a look at that.' He rises from the table.

'Oh,' says his wife, 'let's go. We've miles to go to-day. Let's drive on now.'

Mr. Hardcastle pushes the brand-new Mrs. Hardcastle into her chair. 'You sit down and eat your breakfast,' he says.

'I couldn't.'

'Eat it. It's ordered. We'll have to pay for it— *you'll* have to pay, because you're the housekeeper— so eat it up and be done with it.' He goes out.

Joe Packet's wife looks sympathetically at Mrs.

Hardcastle. 'You must have been up very early,' she says, 'if you came from Sydney this morning.'

'Oh, yes,' says Mrs. Hardcastle airily. 'Mr. Hardcastle likes to make an early start when he's travelling. Even—well, even this morning.'

'A special morning, my dear?' asks the sympathetic wife of Joe Packet.

'Oh, no,' says Mrs. Hardcastle. 'Oh, nothing special.' *Is* it, she wonders. *Is* it? What have I done? He's so rough, he's so burly; blundering through life like a footballer.

'I wonder,' says the sympathetic lady, leaning towards her and dangling a little trumpery necklace of bright flowers made from dough, 'I wonder if you'd like to help me with my good work. These are for the Red Cross.'

Joe Packet's wife does not look like a lady who sells things for the Red Cross. She has a long, ominous nose, which is piercing Mrs. Hardcastle in the bosom; she has a cold, glittering black eye which Mrs. Hardcastle would prefer to see fixed on someone else; she has a stealthy, cat-like tread, which Mrs. Hardcastle wishes would transport her out of the room. But Joe Packet's wife does not move away from the breakfast-table. She stands there still and ominous.

'Oh,' says Mrs. Hardcastle, 'you sell them, do you?'

'For the Red Cross, my dear. Ten shillings.'

Ten shillings. But Mr. Hardcastle, strong, protective Mr. Hardcastle, is not to be seen on the left of Joe Packet's wife's nose, nor on the right of her nose. If only she will go away.

Mrs. Hardcastle fumbles in her purse.

'Thank you, my dear,' says the woman. 'Now would you like another little necklace? Pretty, aren't they? Or some earrings? For the Red Cross.'

'I think,' says Mrs. Hardcastle desperately, 'that will be enough for just now. Perhaps some other time. When we come back. *I think*,' says Mrs. Hardcastle bravely, 'I'll just pay for the breakfasts now and then we can be on the road.'

'Another ten shillings, my dear,' says the lean wife of Joe Packet.

Ten shillings for bacon and eggs! But Mrs. Hardcastle pays it. Shall she face the fox again? She must find Mr. Hardcastle and go.

But Mr. Hardcastle is not outside by the garage door, where the red fox grins at his wife. Joe Packet has him in the store.

'Packet's my name,' says Joe Packet, 'and Packet's my nature. Ham, Mr. Hardcastle, eh? You'll want it for the trip. I'll pack it.' Swift and light in his movements, swift and fluent in his speech.

'Ha!' roars Mr. Hardcastle happily, 'you want to pack me the whole blasted shop.'

'The old red fox, he's dead, eh?' says Joe Packet. 'He's finished, that one. But you and I, we live. Hey, Mr. Hardcastle, we live—and while we live we eat.'

'You got any salmon?' asks Mr. Hardcastle. 'Put it in.'

'Three tins,' says Joe, chuckling. 'Four tins. We'll make it four. The old red salmon, he swims in the sea no more.' He's a hard case, is Joe; his face all wrinkled with laughter, and his upper lip lifted at the corner in a permanent grin that shows a yellow fang.

'What the hell will I ever do with four tins of salmon?' Mr. Hardcastle joyously bellows.

'You're going to Melbourne. With a lady. You take a week for the journey. You eat by the roadside. Plenty, to keep your strength up.'

'Put 'em in then, put 'em in,' says Mr. Hardcastle. 'To keep my strength up.' (Bark.)

Joe laughs. Square head lifted off his chest again, thrown back, and the high whinnying laugh shooting up, it seems, at the tins of biscuits on the top shelf. His hands hold his belly in.

'Right!' says Joe. 'Now then. Fruit, chocolates, cigarettes, what else does the lady like? Biscuits! Gingernuts, wafers—no, chocolate fingers.' He climbs a ladder to the top shelf. Force of habit alone prevents his blue dungarees from slipping off.

Mrs. Hardcastle is astounded. The pile of foodstuffs and groceries. Simply squandering money. And him, of all people! What would he say if he knew about the ten shillings for the necklace and the other ten shillings for breakfast?

Why, at the moment, he, Mr. Hardcastle, shrewd, tough, tight-fisted managing director of a factory, he would say nothing at all. How curious; curious. What have he and Joe Packet been saying to each other while they stared at the old dead dog-fox? What male jokes have they cracked? She knows. She knows. The three jolly foxes together.

But here comes that woman behind her; the long, sharp nose is making a hole in her spine. 'Oh, come,' says Mrs. Hardcastle to her husband. 'We must go.'

Joe Packet slithers down the ladder.

'Yes,' says Mr. Hardcastle. 'In a minute.'

'I'm sure you'll have a lovely journey,' says the wife of Joe.

'I think,' says Mrs. Hardcastle to her husband, 'I'll sit in the car and wait for you. Don't be long.' She looks down, over the tops of her horn-rimmed glasses, at Mrs. Packet, who is not now some sliding, sinister animal, but, because Mrs. Hardcastle is departing, merely the avaricious wife of a storekeeper. 'Good-bye,' trills Mrs. Hardcastle sarcastically as she goes out the door, 'I do hope you bring lots of success to the Red Cross.'

Mrs. Packet smiles, her long flickering upper lip, with its faint black moustache, disclosing very small white teeth, like a fish's. Such a repellent-looking woman!

'Quick, then,' says Joe. 'Three at one-and-two is three-and-nine, the biscuits two-and-sevenpence, salmon, pears, three tins of peaches, chocolates, say two shillings, no, half a crown, ham, chicken-paste, loaf of bread sevenpence, then there's the cigarettes; look here, Mr. Hardcastle, I'll throw in a packet of matches; now that's two-pounds-ten the lot. And no charge at all for looking at the old red fox.'

'Ha!' laughs Mr. Hardcastle. 'I know who's the old red fox. Two-pounds-ten!'

'But isn't it worth it?' said Joe. 'Life is worth it! Picnics by the road are worth it. You and me, we know, Mr. Hardcastle. You're only old once.' His whinnying laughter.

'Two-pounds-ten, then,' says Mr. Hardcastle, a little sadly, for, after all, money is money.

'And ten shillings for the breakfasts, don't forget,' says Mrs. Packet, her long nose entering the conversation.

'Three quid,' says Joe. 'Three jolly old quid the lot.'

Mr. Hardcastle pays him. 'I'll tell you what,' he says, 'that damned old fox-skin won't be worth a cracker to you, anyhow. You saw the holes where the ticks had got into it.'

'Never mind about that,' says Joe. 'We'll find a use for him somehow. He was a good fox in his day. Good-bye, Mr. Hardcastle.'

As Mr. Hardcastle drives off Joe Packet waves, and the red fox, on the garage door, is grinning.

'I thought we'd never get away,' says Mrs. Hardcastle, looking back from a bend in the road at the store by Fat Chow Creek. 'Those awful people. They robbed us.'

'I told you they'd do pretty well there,' Mr. Hardcastle answers. 'Three quid they got out of me. Well, it was worth it.'

'*What* was?' asks the brand-new Mrs. Hardcastle. 'Three pounds just for that box of groceries.'

'Ten bob of it was for the breakfasts,' says Mr. Hardcastle.

'But I paid them for the breakfasts!'

'Damn it, I did!'

'We both paid!' Mrs. Hardcastle is aghast. 'We've paid them twice for it. Oh!'

'Ha!' laughs Mr. Hardcastle, placing his hand on her knee as, doubtless in error for the gear-lever, he so often does. 'Diddled us, diddled us properly.'

'We'll put the police on to them!' says Mrs. Hardcastle.

'No,' her big husband scorns her. 'I can afford it. Let 'em go.'

'I think you should drive straight back to that shop and demand your money back. You must have gone absolutely mad to take it so calmly. Laughing.'

'I like to see it!' Mr. Hardcastle shouts with his bark of laughter. 'The old fox and the vixen! They'll do all right, that pair. They'll make money. I'd like to have that old fox on my sales staff.'

'You're a bit of a fox yourself,' says Mrs. Hardcastle softly. She looks at him archly, over the rims of her glasses. 'But you want to look out, you know. More than one old fox has put his foot right into a rabbit-trap. And that was the end of him.' Her wedding-bells peal and peal.

Mr. Hardcastle begins to laugh, then does not. He stares at his brand-new wife. There is something strangely steel-like in Mrs. Hardcastle's appearance. Bones, wires, those horn-rimmed glasses, that frizz of springs on her head, those enormous teeth. And the old fox in a trap. He stamps his foot on the accelerator.

DRIFT
By PETER COWAN

IN the morning the Bren-gun carriers had been through the fields and their flat tractor-like marks were scored across the paddocks and into the timber, where they had gone from sight. In the house the woman put the lunch dishes on the table and the girl crossed over from the stove with the teapot she had filled. They sat down, and the men edged their chairs in.

'Wish I'd been in one of them,' the boy said.

'One of them ran out of petrol out on the other side of the gully,' the girl said. 'I heard the men in the truck say.'

'That's what I'm going to try and get into.' The boy looked away from the window. His mother smiled.

'They haven't taken you yet,' his father said.

'There might be a letter this afternoon.'

'They took Roy Jones,' his mother said. 'I think Harry'll get in all right.'

'They got to have food,' the man said. 'They got to

have food, don't they? If they go taking all the farmers
what the hell's going to happen to the place.'

'That's why they wouldn't take me before.' The boy
nodded. 'But they might now I've written about it.
And you said you'd let me go.' His eyes were
restless.

The man did not say anything. He looked at the
food on his plate and his moving knife and fork as
though he would shut out all the rest about him by
forcing his attention to that.

'Well, if Harry goes,' the girl said, 'I'm going too.'

'What'd you do?' Harry asked.

'There're plenty of things I could get into. They're
wanting women all the time.'

'You'd be a land-girl, I suppose.'

'Thanks. I'm that here. No, I can drive a car. I can
drive the truck, too. There's plenty of things I could
do.'

'What you can do now,' Harry said, 'is get me a bit
more potato.' He pushed his plate towards her. The
girl got up and went across to the stove. Her short red
jumper made a splash of colour against the dark
shining stove and the whitewashed stove place.

'I won't be sorry when the Army has to feed you,'
she said, putting the plate down in front of him.

He grinned and flicked the tight seat of her skirt
with his finger as she turned to her own chair.

'It's the women put on weight in the Army.'

'Yair?'

The man sat looking down at the table while the
woman and the girl cleared away the plates and
served the pudding. He ate quickly.

'I suppose I'll hardly know you when you both
come back on your leave in uniform,' the woman said.

'You won't be able to miss Bet.' The boy grinned.

'Very funny. I think the women's uniforms look better than the men's anyway.'

'You'll probably both seem quite strangers,' the woman said. Something in her tone made the man look up quickly, but she was looking at them, and he lowered his eyes again unobserved.

When they had finished he got up and went outside. The early rains had brought the grass up and the fields were a vivid green. In the paddock by the rise there were ewes with lambs. As he went over towards the sheds a dog came out, stretching, hollowing its back, its tail beating slowly as the man spoke to it, and they went across to the low rails of the pig-pens. The man began working on the fence where he was replacing some of the old boards with new timber. The dog lay in the sun by some of the new wood on the grass. Inside the other pens some of the older sows lay basking, dug in the softened earth. For a time the man worked, and then he saw the boy come out and go over to the stables and then across the paddock to catch the horse. He watched the boy lead it in and harness it in the sulky and drive across to the house gate, where the girl came out and got up into the sulky. They waved good-bye to the woman and drove down the track towards the road.

As the man worked the sun drew across the sky so that the colours of the land changed and deepened, and the distant hills darkened. The ewes with the lambs had grazed down towards the fence, and out by the belt of timber he could see the cattle. He left the work he was doing and went across to the house. The woman had the kettle boiling and she made the tea. He sat down by the end of the table where he could see out of the window.

The woman poured his cup of tea.

'Listen, Jim,' she said. 'It's no use worrying about it on and on like this.'

'No,' he said.

'He'll be all right. It's not as if we were the only ones had to worry these days.'

'Why's he want to go?' the man said abruptly. 'Why d'both of them, come to that.'

'If he didn't want to go I'd think it much stranger. Of course he wants to go, like everyone else. They both do.'

'Y' don't see,' the man said. He drank from the cup, looking out the window, sipping the hot tea. Across the fields he had spent his lifetime clearing he could see the flat squashed tracks of the Bren-gun carriers. They ran straight, not turning aside till they reached the timber, where they went out of sight. In the way they went across the property that had absorbed his effort and his work and his thought, and with which he had so identified himself that he seemed as nothing without it, he saw the symbol of something beyond him and which took no account of him, something he was powerless to halt. It was not war, but something which war had merely hastened. His mind sought for words to bring his feeling into clarity before the woman.

'Y' don't see,' he repeated. 'Why can't they stop here? We got to produce food. They got to have food. Men can't fight without food, though you'd think they could the bloody stupid way the manpower people go on. And the cities can't starve. He's doing work that's got to be done if he stays here.'

'But he's young and he doesn't see it like that. He wants to be where the other young men are, and where a lot of his cobbers are. You don't seem to understand——'

'It's you who don't understand,' the man said. 'Don't you see if he goes, if they both go, they won't come back.'

'That's the sort of chance we all have to take now, Jim.'

'I don't mean that. I don't mean that. Look, it's this place they're both leaving. Don't y' see? They won't come back.'

The woman shook her head. 'I think you're being a bit silly.' She moved her hand uncertainly.

He pushed his cup towards the centre of the table and stood up. 'Well,' he said, 'I'd better get started on the milking.'

He went outside and across to the milking sheds. He had almost finished in the sheds when he heard the sulky coming up the track. He was going over the yard to the gate to the paddocks when he saw the boy come into the shed. He waited by the gate. The boy came up to him.

'I got the letter,' he said. He had it in his hand, a light-brown envelope. 'They'll take me. They said they'd notify me.'

The man pushed the gate. 'They say when?'

'No. But it prob'ly won't be long. They called Roy Jones up in about two weeks.'

'Yes.'

The boy kicked the damp gravel. 'You'll be able to keep the place going—it's not as if——'

'I can work it, I suppose.'

'Well——'

The man shook his head, and then he said quietly: 'You're in a hell of a hurry to go. Both of you, come to that.'

'It's not that.' His denial came quickly.

'I been here thirty years since my old man died.'

The man gestured his hand towards the paddocks, the green deep in the fading light. 'This was bush but for a couple of acres the old man cleared.'

The boy's eyes were restless. He marked the damp earth with his foot.

'Yes but——'

'You don't see it, like that, do you?'

'After—when this is over——'

'Don't matter,' the man said. He pushed the gate open. 'I'll bring the cows in.'

'Righto.'

'You needn't come. You take the horse out. I won't be long. I got everything ready in the shed.'

The boy nodded. 'Right.'

He went back towards the shed. The man walked across the grass that was lengthening in the paddocks. The belt of timber was over to his right. The last of the light was shining on the hills, so that patches stood out clearly against the depths of shadow. Where the light caught he could see the individual trees and the shapes of the rocks. He walked on towards the belt of timber.

TWENTY STRONG
By Margaret Trist

Della Parkins, The Ten-mile Farm, Branch Creek, via Woonganattie, was painted in thin black lettering on the tin trunk. Della looked downward at it from the high seat of the buggy on which she sat, the lettering blurring and distorting through her tears.

'Here,' said the driver of the buggy, who was also

the mailman, and who was at present unwillingly
escorting Della to school in Woonganattie, it being
shearing and no one else having time, 'put your feet
on it.' He juggled the trunk into position with his foot
and she rested her black buttoned boots on it, placing
them sadly and sedately side by side. 'Aren't you going
to give your folks a wave?' he asked.

She turned and waved forlornly through the flap at
the side. Her mother on the back steps, her father by
the boot-scraper, waved back. A flannel-singleted
shearer washing his face in an enamel dish on a tripod
outside the shearer's hut raised his arm and waved too.
Other shearers smoked outside the shed, filling in the
moments before they must go inside. She could still
feel the throb of the engines from the shed as the engine
heated up. The sheep were restless in the yards. A bird
note trembled intolerably in the air; the pumpkin
vines flaunted yellow flowers and the clover was
tenderly green beside the smooth silver of the dam. It
made her feel sad as she drove away from it all in the
clear bright light of the early spring morning. A tear
pressed from under one eyelid and slid slowly down
her cheek. She turned her head away from the white-
painted house, the gently rolling paddocks, and
resolutely faced the road ahead, a grey road, soft with
the dust of a rainless winter, winding away for ever
across the plains. With one hand she smoothed her
green crepe dress over her thin, hunched-up knees. It
was a smart frock. She had picked it herself from the
catalogue. 'In shades of olive, rose, saxe and navy,'
Mother had read out to her. 'Olive,' she had said. And
now here she was riding to the end of the world in the
stiff new dress, and watering it with her tears. Was
this the outcome of picking a dress in which to be
happy? It showed you never could tell. How many

other girls were riding up or down Australia at this very minute, weeping down the front of their Sunday finery?

The mailman's name was Tom. He was a thin, old man, with tea-stained whiskers and a brown neck hanging in folds above his collarless, striped shirt. He glanced at Della uneasily. 'People haven't any right,' he thought, 'sending a kid out done up like that. Them buttoned boots. Not worn any more, button boots aren't. Won't she have a time of it, landing at school in buttoned boots.'

'Don't you want to go to school?' he asked.

'No,' she answered.

'Come now. You've got to be learned you know. Lessons aren't so bad once you get the hang of them.'

'Oh, I can do lessons,' Della replied loftily.

'What have you got to go to school for?'

'I'm too bad to stop home any longer,' she told him mournfully.

'Bad! You don't look bad to me.'

'Don't I? Well, I am. I'm awful bad. I've given Mother nerves.'

'You don't say! What was it you did that was so bad?'

'Oh, everything——'

'For instance now?'

Della stopped crying to pick and choose amongst her misdeeds. 'I nearly got drowned in the dip last week,' she said.

'Pooh! Did that once myself,' replied Tom.

'Did you? What did everyone say?'

'Didn't say anything. They didn't know.'

'But how did you get out?'

'Brother of mine. Big bloke. Pulled me up the side.'

'Maybe if I'd had a brother——'

P

'They're handy when you're a kid,' admitted Tom.

'Then I fell in a tank through a hole in the top. Gee, it was terrible wet and dark——'

'You seemed to be set on getting yourself drowned.'

'I've nearly been drowned most ways,' replied Della modestly. 'In the creek and in the dam and once in the horse-trough.'

'Kind of slimy,' murmured Tom.

'Ugh.' Della shivered, then looked at Tom suspiciously. 'How do you know?'

Tom nodded his head. 'Me too, once.'

Della's eyes were bright with interest. 'Have you ever been bitten by a snake?' she asked.

'No. Have you?'

'Not quite, but I pulled one out of a log by its tail one day.'

'How was it it didn't bite you?'

'The devil looks after his own, Father said.'

'I don't know as how that was a nice thing to say to a little girl,' replied Tom thoughtfully. 'Not that I'm any judge. I was never a hand with children.'

'Didn't you have any children?'

'Lord love us. I had ten.'

'Well, how was it you never got your hand in?'

'I can't rightly remember. It was a long time ago and I was only home Sundays. A mail run used to be a mail run in those days.'

'They couldn't have been bad like me.'

'No worse or no better if you ask me. All kids are the same. Not good and not bad.' His hands tightened on the reins and the horses came to a stop. 'You just take a squint back that way. See them tin roofs. That's the last you'll see of your place for a few months. Now take a look over this way, across what we used to call the Prairie. That's McAlistars' stockrails in the distance. Shift your eyes a little to the north, that belt of timber, that's Munros'. And in front here, where the road curves by the river, that's Ryans'. Big places, all of them. In the old days large families were reared on them. Nine kids here, ten kids there, twelve somewhere else and so on. Fine kids, too. What they didn't know about sheep and cattle and horses, wasn't worth knowing either. You couldn't ride this way this time of the morning then and see the plains empty on every side of you. Shut me eyes now and I can see them mad McAlistar boys galloping straight for me, putting their horses at the fences, standing straight in the stirrups, their black hair waving upright in the wind. Many's the time I threatened to tell their father of their wild ways. And what did they do? Laugh at me till the morning echoed, and I guess I deserved it.' Tom lapsed into silence and sat quietly looking at the reins in his thin calloused hands. Della watched him covertly. She'd heard tell of the McAlistar boys, too, but most of them had been dead before she was born.

'You were telling me something,' she said politely after a long time.

'Was I?' asked Tom and jogged up the horses. They ambled forward and broke into a brisk trot, spiralling the dust softly into the sunny air. 'I'm an old man and I forget.'

'About all the children who used to be around here once,' prompted Della.

'They're here no more,' said Tom.

'There's me. But I'm bad.'

'I guess I'd be bad too if I were the only little person for miles around.'

'Would you?' asked Della delightedly.

The buggy swept down a slope and clattered over the bridge. Murphy's lay behind them, its roof burnished silver under the sun. 'Time was,' said Tom sorrowfully, 'and five little girls used to wave to me over the bridge railing. They used to wear pigtails and pinafores.'

'I guess it was a long time ago.'

'It was, but it weren't so quiet. Australia's a quiet place these days. I'm not the kind to want to tell the young people anything. The young people always know best, I reckon. But it's kind of funny.'

'What's funny?'

'You, for instance. You're the only little girl for miles around. Four places that reared families and now among them all there's only you. What happens? You've got to be sent to school because you give your mother nerves, and your father——'

'I give him a headache.'

'There! Don't you think it's funny?'

'No,' said Della puzzledly. 'It's not funny. Not at all.'

Tom sighed. 'Perhaps you're right,' he said.

They went on endlessly over the winding road. Now and then a stunted gum flaunted its twisted trunk and abandoned curved leaves by the roadside, or a log hollowed greyly among the riotous spring grasses; they passed over culverts, and bridges that spanned waterless creeks. There was a wayside post office, into which Tom disappeared for three minutes, and a wayside pub that held him captive for fifteen. He came back wiping his whiskers. 'They want to put a car on this run now, but it's going to be over my dead body they do it,' he told Della boastfully.

Della wasn't interested. 'What's school going to be like?' she asked.

'School. Oh, school's all right. There's singing comes from there in the daytime. And at night the kids laugh and skylark on the lawns till bedtime. The sound floats across the creek and into the township. Look, that's the township, down there, Woonganattie. A good little town, Woonganattie. As up to the minute as they're made. My, the kids are going to laugh when you hit Woonganattie in those buttoned boots.'

'What's up with my boots?' asked Della ominously.

Tom looked at her. For the first time he noticed the set of her mouth and the light in her green eyes.

'I guess I was wrong,' he muttered. 'It's not the boots.'

'What's up with my boots?' repeated Della.

'Nothing. Nothing.' Tom averted his eyes hurriedly and whipping up the horses they fled along the curve that led into Woonganattie, drawing up with a flourish in front of the school. Della Parkins, of the Ten-mile Farm, Branch Creek, via Woonganattie, had arrived at school. No princess of old was ever delivered with more aplomb to the austere way of learning, tin trunk, green crepe dress, buttoned boots and all. 'What's up with my boots?' said the light in her eye. She was twenty strong. The kids everyone should have had, but hadn't.

THE KID
By KEN LEVIS

No wonder the blokes were sore. You know how they get, all worked up and indignant. They always do when they're dragged out early. And this time there really was good reason.

'Just like the blasted Army!' the men said. 'Twelve hours after they know the kid's lost they pitchfork us out into the night—the night, mind yer—when we can't do a damn thing in these hills.'

It's times like that you feel mad and would like to kick someone hard. There was the kid lost out in the hills, and there we were, bottled up in camp because the loon in charge couldn't get the order signed for the trucks to leave. The bloke that should sign it was away, and the bloke left behind wasn't game. Red tape! You know what it's like. Blokes busting to be doing something, and can't, and then blokes made to work when it's the last thing they want. That's how it always is in the Army. At any rate in the bits of it I've been in.

At last they'd got us crammed into the lorries with the cold wind curving past our cheeks. Our lorry hadn't any canvas top like the others. They'd just grabbed whatever trucks happened to be about. They'd grabbed whatever men there were, too, to make up their number. There we were, stacked into the trucks. Water-bottles and iron rations, and our cheeks like smooth stone in the dawn wind.

Not that we minded the cold. It felt pretty good sitting there under the stars, looking down on the hooded lights of the convoy wriggling up the steep climb. Just as if they were threaded on a string and tugged along out of the valley. Then they would disappear as we swung round to miss the low trunks of the twisted mountain gums. As the lorry lurched over the road boulders the greatcoats opposite would stand up against the sky, while our side sank down in the ruts and the blokes cursed the driver.

'Yer bloody fifth columnist,' they said.

The driver offered to fight the bloke that said that.

Yes, it's pretty good out driving in the dawn. You sort of feel good, as if you were a bit of the night and the country—if you follow me. At any rate the blokes got in better spirits. Of course they kept grumbling.

'You'll find, sure's hell, when we get there,' they said, 'some nitwit of a loot's in charge that don't know a bush track from Pitt Street. See if the loon don't!'

Well, it wasn't long before we were over the spur, and the truck side-stepping down the other side. Bushes began to take shape, and you could breathe the smell of wet gum-leaves. Right down into the valley the convoy wriggled. We looked up at the great mountain wall towering black above us, clearly marked where the stars were getting faint. The fellers didn't say much now. Funny how you don't feel like talking much in the dawn, isn't it?

The truck kept moving along the valley. Past the outlines of a house. A dog rushed barking out of the darkness. He'd have plenty of work ahead of him before the convoy got past, we reckoned. On we went past great clumps of Lombardy poplars. You couldn't miss picking their outline. 'Poplars!' the men said. People must've lived here a long time to have poplars that size. These valleys were all pretty old. Settlers there right from the time of the Ophir gold-rushes. Wonder why the old people grew so many poplars and elms. Did it everywhere. Reminded them of what they liked, I suppose.

Suddenly the lorry bumped to a stop. Curse the driver. Without waiting for orders the men scrambled up from their cramped seats. We swung to the ground. Shapes of several cars stood about. Voices from a little distance, left front. A lantern came swinging towards us. The lamplight from a doorway lay pale on the bush track.

Funny how scenes like that stick in your mind! Everything quiet; the bush dark, stretching away on all sides. Somewhere in that quietness was the lost kid. I suppose all the blokes had some picture in their minds of the poor little beggar. I did, at any rate. Now we were there, we wanted to get on with the job. We hated standing about when we knew the kid was somewhere in that quietness.

The house from which the lamplight came was a two-roomed shack. The sort you find in old dead prospecting dumps. No paint on the walls, the back doors made of bag, and the old enamel wash-basin standing outside on a soapy wood-block. You're never sure whether the fellows that own such shacks are blokes trying to be farmers and doing a bit of fossicking, or chaps after gold, kidding themselves they're farming in their spare time. They don't seem to do much of either.

Some of us pushed into the room because we found they were making a bucket of tea in the fire-place. If you get in early, there's always a chance of doubling up later on, when the mob finds out what's doing.

It was the sort of room you find in any of these two-roomed shacks. A broken sofa with its cover worn through and the pattern rubbed off; two broken-legged chairs mended with boards from a Plume kerosene case, the brand still on them. And there was the usual greasy table. It was a dingy hole all right, with a feeble kerosene lamp trying to soak up some of the shadows in a half-hearted way, as if the job had made it tired.

The powdery red from the fire-place kept on rubbing the woman's black dress. She was a big Irish sort of woman with a square red face and her hair all ruffled; and she wore boots. She dipped us out a mug of strong black tea from the kerosene tin on the hob. We asked whether it was her child that was lost.

She seemed to think she'd been insulted, for she stopped dipping as she stood bent over the can of tea.

'No kid of mine!' she roared. 'I've had twelve and none of them ever got lost. If they did, they pretty soon found themselves, don't you worry. My kids don't get lost.'

After that she went on with the tea-dipping. A couple of mugs later she said, 'It's me sister-in-law's kid that's lost. She come up from Sydney yesterday. Scared the Japs might come. Next thing the kid's gone.'

By this time the mob was after the tea, so we had to get out. We didn't see the woman again, or the kid's mother at all. They reckoned she was in the other room trying to sleep. Lord knows where all the kids were. Perhaps the neighbours had taken them out of the road. Perhaps they were all grown up. It's hard to tell the age of a woman like that.

Outside it was still quiet, though the bush was taking on its proper shape. It's the quietness that gets you. You think of the kid out there alone. You wonder why he doesn't holler. But of course he was only six and the sound wouldn't carry far, although it's so quiet. The bush'd soak up the sound. Perhaps he was asleep. In that case we might find him soon after he was awake and he wouldn't be much the worse for wandering off. You think of all sorts of thoughts like these when you're waiting for the search to start.

As the light grew stronger a whistle blast drew us together. The lieutenant in charge spoke to us. He was a young fellow with deep blue eyes and fresh-creased giggle pants. The blokes nodded at each other. 'Told yer so!' they said.

'Extended lines!' he ordered. 'Five paces interval. The boy lost will not answer you. He has no roof to his mouth. He knows nothing of the bush, the police tell me. We'll move through the bush to Stanley Gap road. Search thoroughly. It's a matter of life and death.'

No roof to his mouth, eh! Strange the difference that made. A special kind of kid, then, almost unreal. Wouldn't answer when called. You see none of us had thought of him not answering. It upset the picture we all had in our minds.

The men disappeared in the thick bushes. Funny how bush swallows up an extended line. It's an awkward damn thing, too. At one moment when the bush thins, you suddenly find everyone bunched together. Then you get widely separated, and one wing loses direction and big gaps are left uncovered. Particularly in broken country. Of course that's what happened here. Up the quartz outcrop we scrambled, our iron-shod heels ringing on the morning gravel. Dry bushes cracked, and the search was on.

Down the steep quartz-strewn ridge we crunched, gripping the spindly saplings, digging our heels into the rock-hard crust. At the bottom the dead stream had hacked its thin trench through the rock many feet deep. Where clay remained, it had licked out the softer layers beneath, leaving the treacherous crust. The place was a nightmare. No wonder we hadn't left earlier. How far could the kid get in this country, we wondered, and barefoot?

Up the opposite steep slope we sweated, striding indiscriminately in our heavy boots through the dry stubble above. Another gully, steep as the last. Peering beneath logs, among tangled roots in deep water-crevices, thrusting poles in the few stagnant pools, we toiled over the country.

'The bloody fool's going too fast,' the men cursed. 'The poor little beggar might be anywhere here and us not see him.' But they were eager to find him and pressed on at the same mad rate themselves. By now our bodies were dank with sweat, our boots rubbed raw of polish on the toe-caps.

'Bare feet,' said the men. 'How the hell?'

The whistle shrilled a halt. We sat in the sunlight, short-winded.

'The cops,' the men said. 'They've got the blood-hound.' A great hulking black dog went by on a lead. It looked mournfully at us. Two shirt-sleeved coppers followed reverently. Conscious of its importance it moved on. In silence and deep respect we observed. Here in this heavy, queer-shaped organism was hidden the power that would render unnecessary the efforts of two hundred trained troops. The search was as good as over.

The dog, however, became uncertain. He hung his forepaw pensively, then made off at an angle to the line of search. On we sweated over country still more lacerated than before. It became harder to keep the line. Over the narrow hills it became broken, so that by the time Stanley Gap road showed, at the foot of a steep spur, the men were separated in bunches cut off by rock-faced water-beds.

An hour later, most of us had toiled back to our base. In a clay-carved watercourse we washed down the bully and Army biscuits with water. The biscuits stuck in our necks. The men made their usual jokes.

'My old man,' said one, 'made a photo frame out of one of these biscuits last war. It's still hangin' at home.'

But we weren't very enthusiastic over the jokes. The men were worried about the kid. The affair was becoming a personal matter between us and the bush.

'He couldn't have gone far that way,' the men said. 'His feet'd be cut to ribbons.' 'He could've been in a hundred places this morning, and us not seen him,' we said.

Soon we were off again. The sun blazed down. We took the opposite direction, along the valley floor and flats. 'Watch out for old shafts,' the police officer directed. 'A lot are tangled over with weeds. Look out for marks at the mouths of shafts and for stones that have been dislodged.'

Funny how business-like a copper becomes when he gets his coat off.

We pushed on through the dry grass. There was need for care all right. The ground was pitted with shafts—dark holes without cover, some with rotten wood pretending to make them safe, sunken grass and matted leaves. No solid ground anywhere for twenty yards. In some shafts the sun showed dead leaves floating on stagnant water. The men gathered at one to look at the swollen carcass of a beast nearly submerged in the black shaft-water.

'Yer'll niver find him,' crooned a crazy old hermit we met there. 'They wander away,' his thin voice piped. 'He's in one of them, eh?' His thin hand stroked the scanty white hair on his sunk cheeks and he cackled a nervous laugh. 'Yer'll niver find him!'

We were ready now to agree with the blue-eyed old simpleton, but somehow were glad to leave him behind. We were determined to see this thing through. The odds against the kid were too great. Not a fair go.

Suddenly the line halted. The crumbled lip of a shaft showed traces disappearing in the blackness.

Someone let drop a piece of quartz. A faint click as it hit rock and soft splashes deep down. Some bloke said he'd like to make sure the kid wasn't there, so we passed the rope round his waist and knotted it. 'Wot's yer last wishes, mate?' the men said, not so much for the joke. They felt it was the sort of joke they ought to be making. But no one laughed much, because, you see, every bloke had a picture in his mind how the kid would look if he was down there. And the fellers that did put up a show of being unconcerned only made it more plain that the men were getting anxious about the kid.

The chap in the rope pulled off his shirt and pushed himself stiff-legged over the lip of the shaft, body-muscles tight beneath sunburnt skin. Out of the sunlight he swung, his boots sending loose stones shooting into the blackness. When I think of the search for the kid the picture of the bloke pushing himself over the shaft's lip, down out of the sunlight, always comes into my mind; with the line of men taking the strain, looking like chiselled statues in the strong light, and the rope rippling over the log we had put at the shaft's mouth.

Pretty soon the bloke signalled with the torch to be pulled up. He looked green about the gills when we got him in the sunlight again.

'I don't think anything's down there,' he said. 'The air's too rotten to look about much. Paugh! You need your gas-mask.'

On the line went down the valley, our shirts sweat-soaked under the midday sun. We wheeled through the scrub and back to the clay-washed watercourse without result.

Bare-chested we lay in the thin shade, munching our bully and biscuits. We had to go easy on the water.

There was a whole afternoon ahead yet. The blokes
we had left behind with the gear told us about the dog.

'Did yer hear about the bloody dog?' they said.
'He's scabbed on us! Up in the hills,' they said, ''is
bloody 'ighness is snuffing along, when thump! thump!
First time he'd seen a blasted roo. The coppers hadn't
taught him what a roo was, yer see. Woof! woof! 'e
goes, and off like hell after him. The coppers just got
him back now. He's fair busted. All in,' they said.
'He's asleep in their truck. . . . Aw, the hell!' they
said.

Every bloke looked round to see where the coppers
were, but they weren't showing themselves. Oh, no!
Wonderful, isn't it, how a bit of sarcasm freshens you
up?

Somehow our feelings towards the kid were changing. In the morning we had thought of him terrified,
out there in the stillness. We had thought of him
wandering, lost in the bush, alone. We would search
the bush, someone would pick him up and cart him
home. Straightforward, wasn't it? Things usually are
until you get to work on them.

Then the loot had said he had no roof in his mouth.
That knocked cock-eyed the little picture we had in
our heads. Made him hard to imagine. Unreal almost.
And then we had all been through the bush to the
Stanley Gap road, and the bush had beaten us, and
we had found all those devilish shafts, and the old
loon with the nervous laugh, 'Yer'll niver find 'im!
He's in one of those, eh?' And now the bush had made
the police-dog a silly fool—just by sending along a
kangaroo to meet it. And the notion came into my head
as we lay there that the bush was just mocking us. It
had hidden the kid away somewhere and was amusing
itself with our efforts. Stupid idea, of course. But you

know how it is with these thoughts. They just come
into your mind, and there you are. Remember, the
day was a scorcher and we'd been going hard since
three o'clock and the water was warm in our bottles.

At any rate there I was thinking of this silly feeling
of mine—that the bush was playing with us—when
our N.C.O. got some of us together. Not a bad bloke,
our N.C.O. 'Stagger this way, men,' he said. 'They
want us over at the dam.'

There was an old muddy dam on the side of the hill
that had been used when the gold was there. Just the
sort of place a kid would like, the johns reckoned. We
put the irons through it without result. But the police
weren't sure and ordered us to cut the bank. We dug
through it and two bronze-backed fellows stood knee-
deep in the slush, shovelling stinking mud from the
new cut. The water swirled silently through. . . . We
all sat on the bank to watch.

'That's the old man,' the men pointed out, 'there on
the bank. He come up from Sydney. He's given up
hope of gettin' the kid alive,' they said.

He seemed a pretty decent sort of cove, too. Tried
to show no weak anxiety before the men. It had hit
him hard, though. You could see how weary and
worried he was, and he looked about all-in now. We
were sorry for him standing there by himself, his
brown eyes searching the emptying water. Poor devil!
A soldier moved over near him in case he toppled.
The blokes would keep glancing at him as the mud
started to show in the shallow parts—glance and look
away quickly in case he should think they were
watching him.

Patches of wet mud began to shine in the sun. Tad-
poles slithered everywhere in the soft mud. Two deep
holes showed. A huge fellow, trousers tucked high on

his thighs, waded through the sucking mud to the deeper parts. He held a shovel, which he thrust before him and on each side. The soft mud made his task difficult. He thrust hard with his shovel at each stroke so that he would know if anything lay in the deep sediment. Suddenly he hesitated, struck several times. We all searched his face. The father winced. His face was white. The fellow thrust uncertainly, decided nothing was there, and moved on.

Of course the dam was empty. It seemed as if we'd known it would be all along. All through the afternoon we searched, along the creek, forcing poles through the water-holes, under the matted blackberry-bushes, in the reed-beds, in hollows scooped out by the water under the clay banks. Up the mountain side the men spread and the police dragged the old drinking wells.

And the notion that had put itself inside my head kept on coming back and fixing itself there. Not only was the bush mocking our efforts, but the kid was becoming identified with it. We didn't talk now of finding the kid, but where we might find his body. The six-year-old had us licked. He and the bush were working together to make fun of our efforts.

Stupid notion, wasn't it? But that's how it seemed when the search was stopped for the night. Whatever we'd tried was useless. We were beaten everywhere, licked. And now the dark stopped the search. We made fires for ourselves and slept near them that night, for a cold breeze crept up the valley, shaking the poplar-leaves. Wrapped in their greatcoats, the men murmured in broken sleep. Every now and then one would curse, stretch his cramped body, rise and throw more wood on the fire.

It was hard to get much sleep, and when I did, confused dreams of the kid and the old hermit with his skinny hands stroking his sunken cheeks would come. The grey-haired old loon was sitting on his knees. They were yabbering to each other, but you couldn't tell what, because the kid had no roof to his mouth. And then I would wake, feeling the place was evil and that the crazed old loon was somehow the spirit of the place, leering at us, and the kid was mocking us with him. Then I would tell myself what a damn fool I was for having such fancies even in sleep; and I'd try to move my body so it wasn't so cramped— you know how you do when you're not used to much bivouacking. And then I'd try to get to sleep before I got cramped in that position.

Well, the N.C.O. shook us awake before the sun was up. A fog had crept up the valley with the dawn, and everything was wet and the bush blotted out—even the line of poplars. The trucks had come to carry us back to camp, and the men were in pretty bad humour as they lined up for a mug of black tea from the shack fire-place. They looked a tough crowd, too, with dirty unshaved faces and wet greatcoats and boots rubbed raw from the quartz.

All around us the bush was quiet as it had been when we first came to the valley. But it was now a mocking quiet. The bush had scored. As the lorry scrambled up the rough bush track, we stared out into the fog. The bloke beside me spoke. He put into words as well as anyone could the feeling we all had.

'The kid was too good for us,' he said, and he poked in the ends of the cigarette he was rolling. 'Right from the word go he had us licked.'

HULLO, JOE

By JON CLEARY

NOTHING is the same.

The street hasn't changed. No new houses have been built, all the old ones still stand as before, unchanged; the house opposite still has the bent iron railing in the fence; the telegraph pole Neale's kids used to play cricket against is still marked with smudges from muddy balls; the tree in the front garden of Shorter's place still needs lopping. Only—I have forgotten—it isn't Shorter's place any more. They moved the year I went away. And—will I always keep forgetting like this?—Neale's kids aren't kids any more. The elder boy has just gone into camp and the other boy and the two girls, the freckle-faced, spindly-legged, bobbed-haired girls, are all working now. That is it—everything is the same on the outside, familiar and unchanged as it was then, but inside, in the houses, with the people and the way they lived and the way you remember them, which is the real memory of a place, nothing is the same.

Back in the house I can hear my sister singing. Even the songs aren't the same. What were they singing when I went away? *Begin the Beguine*, I think it was. I hum the first few bars of it. Maybe it was *Daisy*, maybe it was *Home, Sweet Home*. It was all such a long time ago, when I was a young man. It doesn't matter, anyway. I wonder if they sing them now? Probably not. Songs are forgotten. Like other things.

'Joe, dinner's ready.'

That is my mother, back in the house. My mother calling me in to dinner. And I'm scared. It has been like this ever since I came home a week ago. I sit at the

table with the family—my father, my mother, my
sister, my two young brothers—and I don't know what
the hell to talk about. I feel like a stranger. Twenty-
three years of living with people, loving them because
the same blood courses in our veins, because we have
had so much fun and understanding, because they
are my family and that is enough, and then going
away for three and a half years and coming back to
feel uncomfortable with them, like being in the
presence of a memory and not sure they will remember.
It is all so cock-eyed. But that's how it is. Scared of
being alone with my own family.

I linger for a moment, looking down to the bay
where the sun is gold on the water, reluctant to go in,
and then I turn and enter the house. It is the same
again to-night. They are all sitting in their regular
places, the same as when I went away—Dad with his
back to the window—and they all look up as I come
in and sit down, but I can't see behind their eyes. I
wish I knew what they are thinking.

Mother has cut up my food for me. That helps to
make me uncomfortable. Everything—washing, shaving, dressing, eating—brings the same thought to
mind. The sleeve of my coat is dangling and Mother
leans across and stuffs it into a side-pocket. Oh God,
Mother, don't do that! But what's the use? She
wouldn't understand. So I say thanks and give the
helpless smile the helpless are supposed to give and
let it go at that.

My mother mentions a Mrs. French. She speaks as
if she knows her very well, as if they are the best of
friends. I used to know all my mother's friends once.
But I don't like to ask who Mrs. French is. Everybody
else in the family knows her. But she is just a name to
me. And somehow that is all I want her to be.

'You must meet her, Joe. You'll like her.'

'Will I?'

Only Dad notices the apathy in my voice. He looks up and catches my eye and quickly looks back to his plate. Mother chatters on. Mother never notices anything about anybody. A midget could walk into our house and Mother would say, 'What an odd-looking little boy!' and go on talking. She is starting to irritate me now. Fran, my sister, is asking if her frock has been ironed for the dance to-night. So people still go dancing. Fran's fiancé, Dick Shorter, who used to live down the road, is up in New Guinea now. They became engaged when he landed back from the Middle East with the Ninth Division. I wonder if he minds Fran going out like this. I wonder if she tells him in her letters. I open my mouth to say something and shut it again quickly. All of a sudden I want to get up and scream. I am hating the family. I can feel it growing inside me, eating the love I had for them. I must get out of here.

'Excuse me. I don't want any sweets, Mother.'

I stand up and go out of the room quickly.

I hear my mother say, 'What's the matter?'

And then Dad's voice, very quietly, 'Let him go. I think I understand.'

I wonder if he does. I hope so. I want someone to understand me.

I go out of the house and down the street. It is still light. I look at my watch. Seven o'clock. Time for the news. So everybody will sit about their radios and listen to how the war, the war I was in just a short time ago, is going, and they will hear that the Russians are still advancing, or the Eighth Army has outflanked the Germans, or we have lambasted Rabaul again, and they will sit back in their deep comfortable chairs on their well-shined behinds and say, as they drink their coffee, their voices smug and complacent and so wise, 'We've got 'em on the run now', and 'It won't last long at this rate', and so what the hell do they know about it? Maybe when you're in the war, in close, you don't think about it. And maybe when you're out of it, away from it, but with your arm left there, your good left arm that was brown and muscular, maybe you don't care.

Maybe you have to be right away from the war, back home in the safety and comfort of the four walls of your home, not knowing the horror of bombs falling close, or men and sand and gun disappearing in a brown-yellow cloud that hits you as visible sound, or mud that drags you down as you cross the open space with the M.G. lined on you, its fire going past you so close, so swift, so sharp, you can't believe you're alive, maybe you have to know none of that to know all about the war.

There are a few people coming up the street, coming up from the tram-stop at the bottom of the hill. I don't know any of them, but a couple of them glance curiously at me as they pass. I know what they're looking at.

I turn the corner at the bottom of the hill and I bump into her. I haven't seen her since I landed back, but I knew her well in the old days. She was Fran's best friend.

'Hullo, Margaret.'

She is still getting her breath from the collision. Then she laughs. She is a tall girl with a good full figure. She is blonde, her hair swept up so that you can see the high curve of her cheek and the long graceful column of her neck, and her laugh is warm, tumbling sound, sun-flecked and musical. I notice she is still wearing her wedding ring.

'Hullo, Joe.' The laughter is still there, behind her voice. 'I heard you were back. But I didn't come up. I thought you might like to get settled in first.'

'You're looking well.'

She is. She is in black and it sets off her hair. I wonder does she always wear black now.

'So are you. From the way your mother spoke I thought . . .'

'Yes. But you know what mothers are.'

'Yes.'

'How's the little girl—what's her name?'

'Kerry. She's fine, thanks, Joe.'

'How old is she now?'

'Going on three. Fran has asked me to dinner to-morrow night. You can see her then.'

'I'd like to.'

'I'll have to go now, Joe. Good-bye. See you to-morrow night.'

''Bye.'

She goes up the hill. She walks very nicely, with lovely long strides.

I turn and keep on down towards the beach. Not a word about Michael, not a glance at my sleeve. Two people picking up where they left off. Nothing about her marriage—that happened after I left—and Michael being killed in Crete and leaving her and the baby, the baby he never saw, and nothing about me losing an arm at Wau. Just two normal people meeting and saying hullo. I feel much better, just for meeting her.

I am down near the beach now. I walk along the promenade. The surf is quiet, the water rolling in and curling slowly up as if it were tired and then flopping with a hard flat sound on the sand. Right out on the sea-line there are some big clouds stepped in towering masses, shot with fast-dying colour from a fast-dying day, the night hiding deep at their base in soft blue shadow. Gulls hang on the breeze, motion suspended in white triangles against the dusk. The street lights are on, yellow pin-heads climbing the hill from the bay road, and already there are a few people coming along the promenade for their after-dinner stroll. I count them as I pass. I walk the length of the promenade and I pass twenty-eight people and I don't know any of them.

Suddenly I feel very lonely. This is my home town, the suburb I was born in and lived in for twenty-three years, the suburb where I could go for a walk any time of day and meet someone to say, 'Hullo, Joe.' And now nobody knows my name, nobody knows me even to nod to. I'm here, but I don't belong.

The next night we are all sitting at the dinner-table. There is the family and Margaret and her little girl and my uncle and aunt. The little girl, Kerry, is sitting between Margaret and me. My uncle and aunt are opposite. Aunt Kath is my mother's sister; the only difference between them is that my aunt carries more weight. Uncle Jack is built like a pillar-box and has as much personality—he takes everything in and nothing comes out. Everybody is talking at once. I just sit and the noise is giving me a headache.

'. . . are cutting down our meat, too.' That is my aunt talking. 'We won't be able to get a thing soon. They told me last week I'll be lucky if I get beef again.'

No beef! Too bad. Too bloody bad. No beef! And the only thing I haven't is a left arm.

'. . . you start to realize there's a war on.'

Four years of war. Four long years, and I saw Bud

die, and Ted and Mac, and I saw Morry blinded, and they can call me Wingy now. I saw two hundred planes in the sky and none of them ours and all of them out to kill us, and I saw a destroyer go down with wounded men sliding off her decks to drown, and I saw a land-mine burst under nine men and when the dust cleared there was nothing, just nothing but the roar in your ears and the stark memory of them in the last moment standing there, and you can't remember anything else about them but the figures standing and the one kneeling, just figures alone in a void of memory without sky or desert or background of any sort, and I saw a kid in a battered old Gladiator fight twenty-seven Stukas till they sent him down to the hard red earth of Crete and the glory that you can't tell to people who didn't see it, and I saw a man, wounded in the thigh, a gaping wound that bled and bled, walk for three days through rain and mud and cold back to the C.C.S. because no one could be spared to carry him. And Aunt Kath loses her ration of beef and realizes there is a war on!

My fork clatters to my plate and I open my mouth. But I don't get to say anything. I feel a hand on my thigh, pressing it, and it is Margaret, leaning across the little girl. She is looking straight at me and the look in her eyes shuts my mouth.

'Having trouble, Joe? she asks.

'No. No, the fork just slipped. I'll be all right.'

She presses my thigh again and sits back.

The rest of dinner I am eating my food and not knowing what it is, my mind full of Margaret and the look in her eyes. It was an understanding look. It is the first time I have seen that look since I landed back.

We are in the lounge-room after dinner. We are all

sitting about and Fran is at the piano. Margaret is standing beside her.

Margaret says, 'Come and sing something with us, Joe.'

I get up and go and stand beside her. Fran starts to play something and she and Margaret sing it and I can hear the others behind me humming it, even Dad. And I stand with my mouth open and nothing coming.

'What's the matter, Joe?' asks Fran, breaking off.

'I don't know it. I've never heard it.'

'Oh, don't be silly! You must have heard it. Why, it's topped the list for the last three weeks in the Hit Parade.'

'Has it? What's that?'

'What?'

'The Hit Parade.'

Margaret says, 'Move over, Fran,' and she sits on the stool and starts to play. It is *Night and Day*. 'Remember that, Joe?' She winks at me and starts to sing. I pick her up and from there we go to *Charmaine* and *The Desert Song* and *Stardust* and I feel better than I have felt since landing home.

Then it is late. I stand in the hall while everyone says good night, then I say, 'I'll see you home, Margaret.'

'It doesn't matter, really, Joe. We'll be all right.'

'Leave the key in the door, Mother. Come on, Margaret. I'm seeing you home.'

She laughs and kisses my mother and Fran. We go down out of the gate.

'Here, give me Kerry. She's too heavy for you to carry.'

'But what about—?'

'I can manage. She can sit up and hang on to my neck. There. How's that, Kerry?'

The little girl smiles sleepily and leans her head on my shoulder. We don't talk much on the way to her place. It isn't far and we are soon there.

'Would you like to come in, Joe?'

It is a beautiful night, moon and stars and quiet.

'Let's stay out here. We can sit on the veranda.'

'I'll take Kerry in and put her to bed. I won't be long.'

She goes inside and I sit on the steps. I take out a cigarette and, holding the match-box with my chin against my throat, I strike a match. I haven't learned yet how to do those match-lighting tricks with one hand.

She isn't long. She comes out and sits beside me on my left side. The moonlight is soft on her face and I can smell the crisp smell of her hair.

'Well?' she says.

'You say something. Anything. Just go on talking. I'll listen.'

'What about? Me? You?'

'You.'

'No.' She looks up at the sky for a moment, then directly back at me. 'No, Joe. We'll talk about you. There's something wrong with you, Joe. Something terribly wrong.'

'Yes. . . .'

'No, not . . . I don't mean that. I mean inside you, in your mind. I noticed you to-night. You resented practically everything anybody said.'

'Is it as obvious as that?' I flick my cigarette away, a falling red arc in the darkness.

'I don't know. It was to me.' She is sitting with her hands clasped, her elbows resting forward on her knees, and now she is looking straight out into the night. There is no sound but the rumoured rolling

of the sea, a long way off. 'I wonder if Michael would
have been like you had he come home.'

'How?'

'Soured and bitter.'

'Am I like that?'

She nods. Her hair falls forward with the gesture
and she leaves it hanging; it is smooth, falling sleekly
in a soft rhythm of beauty, the moonlight a sheen on
the blondeness. I want to lean forward and touch it.
'Yes, Joe. And you know it. I saw your lip curl to-night
when your aunt mentioned losing her beef ration. If
I hadn't touched you, you'd have insulted her.
Wouldn't you?'

'I guess so. That got me completely. I don't know—
why have people got to be so ignorant?'

'That's it, Joe. They're ignorant. All of us here at
home are ignorant. Very ignorant. We don't know a
thing about war, Joe—not real war, not war as you
know it. We read about it in the papers but they only
tell you how it is going, whether we are winning or
not. They don't tell you what it is like to get shot, or
anything like that. I don't suppose it would be any
good, anyway. Some of the girls used to tell me what
it was like to have a baby, and I used to listen to them
so that when it came time for me to have a baby I'd
know all the ways of making it easier. And then when
it came time for me to have Kerry, I found all they
told me didn't help at all. Because I really didn't know
anything about it. I had to find out by experience.
They couldn't tell me what the actual feeling was
like, and I'll never be able to tell anyone else. That's
the way it is with the war and us, Joe.'

She is quiet for a moment. I am looking at her and
something is happening to me. I can feel it as surely as
I can feel the gentle night breeze on my face.

'Look. I lost Michael. I loved him, Joe. I loved him very much. But I lost him. They sent me a note one day saying he had been killed. I know where he was killed, Joe. Crete. But I don't know *how* he was killed. You'd have a better idea of that. I've never heard a bomb fall or even heard a rifle fired, but I've lost my husband and people expect me to know all about it. All I know is that I don't get his letters any more and that now I look across the table at young Kerry instead of him. I'm ignorant, too, Joe, but is that so bad?'

She leans forward on her arms and cries quietly. I reach across with my right arm, awkwardly, and press her shoulder.

'Please, Margaret. . . .'

She sits up and dries her eyes.

'I'm sorry, Joe. I don't get like that very often.'

'Do you miss him very much?'

'Sometimes I miss him a lot. In the night-time. The days I can take, but sometimes in the night I get so lonely I can't help crying.'

'Will it always be like that?'

She looks at me. Her eyes are still dark from her tears, tender and deep like night without moon, and they are all I can see. There is a light feeling at the back of my head and my mind is somersaulting.

'I hope not, Joe. I still love him, but it is something that isn't alive any more. I'm not going chasing it but sometimes I wish that I could fall in love again. I wasn't built to let my love go unanswered. Can you understand that, Joe?'

I stand up. 'I understand. I'm beginning to think you're about the only person about here I do understand. Look, Margaret. To-morrow is Sunday. Could I take you and Kerry somewhere for the day?'

She stands up on the step above me. She looks very lovely in the moonlight, her eyes and her mouth soft shadows. I move close to her and I raise my arm. Then I drop it and step back.

'What's the matter, Joe?'

'Nothing. I'll see you in the morning about ten.'

She comes down off the step and takes hold of my coat lapels with both hands. I can smell the clean freshness of her, she is so close, and the blood is pounding at the back of my throat.

'Joe, what is the matter? You were going to say something then. Why did you stop?'

I look down at her. Go on, tell her. Say it. Now is the time. Say it.

'I was going to put my arms around you and kiss you. And then I remembered. . . .'

She looks up at me. The tenderness in her eyes is bursting my heart.

'I wouldn't know if you had two or a dozen arms about me. I wouldn't care.' She raises her face. 'Kiss me, Joe.'

I put my arm about her. I kiss her softly on the warmth of her lips, then I pull her to me and her arms go round my neck and her mouth opens slowly and sweetly, taking the heart out of me, and this moment is music and sunshine and voices in the sky and all the beauty that I've never had before. It is so quiet that I can hear nothing but the beating of my heart, hollow as footfalls in a cathedral, and I feel like crying.

She draws away from me and holds my face in her hands. She can read the question in my eyes.

'Perhaps, Joe. I don't know now. . . .'

The next day we go down to National Park. It is a lazy day, unbroken blue sky falling down over the hills, the sun warm and languid, moving patterns of sunlight coming down through the trees that slowly dance in a breeze that doesn't come below the tree-tops, and the air is clean with the scent of gums. We have had lunch and I am lying back on the rug, Kerry asleep beside me, her head cradled in the crook of my arm, and Margaret is sitting with her arms wrapped round her drawn-up knees. She turns her head and I wink at her and, smiling, she winks back. I feel contented, almost sleepily contented, as if I have gone out of myself, as if I am lying in a cloud and way down there below me, in the body I used to have, is the restlessness I don't want, that I want to forget. I turn my head and look down at Kerry. She looks so peaceful and calm, as only sleeping children can.

'I wish I were a kid again.'

'Would it solve so much?'

'Maybe. Children never have to worry.'

'You mean children don't get soured and bitter.'

'Please, Margaret. Let's forget about that. Let's forget there's a war on.' She looks at me at that, and there is the start of a smile at the corners of her mouth. I grin back at her. 'Did I say that?'

She puts her hand on my throat and runs her fingers round my chin.

'You can be nice, can't you?'

'Just the personality boy. On and off like a light.'

She laughs and clips me under the chin. I laugh with her, the laugh warm all through me, and I love her very much.

Going home in the train the carriage is full of song and laughter. They are all young people, and though there is a part of me that wonders that there are still so many young men here in the old peace-time way of life it does me good to look at them. I am twenty-six and I feel old amongst these other young men. I'll bet they'd think that damn funny.

'Remembering?' asks Margaret.

Sure, I remember. Here before me is life as I knew it once. The companionship and the lusty gaiety and the song of the young in heart. I look out the window at the country going by in swift silhouettes. The sun has gone, only the tips of the trees still holding the light and the mass of them black and heavy against the green early-evening sky. Here in the train there is the sound of youth, loud and alive, but out there I know all the sounds in all the world have gone and earth is just a blue dusk coming fast and I know that this is a dying beautiful day, the day I remembered those times in the desert and in the mountains of the Lebanon, when loneliness came with the night, and I sat there listening to the bombers going over or to the jackals howling, and wished that at that very minute I could go back to the peace and the beauty and the living of the days I used to know. This that I am looking at, the laughing life of a young people and the sun going down on a young country, is Australia, the land and the life I remember.

'Know something, Margaret?'

She shakes her head.

'I've just fallen in love again—with a country.'

She takes my hand and squeezes it.

'Stay that way, Joe.'